UNHOLY INNOCENCE

by Stephen Wheeler

Text © Stephen Wheeler
Cover photograph of Binham Priory, Norfolk
© Philip Moore

By the same author

THE SILENT AND THE DEAD

Brother Walter Mysteries:
ABBOT'S PASSION
WALTER'S GHOST
MONK'S CURSE
BLOOD MOON
KNIGHT'S HONOUR
NINE NUNS
FALLEN ANGEL
DEVIL'S ACRE

Prologue

He led us through the kitchen and out into the back garden. It was a relief to get into the sunshine after the depressing bleakness of the interior. I was expecting him to take us to an outhouse of some kind but he stopped by the midden in the centre of which was a large filthy sheet that looked as though it had been thrown away. The smell and the swarm of flies were appalling and I had to cover my mouth and nose so as not to cough. Only then did I realise what was under the sheet.

'You mean this is the body?'

He lifted the sheet just enough to show me the lower half of a child's bare leg, the heel and calf clearly discernible and of a colour no child's body should ever be. At the sight of it I felt a sudden surge of anger rise up in me which I had difficulty in suppressing.

Moy must have seen the disgust in my eyes and lowered his own. 'I didn't do it, Master Walter,' he said quietly.

My mouth was dry. I swallowed hard, unable to speak. All I could do was nod not knowing whether or not I believed him.

Chapter 1
THE GATHERING STORM

It is many years now since my dear friend and brother in Christ, Jocelin of Brackland, wrote his chronicle of Saint Edmund's Abbey. Perceptive though his account was, it was never a complete history as I'm sure Jocelin himself would have been the first to admit. One glaring omission stands out although I cannot in my heart blame him for choosing not to record it since it caused him many wakeful nights of soul-searching, not least because of his own part in it. Perhaps for that reason he thought it better to say nothing than to speak falsely. Nevertheless, innocent people suffered and they too deserve to have their story told. For four decades I have remained silent on the matter, largely out of cowardice, for among those involved were some of the most powerful in the land and they will not thank me for stirring it up again. But now in my extreme old age I no longer fear for my own mortality which in any case will end soon, and when I come to my Maker I should like to do so with a quiet heart. And so it falls to me to fill the gaps that Jocelin so meticulously left vacant, a task for which I judge myself uniquely qualified, for I am Walter de Ixworth, for many years physician to the monks and people of Edmund's town, and I do not have Jocelin's scruples.

The first ripple of the wave that was about to engulf us arrived from an unexpected source. I was on my way to my brother's shop when I encountered it. To get there I have to cross the market square which on this sunny May morning was thronging with pilgrims as usual. They come to venerate the holy martyr after whom the town was named and whose shrine stands behind the great altar of our abbey church. Most of what happens in the town is the concern of the abbey in one way or another and as such there is often friction between the two. So when I do manage to get out I try to keep my head down and hurry through the market as inconspicuously as I can, although there is no disguising my monk's robes.

'Come to get your blood money, brother?'

This from a foul old hag with an eye-patch who I knew from past encounters to be female, though from her dress and manner you would hardly guess it.

'No Mother Han, I am not here to collect your dues. You know me: Master Walter, the physician. How is your eyesight these days? None too good by the sounds of things.'

'Oh, not good at all, brother,' she simpered. 'I'm practically blind. Look!' She stretched out her arms and started to stagger between the stalls bumping into objects as she went, though nothing that could cause her actual bodily harm, I noticed.

'Let me see.' I took her head in my hands reeling from the stench of onions on her breath. 'I fear there is little I can do for you, daughter,' I coughed. 'Have you tried praying to Saint Jerome for relief? He was a doctor too, you know. Or better still, Saint Lucy of Syracuse. I'm sure a ha'penny in the abbey's poor box will secure a good hearing.'

'Oh, bless you brother, I have little money for cures. I'm just a poor blind widow-woman with a crippled husband at home.'

'You can't be a widow and have a husband, daughter.'

'Can't I?' She pulled a face. 'Well, a crippled father then.'

The young man on the neighbouring stall blew a mocking raspberry. 'Prrff! Don't believe a word she says, brother. She can see all right when she wants to. Spots a pilgrim with a fat purse well enough from the other side of the market place. Have you seen what the she's selling today? Hairs from the goat that sat in Christ's cradle. Last week it was angels' tears. I ask you!' He shook his head and laughed.

'You mind your business,' sneered the hag sticking her scaly tongue out at the man.

'As I remember the story,' I said stepping between them, 'it was an ox-stall that the Holy Mother used for a crib, not a goat-stall.'

'Yeah?' sniffed the man. 'Well she's got a half-bald goat at home that says otherwise.'

At this the hag made a grab for the man and let out a stream of filthy language cursing him, his wife, his children, and calling into question his own legitimacy.

'Mother Han, please mind your words!' I said fending off her flailing arms. 'And you sir, kindly desist. If you can't keep civil tongues in your heads I may have to have you both removed until next market day; maybe even with a fine. Mother Han, you really cannot go around calling people – names - like that.'

'Why not? It's the truth. He is a bastard. Ask him who his father was. Go on. He don't know.' She sneered again at the young man.

'Now, that really is enough!' I insisted. 'One more word Mother Han and I really will speak to the market reeve.'

'Oh, it's all right brother,' said the man wiping a laughter tear from his eye. 'She's right, I am a bastard. In fact, I'm *her* bastard – en't that right, ma?'

'That's right son,' she cackled and the pair of them collapsed laughing in each other's arms.

Before I could respond there came a crash of cymbals from another corner of the market and I found myself being swept in the press of the crowd towards the music. The source was not hard to find. A gaggle of onlookers had formed themselves into a circle in the middle of which was a troop of French *jongleurs* - singers, musicians, dancers - all marvellously got up in brightly coloured clothes and dancing to a song the like of which I had never heard before and sung by a beautiful young woman. The song was all about the month of May - and love, of course - sung in French, the language of love. Not the French of the cold north but that of the sunny south, the *langue d'oc*, much to my delight since I understand it. As I fished in my robe for a penny I thanked the lead player in his own language. His face immediately broke into a smile.

'How do you know the beautiful tongue of the troubadour, brother?' he asked, as I hoped he might. I told him that I had once been a student at the famous medical school at Montpellier. This impressed him even more and he started to lament his native land - the sun, the sea, the food.

'Here everything is cold,' he said with an exaggerated shiver. 'The weather, the beer, the *women*. Especially the women, eh brother?' and he gave me a lascivious wink.

'So why are you here?' I coughed quickly.

'To entertain the King, of course.'

'The *King?*' I snorted. 'My dear friend, I fear you must be disappointed. The King is a very long way from here - in London being crowned.'

'*Non non*,' he said with a serious frown. 'He will be here tomorrow.'

'I doubt that,' I replied as kindly as I could. 'King John has only just arrived from France. I'm sure he has far more important places to visit before he comes to Bury.'

'Ah yes,' he insisted. 'Yesterday he was in Col-ches-ter,' he pronounced the difficult word carefully. 'Less than two days' ride away. Believe me, *mon frère*, he will be here tomorrow. I know, I have seen.'

My mouth dropped open. 'You've seen him?' I asked incredulously. 'King John?'

'Why yes, of course. We keep one day ahead of him. And tomorrow evening we will perform for him in the abbey *comme ça!*' and with a backward flip he disappeared back among his compatriots.

This was news indeed. The King coming to Edmundsbury. Was it possible? It would certainly explain some of the odd goings-on in the abbey over the past few days and with Jocellus the Cellarer out before cock crow each morning buying the pick of the produce from the market. But why keep it a secret? Normally such matters are discussed openly in Chapter, preparations made and much more beside. And why was he here?

Goodness gracious! I could not wait to tell my brother the news and I hurried out of the town through the Risby Gate.

My brother Joseph's shop is a bit of a make-shift affair not much more than a lean-to against the outer wall of the town. He used to have a more substantial property in the Jewish quarter until a few years ago when all Jews were banished from the town's precincts by order of the Abbot. He keeps talking of rebuilding more permanently but I think he secretly hopes that one day he will be allowed to return to his former premises within the walls.

Joseph and I are not really brothers at all; we just call ourselves that by virtue of having grown up together. That came about because my father, while still a young knight, had gone to fight in the wars in the Holy Land; but what he saw at the gates of Damascus so sickened him that instead of fighting he spent his time helping the sick and wounded of both sides. Among the other medics doing the same thing was Joseph's father whose skills as a healer so impressed my father that he was invited to return with him to England and teach him all he knew. He came with his wife, a Damascene Jewess, and in time Joseph and I were both born here, Joseph first and me three years later.

In due course as I went off to study medicine in the great schools of Europe Joseph had to be content with opening an apothecary shop here in Edmund's town, for even had he gained formal medical training he could not have succeeded as a physician. People are happy to buy his herbs and potions but administering them is another matter. He is, after all, a Christ-denier twice over being both Jew and Arab, and therefore his prayers, so vital a component of the healing process, would naturally be ineffectual. Actually, I'm not sure he follows any faith anymore preferring instead the purity of logic and deduction. It has long been a sadness to me that I have never been able to convince him of the undoubted truth of Christ's message, so until he sees the light I'm afraid he must suffer the consequences of his idolatry and put up with the inconvenience of living beyond the town limits. Still, he has managed to build for himself a formidable reputation as a herbalist and his shop provides me with a good many of my healing potions, the purchase of which was the chief purpose of my visit this day.

'Greetings brother,' I said, making the sign of the Cross as I entered. 'God bless all in this house.'

'Greetings indeed, brother,' Joseph replied, 'and thank you.'

The formalities out of the way, I flopped gratefully down onto the nearest pile of cushions which are always scattered about the place.

'God in Heaven, Joseph, when are you going to get some decent sticks of furniture in here? I swear the abbey benches are more comfortable than these pillows.' I threw several away from me in disgust. 'And give me a drink before I wilt. It's hotter than Hades out there.'

He clapped his hands together. 'Is this how you honour your God, by blaspheming and cursing?'

'Oh, don't chastise me,' I grimaced. 'I'm hot and irritable. I'll confess and do penance tomorrow. But listen, I have other hot news all the way from London.'

'About King John's visit tomorrow?'

My jaw dropped open - an unfortunate habit of mine which I have never been able to conquer. 'God damn you Joseph for a necromancer! How the deuce did you know that? I've only just heard myself.'

He shook his head. 'No necromancy. A party of French jugglers came into my shop this morning. They were full of the news.'

'Ah yes,' I nodded. 'I met them in the market. Damn good music, and a damn lovely girl singing it, too.'

'Curses, blasphemy and now lechery,' he sighed shaking his head. 'I fear, my brother, you are rushing headlong into the arms of the Devil. Where now is your oath of chastity?'

'You don't believe in the Devil,' I reminded him. 'And I can admire God's handiwork without wishing to partake of it.'

He grinned back at me and clapped his hands again. This time a lissom youth I had not seen before entered through the silk partition with some steaming beverage and sweetmeats on a tray. I cannot explain why but I took an instant dislike to the boy. He seemed shifty to me, his eyes deliberately avoiding mine as he placed the tray on the floor between us. Joseph was always changing his servants and perhaps this was the only type he could find out here beyond the town pale - another reason to bring him back inside as soon as possible. But it was none of my business whom he chose to employ and so I kept my misgivings to myself. As you will see, I was later to regret my reticence.

'Much as I am delighted to see you, my brother, I do have a business to run. Was there some particular reason for your visit today?'

'What? Oh yes - I need to replenish some of my oils.'

As usual he had anticipated my request and handed me a parcel he'd already made up. Then almost as an afterthought he took a small phial from a shelf. 'Take this as well,' he said handing it to me. 'It's an opiate that I've been experimenting with.'

I took the stopper out, sniffed the contents and nearly choked. 'God's breath, what's in it?'

'Oh, various things: The gall of a boar, hemlock, opium, vinegar, plus a few other ingredients that I've added myself. It will make a man drowsy and deaden the pain of any surgical procedure. But mark me, only give a few drops at a time. Too much and it will suppress the action of the lungs and you may have a dead patient on your hands.'

'Surgery?' I scoffed putting the phial in my belt pouch. 'I doubt I will have need of it. I'm a physician not a surgeon. I leave slicing to barbers.'

'You never know,' he said sternly. 'With so many about to descend upon the town it may be useful in the coming days.' He held open his arms. 'Well, brother, it has been good to see you.'

'You too, brother.' I said hugging him to my breast.

So saying, I stepped out into the bright sunshine again and started back towards the town little knowing just how prophetic his words would be.

Chapter 2
THE ARRIVAL OF THE KING

An event as momentous as a royal visit is not something that can be easily concealed - at least, not without much subterfuge and cunning. And since the King would be staying with us at the abbey during his visit it would have been a courtesy at least to have told us first - an oversight that irked some of our less phlegmatic brethren. But before voicing our complaints we decided to give Abbot Samson the opportunity to explain himself, which he did the next morning in the chapterhouse beginning with a lie:

'Brothers forgive me, I apologise for the confusion. Until today I had no more knowledge of the King's impending visit than did you.'

This we knew to be false since the Abbot had himself been in London until a few days before so he must have known of the King's plans. As Baron of the Liberty of Edmundsbury he was, after all, one of the King's chief advisors.

'How fortuitous, then, that so much extra provision has been bought by the cellarer in the market these past few days.'

This from Brother Egbert who, being something of a natural rebel, was often the first to speak his mind. Several other monks murmured their agreement.

Abbot Samson pursed his lips and nodded. 'No, you are right, Egbert. I did know the King was coming, I admit it. Forgive this poor servant for trying to deceive you but Prior Robert and I were sworn to absolute secrecy. These are dangerous times and the King's safety was our first concern. But, for love of God and Saint Edmund, I will tell you now all that I know and that is this: For those of you who have not already heard the dreadful news King Richard, our beloved Lionheart, is dead, killed most foully by an assassin's arrow. But before he died he named his brother, the Prince John, as his successor.'

Gasps of horror and disbelief went up among the congregation. Frankly I was astonished at this. The news of Richard's death had been the hottest gossip around the town for a fortnight. But I was forgetting how few of my brother monks ever ventured further from the abbey precincts than the cloister garth. News of the outside world was often slow to penetrate the abbey walls. And this particular piece of news they might have preferred not to hear for all knew John's reputation. While King Richard was away fighting in the Holy Land John had been left in charge and his hopeless mismanagement of affairs had brought the country close to civil war. Worse, during Richard's captivity in Germany John had openly conspired to keep Richard permanently locked up and to have himself declared King. It did not bode well for the future peace of the land.

'So it is not King Harry who is coming?' piped up Old Simon who was in his eighties and a bit confused.

'No, Simon,' said Brother Allen seated next to him. 'The new king is Henry's son, John.'

'Little Prince John?' queried Simon still looking puzzled. 'He's but a child.'

'Old enough to be King,' said Allen kindly, 'as of last Thursday,' and nodded toward the Prior.

'There is a new government now, Simon,' said the Prior shortly. 'We must all get used to the change.'

But Simon was having none of that. 'Change, always change,' he grumbled. 'No good ever comes of change. First Stephen then Matilda then back again. That was change and look what happened: Civil war.'

'That was fifty years ago,' reminded the Prior. 'We have peace now, brother.'

'Peace – *piss!*' muttered Simon before settling down again.

Unperturbed, Samson continued: 'But the good news is that King John has chosen to give thanks for his elevation here at our abbey of Saint Edmund.' He beamed encouragingly all round the assembled monks. 'It is a great honour, is it not, that he has chosen us for his first great visit of state? Naturally this had to be arranged with all speed and in the greatest secrecy for the King's safety, hence my inability to share this sad but also, I think, happy news with you until now.' He beamed again and nodded to show his sincerity.

No-one believed a word of it. We all knew Abbot Samson's opinion of John. During Richard's incarceration he had openly opposed John and had defended Richard's honour in the council meetings, even offering to make the hazardous trip himself to the German prison where Richard was kept to verify his identity. But now with Richard dead, all that was in the past and as a member of the King's Council Samson felt obliged to demonstrate his commitment to the new government however reticent he may have felt about it.

Further discussion was curtailed, to Samson's obvious relief, for events were already overtaking us. Outside on the cobbles could be heard the sound of many horses arriving and we all rushed to the windows where we were met with the ominous sight of soldiers, exhausted from several days' march, falling out of line and collapsing onto the ground. They were followed by wagon after wagon of the King's baggage train. The rumpus went on for the rest of the day and it was evening before the last of the wagons rumbled into the abbey grounds. By the time they had finished it seemed as though an entire city had entered through the Abbey Gate and set up camp in the Great Court. The noise of a thousand voices was tremendous as dozens of fires, tents, corrals for horses, workshops and make-shift kitchens appeared as if from out of the mouth of hell beneath us. Only then as dusk began to fall did the King himself canter casually in through the Abbot's gate and up to the palace, along with his retinue of courtiers and bodyguards. Thus in the space of a single afternoon the town and abbey had been transformed from a peaceful haven of pilgrimage and commerce into a garrisoned fortress. All five gates of the town were locked and manned and dozens of soldiers in full battle array and with weapons drawn were nervously patrolling the streets, ready to strike first and ask questions later. Nothing was to be left to chance to ensure the King's safety. Edmund's little town was sewn up as tight as a nun's undergarments – no way out, and certainly no way in.

The following day the whole town was invited into the Great Court of the abbey to hear the King greet his people. I say 'invited' but there was no real opportunity to refuse, though many would have liked to have done so, for John was no more popular with the townsfolk of Edmundsbury than he was with its monks. Few accepted the story of how Richard came to meet his end. Most suspected that he was either languishing once again in some European dungeon or had been murdered. In either instance the culprit was undoubtedly the garishly-attired little man now standing on the podium before them. Still, John's speech that day stirred something in the hearts of those who heard him. He said all the right things: He confirmed the rights and privileges of our blessed martyr, Saint Edmund - very keen was Abbot Samson on this point - and he promised to smite our enemies abroad, by which of course he meant King Philip of France. Then he ended with these words:

'Many of you, I know, do not credit me as a worthy successor to my brother. You think me weak and ineffectual. To you I say this: I am of the same stock as Richard. His blood runs in my veins as it did in the veins of our father and in those of the Lady Eleanor, my mother, who sends her greetings to you all. From Scotland to Navarre ours is the greatest empire since Rome and together we can be greater still. But grant me your trust and I promise you will not be disappointed. There may be worthier princes who have sat upon this sacred throne of England but never was there one who loved thee better.'

The crowd was entranced, charmed even. Where was the snivelling princeling who less than a decade earlier had been forced to humble himself before great King Richard? Where the arrogant boy-lieutenant of Ireland who had been chased back to London for pulling the beards of Irish chieftains? John's words dazzled them. Perhaps better times really were ahead. Perhaps at the magical moment when the Archbishop placed Saint Edward's sacred crown upon his head he had indeed been transformed by the miracle of consecration. How desperately they wanted it to be so. The taxes and the treachery now forgotten, when King John finally turned to Abbot Samson and gave him the Kiss of Peace the crowd roared as one: *Vivat Rex*! Long live the King! Why, even Egbert, I saw, was cheering. Such is the magic of royalty.

But it was all an illusion, for bad times were indeed about to descend upon us.

Chapter 3
ABBOT SAMSON

Bad times began for me personally the very next morning when I found myself summoned to Abbot Samson's study immediately after Chapter. Not that there was anything unusual in that. I was often being reprimanded by the Abbot for something or other, usually to do with my inability to keep my private thoughts to myself. I had a good idea what it was about today.

'Do you know what these are?' he asked tapping the paper on the desk in front of him. 'Plans for my new towers for the west front of the abbey church,' he supplied before I could answer. 'The work will begin this week, God willing. You've no idea the difficulty I had finding the craftsmen capable of doing the job.'

I stood facing him on the other side of the desk like a recalcitrant schoolboy and had to rotate my head to see. 'Interesting shape, father. What are they - octagons?'

He ignored me. 'In a thousand years from now, Walter, when all of us – you, me, even the King – are dust and forgotten my towers will still be here. And in that far off and impossible world of the future - assuming there is still a world for people then and Christ has not already returned to judge us – when men look at my towers they won't be asking who designed them, what was the mason's name, how many tons of stone were needed or where it was quarried. All these are details. The important thing will be my towers and the message they convey. That will endure. Everything else is…' he twiddled his fingers in the air as if playing an imaginary flute, '… flotsam.'

I nodded, trying to look interested but wondering what point he was trying to make.

Abbot Samson sat back heavily in his chair and sighed wearily. 'You seemed confused yesterday afternoon, Walter.'

'Confused, father?' I smiled pleasantly. 'How so?'

'About the events of last November.'

He was referring, as I knew, to the night he presided over the opening of Saint Edmund's shrine. Following a fire in the abbey church the previous year the old shrine had been damaged and Edmund's body was being transferred to a new one specially constructed for him. Samson had taken the opportunity while the coffin was open to examine the remains of the saint, the first time this had been done in fifty years. As one of the senior obedientiaries I had been invited to witness the event along with eighteen of my brother monks. It had been a moment of great mystery and awe and one to which the King had made reference in his speech at the banquet the previous afternoon. He'd been in buoyant mood ever since his successful reception by the people earlier in the day. Maybe it was the abundance of fine wine and rich food which we cloister monks are not used to in our normal afternoons of quiet prayer, rest and work. Maybe it was just the hubris of the moment. Whatever the reason I had allowed myself an indulgence which I should not have done. In his address the King had commented that since he was a direct descendent of Saint Edmund the family resemblance must be remarkable, and to illustrate the point he raised his chin high in profile striking a heroic pose and placed a chicken bone at the end of his nose. It was a good joke and one greatly enjoyed by the banqueting guests who demonstrated their appreciation with much cheering and thumping of tables. It was during the ensuing hubbub that I had passed some asinine comment of my own thinking that no-one could hear. It seems I had been wrong.

'I don't think I was confused, father,' I bluffed. 'I remember the event very plainly: We all stood around the tomb while you opened it. A very sombre occasion, very moving. A cold night but, erm, wet - yes, *wet* I remember. The moon was…'

'I am referring to the condition of the saint's body,' he interrupted shortly. 'I saw it, Hugh saw it, Richard, Thurstan - we all saw it. The only person who apparently did not see it, Master Physician – was *you*.'

I tried to smile benignly. 'Father, I –'

'Ask them. They will all say the same. We opened the coffin, we touched the blessed limbs, unwrapped the sacred breast, counted the hallowed toes. I even entwined my fingers with those of the holy martyr,' he twiddled his own in the air once more to demonstrate the point. 'They were warm, Master Physician. The body was as vital in death as it had been in life.' Then he leaned forward: 'It was not, as you were overheard to remark, *a sack of dried up old bones.*'

I could feel my face reddening. It was true I had mumbled that phrase, or something like it. I had been sitting too far from Samson's table for him to have been able to overhear, so someone else must have tittle-tattled my words to him. Ah, but of course: Faithful old J-J-Jocelin, the abbey Guest-master and Samson's little ferret. Who else? He had been sitting opposite me. Yes, I could quite believe Jocelin would have reported my words to Samson. Well, the ferret was now out of the bag, so to speak, so there was no point trying to shove it back inside again. All I could do was look contrite and grovel.

'My Lord Abbot,' I began obsequiously. 'We all love and cherish the blessed Edmund's sacred memory and the marvellous stories of his martyrdom. But it was three hundred years ago. He has been lying in the chancel ever since. No body can survive that long intact however well it is tended. When the coffin was opened I saw clearly -'

'It was the middle of the night,' he snapped. 'You could not possibly have seen anything *clearly*. I was closer and I am telling you that the saint's body was as fresh and incorrupt as the day Alwyne laid him there to rest. The skin was flushed, the veins bled, the hair and fingernails grew. And how could it be otherwise? When a man becomes a saint he is washed clean of sin by the power of the Holy Spirit and it is sin which corrupts, is it not? Since *Saint* Edmund was without sin it follows that he could not have been corrupt.' He leaned forward eyeing me closely. 'Unless of course you disagree.'

It was a trap and one typical of the wily old Samson - he wasn't known as the Norfolk Trickster for nothing. If I disagreed I would be denying Edmund's canonization which had been sanctified by the Holy Father in Rome and was therefore irrefutable. To try to do otherwise would be profanity. I grimaced unable to think of a suitably clever answer.

Samson sat back again with a pained expression on his face. 'Walter, Walter. When will you learn to keep your more *unconventional* thoughts to yourself? You know how they disturb your brother monks. And it's not the first time, is it? Last time, I seem to remember, you had the temerity to question Saint Matthew's version of the Crucifixion.'

That was a slight exaggeration. I'd merely pointed out that if, as the Gospel asserts, people were raised from the dead at the Passion, and since they were no longer alive now, it followed that they must have had to do their dying all over again which seemed to me a little harsh. I thought I was being sympathetic to their plight. I certainly hadn't intended questioning the words of the evangelist. But some of my fellow monks thought otherwise and rebuked me for my irreverence. It had been a thoughtless observation for which I blame Joseph since he is always putting such foolish questions in my head.

'Your brother monks were very upset,' Samson continued. 'But more importantly, the King was upset, too.'

I shrugged. 'I cannot think why it should matter to the King what I thought.'

'Oh, can you not? Then answer me this: Why do you think he is here? Consider: The coronation was just a few days ago, the orb and sceptre hardly back in their boxes, the ink on the instrument of accession barely dry. Urgent matters of state demand the King's attention in London, possible war with France, discontent among the barons - and yet he decides to visit our humble little abbey here in the Suffolk countryside as practically the first thing he does. Why do you think he would do that?'

"Humble" isn't quite the word I would have used to describe one of the richest religious establishments in Europe. However, relieved that I had a question at last that I could confidently answer, I repeated the stock reply:

'The King felt impelled by a vow to make pilgrimage to the shrine, to show his devotion to Saint Edmund, and to give thanks to Almighty God for his accession to the throne of England.'

Samson snorted with contempt. 'King John has barely got one cheek of his arse on the throne of England and it wouldn't take much to dislodge him.'

My mouth fell open in astonishment at his forthrightness and I shut it again quickly with a plop. I glanced at the door half expecting it to cave in at any moment and a score of soldiers to haul us both off to the torturer's rack.

Samson seemed unperturbed. He eyed me steadily. 'He's not secure, you know, not at all. That little display out there in the yard yesterday was all bravado. He's not trusted. Some of the

French barons are even talking about putting his nephew, Arthur, in his place.' He grimaced painfully. 'That's just what this country needs right now, a twelve-year-old child sitting on the throne. Fortunately, the English barons are for John, as is the Archbishop - *as am I*.'

As a senior member of the King's Council it mattered what the Abbot of Edmundsbury thought on such issues, as I knew only too well, so I nodded my assent.

'Don't misunderstand me,' he continued haughtily, 'John is no Lionheart. He has neither Richard's soldiering skills nor his ability to command the love of his people. John is a schemer, an embezzler and a whoremonger, but he at least has had some experience of statecraft, certainly more than a twelve-year-old boy.' Samson ran his hand over his pink bald pate contemplatively. 'Mind you, he'd make a better fist of it if he spent a little less time in bed and a lot less time in his bath.'

'Father,' I said glancing nervously at the door again. 'Do you think this talk is wise?'

Samson casually waved aside my protest. 'It's early days. We can only pray that time will improve matters. But given the precariousness of his position it is understandable that he will clutch at anything that might strengthen his grip on the crown. And what better way to do that than to associate himself with Edmund who is, after all, the patron saint of the English, a martyr and a national hero who died defending his kingdom from the Great Heathen Army of the Danes. Put baldly, King John is here in Bury not so much because of his love for our revered and blessed martyr, but because Edmund was a *Wufinga*.'

He spoke the name as though that were sufficient explanation in itself. I'd heard of the *Wufingas*, of course, what student of the liberal arts has not? They were the almost mythical lineage of kings dating back a thousand years to the pagan Saxon gods of England. But what had that to do with the modern world? King John was a Norman, not a Saxon.

Samson seemed to read my thoughts: 'King John also traces his descent along this same line through his grandmother who was of the Confessor's lineage and through him to the ancient royal lineages of Wessex and East Anglia all the way back to Woden himself.'

'Ah,' I murmured.

'Ah indeed,' nodded Samson. 'John heard about the opening of the tomb last November and he simply wants those who witnessed the event to confirm the family likeness. Now, that's not so difficult, is it?'

He looked askance at me as though he was not sure himself if he quite believed what he said next:

'Despite appearances King John is something of a scholar who admires learning in others. He was particularly keen to have your endorsement since a physician is supposed to view these things with a certain *scientific* detachment.' He wrinkled his nose at the word. 'So it follows he is not best pleased to hear that you think his….relative….was in such a state of disintegration that he bore no more resemblance to the King than to his pet marmoset.'

I stifled a laugh. King John really must be clutching at straws if he needs my approval. Still, at least it proves I was right: Edmund's body was a sack of old bones after all, even Samson thinks so. But something still puzzled me:

'Forgive me father, but if Saint Edmund gives legitimacy to King John, then surely he gives the same legitimacy to his brother Geoffrey's son - the twelve-year-old Prince Arthur who you do not think fit to reign.'

'Well done,' smiled Samson. 'You're starting to think like a politician at last.' He breathed in deeply. 'The difference is symbolic.' He tapped his drawings again and smiled triumphantly. 'Like my towers. They are symbols, too. Put simply, John is here, Arthur is not. That is a fact, but it is also a symbol. Never underestimate the power of symbolism in politics, Walter.' He sighed heavily, heaved his not inconsiderable bulk off his chair and walked over to the open window. I couldn't help noticing as he did so a ring-shaped cushion on the seat he had just vacated. Piles, I thought. That's what comes of too many eight course lunches. It probably also explains his bad temper, nothing to do with me at all in fact.

Samson stood gazing out across the Great Court at the tents and fires of the King's followers billeted below him. 'These are dangerous times, Walter. Plots and intrigues everywhere. We have a duty to do what we can to hold society together.' He glanced over his shoulder. 'You are too young to remember King Stephen and the Empress. I wasn't much more than a child myself but I saw the fear, the lawlessness. We cannot go back to all that.'

'But surely, father,' I said gently, 'we have a duty also to tell the truth.'

He guffawed. 'The truth? The truth is God's Word as written in Holy Scripture and interpreted by us, His representatives on earth. The truth! Most men cannot read their own names so how can they possibly know what the truth is? Why do you think they come to church week after week? It's not because they know what's written in the Bible. They come out of habit; they come for comfort and because we fine them if they do not. That is what the clergy is for, to intercede, to guide man's innocence as the good shepherd guides his lambs and ensures they do not stray into danger. The truth! If we all went around deciding for ourselves what is truth and what is untruth there would be a different truth for every man on earth, and then where would we be? Anarchy again. There is only one truth and that is the truth that we decide here in this place - with God's guidance, of course,' he added as an afterthought.

Phew! That little speech fair took my breath away. I thought for a moment and then said slowly, 'In that case, why did God give us free will if not indeed to decide for ourselves?'

'Adam and Eve had free will and it got them expelled from the Garden of Eden,' he sniffed.

'Oh, but surely the expulsion from the Garden of Eden was due to temptation by the Prince of Darkness whom our free will permits us to accept or reject.'

Samson sighed heavily. 'Walter, why do you have to take such a skewed view of things all the time? Why can you not accept plain facts?' He looked at me with disappointment. 'Well, I am not going to debate theology with you, I have spent enough time on this. Mankind may have free will but as a member of this community you do not. You will therefore honour the vows you made to me when you entered our order, in particular the third one, and *obey*.' He leaned forward across the desk and looked me straight in the eye. 'Which means that if I say Edmund's body was incorrupt, then incorrupt it was.'

I winced. 'But in addition to being a monk, Father, I am also a physician. Every day I have to ask questions: How did this fever start? What caused that injury? Where may I find a cure for that man's belly ache or this woman's boils? How am I to do that without having an enquiring mind?'

'Maybe you can't,' he said wearily. 'Maybe you will have to choose between your Hippocratic Oath and your oath to God.'

I, too, would have liked to debate the point further but just at that moment the door to the study burst open and one of the novices rushed in, his arms waving wildly in the air, his eyes wild with fear.

'Murder!' he yelled. 'Murder!'

'What?' said Samson rising quickly to his feet. 'Who?'

'The King!' blurted the boy breathlessly. 'He is poisoned!'

Chapter 4
CONSPIRACY

We both rushed out of Samson's office and along the passage into the annexe where the King had taken up residence. Being half Samson's age and considerably fitter, I arrived at the door to the King's bedchamber ahead of him. Two beefy guards wearing chain hauberks and iron helmets and looking extremely nervous crossed their lances in my face as I tried to enter, nearly slicing off my nose in the process.

'I'm a doctor,' I remonstrated with them. 'I can help.'

But they were not to be persuaded and ordered me back on pain of being skewered. Anxious as I was for the King's good health, I was even more anxious for my own, so I stood back and waited for Samson to arrive. A few seconds later he came puffing up behind me and waving the guards aside. Even then they hesitated.

'I am his grace the Abbot,' he bellowed at them breathlessly. 'If you do not let us in I will have you both flogged. *Now open this door at once!*' They looked at each other. At last they relented and admitted us.

Inside the room there were more guards looking even twitchier than the two outside. They reluctantly allowed Abbot Samson through but me they continued to hold at the door. I had to content myself with trying to see over their

31

shoulders. From my position I could just make out the King's bed on the far side of the room. Standing around it like angels of the Apocalypse were three people I recognised from the banquet. One I knew was the Chancellor, Archbishop Hubert Walter of Canterbury, a bluff-looking man with a strong jawline and tonsured like a monk, though I think by nature's hand rather than his barber's. Standing next to him was a much younger man, handsome and with a noble bearing who Prior Robert, discreetly identifying the guests at the banquet for our benefit, had named as Earl Geoffrey Fitz Peter, the Chief Justiciar of England. Who the third man was there could be no doubt for there was no other quite like him in the land. Towering well over six feet in height and with a commanding military bearing was the formidable William Marshal, the Earl of Pembroke, probably the most powerful man in England after the King himself – though some said more powerful than the King. Unlike the others who were looking very worried, Earl Marshal's face wore an expression of stoic inscrutability - as much because most of it was hidden by his ferocious red beard as anything else.

Bending low over the bed was a fourth man who I took to be the King's physician, a Frenchman judging from his garb and waxed whiskers. Well, I thought, the King cannot be quite murdered yet since a dead man has little need of a physician. And from the screams and foul language coming from the bed it appeared his highness wasn't about to expire any time soon - his lungs at least sounded in excellent health. I could just make out their owner propped up in the bed against a bank of pillows. King John's dark hair was made all the darker by the pallor of his skin and the sweat plastering it to his brow while his mouth was contorted as though sucking on a particularly sour lemon. He was clutching his stomach, rolling from side to side and moaning all the while. From all this I made my preliminary diagnosis that the problem was likely to be with his belly.

'God damn you man, stop fussing. I'm not a woman in labour. Get *off* me!' The King violently shoved the French doctor away from him. 'Lucifer and all the dogs of hell curse you for a useless Frog!' he yelled slapping the physician hard about the head.

'Oh *sieur, sieur*,' whimpered the physician lifting his hands timidly in defence and supplication.

The King turned on his other attendants, the three most powerful men in the land, and growled at them. 'Look at you, like a pack of hyenas waiting for a corpse to devour. Aow! My bowels feel like someone's shoved a hot poker up my arse. Can't you give me something for the pain?' He turned manic eyes up at the Archbishop. 'Where is he? God damn his eyes I'll strangle the whore's whelp with my own hands! *I want that monk here now!*'

For one dreadful moment I thought he might have meant me, and from the sidelong glances I was receiving from my two guards I could see they were wondering the same.

'Not here yet, sire,' the Archbishop replied placatingly. 'He is being sought. But look, Abbot Samson is here.'

'I don't need a damned abbot,' he growled. 'I want the murdering monk who's poisoned me! And when you find him I want him flayed alive! You hear me? Like Richard's murderer. Am I to be disobeyed in my dying hour?'

He yelled and screamed and kicked his legs in the air and threw all his pillows out of the bed. It was quite a lively performance for a dying man and clearly demonstrated the famous Angevin temper of which I had heard. They all had it, apparently: John, Richard, even Bluff King Harry who was supposed to have chewed the carpet when taken by an uncontrollable fit of anger. Any child creating such a fuss would have been sent to bed without its supper – which is probably what used to happen to John, come to think of it, and which in turn explains his behaviour as an adult. Joseph with his taste for contortions of the mind would love to be here right now to witness this, I thought. I could see his wise brown head analysing and nodding sagely. I suppose such behaviour is a necessary attribute of any megalomaniac, but I did also wonder what had happened to the gentle and accommodating King John we had been presented with at the pageant the day before. It seemed the public face of the King was different from his private persona.

There was one other person in the room who I hadn't noticed until now. He too had been at the banquet sitting on the King's table, though somewhat distantly from the others. He was perhaps a decade older than me and noticeable because of his hairstyle which he wore shaved at the back in the old-fashioned Norman manner. This style, I remembered from my history lessons, had been adopted by our Norman conquerors so that their enemies could not grab their hair in battle, unlike their Saxon opponents whose long hair and generous moustaches had placed them at a disadvantage in close-quarter fighting. When he came to identifying this gentleman Prior Robert had lowered his voice further and whispered discreetly behind his hand the name of Geoffrey de Saye, uncle of the Justiciar. That probably explained his presence, which seemed otherwise superfluous, for de Saye was not among the group around the bed but was skulking alone by the window and wearing an expression on his face somewhere between boredom and disgust.

I could see that my services were not needed so I was about to unobtrusively take my leave when the said Lord de Saye spotted me.

'Well, look who's here. The bone-breaker.'

'Who?' I stupidly replied.

'You, idiot.'

Earl Fitz Peter glanced briefly at me then turned frowning to de Saye: 'Uncle, please.'

I was shocked at being addressed at all but the more so for the manner in which de Saye had spoken, almost as though he knew me. I racked my brains but could not think that we had met before. I'm sure I would have remembered if we had. When I think of it now, I did seem to remember him staring at me once or twice during the banquet although at the time I'd put it down to my fancy. Now I was not so sure.

Well, there was no time to dwell on it for

without my noticing the French doctor had sidled unobtrusively up to me. 'You are a physician, *mon frère?*'

I winced. 'Yes.'

'*Bien. Viens ici.*' When I hesitated, he smiled in amusement. 'Come. Do not be afraid,' whereupon he took my elbow lightly in his fingertips and led me to the other side of the room where he flourished a glass bottle half-filled with yellow urine. The light shining through it showed it to have a cloudy green hue. It didn't look at all healthy to me.

'Well?' he demanded.

I cleared my throat. 'The King's?'

'Yes of course, the King's,' he said indignantly, then lowered his voice. 'It is disgusting, *non?*'

'Er – *oui.*' I felt like I was a student again and back at anatomy class in Montpellier.

'And,' he said cocking an elegant Gallic eyebrow, 'what does this tell us?' He twitched his moustaches suggestively.

I took out my vademecum which I always carry attached to my belt. Among its many charts is one for the analysis of urine samples. Comparing the colours on the chart with that of the specimen I concluded that the King's humours contained far too much black bile which might explain his temper and I said as much to the French doctor.

'*Bon,*' he nodded approvingly. 'I concur.' He then sniffed the specimen and held it out for me to do the same, which I did and nearly choked.

'Urgh! Fish.'

'Aha!' squealed the Frenchman delightedly. 'You noticed.' Then he did what I was expecting next but had been dreading: He dipped a manicured finger into the warm, viscous liquid and sprinkled a few drops of it on to his tongue. But before he could offer me the bottle to do the same we were mercifully interrupted by shouting coming from outside the bedroom door which burst open and one of our brothers fell heavily in followed by one of the beefy guards. The man's eye was swollen badly and he had a large cut on his lip from which blood was oozing. His hands had been bound in front and a stick inserted through his elbows behind thereby thrusting his chest painfully forward. The guard kicked the hapless monk onto his knees in front of the King's bed where he scrambled to look up, absolute terror contorting his eyes.

'This is the pervert who poisoned the King,' growled the guard.

'Brother Alric!' said the startled Samson and immediately turned to the Archbishop. 'What is the meaning of this outrage? This man is one of my congregation. How dare he be treated this way?'

The Archbishop merely shrugged and walked away. But Samson would not be fobbed off so easily.

'You!' He pointed at the guard who had kicked the monk. 'Whose man are you? I'll have you horsewhipped for this impertinence. Release Brother Alric at once!'

The guard hesitated and looked to de Saye who with a resigned gesture waved him aside. The guard immediately released his hold on the hapless monk who fell towards the bed. So, I thought, not only an ill-mannered rogue this uncle of the Justiciar, but a bully too.

John scrabbled to the edge of the bed to peer at the man more closely. 'Is this him?' he gasped looking at the terrified monk. 'Is this my poisoner?'

'No poisoner, I beg of you, sire,' whimpered Alric pathetically. 'I am the baker. That's what I do. I bake – bread, cakes, biscuits. Pretty little confectioneries to sweeten your tooth. Why would I want to poison the King?'

'Why indeed!' John wrinkled his nose and grabbed Alric by his robe. 'I'll have you roasted on your own spit, you murdering knave. Whose pay are you in? Eh? His?' he pointed at Abbot Samson. 'Philip's? God's bowels!' he bellowed. 'Will no-one protect me from this nest of traitors?'

Right on cue de Saye stepped forward again. This time he grabbed the unfortunate Alric by the throat himself and started to throttle the poor man twisting the ropes to make him scream. Fortunately for Alric, at that moment John had another attack of colic, gasped and let out a terrible final cry then rolled onto his back distracting de Saye long enough for Alric to wriggle from his grasp and scuttle as fast as he could to the other side of the room. De Saye made a grab for him but Samson stepped between them, to de Saye's evident fury.

But now another quarrel had broken out, this time between the Archbishop and the Justiciar. It appeared to be over the ability of the King in his current condition to continue governing the country, the Justiciar saying he wasn't competent, the Archbishop insisting that he was.

While this new distraction was going on I took

the opportunity to make a more detailed diagnosis of the King's condition now that I was closer to the patient. My mind had gone back to the banquet the day before and suddenly all became clear to me. What had 'poisoned' the King were all those lampreys he had eaten. He'd certainly had enough. Loathing the slimy creatures myself, I had taken a particular interest in the King's evident relish of them and had watched with growing revulsion as he consumed plate after plate of the slippery worms. No doubt for those who have a taste for them they are a delicious delicacy but I can't abide strong-smelling fish. But it was definitely the smell I detected in his urine just now. In addition there was a jakes bucket by the King's bed which I had already noticed was empty and unused. Lampreys are notoriously rich and fat-filled which, if taken in sufficient quantity, can block even the most robust digestive system. Somewhere in the back of my mind I seemed to remember that one of John's ancestors – was it his great-grandfather King Henry the First? – had died from eating a surfeit of the wriggling parasites. Not wishing to interrupt the *contretemps* between the Archbishop and the Justiciar, I leaned towards Abbot Samson and whispered my conclusion in his ear. Unfortunately Samson, being a little deaf, did not hear me the first time so I repeated my diagnosis louder just at the moment when my warring lords spiritual and temporal paused in their wrangling and the word *CONSTIPATION* rang out in the silence, as clearly as a rook's caw on a crisp winter's morning.

Every eye in the room fell upon me. If the

floor could have opened at that moment and swallowed me all the way down to Hades I would not have protested.

The first to break the silence was Archbishop Hubert. 'What nonsense is this?' he scoffed glaring at me angrily. 'What do you know of it?'

'My lord Archbishop,' droned Abbot Samson pedantically. 'Master Walter is a trusted physician and academician, let me assure you -'.

'And your prescription?'

The voice cutting short the Abbot, deep and filled with gravitas, was that of William Marshal. It was the first time he had spoken and clearly he wanted a straight no-nonsense answer to his question. He looked at me with steady eyes. The stage, for good or ill, was mine.

I quickly repeated my conclusion and my reasoning over the lampreys. De Saye snorted contemptuously while everyone else looked merely bemused. Only Earl Marshal, I saw with gratitude, was nodding and stroking that fearsome beard thoughtfully. But having talked myself into a diagnosis I had no suggestion for a remedy which was what the councillors now demanded. They looked at me expectantly and I could feel my worth plummeting fast as I fought to think while the French doctor pursed his lips and cocked that inquisitive eyebrow of his again.

It was then that I remembered the opiate that Joseph had given me three days earlier. I had completely forgotten about it until then but fumbling now in the folds of my habit I found it was still in my belt pouch where I had put it. I drew it out and flourished it triumphantly aloft. The effect could not have been more dramatic than if I'd produced a rabbit from my undergarments.

'This,' I said with more confidence than I felt, 'will alleviate the King's discomfort and facilitate his recovery.'

Behind me I heard de Saye lightly clap his hands together as though I had performed a magic trick for children. But another hand, this one exquisitely manicured and be-ringed, came up and delicately plucked the phial from my grasp.

'What is in it?' asked the French physician uncorking the phial and sniffing the contents.

'Oh, various things,' I bluffed trying to remember what the hell it was Joseph had told me was in it. 'Hemlock, opium, that sort of thing - plus a few other ingredients of my own concoction. It will make the King drowsy and deaden his pain. But only a few drops at a time as too much and the effect could be …dangerous.'

My words faded away because to my horror at that moment the King had opened his eyes and, seeing the phial dangling above his head, seized it from the French doctor's grasp and poured the entire contents into his mouth swallowing the lot in one gulp.

The King slumped on the bed, dropped the empty phial onto his chest and let out a terrifyingly final-sounding exhalation of breath. De Saye roared and stepped forward, grabbed my cowl and lifted me bodily onto my toes practically choking me in the process while the Justiciar pulled a dagger from somewhere beneath his robes and waved it unnervingly close to my nose. Just in time to prevent me from being perforated or garrotted the King snorted in his sleep, rolled over in the bed and let out a loud and satisfying fart the aroma of which confirmed as nothing else could that my diagnosis had been the right one and it was indeed the lampreys that were the cause of his problems.

'Ah, *merveilleux!*' squealed the French doctor sniffing the air delightedly as though it were some exotic French perfume.

'The King,' I choked as de Saye dropped me back onto my feet, 'should sleep for a day or two now. Then, God willing, he will have a goodly motion and expel the offending blockage. In the meantime I think rest and quiet is the best, erm, *prescription*,' I said, deliberately using the Earl Marshal's word and praying he agreed. He immediately went into a huddle with the other two courtiers and Abbot Samson. All I could hear was the thumping of my heart which I was sure everyone else in the room must hear as loudly as I did. They then called the French doctor over and all five had an animated conversation conducted at the level of a whisper. Finally, they emerged from their deliberations.

'We agree with Master Walter's conclusion,' said William Marshal with his patrician voice again. 'The King will be allowed to rest and recover. But none of this must get out. If it becomes known that the King is incapacitated it may persuade some to try their luck. I therefore direct that all who witnessed the events in this room today are on forfeit of their life not to reveal what they have seen here.' He turned to Hubert Walter. 'My lord Archbishop, will you administer the oath?'

The Archbishop nodded and asked everyone in

the room to kneel. One by one each of us solemnly swore ourselves to silence and then a prayer of supplication was said for the King's speedy return to health and for peace in the world. We recited the *Paternoster* and the *Ave Maria* and finally the Archbishop gave his blessing to seal the oath.

'Father Abbot,' said the Earl rising to his feet again, 'you will ensure that all servants who wait upon the King are known by you personally.' Samson bowed and nodded. 'The story to be given out is that the King is tired after the events of recent weeks and will remain in the abbey a few days to recuperate. I will return to London with the Archbishop to secure the capital. You, my lord,' he said to the Justiciar, 'should remain here with the King.'

Earl Geoffrey opened his mouth to protest but shut it again and reluctantly bowed his assent. Earl William then turned back to Samson. 'Father Abbot, please have a proclamation drawn up to the effect I have directed and posted on the abbey gate.'

Abbot Samson bowed his agreement, too. Then upon a gesture, the servants were let back into the room to adjust the King's bed for his comfort and the assembly quickly broke up. As I scurried, thankful at last to be able to get away, I felt a restraining hand grip my shoulder. It was de Saye again.

'If the King does not recover, bone-breaker,' he whispered in my ear, 'and you turn out to be a very clever assassin, I will personally pull out your entrails and make you eat them.'

'Have I done something to offend your

lordship?' I asked in all innocence, but seeing Samson approaching de Saye merely let go of me and walked swiftly away bowing to Samson as he passed.

'What did he want?' Samson asked watching de Saye walk over to speak to the guard who had manhandled Alric.

'In truth, father, I do not know.'

Samson frowned and tutted. 'Be careful of that one. Geoffrey de Saye is the King's new bullyboy, keen to demonstrate his loyalty to the new regime.' He snorted. 'As loyal as a dog is to the hand that feeds it. I hope you know what you are doing, Walter. If the King's condition does not improve Brother Alric's fate will be as nothing compared with yours.'

I watched as the guard came to attention and saluted before following de Saye smartly out of the room. I wasn't too worried by Samson's words. I was confident that Joseph's potion would work and the King would recover in a day or two and then the whole royal circus would up sticks and be gone, de Saye with them. He had shown himself to be someone who took pleasure in the suffering of others and was therefore to be avoided. That would not be difficult since there would be no reason for our paths to cross again. I resolved to dismiss him from my mind, convinced that whatever the reason for his hostility it had nothing to do with me personally. But I was wrong in this as I was to be in so many things in the coming days, for there was indeed a particular reason for de Saye's dislike of me and it would be a while before I found out the truth of it.

Chapter 5
A FOOTBALL MATCH

Looking back now with forty years' hindsight, it is easy to see how the clues pointing to the impending disaster were steadily mounting although at the time there was nothing obvious to connect them. I doubt, for instance, if anyone would have thought the King's ailment had anything to do with it for it had the air of farce about it. Those of us who had been witness to the bedroom scene kept to the official line that he was suffering from fatigue as we were bound by oath so to do, but frankly if any of King Philip's spies truly were about they must have been laughing up their conspiratorial sleeves.

For once John's well-known fondness for his bed actually worked in our favour since incredulous eyebrows were raised and knowing winks exchanged. After a few days even Abbot Samson was beginning to find the reports of the King's progress embarrassingly implausible and eventually he gave up, leaving it to poor old Prior Robert to impart the daily bulletin. Since I heard no more from my lord de Saye, I presumed the King's condition at least had not worsened. Still, we all prayed sincerely for the King's speedy return to health if only to see the back of him and his entourage. But the King seemed in no hurry to go despite the undoubted pressing needs of his government. I could not help but reflect that this was one more aspect of John's personality that contrasted with that of both his whirlwind father and his firebrand brother. Henry and Richard had both kept hold of their vast possessions by being – or seeming to be - everywhere at all times. In that respect John had more in common with another of his forebears, Ethelred called *Unready,* who through indecision and timorousness lost his kingdom to King Cnut of Denmark. Some wag even went so far as to suggest a new soubriquet for John himself: Not so much *Lackland* as *Lackaday*.

This dithering was very frustrating as Earl William's security arrangements severely restricted movement. I felt this more than most of my brother monks as I was accustomed to passing freely between abbey and town in the pursuance of my medical ministry. I had patients that needed my urgent attention but instead I had to spend much of my new enforced leisure time in either study or preparation of various potions for use when I eventually did manage to get out and about again. There comes a point when reducing yet another solution of pig bile to paste begins to lose its novelty value. By the time the King's health had fully recovered I should have collected enough magpie beaks to cure every case of toothache in the Liberty.

I did, however, have one new patient I was able to see. After I'd left the King's bedchamber I'd gone down to the kitchens to see how Brother Alric was faring - the brother so badly mistreated by de Saye's lout of a guard. No bones broken, God be thanked, but he had some nasty cuts and bruises which I duly dressed. I complained once again to Father Abbot about his mistreatment but Samson, ever one to smooth ruffled feathers, was of a mind to play down the whole affair reluctant as he was to prompt any more ill-will than already existed between the abbey and the King's men.

And that was another bone of contention. With so many young men with nothing to do billeted within the abbey grounds tempers were beginning to fray. Drink was the main problem. Complaints from the cellarer's office about drunken brawls had already led to a banning of alcohol within the abbey precincts. Needless to say this ordinance had no effect whatever. The men simply went out into town to get their drink there. And they returned, inevitably, with women.

Now, licentiousness within the abbey precincts was not something to be taken lightly. We are a celibate order and such behaviour brings disgrace upon the name of our virtuous – and reputedly virginal - saint. And our tonsures did nothing to shield us from the attentions of these…ladies. One evening as the light was beginning to fade I happened to be in the Great Cemetery behind the abbey church – I'd gone there for a legitimate purpose, it being too much of a trudge to the necessarium just to make water - when I heard a noise and out from the bushes emerged a soldier with two girls in tow. Startled, I had to finish my business quickly and just managed to hide in time to see him hand the two girls over to a grotesque creature perched cross-legged upon a coffin tomb. I crossed myself quickly, wondering what manner of devil this was when I recognised its shape: It was Mother Han, the woman I found selling fake relics in the marketplace a few days earlier. The soldier was just too much of a brute for me to tackle on my own, but Mother Han was not. She was so busy examining the coins the soldier had given her that she didn't notice me scuttle over. Glancing quickly at the two girls who were quite unperturbed at seeing a monk in a habit, I challenged her:

'Mother Han, what is the meaning of this outrage?'

'Eh?' she stared up at me with her one good eye. 'Ah, the bone-breaker,' she nodded. 'It's tuppence for you as for anybody else.'

'Mother Han,' I protested. 'These girls can be barely above nine or ten summers!'

She shrugged. 'A penny each then.'

'Mother Han!'

'We all have to make a living, brother. Anyway, these two are eighteen. Ask them.'

I bent to examine the smallest girl more closely. 'This one still has her milk teeth!' I said rising up again.

Mother Han squinted at the girl through her one good eye then tutted. 'I thought they looked a bit small for eighteen. Ach, you can't believe a word anyone says these days.'

I started spluttering again.

'Oh, all right, keep your tonsure on. We were going anyway. It's too quiet here. Quiet as the grave,' she cackled and heaved herself laboriously off the tombstone. With the bell tolling vespers above us I watched with dismay as she corralled her two young charges out through Anselm's gate tipping the gatekeeper a coin as she went. As they disappeared into the gathering gloom I realised something had to be done to distract so many idle young men before even worse befell us. But what?

I'm not sure whose idea it was to hold a football match but it certainly wasn't mine. I had witnessed too many such tournaments when I was a student and there are fewer maimings in the aftermath of a battle than after a game of mob football. That is because on a battlefield there are strict rules governing the slaughter while on the football field there are none. The proposal was much debated in Chapter before agreement was finally reached. No-one was under the illusion that the whoring and the brawling would cease after the match but it would perhaps resume with a little less vigour than before - at least for a while. But it was agreed that a well-policed contest between the two teams – one from the town and one drawn from among the King's men – would be a welcome distraction.

The game kicked off shortly after sext in the after noon. I had my work cut out coping with the multitude of injuries among both the players and the spectators - not that there was much to distinguish between the two since every townsman under fifty seemed to join in the game at one point or another. As usual these were mostly knife wounds, some malicious but most due to players and spectators carrying their weapons loosely about their persons. I vowed that if another game like this was ever arranged I would make it my business to insist that daggers be unstrapped and left in the sacristy. The game did manage to end more or less on time mostly because someone – I think it was the Prior – simultaneously got all the bells of the abbey to ring for compline while the army heralds trumpeted assembly at the other end of the ground. The only people still left playing at dusk were the town boys who had far too much energy and didn't know when to go home. I have no idea what the final score was but Gilbert, my assistant who had been enthusiastically rushing in and out of my make-shift treatment room with progress reports all afternoon, thought we had scored thirty-seven goals to the army's ten. In any event it looked as though our side had won the day, and judging by the rather boozy singing and chanting it had been a successful one.

With the last patient patched up and sent on his way I dismissed Gilbert with my thanks while I finished tidying up. By and large it had been a joyful day. As I stood at the door winding bandages and looking out over the long June twilight I saw a hooded figure standing by the gate. From his height and his stance I could see that it was Joseph. Surprised and delighted, I waved furiously and rushed over to him.

'Greetings brother,' I said breathlessly. 'What's the purpose of the hood? Are you in disguise?' I was still exhilarated in the aftermath of the football match.

'Greetings indeed, brother,' he replied coolly. 'It is a relief to see you too. When I didn't hear from you for a few days I became worried.'

'Worried about me?' I chortled taking him to one side. 'There was no need. Apart from being bored out of my mind. With the King ailing everyone's movements are restricted.'

'You don't have to be coy, Walter,' he said softly. 'I know that it is your movements that have been restrained. And I know why.'

'You've heard the news, then?'

'Regarding the King's rheum? Of course. Everyone has heard it and no-one believes a word of it. What's really wrong with the King? I've heard he's been poisoned.'

I laughed dismissively. 'Poisoned? My goodness me, no! Where did you hear that? Poisoned indeed! Huh!' But Joseph was not fooled by my denial. 'I'm sworn to secrecy,' I conceded seriously. 'But no, not that. Suffice to say your divining is as uncannily accurate as ever.'

He frowned. 'Brother, you do my reputation no good by this constant inference of my sorcery.'

'Doesn't do it much harm either,' I grinned. 'Ah, it is good indeed to see you,' I thumped his shoulder. 'I have been so bored kicking my heels these past days. What news of the outside world?'

He waved a dismissive hand and looked at me seriously. 'Walter, I have come to tell you that I am going away for a while.'

'Hm, must be serious if you're calling me Walter. Why? What has happened?'

'Nothing – yet. But it is not safe for those of… my persuasion here in Bury while so many armed men are in the town.'

'Jews, you mean,' I said fixing him with a stern look.

'Anyone who looks a little different. And I am hardly invisible.'

Taller than most and certainly darker, he had a point.

'But you have the King's protection.'

'Such arguments are for lawyers,' he dismissed. 'It will be safer not to tempt fate.'

I was sad that he should feel so threatened. If he thought there was real danger then there must be.

'Where will you go?' I asked.

'Best you don't know, but I will be safe.'

'It's a pity you can no longer come here,' I said indicating the strong walls of the abbey buildings. There was a time when he would have been able to find refuge within the abbey precinct. But since Abbot Samson banished the Jews from the town and abbey they can no longer find sanctuary here. Besides that, many of these soldiers must be veterans from the recent wars in the Holy Land. It would only take one man with a grudge to put a length of steel through Joseph's superb brain. Yes, I could see that he might well feel safer with friends further afield.

'You could go to my mother,' I suggested.

He shook his head. 'No, the lady Isabel is not in good health. I would not wish to burden her further. And it is unnecessary,' he added quickly before I was able to protest. He became serious again. 'Walter, listen to me. There is another reason for my coming here tonight.' He looked at me earnestly. 'I have come to warn you.'

'Warn *me*?' I snorted, sitting on the ground. 'About what?'

'There is one among the King's entourage who has no great love for you. Indeed, he wishes you nothing but harm. Your mother, I think, knows who it is but she would not tell me. You must be on your guard.'

I nodded. 'I have an idea who it might be but for the life of me I have no idea why.'

'You have a name?'

'Yes,' I said cautiously, but before I could say we were interrupted by a group of half a dozen boys in high spirits nearly colliding with me as they ran pell-mell towards the river, hallooing at the tops of their lungs as they went. Had the gatekeeper been a little less sleepy he might have caught them as they passed through the gate, but they were too quick for him, dodging his cuffs, and out and across the square before he had a chance to react.

'Come back again, yer little beggars,' he yelled. 'I'll whup the lot of you!'

We heard them disappear up into the town no doubt to cause more pandemonium to some other poor innocent soul.

'I think perhaps you had best get home too,' I said to Joseph.

'They are only boys,' he dismissed.

'I know, but high spirits and alcohol make for a lethal combination.'

As if to prove my point another posse came rushing back the other way down Churchgate Street towards the abbey shouting at the tops of their lungs. These stopped to speak to the gatekeeper. As we watched, intrigued, they stood gesticulating and arguing with great ferocity for a few moments. But instead of berating them the gatekeeper suddenly turned unexpectedly on his heel and ran as fast as his fat legs would carry him towards the barracks. A minute later the posse was back again and shouting in great excitement. I thought at first it was one of the chants for the football match, but then I realised it wasn't that at all. It was just one word they were shouting over and over, and the word was "*Murder!*"

Chapter 6
AN INCONVENIENT MURDER

My initial reaction to the "murder" was that, like the King's "poisoning", it was nothing of the kind but just another piece of mindless violence in the aftermath of the football match. Either that or someone had taken advantage of the general confusion of the game to settle an old score – unfortunately another all-too-common event. I was forced to rethink both conclusions, however, at Chapter next morning when not only the Abbot but also the Prior were absent and rumoured to be in deep conference with the Justiciar who was still at the abbey.

Chapter is the daily meeting when notices are given out and the general business of the abbey discussed, and other than when we recite the offices, it is the only time when all eighty of the choir monks assemble together. As such it interrupts the smooth running of the abbey and can be something of an irritation. Without the Abbot or the Prior present there seemed little point in holding it at all. By common consent, therefore, the meeting was about to break up when we received a message from the Abbot asking us all to remain in the chapterhouse until further notice on a matter of extreme importance. This naturally sparked speculation that the delay might be something to do with the murder. For the Abbot, the Prior and the Justiciar all to become involved the victim had to be someone of unusual interest at the very least and we wondered who it could have been. So we remained on our stone benches lining the walls of the chamber in some degree of trepidation.

After a further hour and in something of a flurry Samson at last arrived, accompanied by a stony-faced Prior Robert and an even stonier-faced Earl Geoffrey. I gathered later that the delay had been largely because of acrimonious wrangling between the Abbot and the Justiciar over who was the most senior officer now that William Marshal and Archbishop Hubert had both returned to London. It was a moot point for the Justiciar officially acts as regent in the King's absence and would doubtless have insisted on doing so today. But Abbot Samson would be loathe to relinquish one scintilla of his authority whilst within the abbey demesne. Only threats from Samson to appeal directly to the King had forced the Justiciar finally to submit, and judging by the expression on his face he did so with bad grace. But now that the correct protocols had been established at last Abbot Samson addressed the assembled community, and he did so in words of utmost gravity beginning with the usual prayer for divine guidance:

'The Peace of the Lord be with you and may He give His blessings on these our solemn deliberations, Amen.

'My lord Justiciar, Brothers in Christ, I have a woeful duty to perform. Yesterday evening during compline word reached us that the body of a twelve-year-old boy had been found in the town.'

Was that it? Was that what had kept us so long from God's work, the death of a mere boy?

'Was the victim known?' This from the far end of the chapterhouse.

'Yes,' answered Samson simply. 'The boy's name is Matthew, son of William the Fuller, a tenant of the abbey.'

Oh, worse and worse. Not just a boy but a *servant* to boot. This caused a good deal more noisy protestation with many frowns and the shaking of tonsured heads.

I should perhaps explain for we are not quite as heartless as my account may make us at first appear. You see, tragic though any death is - and the death of a child particularly so - nevertheless it is hardly so vital as to disrupt the important work of the abbey. We had the souls of the entire nation in our care not just that of a single child. Besides, murder was a matter for the Abbot and the secular authorities not the entire convent meeting in full Chapter. We had better things to do with our time than to waste an entire morning waiting to be told news that could easily have been conveyed with a great deal less disruption to our busy schedules.

'I understand your disquiet, brothers,' said the Abbot raising his voice above the growing clamour, 'but if you would bear with me for just a moment longer.' Here he paused to confer with the Justiciar and the Prior while the restlessness continued. But then Abbot Samson resumed:

'From his injuries and the circumstances of the boy's death I fear it might be…that is to say, it looks as though it could be....' He grimaced awkwardly. 'Brothers, I believe we may have another Robert on our hands.'

This had the effect Samson was clearly expecting. For a moment we all froze, no-one daring to move or to speak as we held our collective breath. Those monks who had stood up to leave sat down again while others looked anxiously at each other and then to the Abbot who at last had our full attention. We all waited to hear his words for we knew well enough to whom – and to what - Samson was referring. Ah yes, we all knew what Samson was talking about all right, and as I remembered the details all in a rush a tingle of anticipation ran down my spine, for eleven years earlier the body of another twelve-year-old boy had been found murdered in the town, and that time there was no doubt about its significance.

His name was Robert and his death had led to one of the most disturbing episodes in the entire two hundred year history of our abbey. No culprit was ever found for the murder but it was widely believed that the Jews had killed him in mockery of Christ's Passion. Whatever the truth of it, many miracles were ascribed to the boy and he quickly became venerated as a martyr - indeed, his shrine still stands in the crypt of the abbey although these days largely forgotten. But the tragedy that followed his death and the shame that so many still felt as a result was that a few years after Robert's death, on Palm Sunday *anno domini* 1190 to be precise, riots had broken out in the town and fifty-seven Jews were massacred, some at the very gates of the abbey trying to find sanctuary within our walls.

In mitigation, if defendable such an appalling episode could be, it was a time of great religious anxiety. Jerusalem had fallen to the heathens three years earlier and the new king, as Richard was then, was eager to win it back for Christ. The entire country had been roused by his call to arms against the infidel and emotions were running high. Local resentment against the Jews, never entirely stilled after the death of the boy-saint, erupted again with tragic consequences. Those Jews who survived the butchery were later expelled from the town, my brother Joseph among them. And the Abbot who had ordered the expulsion was none other than Samson de Tottington.

'Was he crucified?' inquired one lone voice once we had at last collected our wits.

'It is too early to say,' replied Samson.

'Have there been miracles?'

'To my knowledge, not yet.'

'Who is keeping watch over the child's body?'

'His family, and my lord Essex here has posted a guard.' Samson bowed in deference to Justiciar Geoffrey.

'It is only a precaution,' said the Justiciar. 'Our priority must be to maintain order while the King's person is in the town.'

'It is God's priority we are concerned with, not the King's,' came an angry voice.

'Who did it?' came another. 'The Christ-killers?'

'You mean the Jews!'

This provoked a storm of protest among the brethren and much angry argument. Samson frowned and shook his head. I looked on in dismay for the news had hardly been announced and already the old passions were coming to the fore. I could see now that Joseph had been right to fear for his safety and I thanked God that he had chosen to leave the town the previous night. I could only hope he was a long way away by now.

Samson held up his hands beseechingly. 'Brothers, I know no more at the moment. Please, speculation is unhelpful. Let us wait until we have confirmation and more details.'

'The body must not be touched!' yelled another angry voice.

'His purity must not be violated!' came yet another.

'Yes,' said Abbot Samson wearily sitting down. 'I know.'

An hour later I was once again standing before Samson's desk in his study. He was slumped disconsolately in his chair exhausted and looking as though his haemorrhoids were giving him even more discomfort than usual. On the desk this time were not drawings of towers but the yellowing pages of a script written in a neat, small and precise hand. The author, I had no doubt, was the man now hovering at Samson's elbow, hands clasped behind him, his pointed nose twitching like a weasel that had just located its supper – the excellent and devoted Brother Jocelin. Could this be the famous chronicle of St Edmund's Abbey, about which we had heard so much but which no-one had ever been allowed to see? If so, whose nemesis was I about to meet? Not, I hoped, my own. I tried surreptitiously to read the thing while Samson had it open but the hand was so spidery it was impossible to read upside down. Besides, Jocelin's writings seemed to be interrupted with odd little quotations from other texts every few lines as a sort of faltering commentary, making it impossible to follow. Good God, I thought, the man even writes with a stammer.

The sound of hooves on the cobbles below drew our attention to the open window.

'The Justiciar,' Samson grimaced without looking up. 'Returning to London. With Earl William and the Archbishop already gone he doesn't want to be the only member of the Council remaining. The last rat deserting the sinking ship.' He sighed then shook himself. 'It is of no consequence. We have adequate resources to protect the King.'

From where I was standing I could see into the courtyard below. Earl Geoffrey was just mounting his fine-looking dappled grey gelding with its harness of blue and gold silk. Already mounted and raring for the off were a dozen troopers dressed in the Fitz Peter livery of red and yellow ochre. Once in the saddle and with the briefest of backward glances the Chief Justiciar spurred his horse and the entire posse set off at a brisk canter towards the Abbot's Gate, tails swishing in the mid-morning sunshine as they went.

But what drew my attention was the man left standing on the cobblestones watching the Justiciar go: Lord Geoffrey de Saye. My heart sank. Why could he not have accompanied his nephew back to London? With the Justiciar gone there was no-one left to exercise a restraining hand on the man, a situation that de Saye no doubt would be relishing. Was it my imagination or did he glance up at the Abbot's window before turning on his heel and returning to the lodging house? I frowned with dismay.

Samson was tapping his desk to regain my attention. 'Walter, what do you know about Saint Robert of Bury?'

I had to think. 'Erm, only what everyone knows, that he is one of a number of boy-martyrs who have been venerated in recent years,' and then I added and immediately regretted: 'To the honour of Saint Edmund.'

Samson nodded. 'Out of favour these days, alas, but a decade back it was a different matter. Pilgrims flocked to his shrine and he performed a great many miracles both before and after his death.' Without looking up he lifted an imperious finger. 'Jocelin here wrote an account of his life. He died in…' Samson squinted at the page in front of him his nose nearly touching the page. 'Jocelin,' he said impatiently. 'I cannot decipher this scribble for ants. When was it?'

'Er, e-eleven-eighty-one, f-father,' stuttered Jocelin bending low.

'Eighteen years,' Samson mused stroking his neatly clipped white beard. 'Was it so long ago? It came at a bad time, I know that. A year before my election.' He glanced up at me. 'We had no moral guide then you see, Walter, Abbot Hugh having died the previous November and the abbacy vacant.' He frowned into blank space. 'That was part of the problem. Prior Robert was in charge until a new Abbot could be elected. A good man,

Prior Robert - devoted, gentle, but a little...' he groped for an appropriate word.

'Lax?' suggested Jocelin.

'Overwhelmed,' corrected Samson. 'Matters got out of hand, which is something we cannot allow to happen this time.' He focussed back on me again. 'That's why I want you to take charge of this. Liaise with Jocelin here. Look for similarities between the two cases, anything that can give a clue, then report back to me.'

My mouth dropped open in astonishment. I must have looked as bewildered as I felt as I glanced helplessly at Jocelin.

'Father Abbot,' said Jocelin softly in his ear. 'If you c-could just explain...?'

Samson raised his eyebrows. 'What? Oh yes. I'm sorry, Walter. I didn't manage to get to bed at all last night. Events have been unfolding so fast I am losing track of who knows what. All right, let's go back to the beginning. Boy martyrs, yes.' He winced and shifted his weight to his other buttock. 'As you say, there have been a number of them in recent years – William of Norwich was the first, I think. Then there was the child Harold in Gloucester - I believe he was the youngest. And our own blessed Saint Robert the most recent of all. There have been others here and in France. They had certain attributes in common – all were boys, all pre-puberty and all killed in a grotesque parody of Our Lord's Passion, it has always been assumed, by Jews.'

Here I felt the need to interrupt. 'Why?'

He frowned impatiently. 'Why what? Why did they do it, you mean?' Samson inhaled deeply shaking his tonsured head. 'Who knows?

Mockery, jealousy. Something about returning to Jerusalem.' He snorted up at Jocelin. 'Not that there's any chance of that at the moment.'

'No,' I said. 'I meant, why would the Jews be blamed in this case?'

Samson lowered his voice almost to a whisper. 'Because of where the body was found, of course.'

'Which was where?'

Samson frowned again and looked at me as though he could not believe I did not know. Fortunately Jocelin saw the danger and coughed lightly to clear his throat. 'I-in the garden of a prominent local Jew.'

I said carefully and deliberately: 'The garden of a Jew? I thought all the Jews in Bury had been expelled some time ago, by your order, Father Abbot.'

Samson shifted uncomfortably in his chair again. 'They had. Most of them. Anyway, that's beside the point now. You saw the response of your brother monks this morning at the mere suggestion that the boy might have been martyred by Jews. I've no doubt the reaction of the townsfolk will be the same. It's a highly emotive subject. People…react.' He glanced at me. 'We need to be discreet but we need a quick resolution. The longer we delay the greater the chance of some…unpleasantness.'

By 'unpleasantness' I presumed he meant the Palm Sunday riots and murder of fifty-seven human beings. An interesting use of the word.

Samson suddenly exploded: 'God damn the boy! Why did he have to choose now to get himself killed? The King here.' He pointed a fat finger at me. 'We must do all we can to ensure

King John is not given any excuse to take over the investigation - which he will, mark my word, given half the chance. At the first sign of faltering he will put in his own men and that cannot be allowed to happen. The honour of Saint Edmund is at stake.'

The honour of Saint Edmund. Is that what was really bothering Samson, I wondered? The saint's honour resided in the hands of his champion-in-chief here on earth who was the Abbot of Edmundsbury, of course. Could it be that Samson's main concern over this boy's death was the threat it posed to his own authority? Or was I being uncharitable?

'Why would the King want to do that?' I asked naively again. 'Interfere I mean. Surely he has more to worry about than the death of a miller's son?'

Samson looked at me with amazement. 'Anything to do with the Jews is the King's concern, Walter. They have no status other than at the King's behest.' He snorted. 'I should have thought you of all people would have known that.'

I looked up rather too quickly. Was he referring to my connection with Joseph? I didn't think he knew anything about that. I could feel my cheeks start to redden and burn. All I could do was nod stupidly, which he evidently took to signal my agreement.

'Good, well that's settled then. Unless you have any more questions?'

'Just one,' I said. 'Why me? Bearing in mind our last conversation on the subject of miracles, I would have thought you'd regard my approach as being too....scientific?' I was referring to the discussion we'd had concerning the remains of Saint Edmund just prior to the drama in the King's bedchamber.

Samson's lips tightened. 'It is precisely because you take such a perverse view of these matters, Walter, that I want you on the case. That and your medical training which I am sure will be decisive. I am confident your approach will get to the truth unswayed by – how shall we say? - *religious hysteria.* And your reputation as a neutral in these matters...' here he put up his hand to forestall my protest '...will help dispel any accusation of bias on the part of the abbey which must be seen to be impartial. If we lean too far one way we will seem to be favouring the King; too far the other way and the King will feel aggrieved and step in. Neither would be a good outcome from our point of view.'

'I see.'

He nodded. 'I'm glad you do. Now, as our resident expert on the subject of boy martyrs Jocelin's input will prove to be invaluable to you. Here's his work on Saint Robert.' He shuffled together the papers on his desk and held them out for me to take. 'You have my full authority to examine all the evidence, call as many witnesses as you think fit, come and go as you please.'

'Oh, but what of Earl Marshal's restrictions on movement?' I said hopefully.

Samson waved an impatient hand. 'The Earl isn't here. And besides,' he shifted uncomfortably in his chair, 'no-one believes all that nonsense about the King's hay fever. This murder must take precedence now. You have my permission to forgo all other duties, including your office devotions where necessary, until this matter is resolved. Be thorough, be fair and above all be objective. Let no-one sway or influence you to any precipitate conclusion. Then come back and tell me that this miller's brat has nothing whatever in common with the blessed Robert but is merely a stupid child who managed to get himself killed. *Dominus vobiscum*.'

'He doesn't like the Jews much, does he?' I said to Jocelin as we strolled back to his office. As Guest-master Jocelin had his own room in the Court of Hospice, not confined to a common cell like the rest of us choir monks.

Jocelin grimaced. 'Th-they opposed his election. He also blames them for b-bringing the abbey into debt.'

'Oh, but that was financial mismanagement on the part of Abbot Hugh, surely?'

'But Hugh was old and easily manipulated,' countered Jocelin. 'The J-jews took advantage. There's no doubt.'

We walked in silence for a minute.

'You admire Abbot Samson, don't you?' I said at length.

'I think he has done many good works.'

'Including expelling all the Jews from the town?'

'Th-that was as much for their own protection as anything else.' He smiled. 'Don't judge him too harshly. One of the reasons he chose you to investigate this matter is the fact that you have a Jewish b-brother and so will be sympathetic.'

'So he does know about Joseph? I wasn't sure.'

'Of course. Abbot Samson has the welfare of all his flock c-constantly in his mind. How can he d-do that if he does not know all that there is to know about each and every one of us?' He stopped by a panelled door set in an arched alcove. 'Here we are.' He took out what was the largest iron key I had ever seen from somewhere under his robe and began laboriously unlocking it. I could see now why no-one had ever seen his famous chronicle and possibly why Samson placed so much faith in him. Security was evidently one of Jocelin's valued qualities. He pushed the heavy door open for me to enter ahead of him.

The room was small and made all the smaller by shelves lining every wall upon which were stacked piles of papers and books of every size and description spilling over onto every available surface. As well as many religious tracts I could see works by Virgil, Horace and Ovid among others that I could not recognise. This was a scholar's room indeed, an impressive library that put my own modest collection to shame.

'You have been to the university?' I asked running my finger along the nearest dusty shelf for this was surely a don's study.

He bowed shyly. 'Alas, n-no. I come from a very poor family.' He hastily cleared a pile of papers from a bench so that I could sit down.

'A local family, judging by your accent.'

'Indeed. I am a Saint Edmund's man body and soul. My f-family still live here – in the lower brackland in the north of the town. Do you know it?'

I did. I'd had many a pneumonic patient in that area of heathland and wood. A poor area indeed. Jocelin had done well to escape it.

'Master Samson t-took me under his wing when I first entered the order twenty-six years ago. I owe everything I am to him. "He grew and the Lord b-blessed him",' he smiled.

I smiled back. I could see I would have to be careful what I said to this man for I had no doubt it would all get back to Samson, the bad as well as the good.

As though reading my mind, Jocelin chuckled. 'Do not worry. I am indebted to Master Samson b-but I cherish truth more. After all, we are all here but for a short span, are we not? The f-future is merely the present continued and the work we begin here on earth will carry on after we have p-passed over. So it follows we must apply ourselves as honestly as we c-can in all we do while we are here. Is that not so?'

I was taken aback by his sudden descent into philosophy. Clearly Jocelin was a man of learning. Such people, as I knew from my student days, value intellectual integrity above personal relationships. Perhaps he wasn't quite the lick-spittle I had taken him for. In that regard he had something in common with Joseph, both men coming from humble backgrounds, albeit worlds apart, and both self-taught. Alas, neither was likely ever to rise very far in this world where men progress mainly through patronage and rank.

'Well,' I said dropping heavily onto the bench, 'since we have been thrust together in this buggers' clinch, I suppose we'd better get on with it. What can you tell me of these boy-martyrs?'

He coloured at my coarseness, which made me smile inwardly. I could see there were some aspects of our association I was going to enjoy.

'Beyond what Samson has already said, not m-much. They all had injuries similar to those suffered by Christ at his Passion. Th-that's the basis of the complaint against the Jews - that they are taking the boys in order to mock Christ.' He went to a corner of the room, dug out a sheet of parchment. 'This is the account of Harold of Gloucester's d-death.' He started to read: ' "On the 18th of March a*nno domini* 1168, the body of a ten-year-old boy was found in the River S-severn at Gloucester, much mutilated, with traces of burning on the flesh and the garments, thorns in the head and armpits, marks of m-melted wax in the eyes and ears, and some of the teeth knocked out…" '

I stopped him there. 'Burning, did you say? Melted wax? Teeth knocked out?' I shook my head. 'This is a strange kind of crucifixion.'

'The G-gospels tell us that Christ was t-tormented in many ways prior to the final act,' said Jocelin. 'Who can tell what was d-done to little Harold? But it's the timing that was the k-key in this case. The murder was supposed to have taken place on Friday, March 17th of that year. The boy was reportedly stolen by the Jews at the end of February and hidden until the day of the m-murder. The date is close to the time of the Jewish Passover.' He looked up. 'The legend is that without the shedding of human blood the Jews will not be able to obtain their f-freedom or return to their homeland – that is what Samson was referring to. It's what all Jews ultimately crave – "Next Year in Jerusalem",' he grinned.

I shrugged. 'So?'

'S-so every year they have to sacrifice a Christian child in mockery of C-christ's P-passion so that they might avenge their sufferings on Him. It was because they killed Christ that they had been exiled from their own country and made s-slaves in a f-foreign land.' He smiled rather embarrassedly. 'We-ell th-that's the th-theory at any r-r-rate.'

I noted with interest that whenever Jocelin was embarrassed or unsure of something his stutter grew worse. I was beginning to warm to him.

'Do you believe all that?' I asked him seriously. He shrugged non-committally, so I let the question hang for now. 'Samson also mentioned the Norwich case – er, William?'

'Ah yes.' He took down another large manuscript roll. 'This is the most d-documented of all the boy-martyr cases. It was written up in great d-detail some years after the event by Thomas of Monmouth, a Benedictine monk at our s-sister house in Norwich. In this case the mutilated body of a twelve-year-old boy was f-found in woodlands outside the town. William was a tanner's apprentice and much used to visiting the houses of Jews in the course of his trade. B-brother Thomas details what was done to the boy, his injuries and abuses, straps and gags and so on, a-and various marks in mockery of Christ's injuries.' He looked up, frowning. 'I have to say, however, that n-none of this was mentioned in any contemporary report.'

'You sound doubtful.'

Jocelin gave a pained look. 'Thomas was writing a g-generation after the event. He was also m-much encouraged by his Bishop who gave him great latitude in order to encourage the c-cult of Saint William.'

'So you think he may have been guilty of... embellishment?'

'Well, B-bishop William was very keen for him to write his history.' He reddened perhaps recognising similarities with his own account of Robert of Bury.

'Why would the good Bishop wish to do that, do you think?' I queried gently.

Once again Jocelin squirmed on his chair. 'The official r-reason is th-that the b-body would become an object of v-v-veneration and worship.'

'But?'

He thought for a moment. 'I suppose the cynical view would be that such an object would bring pecuniary b-benefits to its possessor.' He lowered his voice and leaned forward. 'There was even an attempt to get the b-body removed to a priory in Sussex, I believe.'

'For the purposes of veneration and worship, of course, not for the pilgrim's penny it would attract,' I suggested, tongue in cheek.

'Naturally,' agreed Jocelin.

'Nevertheless, the boy was undoubtedly murdered.'

'Oh yes.'

'By someone.'

'Well – yes.'

'But you are not convinced that it was the Jews?'

Jocelin thought carefully for a moment before he replied. 'I come back to the point that the only real connection with the J-jews is that all these m-murders took place around the time of the Passover, which is also close to Easter, naturally, since it was at the P-passover festival in Jerusalem that Christ was c-crucified.'

'It's June now,' I reminded him. 'Easter was two months ago.'

He nodded. 'And the Jewish P-passover was in the week beginning April the 8th,' he added weakly. 'I looked it up.'

'So it could all be circumstantial. And the fact that this murder was nowhere near the time of the Jewish Passover festival must be a mark in their defence.' I thought for a moment. 'Tell me something else. Why were all the boys so young? Pre-pubescent, Samson said. Robert was twelve, William was also twelve and Harold ten. Why so young?'

Jocelin sat back and made a cat's cradle of his fingers – a typical scholar's pose. I'd seen Joseph do the same a thousand times. 'I think it is their purity that is important. We have to remember what martyrdom is. At base it is an injustice d-done to an innocent victim. A child-martyr, especially one so very young as these boys were, p-pure and unsullied, offers the ultimate representation of the s-sufferings experienced by a faultless human being. This, after all, is what made Christ – Christ.'

I nodded then asked the crucial question again: 'So do you believe these boys really were martyrs?'

Jocelin looked at me and I could see he was now in deadly earnest. 'I believe sincerely with Brother Thomas that by the ordering of Divine Providence these Holy Innocents were predestined to their sacred role from the beginning of time. I believe they are pure and unspoilt and free of sin; that they have been absorbed into the Heavenly Host and even now sit among the Blessed Communion of Saints. If I have doubt it is that they themselves would choose to be made mock of and to be put to death in scorn of Our Lord's Passion. Rather, I believe they were martyred for God's own purpose the which we cannot know and will for ever remain a mystery.'

I held my breath while he said all that, and without a single stutter I noticed. 'But without being martyred for their faith – by Jews - they would not have been recognized as saints,' I suggested.

'Their miracles would have been p-proof if that's what is required by doubters. That is why I wrote Robert's history, to show that he had been ordained for his role at birth and c-continues to reveal himself to us even today.'

'Very well,' I said impressed with Jocelin's evident knowledge of the subject. 'Tell me what you know of our own Robert of Bury.'

Jocelin's face cleared. He looked much more relieved. 'Now I'm on m-much f-firmer ground. I studied this case in great detail and h-have in fact written my own history of the miracles of St. Robert which I entitled, *Miracula multa et magna apud Aedmundum per beatum puerum Robertum*.' He beamed. 'R-rather a neat title, I th-think you'll agree. Th-that's the piece Master Samson gave you to read.' He pointed to the thick wad of papers I had dumped unceremoniously on the floor next to where I was sitting.

'I'll read them later,' I smiled, lifting the pages reverentially from the floor and placing them on Jocelin's crowded desk. 'For now, could you just précis the more pertinent points?'

'Well, it's the familiar story,' he said, warming to his subject. 'Robert was a twelve-year-old boy murdered once again during the Passover week – actually on Good Friday *anno domini* 1181. N-notice this time it really was during the Jewish Passover week.'

'Unlike this fuller's boy today,' I interjected pointedly. 'And the marks on the body in this case? Similar to Christ's?'

'N-no record survives.' He frowned. 'As Samson said, it was a time of great confusion.'

'I see,' I said. 'Continue.'

'Well, the J-jews were immediately suspected although no individual Jew was ever charged. But what interested me, and what I was most c-concerned to do in my book, was to chronicle the m-miracles performed by the saint after his death.' He licked his lips. 'For example, imagine a light shining above the martyred boy's shrine in the darkened crypt when there was no possible source of illumination, and a nun, blind since childhood, looking towards the light, is s-suddenly able to see again. Th-then there was the instant of the girl with a crooked finger.' He held out his own hand to demonstrate the scene. 'I remember she placed her hand on the saint's t-tomb, thus, and -'

'Yes,' I said rising and tucking Jocelin's manuscript under my arm. 'This is all very interesting, brother, and I will read it – later, I promise. But I think for now we should see the body of the murdered boy, don't you? It has lain untouched for eighteen hours and it is another hot day.'

'O-oh, y-yes, o-of c-course,' said Jocelin, reddening deeply and rising so swiftly he nearly knocked over his stool.

'You know where it is? The boy's body?'

'Y-yes. Master Samson g-gave me the location.'

'Right then,' I smiled. 'Shall we go and find him?'

Chapter 7
THE SUSPECT

Before we left the abbey I made a quick detour to my cell in order to drop off Jocelin's history of the life of Saint Robert. Despite his enthusiasm for the subject this sounded like a hagiography and, exemplary though the life of a twelve-year-old boy-saint doubtless was, I needed a different kind of inspiration to solve this murder. Besides, the murder was already eighteen hours old and I had seen enough dead bodies in my time to know that putrefaction begins much sooner in warm weather. As every student of medicine knows, this is because of a build-up of black bile occurring in the body after death which is hastened by warmth. However, I could not but reflect that if this boy truly was a saint then we should know soon enough for by Samson's lights his sins would be washed away upon achieving beatification and his remains should therefore be no more corrupted than those of Saint Edmund. Or maybe Edmund's degree of sainthood was of a higher order than that of a mere miller's boy. It was an interesting hagiological point which I might take up with Samson at some later time.

For now, though, I couldn't spend hours picking my way through Jocelin's neat but indecipherable script. That delight would have to wait for later. I just hoped I didn't forget I had it.

It would be a tragedy if it got mislaid. Armed only with a wax tablet and stylus for making notes we set off into the town to find the murdered boy. Jocelin had with him a heavy-looking hessian bag slung over one shoulder and filled with….Heaven alone knew what it was filled with; manuscript paper for yet another book, I shouldn't wonder.

'Where exactly is the body?' I said, looking at the houses we were passing. It was a highly select neighbourhood, not one I'd normally associate with street violence.

Without slowing his pace Jocelin opened his notebook. 'We are looking for the house of Isaac ben Moy.'

I groaned. 'That's a Hebrew name. I thought there weren't any Jews in Bury any more. I thought Samson got rid of them all.'

'He did,' replied Jocelin. 'Well, n-nearly all. It appears Isaac ben Moy has a brother-in-law. Benedict of Norwich. You've perhaps heard the name?'

Indeed I had. Benedict of Norwich was one of the richest money-lenders in that city - indeed, one of the wealthiest in England. He had made loans to the dowager Queen Eleanor of Aquitaine, no less, as well as to the abbey. Joseph had sometimes hinted that one or two of the wealthier Jews of Bury had been exempted from the general exclusion in 1190. It now appeared that this relative of Benedict's had been one of them. I don't know why I was surprised. Where money is concerned even the most stringent rules can be broken. Samson may have blamed the Jews for getting the abbey's finances in a mess in the past but without their loans few large projects - Samson's west towers of the abbey among them - could be carried out.

Joseph had long ago told me the history of the Jews in England. Until a hundred years ago there had been none at all. It was the Conqueror who brought them over from Normandy in order to finance his extravagant building programme of castles and cathedrals. This was because the Church banned usury – the practise of charging interest on loans. The Jewish faith also banned usury but they somehow managed to circumvent the prohibition. However, useful though the Jews were to the Crown they could never become citizens since that required the taking of a Christian oath which no Jew could do. So instead they were privileged 'guests' of the King - a nebulous status that placed them under his personal protection and exempted them from the normal taxes, tolls and fines that everybody else had to pay – one cause of resentment by their tax-paying Christian neighbours. However, this royal 'protection' was a double-edged sword since by owning the man the King also owned his property and, crucially, all his assets when he died. I had no doubt that that was the real reason for King John's interest in this case, for if a Jew could be shown to have committed the murder of this boy then his assets would be forfeit and revert to the Crown. And if this Isaac ben Moy was half as wealthy as his illustrious brother-in-law then it would be a sum well worth a king's attention.

'Here we are,' said Jocelin guiding us round a corner. There was no mistaking which house we were looking for. A small crowd had gathered outside a very grand-looking residence set in its own grounds. But as we approached it was clear that the house was less the attention of the gawpers than was the curious pantomime that was being enacted in front of it. Four women, dressed identically in white pinafores and coifs, were kneeling in a semi-circle facing the house, holding up their hands in supplication and muttering in some incomprehensible language. The gawpers, mostly young men, were mimicking the women's prattle, but however provocative the men tried to be the kneeling women took no notice of them whatsoever. Indeed, they acted as though they were in some kind of trance.

Overseeing all of this was a captain of the King's guard, a sturdy-looking man in his late forties who was stationed in front of the house entrance with a bemused expression on his face. This, doubtless, was Justiciar Geoffrey's man and so it was him I approached.

'Good day to you, Captain. I am Master Walter, the physician at the abbey. Erm - who are these women?'

The captain shrugged. 'Nought but harmless gabblers. Foreign by the sounds of them.'

'Not so harmless if they draw this much attention to the house,' I said, mindful of Samson's instruction to try to keep the investigation discreet so as not to arouse emotion, particular religious emotion. To little avail it seemed. The Holy Stable in Bethlehem could have lent its star to hover above the spot and the location would not have been more obvious. If I did not believe in such things I would swear there was a conspiracy to make my job as difficult as possible.

'Can't you get rid of them?' I asked the man.

He shook his head. 'My instructions are only to keep the house clear of the curious. Long as they do no more than pray, as far as I'm concerned they can remain.'

I pouted my irritation. 'Has anyone else been?'

The captain counted them off on his fingers: 'The Sheriff, a couple of rabbis, some of the monks from the abbey.'

I was angry particularly about the monks. They should have been told I was in charge of the investigation and ordered to stay clear. 'They had no authority,' I told him haughtily. 'Any of them. Who did you let in?'

'None of them. Not even the Sheriff – I'm Lord Geoffrey's man and he said to let no-one in.' He looked me up and down. 'And you won't get in, neither.'

I drew myself erect. 'I am the Abbot's personally appointed examiner. I need to see the body as soon as possible.' I looked about me. 'Where exactly is the body?'

'Where it's always been. Inside the house.'

I was appalled. 'You mean the boy is still lying where he fell? This is an outrage!'

'Aye, well he can stay there till he rots for all I care. My orders are no-one gets in or out, not even the body, and that's what I'll do until Lord Geoffrey himself tells me otherwise.' He eyed me warily.

I smiled back. 'For your information Lord Geoffrey isn't here anymore. I saw his horse disappearing up the London road not an hour since. I'm afraid you're on your own, my friend.'

I was pleased to see that that knocked the wind out of his sails a bit. I nodded my satisfaction and squinted at the building.

'What about the family? Surely they're not still in there?'

'Aye, that they are. All five of 'em. Too scared to leave, poor bastards. Not sure I'd risk it neither, specially with this lot out here.' He nodded toward the kneeling women. To my annoyance I saw that Jocelin was in animated conversation with them.

'Oh, Brother Jocelin!' I called. 'Could you spare us a few minutes of your time?'

He looked over his shoulder and nodded without interrupting his discourse.

'*Now* brother, if you please.'

He finished his conversation, made a quick sign of the cross over the women and came over. 'F-fascinating!' he said breathlessly. 'Absolutely f-fascinating. D-do you know who they are?'

'No, I do not,' I sniffed.

'Knielers,' he said. 'The Sisterhood of the Passion of Christ, to give them their proper name. B-but Knielers is how they are generally known. It's a D-dutch word meaning to kneel, you see? B-because that's what they do: Kneel and pray.'

'I'd noticed.'

'A-and they talk in t-tongues,' he continued enthusiastically. 'They claim it's the Holy Spirit speaking through them. Can you believe that? Absolutely f-fascinating. Heretics, of course, they'll all end up on the scaffold. But f-fascinating n-nonetheless.' He smiled back at them.

'Well, what are they doing here? And how did they know where to come? The boy's been dead less than twenty-four hours and Holland is at least two days sail away.'

'They claim they saw a vision,' enthused Jocelin. 'A week since. A boy dressed in white and flanked on either side by Saints Robert and Edmund. That's how they knew where to come. A week before the boy was killed. Think of that. You see what this means? It's a miracle. The *first* miracle.' He turned his gaze once more to the women, the light of wonder shining from his eyes.

We did eventually manage to get past the captain but only after I made Jocelin go back to the abbey and return with Abbot Samson's seal of office confirming my authority. While I was waiting for him to return I had time to reflect on what had just occurred.

Jocelin was convinced that what we had just witnessed was a miracle, and on the face of it I had to admit it was the only explanation. How else did these women - these *Knielers* - manage to get here so soon or even to know where to come? They would have had to start on their journey before the boy was even dead. Miracles do occur, of that I have no doubt. I have myself witnessed dozens of cures of the human body inexplicable other than through the intercession of the saints. But the question was, had a miracle occurred in *this* case?

There was one other matter that was worrying me. While I waited outside the house I had the distinct feeling that I was being observed -

watched. It was just a feeling, I put it no stronger than that. I could see no-one lurking about. But it gave me an uncomfortable sensation in my neck. However, I could not concern myself with any of this for now. My duty was to the dead boy. All else must wait.

Jocelin returned at last and presented the seal to the captain who in spite of his earlier protestations gave it little more than a peremptory glance before letting us through the gate and up to the street door.

We were admitted by a short, stocky woman in her mid-fifties dressed in a maid's uniform of a vintage not seen in my mother's house since I was a boy. She did not speak or even smile but ushered us through to a large central hallway.

Inside the house was dark with every shutter closed. It took a few moments for my eyes to adjust to the gloom but when they did I saw we were in a well-ordered and tastefully-appointed hall. The place reeked of understated opulence. Pride of place was given to a large bound copy of what I assumed must be the family's holy book covered in Hebrew script. Such a thing I knew would be enormously valuable, at least as valuable as the house in which it stood, and demonstrated as few other things could the very great wealth of the family who possessed it. Crouching almost invisibly by the staircase in the midst of all this sumptuousness were the silhouettes of five human beings.

'God bless all in this house,' I said stopping myself just in time from making my usual sign of the Cross.

'Amen,' came a man's voice, and I stepped toward the speaker extending my hand in greeting.

'Good day to you, sir. I am Brother Walter and this is Brother Jocelin. I hope you will forgive this intrusion but we come with the authority of the Abbot to investigate…this unfortunate matter.'

'There is no need of delicacy, Brother Walter, we know why you are here. I am Isaac ben Moy and this is my wife, Rachel. These are my children, Jacob, Jessica and Josette.'

I saw before me a man in his mid-forties and the wife perhaps a decade younger. The children, two girls and a boy, were all young, the girls probably eight or nine, the boy older, thirteen or fourteen. They all looked terrified and my instinct – indeed my desire – was to put them at their ease.

'Do not fret, sir. I intend only to remove the body once I have inspected it and then you should be free of the affair,' assuming, I could have added but did not, you are not the murderer. He nodded and walked over to one of the windows over-looking the street. It was shuttered like all the rest but he peered through the slats at the four Knieler women who had resumed their semi-circular vigil and were chanting their unintelligible burble again.

'I suppose we can hope they will leave with the body,' he sighed. 'Each hour they remain the crowd grows more curious. The longer they are here the chance increases of someone doing something foolish.'

At this Moy's wife let out a sudden sob. 'Foolish? You say *foolish*! *Murderous* is what they will be.'

'Rachel,' her husband held out his hands imploringly. 'This is not the time -'

'No!' she spat. 'I will speak. Foolish you say? Foolish is to tether the lamb to the lion and expect it to live. Foolish is to remain here when all our friends have left. Foolish is to trust in the King's protection when there is no protection for the likes of us. Foolish is to think your money will save you from these *goyim*.' She shot me a look of contempt. I must say I was taken aback by the sudden ferocity of her attack and felt my back stiffen a little.

Moy smiled embarrassedly at me then turned back to his wife. 'Chick, the brothers do not wish to hear this.'

But she would not be silenced. 'No, but they will hear while hearing is possible.' She raised her head proudly and defiantly pointed to the window. 'Those women out there are only the beginning. Others will come and not to prattle and pray but to stone and to murder, and then all your precious money will not save you.' She spat with contempt.

'Wife, silence now, that is enough!' he shouted finally losing his patience. The little girls started to cry and the boy stared at his father angrily clenching and unclenching his fists.

Rachel drew the girls towards her stroking their hair. 'Hush, do not cry, all will be well. Mummy is just upset that's all,' and she began to rock the girls in her arms.

Moy turned to me. 'I could not leave. My business is in the town. Besides, with the King here –'

'I can have the guard increased once we've gone, if that will reassure you,' I suggested not knowing if I had the authority to fulfil such a rash offer.

Moy smiled sardonically. 'That will simply draw more attention to us.'

I had another suggestion to make: 'I do not wish to sound impertinent but have you thought of leaving now and going to stay with your family? Your brother-in-law in Norwich, perhaps?'

He held out his arms to indicate the many priceless artefacts in the hall, and no doubt the many others which I was sure were elsewhere in the house. 'And just how much of this do you think would be left when we returned? Besides, I am a suspect in a murder case. Will the authorities allow me to leave now?'

Of course he was right. Even if Samson let him leave, the Sheriff of Suffolk would arrest him as soon as he left the jurisdiction of the Abbey. I was not as good at this as I thought.

'In that case,' I said hastily, 'the sooner our business here is concluded the sooner we can leave you in peace.'

Moy nodded. 'I will show you the body.'

'There is no need,' I said trying to save his anguish. 'One of your servants can do it.'

He gave a wry laugh. 'They were the first to leave – after they informed the Beadle about the body.'

'Oh, but surely -' I indicated the street door.

Moy nodded. 'We still have one loyal servant - Matilde. She is a Christian but she is devoted to the family. Her family came over from France with mine fifty years ago and they have been with us ever since. She would never leave the children. But I'm afraid she would not be much help to you – unless you can speak French. Her English is poor.'

I doubted if she spoke the French that I was familiar with and I didn't trust my northern French enough to question her.

'In that case, sir,' I said, 'I would be grateful if you could now show us the body.'

Chapter 8
THE CASKET

'You mean this is the body?'

I was appalled that it should have been left lying out here on the household midden like a discarded child's doll and glared accusingly at Moy. But then I realised that was unjust. It wouldn't have been his decision to leave the boy's body but a directive from higher up – the Sheriff's office perhaps, or even Earl Geoffrey himself. But at times like these it is not a matter of logic.

The flies and the smell notwithstanding, Jocelin immediately dropped to his knees next to the corpse and taking out a small crucifix began quietly to recite the prayers for the dead. The sound of his trembling but determined voice was pathos itself. I should have joined him but frankly I was too overcome with emotion to do anything but stare. I could only admire his heroism at bending so close to the pile of filth on top of which was this single broken jewel – a child's body.

By the time he had finished I was in command of my own emotions enough to be able to place my hands on his shoulders and raise him up. As I did so I saw that his cheeks were awash with tears.

'Go inside the house, brother,' I told him. 'I will call you if I need you.'

'Yes brother,' he sobbed. 'Thank you.'

In my professional career I had seen many dead bodies often in worse condition than this, but a child's death is always the most terrible. I doubted if Jocelin had ever seen anything so ghastly and I was annoyed at myself for not foreseeing the possibility and preparing him. When he had gone I gently lifted the sheet in order to expose the body fully. As I did so there came a sudden blood-curdling cry. Startled, I looked up to see a woman's face hovering above the fence, a face of utter misery and despair. Before I knew what was happening the woman had scaled the fence with astonishing facility and was even now laying her fists into Moy with such ferocity I was amazed he was still managing to stand. He did nothing to stop the blows other than to protect his face which was already spewing blood in every direction. And now all was confusion as the garden was suddenly filled with people shouting and wailing. Through the middle of it I heard a voice of authority I recognised:

'Hold now! Stop that! Stop I say!'

It was the captain of the guard who had abandoned his post at the front of the house in response to the woman's scream and had rushed through the house towards the source of the commotion. He in turn was followed by half the street. Now the captain placed his arms around the screaming woman and was holding on for all he was worth and still he was having trouble containing her seemingly super-human strength so determined was she to get at Moy. Could there be any doubt that the woman was the mother of the murdered boy?

'Captain,' I said urgently. 'There is danger here of mob riot. We need more men.'

'What would you have me do, brother?' he scowled breathlessly. 'Let her go?'

The situation was impossible. I got between Moy and the men in the crowd and tried to reason with them but far from calming them my efforts seemed to inflame them more. I was being pushed back steadily towards the stricken Moy who was now lying on the ground and apparently resigned to his fate. In a very few moments he was likely to be smothered to death by the numbers if not first being beaten to a pulp and possibly myself with him and I was powerless to prevent it.

And then – a true miracle. Cutting through the shouting and the cursing was a lone voice singing, incredibly, the twenty-third psalm. At first it had no effect but gradually as the singing grew closer so the passion in the crowd began to subside until all that was left was Jocelin walking slowly through the middle of the crowd holding aloft his crucifix in both hands for all to see, the image of the Christ glinting in the sunshine. He stopped before the stricken Moy and faced the mob which had now turned back into a group of ordinary men once again. One by one they went down on their knees so that by the time Jocelin got to the last lines of the psalm, *Surely goodness and loving kindness shall follow me all the days of my life* he was the only one still standing and his the only voice still to be heard - the only voice, that is, other than the quiet sobbing of the grief-stricken mother who was now being cradled like a child in the arms of the captain.

Within minutes order had been restored. The moment the captain had abandoned his station outside the house Rachel Moy had sent her son, Jacob, to run as fast as he could to the abbey to fetch back soldiers who were now dispersing the crowd. The murdered boy's mother, at last subdued, was kneeling before the corpse of her son, oblivious to the flies and the stench and making no sound now at all. Even the tears on her face had dried to streaks. It was as blank as a sheet of parchment. Isaac Moy was sitting on a rock a discreet distance away while his wife bathed a cut above his left eye repeating over and over, 'You see? You see?'

I went over to cast my professional eye over his injuries. They seemed less than I would have expected given the ferocity of the battering he had received, mostly bruising about the head and on the shins from the woman's kicks. Jocelin was trying to comfort the woman but she simply ignored him, her dry-eyed gaze focussed entirely on her child's body. I suggested to the Moys that we all went inside the house, leaving her to grieve alone. Rachel Moy pursed her lips and glared at me as though I had been responsible for the woman's performance.

'I will speak to her,' I assured Moy when we were back inside. 'Tell her there is no evidence to suggest you are her son's murderer.'

'No evidence,' he smirked.

I frowned at him impatiently. 'You must realise that until we know more you remain a suspect – the *prime* suspect.'

'The *only* suspect,' he corrected me. 'I am a Jew. The boy was a Christian. I am not blind to the implications of what that means in the minds of other Christians especially in this town.' He looked into his wife's face. 'We were here when they found the body of Saint Robert. That time there was no one suspect and all the Jews were blamed. Fifty-seven friends and family died. By God's good grace - and good luck - we were among those who survived. But this time they have their suspect and I know what people will think. And it isn't true.'

'Very well,' I said. 'Let us, then, take the correct procedure. Sir, you must indeed be a wealthy man because I noticed you have a copy of the Old Testament on your lectern in the hall.'

'The true Bible, you mean,' he said with a defiant smile.

I could feel Jocelin bristle next to me. I nodded curtly letting the slight pass. 'Whatever we choose to call it, it is sacred to both our faiths. Will you therefore, Isaac ben Moy, before us and before the God of all mankind, swear you did not kill this boy?'

Ben Moy rose instantly, strode unhesitatingly over to the lectern and, shutting his eyes, he mumbled something that I took to be a Hebrew prayer of some kind. He then set his jaw, bared his right arm to the elbow, placed the palm of his hand flat upon the ornately-carved cover of the holy book and looked me steadily in the eye. His voice too, when it came, was steady and firm.

'I swear before the God of Abraham and Moses and all the Patriarchs that I did not take the life of this boy.' He nodded sternly at me then removed his hand from the leather-bound book. But I pushed it back down onto the leather binding and held it there firmly with my own hand.

'And further swear that you did not know him.'

For the briefest moment I thought I felt his hand beneath mine falter, but then he said as steadily as before, 'I so swear.'

I waited a tortuous few moments longer looking deep into his eyes and keeping his hand pressed hard down on the book that we both believed contained the very words uttered by God Almighty Himself. Behind him I could see Jocelin frowning with an intensity I had never seen before. At last I nodded. 'Very well,' and released his hand. He took it back and looked at it as though it were an alien object.

'Well,' I sighed once he had sat down again. 'This unfortunate incident has revealed one thing in your favour. We now know how the body could have got onto your garden. Until that woman appeared I could see no way it could have got there except through the house. However, she managed it and so could the murderer. When she has recovered herself sufficiently I will go down and ask her to show me how she did it.'

'She's already gone,' said Rachel coming in with some wine on a tray. 'Left the same way she came in, over the garden wall.'

' 'Tis no matter,' I said trying to cover my embarrassment. 'I-I will interview her later. We know where she lives. In any case, I don't want to distress her any more than I must. At least those damn Knieler women have also gone, *Dei Gratia*,' I said looking through the window at the front of the house. 'But I must arrange for the boy's body to be removed as soon as possible. He has already been in the open for far too long. In this heat he must be in the ground soon.'

'Before that it must be decided on the form of mass to be said over the body, s-surely,' warned Jocelin coolly.

'By "form of mass" I take it you mean his beatification,' said Moy wryly.

I shifted uncomfortably. 'Sir, I cannot answer for how the Church will regard this child. I will do my best to provide the evidence as objectively as I can. But evidence alone does not always counter prejudice.'

I was thinking of the other child murders and how, even though no individual culprit had ever been found, suspicion remained with the Jews with terrible consequences for them. I placed my hand on Isaac ben Moy's shoulder and was surprised to find him trembling. In all this I had forgotten the emotional impact it must be having on the man.

'We need to find the identity of the killer,' I said to him gently. 'Only then will your name be finally cleared.'

'Thank you, brother. But I know there is little chance of that.' He looked at Jocelin then said to me solemnly, 'Brother Walter, would you come with me please?'

My heart began to pound in my chest. Had he finally realised the hopelessness of his position and was ready to make his true confession? I could see Jocelin was expecting to come too but I held up my hand to stay him and followed Moy alone into the hallway.

He led me to an adjacent room that I took to be his office, the walls lined with shelves and filled with documents and accounts records. Closing the door firmly after us he went over to one of the shelves in the middle of which was a beautifully-carved and ornate casket. He held it reverentially and opened it. I gasped at the contents for it looked like a King's ransom in treasure – gold and silver ingots, bracelets, brooches, rings, jewellery of every kind together with a great quantity of silver coin. Lying on top was a single document sealed with wax.

'This is my final testament,' he said taking out the document and turning it over in his hands for me to see. Then he replaced the document on top of the treasure, closed and locked the casket and then held it out for me to take.

I stepped back holding up both hands before me not wishing to even touch the thing. 'Oh no, sir, that would not be right. You do not know me. I am a stranger to you. I am also charged with investigating the murder. Surely you can find someone else.'

'There is no-one else,' he countered urgently. 'You heard my wife. She is right. All our friends left long ago. I cannot leave the house and there is no-one I can entrust it to. No, you must do it for me. Please. I have thought about this, believe me. If I should not survive the coming tribulation, open the document and act upon what is written there. If, however, I should survive,' here he smiled, 'well, you can give it back to me together with the casket.'

'But surely your wife is better suited for such a task,' I implored him.

He shook his head. 'Brother, I am a Jew. If I die all that is mine reverts to the King, not to my wife. Rachel will be destitute. My children, too. At least this way, even if you keep the bulk of the money for yourself, some of it will go to my family. I saw you downstairs and judge you to be an honourable man. I believe – I have no choice but to believe – that you will be honourable in this thing too.'

I drew myself erect. 'Sir, you insult the dignity of the King and me by your words,' but I could see he was at his wits' end. 'Master Moy, whatever you may have heard to the contrary I do believe King John to be an honourable man who will not take unfair advantage of your situation - assuming matters come to that - which they very well may not.' I beseeched him: 'Look, I held your hand upon the Holy Book just now and I do not think you would have imperilled your soul by taking such an oath did you not believe it to be true. In which case you have nothing to fear from this investigation, certainly not my part in it. And so, you see, there is no need for any of this.'

He put the locked casket down and thought for a moment. 'You know,' he said, 'nine years ago in the city of York on Shabbat ha-Gadol – that's the Sabbath eve before Passover - a group of men, indebted to the Jews, and made up of priests, Christian noblemen and Crusaders waiting to follow King Richard to the Holy Land set Jewish houses on fire and stole all their valuables. It was a moment of high emotion and excitement over the impending crusade – murderous emotion.' He sighed heavily. 'Anyway, the York Jews fled with their rabbi to the castle for safety. For six days they held out but it was clear they could not escape the wrath of the mob. They were offered the choice of baptism or death. Most chose death the men stabbing their wives first then their children. Finally the rabbi stabbed the men before killing himself. The few who remained alive opened the gate and requested baptism in return for their lives. They were massacred anyway. Over a hundred and fifty Jews died that day and the bonds of debts which were kept for safekeeping in York Minster were burned on the floor of the church.' He once again pushed the key and casket into my hands and stared me in the eye. 'Take it.'

I could see there was no arguing with the man in his present emotional state. I did not want this added responsibility but there seemed no alternative. Reluctantly I accepted the casket.

'Very well,' I said pocketing the key. 'But I think it a mistake. I will keep the casket safe for you or your wife to retrieve whenever you feel the time is right. In the meantime I still have my duty to the Abbot to perform. So now, sir, I must ask to see around the rest of the house. Starting with the cellar.'

The land in this part of the town sloped down towards the abbey and the river below it, and so to keep the houses level the road was terraced on one side, beneath which were substantial cellars. An innocent-looking door in the hall led down to this cellar, at the shallow end of which was a false cupboard which hid a chute leading to the surface where an outside hatch opened to a side street.

'What was this house originally?' I asked, intrigued.

'I think it was built on what was the old cattle market before it was moved,' said Moy. 'My father enlarged it.' He smiled sardonically. 'We Jews like to stay close to the abbey for somewhere to run for shelter in times of trouble.'

With the outer hatch closed no light could enter the cellar. But as soon as it was opened daylight flooded in to reveal the subterranean entrails of what must once have been an artisan's dwelling.

'Fascinating,' I said peering up the chute to the world above. I was enjoying myself. 'I love discovering the history of these old houses, don't you? I imagine this must have been a delivery hatch of some kind, but for what? Something big and heavy to be sure.'

'Carcasses?' suggested Moy.

'Of course! It's an abattoir!' I exclaimed looking around at the layout – but then I caught myself remembering the garden and its dead occupant. 'It's an abattoir again today, I fear.'

Jocelin, who had been scrambling around clumsily behind, let out a yelp as he clumped his head on something sticking out of the ceiling.

' "And behold, a ladder was set up on the earth and its top reached all the way to Heaven",' I grinned at him. 'That's what you get for being so tall.'

He was rubbing his head painfully with his right hand but the blank expression on his face told me something else. I followed the line of his other hand and saw that it was holding on to a set of chains that were fastened to the wall. Chains are perfectly reasonable tools to be found in an abattoir where animal carcasses have to be secured ready for butchering. But if this building ceased a generation ago to be a slaughterhouse, why were they still here? They could restrain a child of twelve with little difficulty. I seemed to remember something similar had occurred in the case of the boy William in Norwich. Moy saw where my gaze was fixed and lowered his eyes when I looked at him. I realised then that I had already more or less dismissed him as the murderer in my own mind, but that had been a mistake. I had been impressed with his apparent sincerity upstairs, but it could all have been an act. Was I so gullible? Was the fact that I liked the man colouring my judgement? I could only hope that it did not.

Chapter 9
AN AUTOPSY

I was sitting alone in my cell staring at Moy's casket which I'd managed to smuggle unseen from his house amid the confusion of getting the body out. I'd got Moy to wrap the casket in sacking in order to conceal its identity from Jocelin to whom I'd then given the task of organising the removal of the body so that he'd be too preoccupied to notice. I didn't want anyone knowing about the casket just yet, least of all Abbot Samson who might well think my possession of it compromised my position as investigator. Besides, if I was right and Isaac Moy reconsidered his impetuosity in trusting me with its safe-keeping I wouldn't have charge of it for long enough for it to matter. That's where Jocelin went, to Samson to report on the day's events. He'd scuttled over there just as soon as he'd finished with me. This unbridled sycophancy towards our faultless Father Abbot is the one thing about Jocelin that still irritates me, but at least his absence gives me time to reflect on what had happened and to decide what I need to do next in order to solve this riddle.

The murdered boy's body lay next door in my workshop on a trestle bench having been brought there on a trundle and wrapped in sheeting to protect it from prying eyes. Even so, a small gathering of neighbours had stood in unnerving silence and watched as the soldiers, under Jocelin's fussy direction, man-handled the body onto the cart and pushed it down the hill, followed by those damn Knieler women processing behind us like a funeral cortège. At least if they were following us they were leaving the Moys alone. I had managed to persuade the captain to station another two of his men outside the house. There hadn't been any more trouble but the report of what had happened had spread with the wind and there is nothing more calculated to inflame emotion than the sight of a bereaved mother grieving over the body of her dead child. Not that there had been any sign of the mother since her invasion of the Moys' garden, which was a little odd considering her earlier devotion. I decided, however, to leave her for the moment. She must be given time to come to terms with her loss and to seek comfort from her priest and family. I knew where she lived and planned in any case to interview her once I'd completed my examination of the boy's body. That was going to be a messy business and not something a mother should have to witness.

In light of this and conscious of the need to preserve evidence I had directed my assistant, Gilbert, to watch over the corpse while two abbey servants washed it clean of the filth in which it had lain for nearly two days. I had been reading again the account of the death of Saint William of Norwich in 1144 which had been almost farcical in its incompetence. Between the killing on Maundy Thursday of that year and the eventual burial in the monks' cemetery *thirty-two days later* the body had been buried, dug up and re-buried no less than three times. Any evidence that might have told of how he met his fate, let alone the identity of the killers, had been well and truly destroyed by then. I was determined nothing so negligent was going to happen in this case. I told Gilbert that once the body had been washed he was to fetch me and I would begin immediately the unpleasant task of dissection. Never having witnessed an autopsy before, Gilbert was keen to watch. I never will understand the fascination youth has with gore.

In the meantime I still had the casket. In truth it fascinated me. It was a beautiful thing in itself quite unlike any I had seen before, exquisitely tooled and with that strange square Hebrew lettering of the Jews on the sides. I'm sure Joseph would have known instantly its place of manufacture and been able to read the inscription, too. What did it contain, I wondered? A lot of gold, for sure, but also that intriguing sealed document. If anything, Moy seemed to regard the document as being of more value than the gold which means it must be very valuable indeed. What could possibly be written on it that was that precious? I was sorely tempted to take another look. I'd toyed with the key in my fingers for a good ten minutes before finally summoning the courage to open it which I did with a quick flick of the wrist.

It was exactly as I had seen it in Moy's house, a fortune in gold and silver which made a pleasing silvery tinkle as I ran my hand through it. And lying on top the single document which after a moment's hesitation I snatched from its place and slammed the casket shut again.

I turned the document over in my hands. A testament Isaac had called it. It was like no testament I had ever seen. The parchment was of good quality and the wax deeply embossed with the Moy seal. The paper was so thick that try as I might I could not read around or through it even when held up to the light. The little I could make out of the writing inside reminded me more of columns of account rather than a written will. Maybe, I thought, it was a list of all Isaac's beneficiaries set alongside the amounts they were to receive upon his death. But there was no way I could know, short of breaking the seal, which I was reluctant to do. It was very frustrating.

The sound of shuffling outside my door told me someone was coming. No time to return the testament to the casket I quickly secreted it inside the cover of Jocelin's treatise on the miracles of Saint Robert. The casket, too, I had to hide but it was too big to fit on the shelf. I frantically hunted around for somewhere to conceal it and in desperation hid it beneath a pile of my soiled laundry just as Gilbert's head appeared round the door.

'Master, you said to call you when the body was washed.'

'And?' I said trying to conceal my breathlessness.

The boy shrugged. 'It is washed.'

'Good,' I said swinging my legs over the edge of my cot and guiding him out the room. 'Now go and fetch Brother Jocelin and tell him we are ready.'

Inside my laboratorium Jocelin, Gilbert and I stood waiting, the body of the dead child lying on the trestle table between us. Aware of the gravity what we were about to do, I was hesitant to begin.

To be truthful, I had never carried out an autopsy on my own before, though I had witnessed a few done by others when I was a student in Montpellier. It is still a very controversial practice frowned upon by the Church Fathers as a desecration, but the master of the school there was a keen advocate and could never get hold of enough executed criminals and suicides to satisfy his lust for such butchery. When the city authorities eventually banned the practice on humans the master used animals in their stead, in particular Barbary Apes from North Africa which he said were like humans in all aspects anatomical. That notion, too, was scoffed at by the Church authorities for how could a mere animal be compared to the miracle of God's ultimate perfection, the human body? Yet Galen himself, the greatest anatomist of all, had used the same ape and had drawn similar conclusions. Even I in my ignorance could see these similarities once they were pointed out to me.

Anatomy has long been a source of wonderment to me. What was the purpose of all those myriad parts inside a human body? The functions of some are obvious enough: The lungs aerate the body while the liver heats it; the bones give the body rigidity while the muscles in their turn afford movement to the bones. The heart, of course, is where the emotions are stored and the brain the repository of the spirit. But what of the lesser organs, the spleen and the kidneys, the pancreas and the gall bladder? If, as the Bible tells us, we are made in the image of God, then what need had God of these oddities? And if, indeed, apes and goats are like us anatomically then surely that meant that they, too, are made in the image of God. It was a perplexing and yet tremendously exciting enigma and one which I was sure would one day give up its secrets. But for now, apart from a superficial geography exercise, most of it would have to remain a mystery.

'What is the purpose of the lavender?' asked Gilbert keen to learn all he could of the mysterious art of dissection.

'Have you no sense of smell, boy?'

'What? Oh yes, I see,' he said stepping back from the table and covering his nose.

Though meticulously washed it was not a pretty sight to behold, being grossly discoloured and somewhat bloated from having lain in the open for so long, particularly the face which had swelled up to resemble one of the pigs-bladder footballs our young men had been kicking around only a day ago. Two of the toes had been gnawed off by rats, I noticed, and both eyes pecked out by crows, but otherwise all seemed intact - all, that is, except for the glaring gash across the boy's throat which ran from ear to ear.

'Now,' I said dressed in a leather apron to protect my robe and giving my blade one last strap, 'as far as I remember, this is how we begin,' and in one sweeping movement I sliced through the boy's skin from groin to throat peeling it apart as I went, like an over-ripe pomegranate. Gilbert instantly passed out on the floor.

After half an hour of cutting and slicing we had several bowls filled with the boy's innards.

'Well,' I said to Jocelin wiping my hands of the worst of the gore, 'apart from knowing his last meal was of pease porridge and that he had a full bladder I don't think we learned very much from that, do you? Except to confirm what we already knew, that he had his throat cut. That is undoubtedly what killed him.'

'I'm m-more interested in the external signs,' said Jocelin pushing back the boy's matted fair hair. 'Look here at the scalp below the hair-line.'

'Good Lord, yes,' I said bringing a candle closer. 'Well spotted.'

'T-two marks, see? One above each eye on either t-temple. Saint Robert, I remember, was thought to have been crowned with a c-crown of thorns. Could this be the same?'

I studied the two marks, pressing down on them and trying to stretch the skin apart. 'These are not puncture wounds as we might expect from thorns,' I said. 'They look more like pressure points to me. Do you see?'

I put a finger and thumb on each mark. They fitted perfectly.

'Let's think about this,' I said stepping back. 'If you wanted to restrain someone from behind, isn't that where your hand would go?' I put my hand against my own forehead in the same position as the marks on the boy's head to demonstrate, pushing back my head.

'The assailant w-would have to be taller than the victim,' said Jocelin thoughtfully. 'H-how tall is the boy?'

I measured him. 'About fourteen hands. I'm nearly sixteen so I could have done it,' I grinned.

Jocelin was now frowning at the boy's hands. 'I've j-just noticed something else. Look at his wrists. More p-pressure marks do you think?'

I looked closely. There was a circular red mark around each. 'Possibly,' I agreed. 'Or ropes could have made the marks.'

'Or chains,' suggested Jocelin.

I nodded curtly knowing what he was alluding to: The chains in the Moys' cellar. 'Could it have been achieved without those restraints?' I asked.

Jocelin shrugged. 'I suppose so. B-but it would surely need at least two people. One to hold the boy and the other to administer the knife.'

'Let's try it,' I said. 'You're taller than me. You be the murderer, I'll be the victim. Here, take the knife and come at me from behind.'

We took up our positions with Jocelin placing his left hand on my forehead pulling my head back as I had demonstrated and his right holding the knife against my throat. I brought my hands up to try to prevent the knife from cutting me. Just at that moment Gilbert began coming round from his faint. Seeing Jocelin standing behind me with the blood-soaked autopsy knife at my throat and my equally bloodied hands flailing to stop him, he gasped and passed out again.

'I think if there had been just one attacker the b-boy would have more wounds on his hands from trying to fight off the knife,' said Jocelin letting go of me. 'A-and there are none.'

'Unless he had been surprised and not had time to respond.'

'I-in which case, why the restraining m-marks on the wrist?' said Jocelin. 'No, I think this was a deliberate act. The boy was cornered, his hands held down and then brutally s-slain.'

'So we are agreed, yes? Two people murdered him.' I thought for a moment studying the eviscerated corpse and addressed it directly: 'In which case, why didn't you cry out?'

'Perhaps he did and no-one h-heard him,' suggested Jocelin. 'O-or perhaps he knew his attackers.'

Perhaps he did. But Moy insisted he did not know the boy. More than that, he swore on oath he did not. Lying to me was one thing, but would he lie to his God? It was very frustrating. I wondered if Jocelin was as conscious as I that we were complete amateurs at this. Judging by his bewildered countenance I guessed he was. Not for the first time I wished Samson had engaged someone with a more analytical mind than mine. But for his own reasons he had chosen to yoke me to book-wormy Jocelin as my assistant, God help us both. So I guessed we were stuck with each other – or more accurately, poor Matthew was stuck with us both.

'He was certainly no weakling, this m-miller's son,' said Jocelin casually prodding the muscles in the boy's arms. 'If he could have resisted I'm sure he would have done. Look at his hands. Calloused and rough. He was used to hard physical work w-wouldn't you say? His attackers, whoever they were, m-must have been strong to overpower him.' Jocelin's eyes suddenly filled with tears so that I feared he might start blubbing again. 'What a terrible end for a child.'

We both stood staring in silence across the dissection table with Matthew's body lying between us as Gilbert began coming round again. At last I noticed him.

'My dear child,' I said dropping to one knee and helping him rise. 'Are you all right? I'm so sorry, we got carried away.'

He looked at me with anxious but relieved eyes. 'Master, you are alive.'

'Yes, I am alive,' I said smiling and nodding encouragingly. 'We are all alive, you, me and Jocelin. Let us all give thanks to Almighty God for that, and honour the dead.'

By the time the other monks arrived to translate the boy to Saint Denis's chapel for his requiem mass I had replaced all his inner parts, albeit haphazardly, sewn him up and covered him with a starched clean white sheet. Gilbert washed and combed the boy's hair and placed two small wooden crosses on his empty eye-sockets while Jocelin covered his neck so the ugly gash that severed his windpipe was no longer visible. For the first time since he died he had begun to look human again, although there was nothing we could do about his bloated face. When we were ready four choir monks came and carried the body shoulder-high in procession towards the abbey church. But even before that another group of monks had cornered me outside in the courtyard anxiously wanting to know if the boy's body showed any signs of his martyrdom. I noticed one of them was Egbert again. I was beginning to think that if there was a controversy of any kind he could be relied upon to be at the heart of it. I very firmly told them I could say nothing before I reported to the Abbot, but I did not know how much longer I could fob them off in this way. It was clear that there was a growing desire among many of my brother monks for a new boy-saint and they looked to me to give them one or, failing that, a firm refutation. At the moment I could provide them with neither.

Abbot Samson was waiting in the vestibule as the monks lauded the boy's body in with bells and incense and bowed low as they passed. As I approached, he put out his hand to stop me.

'Brother Walter. A word if you please.' He took me by the elbow and led me to one side. 'How are things progressing?' he asked quietly. 'Are you close to a solution yet? Jocelin was unable to tell me.'

'We make progress, Father, but it cannot be rushed.' I then explained the procedure Jocelin and I had gone through that afternoon with the autopsy and some of our conclusions.

Samson frowned his disappointment. 'I had hoped you'd got further with this by now. Jocelin told me of the trouble this morning at the Moy house.' He shook his head. 'It is very disturbing especially with the King still here.' He glanced over his shoulder as though expecting to see King John standing there.

'How fares the King?' I asked lightly. 'Is he conscious yet?'

Samson grimaced. 'He recovered well enough by yesterday afternoon to eat a dinner of partridge and stewed prunes. Claimed to have enjoyed some wonderful dreams while he was asleep. What was in that potion you gave him?'

'Trade secrets,' I smiled wistfully. 'I am just relieved he is recovering,' adding with more bravado than I felt, 'at least my lord de Saye will not be able to blame me now if the King died.'

'Oh you needn't worry about that,' said Samson. 'That French doctor's claimed the credit for his cure. So he can also accept the blame if it goes wrong.' He shuddered. 'However, that has not made the King a happy man. He was very angry that all his ministers should have left him alone and was of a mind to chase after them to London.'

'*Was* of a mind?' I said. 'I take it that means he's changed it again?'

Samson sighed. 'He's heard about the murder. At first he was completely disinterested as I had hoped he would. But then someone told him the chief suspect was a rich Jew…'

I nodded. 'He found he was concerned after all.'

'He now wishes to remain for few more days to see the outcome. What he's really waiting for, of course, is for us to make a mistake so he can step in and take over. If that happens all your high-minded talk of scientific detachment will come to nothing. The Jew will be found guilty and executed before you can say foul. Then the King will get his money and simply depart leaving us to clear up the mess.' Samson's face took on a pained expression. 'Also…' he looked about him furtively and lowered his voice, '…he has found a wench to his liking and is taking this…hiatus…to amuse himself in his rooms with her.' Samson shook his head. 'He's done this sort of thing before. It's all very inconvenient. So you see, the sooner you can give me an answer the sooner he will get bored and leave.'

'I will try my best, Father,' I nodded.

'Hm.' Samson stroked his beard thoughtfully. 'This Jew. Jocelin tells me he took you into his confidence. What did he want?'

'To unburden himself,' I said carefully.

'Did he confess?'

'On the contrary, he adamantly maintains his innocence.'

'Yes, well he would wouldn't he?' Samson eyed me suspiciously. 'He didn't *give* you anything, did he?'

Now, that was interesting. In Samson's place I would have asked what it was Isaac had wished to unburden himself of, not if he had given me anything. He couldn't mean the casket because no-one but Isaac Moy and I knew I had it. It made my next answer a cautious one.

'He gave me…his trust.'

I thought I could just about get away with that. It wasn't an actual lie because Isaac's trust was the only thing I had personally taken from him. The other two items, the testament and the casket, would either be returned or handed on to someone else. But I could see Samson was unconvinced.

'Hm.' He thought again. 'What of the murdered boy's status?'

'You mean his martyrdom?' Again I was cagey not wishing to commit myself. 'I think God moves in mysterious ways. I can tell you how the boy died but who am I to judge how He achieves His purpose?'

Samson frowned impatiently. 'Damn you Walter for your habitual obfuscation. Will you answer me straight: Does he or does he not bear the marks of the Passion?'

I looked him directly in the eye. 'No father, he does not.'

We got no further for there came from within the church an agonising cry of despair. Monks came rushing out, some in tears, some cursing.

'Well,' sighed Samson, 'it sounds as though others may have come to a different conclusion.'

We went quickly through the church where we found the body of the murdered boy lying on the floor of the choir, its starched white sheet tossed aside and the naked body exposed for all to see. My clumsy attempt at seamstressing made him look like a badly-mended rag doll. It was clear from the angry snarls that were being directed at me exactly who the monks blamed for the outrage. I could hear the word 'desecration' being bandied about. Clearly many of them had already decided the boy was a saint and his relic therefore sacrosanct. By carving him up I had committed the ultimate sacrilege. The mood of my brother monks was ugly.

Abbot Samson, to his credit, stepped into the fray, pushing me out of the way and moving to the altar to face them. Holding up his hands he bellowed: 'Brothers! Remember where you are! I will not tolerate such lack of respect in God's House!'

One of the monks who had collared me earlier stepped forward jabbing a stubby finger towards me. 'We are not the disrespectful ones. He is!'

Samson was having none of it. 'Do not blame Master Walter. I told him to perform the autopsy. If anyone is to be censured it is I.'

Admirable though this claim was it wasn't strictly true. Samson had given me free rein to do what I thought I must, but he had not specifically asked me to slice the boy open. Indeed, I am sure he would have strongly disapproved which of course is why I hadn't told him beforehand. But I was grateful for this display of support at a difficult moment.

'Then you too should be ashamed!' came a lone voice.

'Shame?' said Samson and shook his head. 'Is it shameful to seek the truth of how a human being, so violently and heinously torn from life, met his end? Is it not more shameful that anyone should have to leave this world unaccounted and thus allow his killer to go free for want of knowledge?'

'We know who killed him. It was the Jew!'

'No brother, we do not know that,' snapped Samson rounding on the speaker. 'That is surmise. That is gossip. And anyone who thinks it and spreads it as fact is doing the work of the real murderer for him and is no friend of this child. Master Walter has been charged by me to examine this matter. If in the fullness of time he is discovered to have been martyred we will give him due veneration. Until then he is just another dead child. This is not the Anarchy. We will proceed with due process.'

Here Samson lifted the sheet and covered him up again. He sighed heavily.

'What this beautiful and unique child needs from us now is to celebrate his short life, to comfort his bereaved mother and give him the decent burial he deserves in hallowed ground according to our Christian rites. We are squabbling over him like dogs over a bone. Now, no more of this shameful behaviour. We will give thanks to Almighty God for the gift of this child's life and our solemn prayers for the protection and comfort of his immortal soul.'

Samson then theatrically brought his hands together and bowed his head and one by one the other monks did the same - or most of them did. Perhaps a quarter, twenty, remained seated frowning and shaking their heads in disapproval. Samson chose to ignore them. After a moment more of silence he led the committal prayers for the dead, and when he had finished he bent down and despite his great age, his gout and his haemorrhoids, he lifted the boy bodily in his own arms and carried him out through the south door to the waiting open grave.

Chapter 10
HOW TO MAKE A MARTYR

'Well,' grinned Gilbert when we returned to my cell. 'That certainly put the cat amongst the pigeons.'

'More like a wily old fox among chickens,' I said meaning Samson. I threw myself disconsolately onto my cot and feeling for the first time since this business began exhausted and irritable. 'I noticed loyal old J-J-Jocelin was nowhere to be seen when the b-b-blame was being d-d-d-dished out.'

Gilbert snorted at my poor attempt at mimicry then coughed indicating the doorway. I turned to see Jocelin standing on the threshold.

'I was c-collecting information that m-may be useful w-when we interview the boy's m-mother,' he said coming fully into the room. 'I p-presume that is what you will want to d-do n-next?'

I sat up sharply. 'Yes, erm, thank you Jocelin,' I said trying to cover my embarrassment. 'That's exactly what I had intended doing next.'

I indicated a stool for him to sit then glared pointedly at Gilbert to disappear. He did so with his hand over his mouth. I could hear him sniggering all the way down the passage, damn the boy.

'What – erm - have you managed to discover, brother?' I said to Jocelin.

He read coldly from his notes: 'The family are t-tenants of the abbey. The father, William, worked the abbey's fuller watermill a m-mile south of the abbey on the f-field of Haberdon next to the river. Matthew was training with his father until he d-died.'

'When was that?'

'Eight months ago. An accident involving the m-mill wheel. Which left Matthew as head of the household, the eldest of six ch-children who all live at the mill with their m-mother.'

'That must be the woman we saw this morning at the Moy house.'

He nodded. 'When the father died the t-tenancy reverted back to the abbey.'

'So the family was made destitute. That seems unjust.'

'Father Abbot had n-no option,' defended Jocelin. 'I spoke with the Sacrist's office. F-fulling is heavy work involving much scouring and thickening of wool cloth, apparently. And then there is the fuller's earth to dig…' he looked up, '…that's the clay used to c-clean the wool. No work for a child, even one as strong as Matthew, and certainly no work for a f-female. Brother Hugh has, of his charity, allowed the f-family to remain in the cottage until they can find alternative dwelling.'

'And have they found anywhere?'

He folded his arms over his notes. 'It seems n-not.'

'All right,' I said. 'That tells us a bit about the family but nothing about why Matthew was murdered.'

Jocelin pursed his lips. I was beginning to know that look. He thought the question irrelevant if not actually irreverent. He thought he knew why Matthew had been murdered and it had nothing to do with human frailty; he'd made that clear at the Moy house although he had not come out and said so directly. It was a growing source of tension between us that was threatening the investigation and could not be allowed to continue. I didn't mind him holding different views from me – disputation is what fuels debate and it is debate, as I knew from my student days, that produces solutions. But this constant clamming up amounted to – well, if he were a child I'd call it dumb insolence. There was a crisis looming, the air between us thick with unvoiced grievances. It had to be cleared if we were to make progress.

'Brother,' I said quietly, 'if you think this investigation is pointless then I would prefer it if you said so now. It is going to be difficult enough negotiating through this maze of prejudices. Without your full commitment it may become impossible. So if you feel we cannot put our personal differences to one side then you may as well leave now. I will tell Abbot Samson that it is my fault – which I'm sure he will have no difficulty believing. I'll tell him we are incompatible. You won't be blamed.'

He fumed. He really did look quite put out for the first time since we got together on the case. If

I didn't know better I'd have sworn his bald pate was actually steaming.

'F-father Abbot has ch-charged me to ass-ssist you,' he stuttered, 'and th-that is what I int-tend to do. It matters not a j-j-jot what I p-privately think. I w-w-ill continue to aid you as b-best I c-c-can.'

I nodded. 'Very well. So long as we understand that.'

'Although if asked I would s-say we are w-wasting our time. It seems p-perfectly clear to me that poor little Matthew was m-martyred. All this examining and s-seeking for witnesses is merely confirming the obvious. "What God has wrought no man maketh nought." All else is v-vanity. Nevertheless,' he went on before I could interpose, 'it is equally c-clear to me that the means by which the boy was dispatched was through human agency – or r-rather *two* human agencies – and it is my sacred d-duty to help you discover th-their identity however irrelevant it may be.' He took a deep breath: 'And s-snipe as you might at me and m-my af-f-f-flictions, Master Walter, we will not be able to gainsay God's purpose for this boy whether it be with my c-crooked tongue or your st-st-star-raight one.'

Well! That was me well and truly rebuked and no mistake. He clearly harboured strong feelings about the case and my thoughtless jibe seemed to have provoked him out of his introspection. Good. If nothing else it proved he wasn't such a cold fish after all but had passion in his belly. And what passion! He was almost panting with fury. I chuckle now to think of it. Dear old Jocelin. At that moment I believe I could have hugged him – except that any such physical contact would probably have filled him with horror. Well, we may disagree on the significance of the murdered boy's death but not on the route he came to it, it seems. I could work with that. But there was still a path leading from the watermill to the Moy house along which Matthew had travelled passing from young innocent life to violent and premature death. Along that path there were clear signs of human intervention, and divine purpose or not we had a duty to follow that path until we discovered its source. God may not wish us to succeed in which case we will fail, but we had to try.

The bell for vespers started to toll filling the awkward silence between us and I suddenly felt the need for spiritual renewal having been too much in the world for one day.

'Enough for today,' I said. 'Daylight is long this time of year. We will both rise early tomorrow morning and travel down to the Haberdon together. Let us hope that the boy's mother has managed to recover herself sufficiently to throw some light on why her child should have met with such a violent end.'

He grunted agreement and stood up collecting his documents together.

'Oh, and brother,' I said.

'Yes?'

I smiled. 'Thank you for that.'

He blushed, nodded, then left.

The Haberdon is a damp meadowland adjacent to the River Lark approximately one mile south of the abbey and the fuller's mill occupies the southeast corner. We arrived there early the next morning to find we had already been beaten to it by another delegation made up of five monks from the abbey. These five were the most senior among the twenty who had heckled me in the abbey church the previous day and had been most vocal in calling for Matthew's canonization. They consisted of James the Third Prior, Ranulf the Sub-Sacristan, Walkin the Pittancer, old Jeremiah and - yet again - Egbert. All were fairly second-league in the monastery hierarchy and none very surprising – except perhaps Jeremiah who was one of the oldest, brightest and most respected of the choir monks and who lent the rest a degree of gravitas. The five of them were dispersed around the walls of the tiny one-roomed cottage that was home for the milling family with old Jeremiah seated on the only stool, his walking stick held before him like a caduceus wand. They were all looking pretty grim and none seemed surprised to see me.

There were no windows in the house, the only light entering through the open door. Once my eyes had adjusted to the gloom I could see that half the room was taken up with one huge bed out of the middle of which stared five pairs of bewildered eyes - the three younger sisters and two younger brothers of the dead boy, I presumed. In front of them and perched precariously on the edge of the bed was the woman who had attacked Isaac ben Moy in his garden the previous day, the children's mother. She looked younger today and would be quite pretty once her puffy eyes, swollen from two nights of crying, went down.

'God bless all in this house,' I said making the sign of the Cross. There was a subdued murmur of responses from my brother monks. I stared at each individually. Most had the decency to avoid my eye, except for Egbert who held it defiantly. I was secretly furious - with them for managing to outmanoeuvre me in this way and with myself for not foreseeing the possibility. But I was equally determined not to let them see it.

'Good day to you, brothers,' I smiled. 'I am here to question this woman about the death of her son. May I ask what your purpose is?'

'The same,' replied Egbert.

'With whose authority?'

'With God's,' said Egbert.

'Really?' I smiled. 'Weighty authority indeed. Funny He said nothing to me about it.'

James, Ranulf and Walkin all gasped at my blasphemy and I bit my tongue regretting my impetuosity. Egbert merely curled his lip and nodded.

'Let us not play games,' said Jeremiah in his fluting, old man's voice. 'You know why we are here, Walter, to ensure God's Will is done. That is all Egbert meant.'

'And that is all I meant. But who is to say what is God's Will? You?'

'I should not so presume,' he smiled. 'The interpretation of the Divine Will is in the gift of no single man however well-qualified he may – or may not - be.'

That was a deliberate challenge to me. And strictly speaking he was right. I was no more competent to perform the task Samson had laid upon me than anyone else in the room. But it was to me that he had entrusted it and any challenge to me was also a challenge to him. For the moment, though, Jeremiah had caught me off-guard and I had no reply.

'The more minds bent to the task,' Jeremiah continued more genially, 'the more likely we are to correctly interpret God's purpose. You would at least agree to that.'

But I was not in a mood to be genial. 'So, it's to be beatification by committee, is it? The Abbot and the Pope are not to be consulted?'

'There was no pope when Edmund was canonized,' retorted Egbert. 'It was the people's will then.'

'Oh, so not *God's* authority after all but the *people's*.' I nodded. 'I see.'

'It amounted to the same thing - then.'

'Perhaps. But those were barbarous times. Today we have the rule of law.'

'Forgive me,' interrupted Jeremiah again, smiling. 'This talk of law. Remind me Walter, your accreditation was in *physic* was it not?'

Damn the man! He would keep harking on the same point. 'I admit I am no lawyer,' I stumbled feeling my colour rise. 'Father Abbot asked me to head this enquiry because of my background and training in the science of diagnosis. He thought such skills might be useful in this case. Be comforted that I will let his grace know that you think his judgement misplaced.'

'Ah, well there you have me at a disadvantage,' said Jeremiah smiling sweetly and shaking his clever ancient head. 'I do willingly confess I have no expertise in the *science* of martyrdom.'

'If indeed this is a martyrdom,' I blurted.

'So you have made up your mind,' shot back Egbert. 'It seems we were right to be concerned.'

'And is that your concern?' I rounded on him wondering how I had suddenly become the one having to defend myself. 'That I have a closed mind? If so let me assure you that my concern is only with discovering the truth.'

'As is ours,' said Jeremiah punctuating each word with the point of his stick on the ground.

'Is it? It seems to me that you are guilty of the exact same error of which you accuse me.'

Jeremiah sighed. 'No-one is accusing you of anything, Walter.' He looked over my shoulder. 'Where do you stand on this, Brother Guestmaster? I notice you are keeping very quiet.'

In the heat of the moment I had quite forgotten Jocelin was behind me and that he was one of the senior obedientiaries, too.

'I f-feel I am half-way between the two,' mumbled Jocelin.

'Fence-sitting as usual, Jocelin,' tutted Jeremiah. 'You may find that an uncomfortable place to be in the coming days.'

Jocelin opened his mouth to reply but shut it again, much to my irritation. I suppose I should have been grateful he said that much in my favour and did not declare his true position which it was clear from yesterday's outburst was more with Jeremiah and the others than with me.

'Brother Jocelin is here to help me question this grieving woman about her dead son,' I said indicating Matthew's mother who had said nothing so far but stood silently while we monks bickered between ourselves. 'Whom we all seem to have forgotten. So far you have prevented us from carrying out that duty.'

'Then ask away,' said Egbert standing aside from the murdered boy's mother with a self-satisfied smirk on his face.

I looked at the woman who did not meet my eye but kept her lips set in a tight line. With a sinking heart I could see there was little point in questioning her now. The others had plainly coached her before I arrived so that any answers I might get would be theirs, not hers. Even so, I had no option but to try.

'Mother,' I said gently. 'Do not be afraid, simply speak the truth. Begin, if you would, by telling me what was Matthew doing the night he died?'

Jeremiah replied for her: 'He was preparing for his coming martyrdom, of course. What else?'

'He left the house that night at some stage,' I said to her. 'Can you tell me what time that was?'

'It was at the hour appointed by God for his sacrifice,' shrugged Jeremiah looking round at the other monks who murmured their agreement.

'Did he know the Moy family?' I persisted with her.

'I cannot see the relevance of that question,' answered Jeremiah. 'If he was abducted it would just as likely be by a stranger…'

'You are all very keen to have the boy murdered by this Jew,' I blurted out angrily. 'I wonder why?'

'Ah, I see we all are to be suspects now,' laughed Jeremiah.

'Not all,' I replied too hastily. 'Any one of you could have killed him – or rather, any two.'

Jeremiah's eyes lit up. 'What - with these?' He took from the sleeves of his robe his two hands crippled into useless claws by arthritis. I felt my face flush crimson and the others laughed at my gaffe.

'We know who killed the boy, and why,' said Egbert triumphantly. 'The Jew, Moy, in mockery of Our Lord's Passion.'

Still embarrassed by my *faux pas* I turned desperately to the mother. 'That's what you thought yesterday, mother. Do you still think the same today?'

She did not reply but instead kept her eyes firmly fixed on the floor. There was a long pause as we waited for her response, the silence hanging heavy in the air. Egbert, who clearly thought the argument won, broke the silence. 'Come brothers, let us go. We have what we came for.'

'Oh? And what was that?' I turned on him shaking now with impotent fury.

He casually handed me a piece of parchment. It appeared to be a declaration by the boy's mother detailing Matthew's life. I flipped through most of it my eye catching the last two paragraphs:

'When he had reached his eighth year of life he was taught the fuller's craft by his father. Gifted with a receptive mind in a short time he far surpassed boys of his own age and was the equal of his own father. So it came to pass that when he reached his twelfth year this boy of exceptional innocence, ignorant of the treachery that had been planned for him, befriended the Jew, Moy, who seduced him with cunning words and tricks.

Then like an innocent lamb the boy was led to the slaughter. He was treated kindly at first and, ignorant of what was being prepared for him, he was kept hidden till the day of the Jewish Passover. On that day after the singing of hymns the Jew Moy suddenly seized the boy, bound and gagged him and placed a crown of thorns upon his head in mockery of our Lord's Passion. Finally he slew the boy by the severing of his head from his body. Thus the glorious boy and martyr, Matthew, entered the Kingdom of Heaven where he lives now in glory for ever.'

'This is preposterous!' I blurted throwing the document away from me in contempt. I pointed at the mother. 'She could not have composed that... that *calumny*.'

'She has put her mark,' said Walkin bending to retrieve the document from the floor. 'The oath is authenticated.' He held it out for me to see the woman's cross.

I turned to the woman again in desperation. 'I do not know what these monks have told you but they have no authority. Abbot Samson will reverse any promises they have made.' I had a sudden thought and turned on Jeremiah. 'Where is Abbot Samson? Does he even know of your visit here today? I cannot believe he gave his permission for you all to be excused at this hour.'

'Samson is away today, Walter. It seems there has been some...irregularity...at our manor of Mildenhall that required his urgent attention. He will doubtless be back tomorrow if you wish to take this up with him then.'

I nodded. 'By which time it will be too late. You will have had the boy declared a martyr by then. And you call Samson de Tottington the Norfolk Trickster,' I sneered with contempt. 'It seems this time it is he who has been tricked.'

Now the mother spoke for the first time her face livid with anger. 'Look!' she yelled at me dragging one of the little girls roughly by the shoulder to stand before me. The poor child was so surprised that she instantly burst into tears. 'See her? I've another four like her, eight if you count the three who God in his spite took from me at birth. I have no husband, no man at all now that Matthew's gone too.' She spat on the floor. 'You monks. You don't live in the real world. You have no children. You don't work. You fill your bellies on the toil of others.'

'This oath,' I said going over it again in my mind. 'It speaks of the boy as though he were singled out for particular attention by God. But he has no connection with the abbey other than being its tenant. He has not led a specially holy life. As far as I can see he was just a regular, ordinary boy.'

'Oh, but that is where you are wrong,' sneered Egbert. 'He was being prepared as a postulant training for the priesthood. Ask Ranulf. He was his novice tutor.'

'It is true, Walter,' said Ranulf. 'I have been training him for the past year.'

'That was why the Jews chose him,' Egbert continued triumphantly. 'It's obvious. They recognized that he was already a saint. What greater prize could they have and what a victory for their Christ-hating religion.' He sneered again. 'Where are your cynical theories now, *Master* Physician?'

The five of them left, doubtless congratulating themselves at having managed to out-manoeuvre me - as well they might. It simply had not occurred to me that anyone would wish to manipulate events to satisfy their prejudices rather than seek the truth. It made me think once again that I was quite the wrong person for this task. Maybe someone else would be better suited, someone less naïve and more pragmatic who would accept a simpler path. I had to face it, I simply wasn't up to the job.

The mother was standing before me evidently uncomfortable that I was still there. Her entire demeanour spoke of defiance, her features set hard and her stance resolute. She was clearly expecting an attack and was readying herself to fend it off. In truth, I felt like shaking the woman for her complicity in the deceit. That outlandish document she had signed could never have been composed by her. The wording, the construction, was too scholarly - more like the work of an academic than a simple mother's testimonial to her child. It was probably even beyond the capabilities of those five monks to compose and I wondered where they had got it from. They had made some sort of deal with the mother in return for her signature on it, but what that deal was would not be wrung out of her by bullying from me. What was needed was subtlety - as Joseph was so fond of reminding me, more flies are caught with honey than with vinegar. So I sat down on the stool vacated by Jeremiah and composed my features into what I hoped approximated a smile.

'You must still be grieving deeply for the loss of your child, daughter,' I said gently. 'Have you anyone to visit you? Family? Friends?'

Her eyes narrowed suspiciously. She looked at her hands and realising she had been wringing them, let them drop. 'Father Paul has been twice,' she said.

'Your parish priest?'

She nodded. 'From Saint Botolph's.'

'But no-one closer. A sibling or parent perhaps?'

She shook her head. 'There's no-one. I have a sister living still in Sudbury but that is too far for her to travel. Besides, she and my husband never got on. There was a family rift.'

'Ah yes,' I nodded. 'Your husband. I heard the tale. A dreadful tragedy. Matthew must have been very capable to have been able to step into his shoes. You must have been very proud of him.'

'Fulling is heavy work,' she agreed pushing a stray brown curl back beneath her coif. 'Strong as he was, it was too much for him alone.'

'So, what you said in your testimonial, that Matthew was the equal of his father, was not entirely accurate.'

She shot me a fiery look of anger. 'I see what you are about. Trying to trip me up. I can't remember what I said in that document. But whatever I said I hold to.' She stuck out a defiant chin.

'Of course you do, I never meant to imply anything else,' I agreed, rowing back quickly. 'But you were telling me about Matthew's character. What sort of boy was he? Jolly? Serious? He must have been quite serious to want to train for the priesthood.'

She shrugged. 'He seemed like just a normal boy to me. I had brothers, I know what boys get up to. He worked hard when he was needed. What those monks said about him was true enough. He was a good boy. They're now saying he's a saint. I don't know about that. All I do know is that when his father died he became the bread-winner for his brothers and sisters and me and he never let us starve. For all I know that's what a saint is. And you, brother, will not trick me into saying otherwise.'

I could see I was not going to get any more out of her about Matthew, she was too wily for that. Instead, I asked her about how she had managed to get into the back of the Moy garden since she insisted she had never been there before. She said she had been directed there by a man. What sort of a man? I asked. Her answer was very vague and her response halting as though having to construct each detail from imagination rather than memory. I doubted if any such man ever existed. When I pressed her to describe him, how he was dressed, his age, his manner, she became agitated and insisted that he had kept his face hidden but that he was well dressed like a gentleman. I decided not to press her further but instead went over to her five remaining children and stroked the youngest girl's hair.

'Who'll feed these poor mites now that both your husband and Matthew are gone?'

Their mother gave me a reply I was already expecting. 'Oh, they will be cared for, do not fear for them.'

I presumed she was referring to the money the other monks had given her for her signature, but when I suggested it she snorted contemptuously. 'What those old misers gave me wouldn't keep a beggar alive.'

As Jocelin and I walked back to the abbey I reflected upon the labourers already hard at work in the fields and wondered how many of them knew or cared that a new saint was in the making just yards from their hovels. I also noticed Jocelin was looking pretty pleased with himself.

'Why so smug?' I asked him. 'Did you enjoy seeing me humiliated, too?'

'I was actually th-thinking about that oath,' he said. 'It must have been drawn up quickly to get it to the b-boy's mother so early and I think I know how. I recognised some of it. It's almost identical to Thomas of Monmouth's c-commentary on the life of Saint William of Norwich.'

I harrumphed. 'If you're right it would certainly explain where it came from. I thought it was too sophisticated for Egbert and Walkin to have concocted.'

Jocelin smiled non-committally. 'They seem to have l-lifted sections of it virtually word for word. But in their haste they made a mistake.'

'What mistake?'

'D–didn't you notice? It said that Moy kept Matthew hidden until Passover. Well, William of Norwich may have died at Passover but Matthew certainly did not. As we already know, P-passover this year was in April and Matthew d-died in J-june'

I slapped my forehead. 'Of course! I knew there was something about it that rankled with me. I was too angry to think clearly. Damn! I wish I'd seen it while they were there. So, that means the oath is meaningless,' I said, and laughed out loud. 'I wonder if the boy's mother realised what she was signing was a lie.'

'Probably not. I d-doubt if she can read and since she could hardly have dictated the testimonial herself she p-probably doesn't even know what was in it. And why should she care? It is quite a thing to be the mother of a saint. Imagine that m-mill turned into a shrine. She could make a f-fortune from selling the water alone.'

I laughed again and clapped my hands. 'Why Jocelin, I do believe you are becoming as cynical as I am.'

He shook his head. 'I am no cynic. You haven't proved that Matthew is not a saint m-merely that others are prepared to bend the truth to achieve their own purpose. I am interested in God's purpose, not man's. If the boy t-truly is a saint then there is nothing you or I or Brother Jeremiah or anyone else can do to p-prevent it. Remember the words of Our Lord: A prophet is not without honour save in his own country, *and in his own house*.'

'Well,' I said, 'a twelve-year-old child has died and not at his own hand. Whether the hand that slew him was God's or someone else's we shall have to find out. I think we may achieve both goals – ours and God's. And possibly bring justice in their wake.'

'Amen to that, brother,' nodded Jocelin.

I was feeling lighter already. Maybe I would stick with the case after all – for the moment at least.

Chapter 11
ROYAL EXPECTATIONS

Despite my misgivings about Jocelin I was secretly glad to have him around to bounce my ideas off. Whenever my own prejudices were in danger of soaring too high one glance from his beaky censorious face soon brought me back down to earth again. Whatever I may have thought of his uncritical devotion to Samson and his sometimes exasperating credulity he did have a keen mind which was open to persuasion so long as the argument was well-grounded and thorough which kept me on my toes. It was a great loss to me as well as a sadness when he died all too prematurely a few short years later. But that was to be in the future. For now he was the whetstone that sharpened the blade of my dull wits and I was grateful for that.

In truth, there was really no-one else with whom I could discuss my thoughts about the murder. Gilbert was a fine fellow, useful and willing, but he had no academic training - indeed, I'm not sure he could even read beyond the rudimentary. The one person I would dearly have loved to confer with, Joseph, had seemingly vanished from the face of the earth. Now when I had more need of his sharp brain than ever before he seemed to have abandoned me. Even though I knew he had left I made a special trip out of the town in the hope that one of his neighbours might know where he'd gone. But his shop was shut up and if his neighbours did know of his whereabouts they were not going to tell me. That they were wary about speaking to someone from the abbey didn't really surprise me. These people were not the same as the traders within the town walls, existing as they did on the edge of a society which was as suspicious of them as they were of it. Indeed, their very existence was technically illegal since in order to trade they needed a licence from the Abbot and, more importantly, to pay their market dues. While I was there I once again had the sense that someone was watching me, but though I looked around at the dense huddle of rough traders and vagrants I could see no-one who seemed to be paying me any particular attention. I shivered involuntarily despite the continuing warm weather and walked disconsolately back into town.

Following our frustrating morning at the fuller's mill Jocelin and I agreed to meet up again at midday in the refectory. Now, we at Saint Edmund's have always taken a relaxed attitude towards the Benedictine rule of silence and have never gone in for too much sign-language which can be very confusing - except at mealtimes when we were supposed to listen to some uplifting passage delivered from the pulpit while we ate. Brother Cedric was particularly keen on this rule when he was reader, as he was today, but try as I might I could not concentrate on the – doubtless inspiring - thoughts of Saint Jerome of

Stridonium while so much else was spinning around in my head. I was still fuming over the behaviour of Jeremiah and the rest of the delegation that had ensnared me at the mill but I was mostly angry with myself for allowing them to outmanoeuvre me.

While I sat mulling over the morning's events Jocelin bustled in looking very pleased with himself and sat down heavily on the bench opposite me. Out of deference to Brother Cedric he held his tongue but I could see he was bursting to speak. At last he could contain himself no longer and leaned across the table to whisper:

'I've been taking another look at Brother T-thomas's treatise on Saint William of Norwich. I was right: Th-that d-document the mother signed this morning was lifted from it v-virtually word for word,' he beamed.

His enthusiasm was infectious. 'So the oath is worthless,' I exclaimed. 'This is excellent news.' I rubbed my hands together. 'Ho ho, that's one in the eye for Jeremiah and his crew!'

My outburst caused Brother Cedric to look up from his lectern and give us a stern look of rebuke before turning a page and carrying on reading.

Jocelin smiled apologetically and lowered his voice. 'I would c-caution against celebrating too early. Discrediting Jeremiah and Egbert may weaken their case but it does not eliminate Moy as a s-s-suspect.'

I raised a sardonic eyebrow. 'Do I detect a note of doubt creeping into your voice, brother?'

He bristled slightly. 'I m-merely p-point out an area of w-weakness in their argument. Other evidence against Moy remains as strong as ever –

the chains in the c-cellar; the very fact that the b-body was found in his garden. The legitimacy or otherwise of the mother's oath I'm afraid is largely ir-r-relevant.'

'Even though we know it to be false?' I objected. 'That matter of the date of Easter…'

'…is a d-detail which will be l-lost on most people who will believe whatever they w-want to believe regardless of facts. Such is the nature of faith.'

I wondered if he was conscious of the irony of his last sentence. After all, it was faith rather than fact that had coloured his own attitude thus far. But I let the observation remain unspoken.

'The point I make,' he continued undaunted, 'is that our brother monks are already halfway convinced of Moy's guilt. All they see is that an innocent child has been m-murdered in mockery of Christ's Passion and someone has to be accountable. Isaac Moy - a Jew, a Christ-denier - f-fits the role perfectly.' He sighed. 'In truth, I doubt if they even see this in terms of a m-man's life. To them Isaac Moy is just a name hardly a r-real person at all. After all, they have never met him. The mother's testament, whether true or false, just adds w-weight to their conviction. Th-that, I am sure, was Egbert's purpose in extracting it.'

I could see the logic of his argument. There was no direct proof that Isaac Moy was the killer but without another credible suspect who else was there to blame? And with so much circumstantial evidence against him and the desire to blame someone, the belief that Moy was the killer was growing daily. We continued to eat our lunch in gloomy silence while Brother Cedric's voice droned on and Jocelin chewed for an inordinate amount of time on his cheese and bread before swallowing.

'One thing has been t-troubling me since this morning,' he said at last. 'The mother's behaviour. It was so d-different from yesterday.'

'Go on,' I encouraged.

'Well, if that c-captain had not restrained her in the garden I thought she could have killed Isaac with her b-bare hands. Yet today she did not mention him once. I would have expected, if she truly believed him to be the m-murderer, she would have pressed us to indict him. Yet today she seemed…'

'Indifferent?' I suggested, leaning aside to allow the servant put down our flagon of beer on the table.

'Resigned,' he corrected.

'So, what is your conclusion?'

He took another bite of his cheese and began chewing interminably slowly. At last he said, 'I think someone must be paying her to keep silent. She v-virtually admitted as much as we were leaving.'

I thought back to the interview with Matthew's mother. She said she had no family other than an estranged sister in Sudbury, no pension or means to earn a wage and yet she insisted her children would not go hungry. I agreed with Jocelin, she must be getting help from someone other than the charity of neighbours. So who? Not Jeremiah and his fellows – when I made that suggestion she dismissed it with contempt.

I was about to remind Jocelin of this when we were interrupted by one of the refectory servants bending to whisper in my ear.

'Your f-face has turned suddenly very pale,' said Jocelin glancing nervously at the pulpit. 'Are we adm-monished by B-brother C-cedric again?' He looked anxiously at the pulpit.

'No,' I said hurriedly draining the last of my beer. 'The King. It seems I am summoned.' I quickly intoned my departing grace and added a prayer for myself before scurrying out of the refectory bowing low to Brother Cedric as I passed.

This was the call I had been dreading. I'd been expecting John to try to influence the direction of the investigation and Samson's absence gave him the ideal opportunity to do so. It was in John's interests to have Isaac convicted of the murder in order to get his hands on his considerable wealth, and from what I had seen of the King I didn't doubt he would try. The question was, would I be strong enough to resist? As I hurried to answer the royal summons I cursed Jeremiah under my breath for tricking Abbot Samson into being away just at the moment I needed his protection for there was no-one else remaining in the abbey with any influence over the King.

I hadn't seen John since my attempt to cure his constipation which already seemed an age ago. To be truthful, I'd almost forgotten he was still here, so much had happened since that afternoon. If I needed reminding I had only to look out of the window to see the army still camped on the Great Court of the Abbey although much reduced from the numbers which had arrived a week earlier. Those that had not already left with Earl William and the Justiciar had begun to drift back to their home villages to tend their crops. Even so, enough remained to place a considerable burden on the resources and patience of the townsfolk who were becoming ever more resentful of their presence – and there was little hope of another football match to release pent-up energies. If the King knew any of this he didn't seem to care, apparently preferring to indulge his favourite pastimes of whoring, eating and lying in his bed.

When I got to the palace I found a gaggle of about a dozen local merchants and others milling at the foot of the stairs that led up to the King's apartments, all hoping to win an audience with him. They were being held at bay by a very unsympathetic-looking guard in full body armour who completely filled the stairwell with his vast form and was not about to let anybody past, least of all me. I tried to remonstrate with him but he seemed impervious to reason. I'm not even sure he understood what I was saying to him or what nationality he was – German I suspected, for he didn't respond to either English or French. I was about to give up when I saw with a sinking heart Geoffrey de Saye skulking on the sidelines clearly enjoying the spectacle. I had hoped our paths would never cross again but there was no avoiding him now. Indeed, he was probably responsible for the obstructive attitude of the guard who was doubtless another of his bully boys. Unfortunately with the Justiciar gone de Saye was the most senior courtier still with the King and would therefore have known about my summons. When he realised I'd seen him he stepped out from the shadows.

I put on my most obsequious smile wishing to avoid another altercation. 'My lord de Saye, good day to you,' I bowed. 'Is this one of your men? I can't seem to get through to him. I have an appointment with the King so I would be obliged if you could get the fellow to step aside and let me pass.'

De Saye curled his lips into a smile but there was nothing friendly in that smile. 'And what if I choose not to get the fellow to step aside?'

His words caused a murmur among some of the merchants and I could feel my cheeks colour. 'Then you should know that the King has summoned me directly,' a fact I'm sure he already knew perfectly well. 'He will not be pleased to have his order ignored.'

De Saye swaggered over to me, an insolent smile playing on his lips. 'What pleases or displeases the King is not for you to say, monk.'

He may have been a decade older than me but he was taller and much more powerfully-built. It was all I could do not to back away from him. But I was determined to stand my ground.

'Don't look so alarmed, bone-breaker,' he whispered gripping my shoulder hard enough to make me wince. 'He probably only wants to thank you for saving his life.' He stepped back and raised his voice again. 'But before he does we must make certain you are not going to try to end it, mustn't we? Search him!' he barked at the guard who immediately stepped forward and very roughly handled me all over even to my private parts making me cry out in protest, to no avail.

When he'd finished I was dishevelled, bruised and in pain. It was an outrageous assault and I had no doubt a deliberate instruction of de Saye's designed to humiliate me in front of the cowering merchants. If so, he succeeded admirably. I was indeed humiliated - and angry.

'This is iniquitous!' I protested impotently. 'Get your filthy hands off me, you lout!'

'Well?' said de Saye.

'He's clean, my lord,' replied the insolent creature, smirking all over his face. The merchants looked on in bemusement unsure whether to protest or laugh.

I had no such misgivings. I was absolutely furious. 'This is an outrageous way to treat a senior obedientiary of the abbey,' I said straightening my robe and recovering my dignity as best I could. 'Be assured, sir, the Abbot shall hear of this.'

De Saye laughed softly at my words clearly enjoying my discomfort. 'I thought you monks liked that - a bit of *man-handling*.'

Those merchants nearby who heard this comment sniggered and nodded at the joke to my increased fury. I was too stunned to reply.

'Go on,' sniffed de Saye looking me up and down with contempt. 'You're free to go. But look sharp! The King is an impatient man and will not be kept waiting. So run, bone-breaker, *run*!'

He made as if to chase me and in spite of my anger I ducked out of his way, much to the amusement of the merchants. But there was little point in continuing a fracas I could not hope to win and I was already late for the King. John would not be interested in my excuses. Lifting up my robe I stumbled up the stairs as best I could.

Seething still with anger and shame and with my legs still wobbly from my encounter I arrived outside the King's bedchamber, breathless, confused and hot, not at all in a fit state to greet my monarch, which no doubt was de Saye's intention. More hopeful merchants were waiting at the top of the stairs, richer than the ones downstairs judging from their attire, and mingling this time with some minor nobility. I collected myself as best I could, straightened my robe and presented myself to another armoured guard on duty outside the bedchamber door. He frisked me once more though peremptorily and professionally this time before turning the handle and pushing open the door.

Inside the room there was a fetid stench of sweat and stale sex. Though a hot day no shutter was open and the temperature was uncomfortably high. King John was sitting before a dressing table wearing nothing but a blue silk dressing-gown, his hairy thighs shamelessly on display, whilst plucking tunelessly at a lyre that was resting on his knee. The bed which had been the centre of attention a week earlier when the King was rolling about on it in agony was even more unkempt today. But this time its occupant was a girl – she could not have been more than fourteen – lying on top of the bedclothes completely naked and propped up on one elbow, her long dark hair hanging loose and covering one alabaster-white shoulder. She was quite indifferent to my presence not bothering to cover her nakedness. I felt my face go hot again but this time with embarrassment.

I don't know why I was so shocked. Samson had warned me about this girl who had been keeping the King in his room for days on end. With her free hand she was choosing from a tray of miniature almond macaroons, each topped with a single red cherry and which are known among the abbey servants – disgracefully - as Venus Nipples. I blushed to think of the significance of that soubriquet in the present circumstances. Seeing them, I could not but reflect on the irony that they had almost certainly been baked in our own kitchens by Brother Alric, the very same monk who John had earlier accused of poisoning him. Had he truly wanted to poison the King this would have been the perfect opportunity to do so. But the girl was popping the little golden delicacies into her mouth one after the other with no ill effect.

But the most incongruous part of the entire scene was the statuesque figure propped on a chair against the wall. From its dress it was evidently female with a long dark smock and linen wimple, but its features thus framed were so ugly with a huge nose above a heavy moustache and a thin slash for a mouth that it could have been either sex. It was evidently alive but sat bolt upright and absolutely motionless the expression on the face one of utter disdain. If the mouth had ever smiled it had long ago lost the habit of doing so.

My discomfort at being confronted by the naked girl clearly amused her. She laughed coquettishly before popping yet another macaroon between her perfectly even, white teeth and chewing lasciviously. I had only a second to take all this in before dropping to one knee and remaining there, head bowed, until bidden to rise.

Not that the king acknowledged my arrival directly. 'Lovely instrument, the lyre,' he said whilst continuing to pluck the strings. 'I wish I could play it. Never had the time to learn. I borrowed this one from those *jongleurs* who played at my banquet last week. Were you there?'

'I was indeed, sire,' I said licking my lips which, I noticed, had suddenly gone dry.

'Instrument of the gods, the lyre. Apollo played it, you know? He was the god of music - also of healing, interestingly enough. But then you'd know that already being a physician yourself.'

'I – er - yes indeed, sire. Apollo. Yes. A fellow physician. And a fine musician too.' My throat was also dry. I swallowed hard and licked my lips again.

John continued to pluck away unperturbed. 'He was also a pansy, of course - liked a bit of cock up him. That's what you get for all that nude wrestling.'

Behind him the girl stopped chewing at this and looked up, her dark eyes wide in amazement. She covered her mouth with her hand and let out a weird squeal of laughter.

John ignored her. 'They said the same about my brother Richard,' he sighed. 'But never to his face.' He strummed the instrument one more time with relish before propping it against the wall. 'Well, bone-breaker, what have you to tell me?'

'Tell you, sire?' I felt myself grinning like an idiotic monkey.

'Yes yes. Come along, keep up. Tell me something. Report.' He looked down at me expectantly.

'I – er -' I began desperately trying to think what to say. 'Is your Highness feeling better?'

He frowned. 'Feeling better? What are you talking about, you oaf?'

'Your – erm – bowels, sire. Isn't that what you brought me here to, erm…discuss…?' My voice trailed away.

His eyes narrowed dangerously. 'My bowels? My bowels*?* Good God, man, I didn't bring you here to talk about my *bowels*. Are you trying to make a fool of me? Is that it? Because I'm not a fool. People think I am but I'm not.' He stood up and started pacing up and down. 'That buffoon of an abbot, now he's a fool. He may have his spies but so do I. He thinks I don't know what's going on, but I do. What I want to know is, *did he do it?*' He had stopped pacing and stood arms akimbo staring fiercely down at me still on one knee before him.

So it was the murder then, that was why I was here. I had dreaded as much. I swallowed again noisily. 'It's too early to say, sire.'

He frowned now like a child whose just been told he can't have his favourite toy to play with. 'Well, when will you be able to say?' he pouted. 'I can't stay here for ever, you know? I've got things to do.'

'Indeed, sire.'

'And remember this,' he said leaning closer. 'I can be as generous to those who help me as I can be *un*generous with those who do not.' He cocked an eyebrow. 'I trust I make m'self clear?'

'Perfectly, sire.'

His meaning was clear all right. He wanted Isaac found guilty so he could get his hands on his property. I was praying he would not ask me to commit myself to this conclusion for I truly did not know at that moment how I would answer if he did, or what his reaction would be. Fortunately the girl saved the moment and very possibly my neck. All the while John was speaking she had been making lewd gestures at me behind his back trying to unnerve me. It was indeed very distracting. Now she got up on her knees to play peek-a-boo with the silk cloth she had wrapped around her. I inwardly groaned wondering how and when I would be able to get out of this madhouse.

'I've got a good idea,' she mooed. 'Why don't we do it in front of this monk?'

From my position at John's feet I saw his left eye twitch. 'I am trying to have a sensible conversation here, madam,' he said without turning round.

'Yes, but wouldn't it be a laugh?' She giggled and thrust out her pert little breasts towards me making me wince once more with embarrassment. 'I bet he's never done it. I bet he's never even *seen* a naked woman before.'

'He's a doctor,' said John. 'Of course he's seen a naked woman before.'

'Yes, but never one with bubbies like these.' She thrust the under-developed things up as high as she could and licked her lips salaciously, making me cringe again.

John slowly turned, went over to the bed and smiling, leaned across and kissed the girl fully and sensuously on the mouth. Then with a deft twitch of his wrist he pulled the silk cloth from beneath her sending her sprawling off the bed and landing on the floor with a heavy bump. She screamed more from surprise than hurt which must have been heard in the corridor because the door was immediately flung open to reveal the guard and a dozen pair of minor nobility eyes peering anxiously in.

'Get out!' he bellowed at them.

The door instantly closed again.

John was apoplectic with rage. 'How dare you?' he screamed at the girl. 'I am the King, you foul-mouthed little trollop. You can get out too. Go on, out - *now!*'

Red in the face and shaking with anger, John threw the tray of macaroons at her head making her yell in pain. He chased her screaming and naked to the door and out into the corridor into the gaggle of astonished courtiers and merchants who now scrambled over each other to escape the fleeing girl's path.

'And take your mother with you!' he yelled, at which point the gargoyle that had been sitting so stoically by the wall suddenly came to life, growled something incoherent, picked up her skirts and followed her daughter out of the room. 'And don't come back!' John boomed at the top of his voice slamming the door so hard dust fell from the rafters.

He stood for a moment panting deeply with spittle actually foaming on his lips as he tried to recover his composure. All the while this performance had lasted I had not dared move a muscle and remained on one knee terrified lest he turn his anger on me next. Gradually I heard his breathing return to normal.

At last he seemed to remember where he was and that I was still in the room behind him. 'Your father,' he said quietly without turning round, 'was William de Ixworth, I believe.'

'That is correct, sire.' I had no idea he knew my family. What horror was he now about to perpetrate on me?

He merely nodded. 'There was a William de Ixworth on crusade with my mother. Before my time. Before yours, too.'

He was referring, as I knew, to his mother, the celebrated dowager Duchess Eleanor of Aquitaine, married to two kings and mother of two more, whose fame and beauty the troubadours had been celebrating for decades. She had indeed been in the Holy Land at the same time as my father on the abortive Holy War to Acre, Damascus and Jerusalem. A very elderly lady now, she had been married to King Louis of France, not yet to John's father Henry, as I'm sure John knew only too well.

'We are of an age, you and I, Master Physician,' he said wearily still without turning round. 'We could almost be brothers.'

'Indeed we could, sire.' The suggestion appalled me but I would have agreed the Moon was made of oatmeal had he said so just to get out of that room as quickly as possible.

'Except I am King of England and you are an impoverished monk.' He turned round and I could see he looked tired, drained. 'All right,' he said. 'You can go. But remember what I said.' He fixed me fiercely with his stare before going back to his seat by the desk and picking up the lyre again.

I have never been so relieved to leave a room in my life. 'Thank you, sire,' I mumbled bowing all the way to the door. 'I will indeed. Thank you. Thank you.'

'By the way,' he said as I was about to open it. I froze with my hand inches from the latch. 'You're doing a grand job. Keep it up.' He began once again plucking at his tuneless song.

Bowing continuously, I backed through the door, closed it with the gentlest of gentle clicks, and then let out a long-held sigh of relief.

Turning, I was confronted by a sea of faces - courtiers, merchants and town dignitaries - all staring at me in silent horror.

'Excuse me, gentlemen,' I mumbled politely as I stepped through them. 'Thank you – excuse me - thank you.'

As I got to the top of the stairs and about to descend, I heard the King bellow one last thing through the door:

'And send up my steward of the bath! It smells like a tart's boudoir in here!'

Chapter 12
TEMPTATIONS & TREACHERY

I have just spent a wretched night. I confess it: I could not get the image of that naked girl out of my head. It was a shock to discover that I still had such feelings because I thought that part of my life had been over a dozen years or more. The King was right, of course, I have seen many a naked female body in the course of my professional career, how could I not? But the girl was also right in that this was no mere medical examination when one's mind is filled with compassion for the patient and the cold determination of a cure and all baser thoughts are forgotten. All women patients flirt - they can do no otherwise since their Fall in the Garden of Eden. But never before have I been so brazenly beguiled by such an accomplished temptress, and one so very young. Where did she learn such skills? No wonder Adam had such difficulty resisting the charms of Eve.

My mind was in turmoil all night, racing with unworthy thoughts as I tossed and turned on my cot, longing for sleep. When it wouldn't come I got out of bed and knelt to pray earnestly to a merciful God to relieve me of my turmoil. And when this didn't work I returned to my bed and lay on my back with my arms firmly held by my sides outside the sheets just as our novice master had taught us in the seminary all those years ago in order to avoid the temptation of Onan. Mercifully it was near to midsummer when the nights are at their shortest and dawn is not long in coming.

Of course I am aware that such feelings are natural in any man and they don't go away just because we monks give our bodies to Christ - monks are still men after all. The test is not the abandonment of those base instincts but the rising above them and weak mortals like us try to emulate as best we can the impossible perfection of our lord Jesus Christ, always being aware just how hopelessly inadequate our efforts will be.

Well, that's the theory anyway. Happily I made it through the night unpolluted. But this is not the first time my sacrifice has been thus tested and as I lay trying to divert my mind from these unworthy cravings my thoughts strayed once more to the more honourable side of human desire and specifically to a certain young lady with whom I had been emotionally intimate in my student days. This was in the south of France where all life celebrates love and beauty. I was a much younger man then, with a younger man's passions which are not always so easy to subdue as they are later in life. The young lady concerned was called Emeline and she was the youngest daughter of the Comte de Céret, a friend of my father and a fellow Crusader on that same campaign the King had referred to. The Comte had been badly wounded at the siege of Damascus in July 1148 when his horse was shot from beneath him and had fallen on his leg. My father managed to save the leg although the Comte walked with a limp ever thereafter. In consequence the two men became lifelong friends. Nothing would have delighted either man more than to see their two families allied in the next generation. In truth, I think both our fathers were more keen on the match than we were ourselves although Emeline and I were extremely fond of each other. Of course, the prospect of having a wife did present me with something of a problem if I was to obey my other calling and become a monk. It was still possible then to both marry and to take holy orders despite the papal prohibitions invalidating all such marriages. Indeed, even today I know of several older priests who still keep female "house keepers". But I was ideological in those days. I wanted to save people from both earthly disease and eternal torment. Besides, if my memory serves me correctly Emeline had a young man of whom she had been fond prior to our acquaintance and who had not quite given up hope of a return to favour, as indeed it turned out to be. So in the end the grand alliance came to nought, amicably I'm pleased to say, and everyone got what they really wanted.

Cock crow came just as I was at last beginning to drift into troubled sleep and I dragged my exhausted limbs out of bed and down to the lavatorium to wash before lauds. Had I known just what sort of day it was going to turn out to be I might have stayed in bed and pulled the covers over my head.

Jocelin was as bright and jolly as I was dull and languorous this Thursday morn when he once again sat across from me in the refectory eager to know how I'd got on with the King. Half asleep still, I gave him an edited version of my audience, omitting mention of either the young damsel in the bed or my encounter with the odious Geoffrey de Saye. I did, however, repeat what the King had said about the murder.

Jocelin listened with concentrated attention. 'W-what do you think he meant by that: *He can be as generous to those who help him as he can be ungenerous with those who do not*?'

'He meant he wants Isaac to be found guilty of the murder so that he can inherit his property,' I said gloomily. 'And he expects me to deliver it to him.'

Jocelin swallowed hard. 'W-what will you do?'

'Pray, brother,' I yawned. 'I'm going to pray.'

'Y-yes indeed,' nodded Jocelin thoughtfully. 'Well, all may not be lost. I've been r-reading up about all this in the l-library and I think I m-may have something.' He reached into his sack and took out his notebook which I could see was filled with jottings.

My heart sank. I was in no fit state this morning to deal with these copious annotations of Jocelin's. They always depress me since nothing could more graphically illustrate just how disorganized my own system of record-keeping is. He writes so much and so often that there can be little ink left in the scriptorium for the copying of manuscripts, although it wouldn't surprise me to hear he had a stock of oak apples in his office from which to manufacture his own.

He found his place in his notes and raised a senatorial finger. 'You remember F-father Abbot told us that all Jewish property goes to the King on the death of the owner? In fact that's n-not quite right. It's only property obtained through *usury* that is forfeit. Everything else he can keep - I m-mean his s-survivors can keep,' he corrected himself sheepishly.

I could tell he was not to be discouraged with yawns and sighs. I closed my weary eyes. 'All right. So how is it possible to tell which property is the product of usury and which is not?' It was a superfluous question. I had no doubt he was going to tell me whether or not I wanted him to.

He licked his lips and shuffled enthusiastically to the edge of his bench. 'Nine years ago there was a m-massacre of Jews in York Castle – er, you perhaps have heard of it?'

I recalled with a shudder Isaac's clinical description of the incident. I nodded. 'A hundred-and-fifty innocent souls. What about it?'

'Well, King Richard was v-very angry about it.'

'I should think so too,' I snorted tucking my head into my robes and pulling them up around me. 'It was a disgraceful episode.'

'Oh, n-not about the Jews being murdered,' Jocelin corrected himself. 'I mean, of course he *was* angry about that. B-but what he was more concerned about was their bonds of debt which were b-burned on the floor of the Minster church at the same time. You see, without them there was no proof of how much he was owed.'

'So King Richard was thwarted for once from getting his hands on his – or rather *Jewish* - money.' I sniffed. 'Good. There is at least some justice in the world. Now, what's your point?'

'M-my p-point,' said Jocelin lowering his voice further, 'is that in order to prevent it happening again – losing the proof of ownership I mean - R-richard decreed that a record of all f-future transactions by the Jews was to be kept by his officials and he passed a law to that effect.' He looked at me expectantly but I just shrugged unable to see the point he was making. 'Don't you s-see? It would make an excellent m-motive for Matthew's m-murder.'

I nodded sleepily. 'By anyone who could benefit from Isaac's death – yes, I see that.' I suddenly woke up. 'Good God. You're not suggesting…' I too lowered my voice now. 'You're not trying to suggest *King John* is Matthew's *murderer*?'

Jocelin blushed. 'No no, of course n-not.' Then he grinned slyly. 'B-but it's an intriguing theory, d-don't you think?'

I did not. The suggestion was preposterous, treasonable indeed and I told him in no uncertain terms that if he valued his neck he should not repeat it to anyone. The very idea that a King of England would be complicit in the murder of a twelve-year-old boy - whatever next?

However, Jocelin's ferreting did put paid to my own pet theory about Isaac's testament, for if it was a bond of debt that Isaac had wished me to preserve, as up till then I had been assuming, then under this law of King Richard a record of it would be held somewhere by one of the royal officials. In that case it hardly mattered what happened to the original. Yet Isaac had been adamant that I should keep his document safe. So it followed that it must be something other than a bond of debt, something important enough for him to want me to protect it as though his life depended on it.

But if not a bond of debt then what was it?

There was only one way to find out. I resolved to do what up till now I had been so reluctant to do: I would go to my cell, break the seal on the document and read it, whether Isaac wished it or not. It was clearly more than a mere testament; it was evidence material to the murder and I therefore needed to know what was in it.

Jocelin was busy scrutinizing another set of his voluminous notes and muttering to himself. 'V-very interesting all these old laws. Did you know that when an abbacy becomes v-vacant the King is entitled to its revenues? That would explain why there was a t-two-year gap between the death of Abbot Hugh and the appointment of Samson. I'd often wondered why that was.'

'Yes, I suppose it would,' I said distractedly.

'I bet Samson didn't like that,' he chuckled to himself.

'I imagine not.' I wasn't really listening anymore. I was paying more attention to the scene outside the window. Samson and the Prior were just arriving on their mules and from the expression on Samson's face he was not the happiest of men. They must have ridden since first light from Mildenhall to get here by now. I couldn't resist a slight chuckle. I didn't envy those monks who had tricked him into going to Mildenhall on a wild goose chase. And when he finds out the reason they did it - to get him out of the way while they interrogated the murdered boy's mother and then to manufacture that false oath - he's going to be absolutely furious. Another poke in the eye for Jeremiah and his cohort of conspirators, I thought with glee. Oh yes, things were definitely beginning to look up.

I had about ten minutes before Chapter and it wasn't an occasion I wished to miss. I'd guessed Samson was going to use the meeting to accuse, berate and then punish those monks who had been agitating to get the boy Matthew canonized, among them in particular the five who had hijacked my interview with Matthew's mother the previous day. I could just picture all five of them – Jeremiah included despite his age and his arthritis – lying prostrate on the floor of the chapterhouse before the entire congregation, contrite and begging forgiveness. No doubt they thought the mother's oath made the deception worthwhile. But they miscalculated. Oh yes, Samson was going to wipe the floor with them - literally. Of course, such degradation of one's brother monks is something shameful to our order and to be abhorred – but it was going to be fun to see nevertheless!

On our way back to our cells I noticed some activity near Matthew's newly-dug grave. Among a group of about a dozen people I could see the same four Knieler women I had seen outside the house of Isaac ben Moy three days before.

'God preserve us, what are they doing here?' I said to Jocelin. 'They're like the chorus in a Greek tragedy turning up everywhere unannounced and wailing away. We must get Samson to exclude them from the abbey grounds. Their presence only serves to further inflame prejudices.'

'B-better here than outside the Moy house,' said Jocelin.

I nodded in reluctant agreement to that. It occurred to me again that I hadn't yet been able to find out how they knew to come to Bury in the first instant. With all the other chicanery that had been going on I wouldn't put it past Egbert to have arranged their presence from the very outset. No, I shook myself. I really must stop seeing conspiracies everywhere. There were other explanations for their presence. I just had yet to discover them.

Jocelin said he had some business of his own to see to so we agreed to meet again after Chapter. That suited me because I didn't want to discuss Isaac's testament with him until I knew what it contained. But when I got back to my cell I was in for a shock: The casket had gone. Or more accurately, the soiled bed-linen under which the casket had been hidden had gone. Then I remembered the date. Bed-linen is replaced regularly on the second Saturday of every third month, a practice Sylvanus the Chamberlain was very particular about, personal hygiene being one of Saint Benedict's strictest rules. This must be one of those Saturdays. Sure enough, there on the corner of my cot neatly folded was a complete set of clean linen. But of the casket there was no sign. I was sure I hadn't moved it. I could only hope that the servant who had taken the soiled linen had noticed the casket and put it somewhere safe. On the other hand, if he hadn't noticed it then the casket and its contents could even now be boiling away in the laundry vats. The thought of all that treasure tumbling around among the soiled underwear of eighty monks made me shiver. At least I'd had the foresight to separate the testament from the casket and hidden it among Jocelin's biography of Saint Robert otherwise that could be cooking in the copper as well. I looked on my shelf for Jocelin's manuscript but to my horror it had gone, too. I searched every shelf and cubby-hole and looked through all my own papers but it was not anywhere. The casket may have been taken by mistake but the testament can only have been taken deliberately. But by whom? I hoped against hope that Jocelin might have come into my cell while I was away to retrieve his tract and not noticed Isaac's testament secreted inside. It was surely a vain hope. In any case there was no more time to think of it now for the bell summoning me to Chapter had started ringing. I dare not miss this meeting. Both the casket and the testament would have to wait until later.

Inside the chapterhouse there was a buzz of nervous anticipation. During Samson's absence the *pro*-canonization faction, as I had come to think of Jeremiah and his friends, had been busy its numbers having swelled from the quarter of all choir monks a day or so ago to over half now. Jocelin had been right when he said the mere existence of the mother's testament was enough to win over some waverers. They were all seated on one side of the chapterhouse with the *anti*-canonization faction, or those yet to be persuaded, seated on the opposite side. There was also a rather unpleasant smell in the house today, I noticed.

Samson sat prominently on his dais at the front glowering at every monk in turn as he entered. He waited until everyone was settled then he rose slowly and held out his arms in customary welcome.

'The Peace of the Lord be with you and may he give his blessings on these our solemn deliberations, Amen.'

The united response of "Amen" thundered louder than usual, I thought, and as the echo died away Samson began to speak, his voice quiet but trembling with suppressed emotion:

'My brothers. I do not need to tell you what has been going on. You all know that I have been badly mistreated, sent to hunt coney in a foxhole. There was no maladministration at our manor of Mildenhall. Our tenant there was shocked to see me and professed ignorance of sending any message for help. I was made to look a fool and this when my presence at the abbey could not have been more urgently needed. The King here, paralysed and unprotected. An ignoble pretence unworthy of our sacred institution.'

The King, I thought wryly to myself, was happy enough to have the run of the place without you. But no matter.

'So now tell me - whose idea was it?' He looked from side to side of the room.

'All!' came a lone voice from the *pro* faction.

Samson glared at the speaker. 'Then I am more sorry for that than if you had taken off both my feet at the ankles. What were you thinking of? You have shamed me but even more important than that you have dishonoured the name of the blessed Edmund with your deceit. I tell you now in all candour that I have prayed to him long and hard and with a heavy heart and he expects the instigators of this charade to own up and accept their punishment.'

He looked expectantly around at the eighty faces encircling him but no-one stepped forward. So Samson went on:

'The holy saint knows who you are and he has told me your names but wishes the guilty to admit their fault in person as a sign of their contrition. So therefore speak now.'

He waited but when no-one came forward he continued more angrily:

'Brothers, I do not intend to conduct a witch-hunt but I will hear the names of the conspirators from their own lips before we leave this place today.'

He waited again, but apart from some uncomfortable shifting on benches no-one made a move. Samson glowered his frustration.

'This is intolerable. I will now sit and we will all wait here for as long it takes even if it takes all day. Have the courage to own up to your sins and grovel for forgiveness. Do not punish your innocent brothers by your transgression. I command you as your spiritual leader to speak now!' He sat down again heavily and waited. We all waited.

A minute passed. Another. Then old Jeremiah, a man whose integrity if not his judgement I had never doubted, started to rise. But before he got fully to his feet Egbert jumped to his, his face purple with fury.

'No!' he growled. 'This is unjust. What we did was right, it was necessary. We are being diverted from the path of righteousness. When Herod denied the Christ-child it was the Wise Men who saved him by going a different way. We too must go a different way if our own shepherd will not see the truth!' He pointed accusingly at Samson.

'Aye!' shouted Walkin leaping up beside him, 'Justice for Saint Matthew!' and within moments twenty more were on their feet waving fists at Samson, who was again on his feet, and all yelling at once.

Such strength of feeling - I admit I was surprised. But not as surprised as I was a moment later when Ranulf the sub-sacristan strode behind Samson's dais and pulled back a screen that until then I had barely noticed to reveal a grotesque sight: The exhumed body of poor little Matthew fixed upright to a wooden board in attitude he never would have adopted in life, his head bowed, his feet together and his arms outstretched in imitation of the Crucified Christ. So that was what had been going on at the grave-side earlier, I should have guessed something of the sort. It also explained the foul odour in the air. A gasp went up from every quarter of the house as two more monks joined Ranulf in raising the board to its full vertical position at which point the entire congregation fell to their knees including, I'm sorry to say, Jocelin, which left Samson and me the only ones still standing.

'See!' yelled Egbert, the little man's eyes ablaze with fanatical light as he pointed to the boy's forehead. 'Marks of the crown of thorns. And here,' he held up a discoloured wrist, 'where the nails were driven through, the other hand here too. And here at the feet. Is there any doubting here to test us further? What more proof do you need that this was a mockery of our Lord's Passion. We are not the criminals. It is the Jew, Moy, who did this! Alleluia, brothers! Alleluia!'

Other monks were echoing the alleluias and moaning, some holding up their arms, others grovelling in supplication as though Christ Himself had come to end the world. We were in the midst of a collective hysteria. I knew I had to intervene. If I did not I feared a mob of my own brother monks would have gone out there and then to lynch Isaac ben Moy.

I strode to the front with my heart pounding in my chest. I needed no more than a glance at the so-called 'wounds' to realise what had been going on.

'These wounds are fresh and post-mortem!' I yelled but was immediately shouted down. So I shouted all the louder: 'They were not present when I examined the boy three days ago. See, there is no blood. Someone has fabricated this. Brother Jocelin will bear witness that I say true.'

I searched among the writhing throng for Jocelin to corroborate my words but instead of Jocelin's face my eyes saw that of another – Geoffrey de Saye. Amid the confusion he had entered the chapterhouse with a troop of his soldiers and now stood at the back glaring at me in triumph. In a moment I saw the trap that had been sprung.

'Of course he would say so, wouldn't he?' bellowed de Saye walking steadily and deliberately to the front while his guards barred the door at the rear. I am ashamed to say I shrank a little at his approach.

'What is this outrage?' yelled Samson clearly overwhelmed by events that were now out of his control. 'This is a House of God!'

De Saye ignored him. 'Of course he would say these wounds are false,' he repeated still staring at me. 'That's what he wants you to believe. He wants you to think that the child was murdered by a Christian. But he knew all along that the Jew Moy had murdered the boy.'

To his credit, Samson snorted loudly in de Saye's face. 'Why would he? What possible reason could he have?'

'Because his brother is a Jew of course!' de Saye yelled at the top of his voice. At this several monks gasped and looked at me in horror.

'And if that doesn't convince you,' he went on, 'then perhaps this will.'

He signalled to one of his men who now came forward and produced the casket that Isaac had given me. I almost smiled with the realisation of what was happening. It was beautifully done like a scene from one of the Easter miracle plays. The soldier held the casket high in the air for a second or two to let the image and colour imprint themselves on the eyes of my brother monks before crashing it down on the tiled floor and smashing it open so that hundreds of silver and gold items cascaded in every direction. The monks closest scampered in panic from the scattering coins as though they were tiny goblins chasing them from Hell. The sense of revulsion was palpable but I almost felt like applauding and could have written de Saye's next words myself they were so obvious:

'And there,' he said pointing dramatically at the treasure, 'are his thirty pieces of silver.'

Oh yes, my role in life at last to emulate Judas. I don't know whether I was still light-headed from lack of sleep or simply bewildered, but my only thought at that moment was to regret that such a beautiful object as the casket should have been so wantonly destroyed.

Chapter 13
INCARCERATION

The abbey gaol is on the first floor of Abbot Anselm's tower, a few yards behind the west entry of the abbey church. As prisons go it isn't such a bad place. It's high up so it's dry and quite spacious, certainly roomy enough to share with the other occupants of rats, bats and pigeons. The bats can be a bit of a nuisance since their droppings rain down in a constant drizzle, but otherwise they are no trouble. They hang upside down in the rafters most of the day occasionally squabbling over the available space like bad-tempered siblings in a bed and then as darkness falls they fly out into the night to do … whatever it is bats do at night. I can attest that the notion they get tangled in the hair is a myth, not that my tonsure provided them with much in which to entangle themselves. In fact, they never seem to bump into anything no matter how dark it gets, their nocturnal aerobatics being far superior to those of birds. How they achieve this is indeed a mystery. It's easy to see where they get their reputation for possessing supernatural powers.

My gaoler was an equally harmless fellow though his conversation was somewhat limited. This is because he had his tongue removed as a boy for slandering his parish priest – at least I think that's what he said. Being both illiterate and mute he was ideally suited to his chosen profession since it was impossible for a prisoner to communicate through him with the outside world. Indeed, a man could rot in that place for years and no-one would hear about it. He sat outside my cage in his little cubby-hole drinking and farting which he could do with amazing facility and laugh with great gusto at each noisome explosion. The louder and smellier the expulsion the more amused he was by it. I think he would have liked me to compete but I didn't have his mastery of the art.

I have to admit you do get a good view of the town from up there. I could see the whole length of Churchgate Street right up to the little chapel at the top where we monks congregate on feast days. Another week incarcerated here and I'd have been able to help celebrate the Feast of Saint Vitus who as you know is the patron saint of dancers, epileptics and rheumatics. It can get a bit chaotic, though, all that gyrating about. Nothing as refined as the stately court dances we used to have in my father's great hall in Ixworth. Or if I was still there on the 24th I could have joined in the Feast of St John the Baptist. The night before the feast a leg bone is taken from a - hopefully dead - frog, cleaned and dried over a fire of rowan and then powdered and sprinkled on food as a love potion. I'm told it works. In some places in the north young people jump through the embers of the fire to be blessed, then everyone joins in the dancing until dawn.

Do I sound bitter? Well yes, as a matter of fact, I was. De Saye's men had taken great delight in hauling me off into this miserable hole despite the protests of my fellow monks. For all they may despise me – and that morning in the chapterhouse several of my brethren would have happily seen me flogged to within an inch of my life – it is another matter for someone else to be doing the flogging. The point is that Samson should never have allowed me to be incarcerated at all. De Saye wasn't the Baron of the Liberty of Saint Edmund, Samson was. Not even the Sheriff had jurisdiction here. If Samson had wanted me released there was nothing de Saye could have done about it. Clearly I had displeased his eminence in some way even though I'd had nothing to do with sending him to Mildenhall and had been working hard to limit the hysteria over this boy martyr – not helped, incidentally, by my erstwhile assistant, Jocelin, who was turning out to be a snake in the grass. He came to see me earlier that afternoon. Conscience made him do that:

'H-h-h-h-how are y-y-you?'

'Jocelin, if you're going to stutter there's no point in your being here. I can talk gibberish with him.' I jutted a thumb towards my gaoler who was slouched, semi-comatose with booze, in the corner. But I immediately regretted saying it. 'I'm sorry, that was unkind. I'm fine. Thank you for asking – and thank you for coming.'

He took a deep breath. 'I n-never s-said I didn't think M-matthew was a m-martyr,' he stammered shamefaced. That was presumably a reference to his falling on his knees in the chapterhouse before the grotesque corpse of that unfortunate child who was still being murdered even in death.

'And you do, don't you? Despite what you saw at his autopsy.'

He winced and lowered his eyes.

'Jocelin,' I said, 'you know as well as I do that those marks Egbert pointed out were not on the body when we examined it. Someone is playing games.'

'I've heard it s-said that exceptionally holy people can spontaneously show the marks of the cross on their own bodies as proof of God's love and of their own p-purity.'

'You think that's what they are on Matthew's body?'

He frowned. 'I don't know, I don't know. But why not? Just think - Matthew as the first stigmatic saint. It is b-bound to happen somewhere one day. Why not today, here, now?' He shook his head passionately. 'Why are you always so d-dismissive?'

I sighed and sat down cross-legged on the floor and motioned Jocelin to do the same. 'I don't dismiss it, Jocelin. I long for a sign from God as much as you do. Sometimes I long for it so much it hurts inside me. But there is knavery afoot here. That so-called oath that Matthew's mother was supposed to have sworn. You said yourself it was copied virtually word for word from Thomas of Monmouth's account of Saint William's martyrdom. Egbert and his friends are so keen on having a martyr they will stoop to any trickery to secure it.'

'Even sacrilege? Surely they would not so d-deceive themselves?'

'Sometimes when we want to believe something so badly and are convinced of it so thoroughly we can be tempted to make the facts fit even when they are telling us the opposite. It is then that we must be on our guard lest our enthusiasm overwhelm our reason.' I looked at his earnest face and spoke seriously: 'This is no academic dispute, brother. A man's life depends on our actions. We must follow the evidence wherever it leads however painful that path and however much it contradicts our sincerest held beliefs.'

'What about those chains in Isaac's cellar?' he pointed out. 'Why k-keep them if not to use them?'

'The house was a former butcher's shop. Isaac told us that himself.'

'Well he would say that, wouldn't he? M-maybe it wasn't a butcher's shop at all. Or maybe it's butchery of a different kind.'

'But the shaft,' I protested with exasperation. 'It was obvious that's where the carcasses were delivered in times past. And those chains were decades old, full of rust.'

He shook his head. 'Perfectly serviceable – as restraints for a child. And M-matthew was restrained – we both s-saw that.'

'But we come back to the fact that the marks on the body we saw in Chapter were freshly manufactured, nothing to do with chains. There were no puncture wounds on the boy's head when we examined him, only bruising. Nothing on the hands or on the feet, only on the wrists.'

Jocelin was wearing that exalted look on his face again. 'A sign of divine favour?'

I sighed in resignation. We were going around in circles. There was no point theorizing. Isaac's life hung on the question and the only way it was going to be answered was to find out who the real murderer was. For saint or not, there was no doubt that Matthew's life had been taken by someone's hand.

'You know the stories are growing, don't you?' he said quietly.

'Stories? What stories?'

'Of m-miracles.'

My heart sank. 'What miracles?'

'It is being said Matthew was a devout child, even while still in his cradle.'

'That's nonsense,' I scoffed, but I could see from Jocelin's face that he was in earnest. 'Go on, then. Tell me. What miracle is this babe supposed to have performed?'

His eyes lit up – bless him, he couldn't help himself. 'It seems that as a baby he had been set to lying in his crib in the garden while his mother was b-busy in the house. A horse broke loose from a neighbouring field and g-galloped wildly at the child set to trample it to death. B-but Matthew calmly made the sign of the cross and the horse was immediately quietened. His mother came out to find it passively eating the g-grass at Matthew's feet.'

I almost laughed at the absurdity of it. 'And you believe this? Where did this story come from? Was it in that fabricated oath of his mother's? No. Has she mentioned it to anybody? Again, no. I bet she doesn't even know the tale.'

A sort of sad smile spread across Jocelin's face. 'This is how it was with Robert, I remember. Stories begin. One m-man tells another and soon everyone has a d-different version of the tale. A divine impulse seizes them. They rush to s-see and they find what they seek: An innocent child m-martyred for his purity. They see the injustice. They are indignant and angry. Then they look for someone to blame. Only that time there was no s-single suspect so all Jews were blamed. A-and then came the Palm Sunday massacre as just retribution.'

I shuddered at his words. They reminded me that I still needed to ask about his own treatise on the miracles of Saint Robert and whether he'd been into my cell to remove it and along with it Isaac's testament hidden inside. But how to broach the subject without giving away its significance? If he'd found it he surely would have mentioned it by now. But if not Jocelin then someone else must have taken it – most likely the awful Geoffrey de Saye. Oh, it was a mess and I could see no way of it being resolved, certainly not with me incarcerated in this place.

'Jocelin,' I said earnestly. 'I'm doing no good in here. I have to get out. You must use your influence with Samson to get him to release me.'

'M-my influence?' he asked, alarmed.

'Yes. He thinks more highly of you than you think. He will listen to you. Tell him I know who killed the boy. Tell him if he wants to avoid more bloodshed he must let me out to prove it. Tell him anything you like but *get me out of here*.'

'D-do you know who d-did it?' he asked in awe.

'No,' I said as the gaoler belched and snorted in his drunken sleep behind Jocelin. 'But I'm never going to find out stuck in here.'

He'd gone leaving me hungry, thirsty and with a wind whipping through the open belfry I was also growing cold despite it being a balmy June night. There's not much you can do alone in a cell like that. I tried to follow the order of the services throughout the day as the bell for each office sounded. I could see my fellow monks filing in and out of the abbey just a few feet below me and despite knowing I was there not one deigned to look up. During the day the men working on the scaffolding of Samson's towers were at eye level. One threw an apple core at me. It came straight in through the narrow window, bounced off my naked pate and his colleagues cheered as he hit his mark. Later, a few of the pilgrims down below stood about gawping up at my cell wondering if there was anyone in here. I'd been tempted to moan like a ghoul just to see their reaction which I could easily do since there was a marvellous echo up there. But I desisted. My friend the mute gaoler probably wouldn't have approved. He might even have gagged me.

I was growing very frustrated but I had to learn patience and could only hope that Jocelin was working to secure my release. I must say I prayed more devoutly in my solitude than ever I did in collective prayer in the choir. I was beginning to see the attraction of the austere life of the anchorite walled up in his cell for years on end. Or perhaps as Saint Simeon Stylites perched on high atop his lonely finger of rock, much higher that Anselm's tower but the principle is the same. There again, perhaps not. I'm not good with heights. Bad enough sitting up there barely twenty feet off the ground. I thought maybe in year or so I might get permission to visit the new order of secluded monks at Witham in Somerset, though from the sound of it I wouldn't get to see any of the inmates since they don't even have contact with each other let alone visitors from outside. But it did sound very peaceful – just a bed, a lectern, a tiny garden and the perpetual solitude of your own thoughts oblivious to the intrigues of the outside world.

Who was I kidding? It must be the lack of food addling my brain. I'd go mad if I didn't have someone to talk to. Even as a child I was always being chastised for a chatterbox. I could no more change my character than I could control those damned bat-droppings. The mind plays tricks when left to listen to itself and I had much to keep a clear head about. It is a wise man who knows his own limitations and I have not the strength of will to live the life of a hermit. But I admire those who can.

Oh, why was Jocelin taking so long? Stuttering some apologetic tale to Samson no doubt. I needed to get out of there. De Saye had taken the casket from my cell and presumably the testament along with it. I couldn't even admit to the testament's existence for fear of antagonising Samson further, having already lied about the casket. If he found out I also had Isaac's testament and had not told him he might easily keep me in that filthy hole for a whole year. It was so frustrating just sitting about unable to do anything.

But hold fast. Who was this coming down the hill now? I recognized that rolling gait. It was Mother Han again. What was she doing out at this time of night? Curfew was hours ago. If she was back plying her wicked trade in the abbey grounds again I swore I'd have her arrested and gaoled – just as soon as I got out of the place myself. She stopped, looked about – *furtively*. Damn those prison bars. I couldn't quite see what she was doing. Now she was beneath me. I was sure she was going in through the tower gate again. In a moment I'd see her emerge the other side. She stopped. Now what was she doing? My God, she was coming up here!

I was right. Mother Han had indeed entered the tower and had climbed the stairs in order to keep a rendezvous she clearly had arranged some time before. She had come to visit my gaoler for which purpose good taste and limited vocabulary prevent me from attempting to describe. I was appalled at what they were doing. Even King John had not been so shameless as to actually *perform* in front of me. The sight – and the sound – of those two going at it like slavering dogs up against the bars of my cage was enough to confirm a man in celibacy for life. If ever I have another night trying to resist carnal temptation I will need only to conjure visions of Mother Han and my gaoler grunting and pawing each other to dampen the fiercest ardour.

God in Heaven, is the whole world, from these two rutting mongrels all the way up to the King, obsessed with this one thought?

The woman must be in her seventh decade and the man hardly less. They took not the slightest notice of me watching – or rather, trying not to watch – from the other side of the bars whence I had retreated to the furthest corner of my realm.

And when they had finished they calmly sat down and proceeded to share the meal that Mother Han had brought wrapped in her shawl. She was still wearing her eye-patch, I noticed, which she now took off and lay to one side, her supposed bad eyesight evidently just another of her many shams. There was nothing wrong with her eye. I snorted loudly. I don't know why I never guessed.

'Oh, it's you,' she said squinting at me through the half-light. 'Thought I recognised that snooty laugh.'

'I was merely lamenting just how far we have fallen since Adam was expelled from the Garden of Eden.'

'Were you so?' She looked about her. 'And how far would you say you've fallen to have landed here?'

'About as low as it gets,' I nodded drawing my robes about me and eyeing her mutton chop covetously. She was making some disgusting noises as she chomped. I wrinkled my nose. How anybody could eat like that was beyond me.

'Hungry?'

'No.'

She grunted and carried on chewing. She must have known I hadn't eaten since breakfast, her gaoler-lover not having offered me so much as a taste of his drink - not that I would have accepted any if he had. It smelled like the stuff shepherds pour on sheep to kill ticks. But Mother Han's juicy chop was another matter. I looked at it dripping with fat and dangling provocatively just inches from my nose. She belched again, wiped her own mouth on her sleeve and then held the half-eaten mutton joint through the bars. After a moment's hesitation I grabbed it and started to gorge. Within a minute I had the bone stripped clean. It tasted like ambrosia.

'You've caused quite a ruckus up on pennypinch hill.'

I took her to mean the area of select dwellings above the noise and smells of the town where Isaac ben Moy had his house. 'Why do you call it that?' I asked.

'Because that's what they are what live up there. The mean beggars. Folk with too much money. Pennypinchers I call 'em. Your Jew friend for one.'

'Isaac Moy? He's not my friend. He's not even a client. I hardly know him in fact.'

'That's what Peter said the day our Lord was hanged.'

'No really, I don't know him,' I insisted. 'I only met him a few days ago.'

'Yep, he said that too.' She wiped a filthy sleeve across her mouth.

I pursed my lips. 'Mother Han, if you've come to torment me I'm sorry to disappoint you. More accomplished practitioners are already on the job.'

'I haven't come for you at all,' she snorted.

'So I saw,' I said eyeing the dumb gaoler who was gnawing happily away at another bone in his corner.

'Well, he is my husband. I can't stay and he can't leave. What would you have us do?'

'Your *husband*?' I said nearly regurgitating my meal.

'Yes, my husband,' she insisted indignantly. 'Hard to credit me with a husband, isn't it? Well, the father of my children at any rate. Same thing,' she sniffed.

That's who the gaoler reminded me of, the young man on the market stall. I knew there was something familiar about him. Maybe these two really were husband and wife.

'The ruckus you say is up on pennypinch hill. I presume by that you mean those Knieler women. Are they still there?'

'Indeed they are,' said Mother Han. 'And a right pain they are too.' She narrowed her eyes. 'I told that Agnes she should go home and piss in her own yard.'

'You *know* these women?' I said, dumbfounded.

'Course I do,' she grinned with satisfaction. 'I know everybody.'

I looked at her doubtfully. 'And when did you have dealing with Dutch zealots before?'

She stopped chewing and guffawed nearly spilling her food from her mouth. It was a not a pretty sight.

'Dutch my fat arse!' she snorted. 'They's Scotch herring girls.' I must have looked as bewildered as I felt for she clarified: 'Them as follow the herring shoals down the coast every year to gut on Yarmouth quay.'

Now it was my mouth that fell open. 'But I was told they came over here from Holland following a heavenly presentiment and speak in myriad tongues.'

Mother Han looked at me as though I were soft in the head. 'Well they ain't. They's Scotch. And that gibberish they talk, 'tain't God's chatter, neither. It's Gaelic.'

'I'm sure you're wrong there,' I said indignantly. 'Brother Jocelin spoke to them. He wouldn't have made an error like that.'

She sniffed and wiped her mouth again. 'Suit yerself. I'm telling you what I know. Them girls is Scotch herringers from Abderbin.'

'I think you mean Aberdeen,' I corrected her, pompously.

'Wherever 'tis 'tain't Ompsterdomp.'

'Amsterdam,' I grimaced. 'Then someone must be paying them.'

'Oh I dare say,' she said rubbing her calves. 'Nasty work, gutting herring. This'll be a holiday for them.'

'A holiday provided by who, though? Who is paying them?'

'Ah now,' she tapped the side of her nose. 'That would be telling.'

'Mother Han, if you know you should tell the Abbot. In fact, I *insist* you tell the Abbot,' I said indignantly.

'Or what?' she challenged aggressively sticking her chin out at me. 'You stuck in there and me out here. Besides, who'd believe a deaf and blind old woman like me?' She held her eye-patch over her eye and put on her most pathetic look.

'You're not blind,' I snorted. 'And you're certainly not deaf.'

But she was right. No-one would think her a credible witness. I wasn't sure I did either. Half of what she said was gossip and the rest plain lies. And if I'm not careful my stupid threats will have closed her mouth for good. I decided to try a different tack, appeal to her maternal instincts – if the old sow was capable of any.

'May I have some cabbage please, Mother Han?'

'Give you the squits,' she warned.

'I'll risk it.'

She dolloped a spoonful onto a slice of bread and handed it through the bars.

'This is quite a jolly picnic we're having,' I grinned sinking my teeth into the squishy mess. 'I haven't had this much fun since I was a child.'

She gave me a sideways look.

'So, erm, what is your story?' I asked conversationally. 'How is it you know so much of Yarmouth?'

She swallowed. 'That's a tale easily told. My mother was a dockside whore, same as my sisters and me. She put me to whoring first when I was six.'

I was truly shocked. 'That's terrible. Where was your father?'

'Ah now,' she said enthusiastically licking a filthy thumb. 'My father was a sailor. Russian by all accounts. I even have an idea who he was. I've got him pinned down to one of fifty,' she guffawed at her own joke. 'Oh don't you shake your head in that holier-than-thou way, you pious prig,' she admonished. 'I don't need your pity. Remember, I'm the one out here and you're the one in there. I did all right. Not many get to my age starting from where I did. I've had five husbands and ten children,' she said proudly. 'Though only one lived past the cradle, God save 'em,' she added and crossed herself.

'The boy on the market,' I said.

'Yeah, that one.' She pulled a face and let out a stream of invectives only a quarter of which I understood. 'It's his wife I blame. Drunk all day and a shrew by night. I've no grandchicks alive nor never will have now,' she sighed.

'In that case, why are you called Mother Han?'

'Mother Hen, Mother Han. It's because I look after the waifs and strays,' she said seriously, then added apparently as an afterthought: 'Like that murdered boy.'

I looked up. 'Matthew?'

She grinned a toothless grin. 'Yeah, I thought that'd interest you.'

'But he has a mother of his own. I've met her.'

'Yeah? Well that's well enough, then.' She sniffed and turned away to find a jug of the same foul liquid the gaoler had been quaffing.

I tried to understand the implications of her words. 'Are you saying Matthew was abandoned by his mother?'

'Never said that. No, never said that. Just that he was more away from his home than in it. Liked to run with the strays, that one.'

That didn't sit well with the impression Jocelin and I were given of the boy when we visited the mill, and it rendered the image of him from the oath as a saintly child, hard working and devoted to his family even more absurd. I was sure Mother Han could tell me more but I sensed her reluctance to do so. She unstopped the leather bottle, took a long satisfying swig and wiping her mouth again looked at me askance.

'What you in here for anyway?'

'Oh, it was a mistake,' I said vaguely.

'Huh!' she snorted. 'Every caged bird says that.'

'In my case it happens to be true,' I said indignantly.

' 'Course it is. And trees can talk and rainbows sing and angels dance upon a pin.' She grinned at me slyly. 'Something to do with that boy?' She nodded when I demurred. 'They're saying he's a martyr.'

'What do you say?'

She shrugged. 'Could be.'

I smiled. 'Saint Matthew of the Haberdon. He's already got half a dozen miracles to his name. I shouldn't wonder if there's a shrine built in the abbey and a holy day declared in his honour within the year.'

'Ha!' Mother Han rocked with laughter. 'That'll be worth seeing!'

'Why so scornful?' I pressed her.

She took another long swig of her bottle. 'Because he was a vile little devil, that's why.' She spat.

'A devil in what way?' I asked trying to keep the urgency out of my voice.

She rocked on her buttocks. 'Nah,' she said suspiciously. 'I've said enough. It's nothing to me.'

'You can't stop now,' I said desperately, but she was already replacing her eye-patch and heaving herself off her haunches.

'Time I was getting back to work.'

'I hope by that you do not mean your usual immoral trade,' I said in frustration and immediately regretted it.

Mother Han stopped and gave me a stern look of rebuke. 'I am an old woman with a useless son and an idiot husband. I get by any way I can.' She snorted down at me. 'I never met a beggar yet refused a crust on moral grounds. Or a hungry monk a chop for all his high and mightiness.'

I looked at the piece of leg which I had picked completely dry but which even now was being sniffed by a rat and found I had no words to reply.

She nodded knowingly. 'I'll bid you good night then, brother.' She looked up at the darkened sky, pulled her shawl up over her head and lifted her skirts to descend the stone steps. In a moment she was gone.

Chapter 14
SOME NEW INFORMATION

'I trust you found your night of confinement rewarding, Master Physician, and that you took advantage of the time for reflection and self-examination.'

Once again I was standing before Samson in his study. Between us on the desk this time was the casket Isaac had given me, broken and hastily repaired but still with the treasure in it - or half of it. Someone had clearly helped themselves to the other half. De Saye, I imagined, or one of his henchmen.

'It was a very uplifting experience, Father Abbot. I am grateful to your grace for allowing me this unique opportunity to meditate upon my faults which are many and onerous.'

He chuckled. 'I bet you are. Jocelin told me how desperate you were to get out. I would have had you released sooner but Lord de Saye insisted on your incarceration. And frankly I could find no reason to disagree with him.'

Ah yes, I could quite believe de Saye had enjoyed the prospect of locking me up. I was still furious with Samson for going along with it but decided to keep my own counsel. I was out, that was the main thing, and antagonising Samson now might put me back inside again. But there was no disguising my face.

'It's no good looking at me like that, Walter,' he said studying me through narrowed eyes. 'You've only yourself to blame for all this. The fact is you should have told me about the casket.' He tapped the thing with a fat pink finger.

'It wasn't something I thought would interest your grace,' I attempted weakly, but he merely shook his head.

'No, Walter, that won't do. The day we buried the boy I asked you specifically if Moy had given you anything and you told me he hadn't. You lied.'

I squirmed. 'Not *lied* exactly, father. He didn't actually *give* me the casket. Rather he *deposited* it with me.'

'However you choose to dress it up you deliberately kept the existence of the casket from me and from everyone else. Not even Jocelin knew of it. And what a stupid thing to do! Good God, man, don't you see how it looks? Here you are interviewing the chief suspect in a murder case and the next thing is you've got a box full of his trinkets hidden in your cell.'

'Half full.'

'What?'

I nodded towards the casket. 'Half the treasure's missing. Hadn't you noticed? I can assure you it was all there when I had it.'

Samson looked at the thing and shifted awkwardly on his chair. 'Yes, well we've only your word for that, haven't we?'

Despite my Herculean efforts to control myself I'm afraid I just lost myself then. After a night locked in a rat-infested cage I'd had enough.

'If you think I'd steal it,' I exploded. 'If you truly think that then put me to the test. Come - bring book, bring candle. I will swear on all I hold sacred....'

'Oh, calm down,' he said flapping a languid hand at me. 'Do you think you'd be standing here now if I really thought you'd stolen the thing? Besides,' he sniffed. 'I've had your cell searched. And don't start blustering again. De Saye would have had you racked if I hadn't. As it is I've told him that I already knew about the casket and asked you to look after it, so you're off the hook. But heed me,' he said wagging a stubby finger at me. 'This is what happens when you take matters into your own hands. Perhaps it will teach you in future to be completely open with me.'

'I can take it, then, that my brother monks who sent you to Mildenhall on a wild goose chase will have received similar punishment – a night in gaol for not being "completely open" with you, father?'

'Oh, they will be dealt with, never fear,' he said irritably. 'I'm fully aware of what they were up to. You're not going to be the only one to pay for your deceit.'

He got up and poured us some wine for which I was grateful not having had anything pass my lips since Mother Han's supper the previous night. He studied me thoughtfully as he handed me my goblet.

'Out of curiosity, why did Moy give you the casket?'

'Insurance,' I said wiping my mouth. 'If anything happened to him I was to make sure it got to his wife and family.'

Samson wrinkled his bulbous nose. 'That sounds suspiciously like a confession to me.'

I shook my head. 'He's a Jew. He doesn't expect to get a fair hearing.'

'Oh, he'll get that, all right,' said Samson ominously.

'What does that mean?'

He brushed the question aside. 'Just tell me now, did he give you anything else? Anything at all?'

'Like what?'

'Oh, I don't know,' he blustered. 'You tell me.' He stared hard at me.

I hesitated sipping my wine slowly to give me time to think. Did he mean Isaac's testament? I couldn't think what else he could be referring to. Would he even know of its existence? Isaac had given it to me and I had mentioned it to no-one. But if Samson knew about it then surely that confirmed its importance. If only I'd opened the damn thing sooner I'd know the answers to all these questions. Should I mention the thing now in the hope that Samson might somehow be able to retrieve it? But then I might not see it again, in which case I'd never know what was in it.

I lowered my eyes. 'No, father, there's nothing.'

Samson narrowed his eyes. 'Why do I think you're still holding something back?' He sighed heavily. 'You disappoint me, Walter. I am not at all happy with the way you have handled things. And I am not alone in that opinion.'

I looked up. 'Why, who else have I displeased?'

'The King. I understand he has already spoken to you on the matter – and that's something else that's happened while I was away and seems to have slipped your memory.'

'He told me he was pleased with my work,' I said petulantly.

But Samson was shaking his head. 'Don't be fooled by royal flattery, Walter. This time next week he won't even remember who you are. Well, for your information the King has now spoken to me. John is not the most patient of men. He is anxious to be leaving here and wants a resolution before he goes – preferably one in his favour.'

'You mean he wants to get his hands on Isaac's money.'

Samson looked at me severely. 'The King has a perfect right to the property of any defunct Jew. Like it or not, that is the law. It's not just his assets but his debts too, remember. The King would be liable for any outstanding monies owed.'

I scoffed. 'Isaac doesn't owe a thing to anyone.'

'Except to God, perhaps. You know, it seems to me that you are grown far too fond of this Jew. That is unprofessional. Your loyalty is not to him but to me.' He inhaled deeply. 'Well, matters have moved on a pace during your confinement.'

My blood ran cold. 'Meaning what?'

But Samson merely drew himself erect. I thought for one dreadful moment he was going to remove me from the case. But it was worse than that.

He looked me in the eye. 'Master Investigator, the King has charged me to ask you formally: Do you have any suspect for the murder of the boy

Matthew, son of William the Fuller, other than Isaac ben Moy?'

'Not yet. But I'm working on it.'

'Then know that the King desires most earnestly that this matter be resolved as speedily as possible. He therefore requests and directs that the issue come before a formal judicial assembly to be held here at the abbey court to decide it once and for all. And,' he added ominously, 'as his highness's chief legal officer within the Liberty of Saint Edmundsbury, I agree with him.'

'A *trial*?' I was stunned. 'When?'

'Monday.'

'Three days - but it's too soon,' I protested. 'I have hardly begun to collect the evidence.'

Samson busied himself with his papers. 'Evidence will not be the deciding factor in this case.'

'Not the deciding factor?' I guffawed. 'What babble is this? How can there be a trial without evidence? Who is to be the judge? The King? *You?*'

Samson shot a look at me that was so violent it made me cringe. '*God* is to be the judge in this case, brother. God.'

I could feel my shoulders sag as the implication of his words struck home. 'You mean trial by ordeal. I should have guessed.'

'Are you doubting God's justice?' he asked facetiously.

It was another of Samson's trick questions. How else could I answer? I pursed my lips. 'No.'

He nodded knowingly. 'If Moy is innocent, *Deo volente,* God will protect him. If not then his punishment will be righteous.' He leaned forward.

'It's his God as well as ours, remember.' He sat back again in his chair. 'In any event, it is far better that we have someone to focus upon. Last time we had no-one and fifty-seven innocents died. This way at least there is a...a...'

'*Scapegoat* I think is the term you're groping for, father. I believe it's a Hebrew concept.' I pursed my lips again. 'May I continue my investigation up to the trial?'

He waved a dismissive hand. 'Do as you wish. You don't have very long.'

'Then I had better begin.' I turned to go.

'Just a minute,' he said. He looked me up and down critically and wrinkled his nose. 'You're filthy. And you smell as if you've been in a sewer. What's that stuff in your hair?'

'Bat droppings, father.'

'Really? Well tidy yourself up. You're a disgrace to the abbey. Now run along, I'm busy.' He turned sharply in his chair to attend to a pet dormouse that he kept in a cage by his bookshelf.

'We don't have much time,' I said to Jocelin as he poured a second bucket of hot water over me. 'Ayeee! Hell's fire, Jocelin, are you trying to scald me to death?'

'I-I'm s-sorry, brother, I d-didn't see where I was p-pouring.'

The servant who had brought the hot water sniggered from the corner of the room. I looked up at Jocelin from my bath. 'It might help if you opened your eyes. Have you never seen a naked man before? It's not a sin you know.'

'I have n-never even seen my own b-body...' he glanced nervously at the servant and lowered his voice, '...*in puris naturalibus.*'

The servant sniggered again.

'You saw Matthew's body naked,' I reminded him scooping a bowl of water over my head to swill the bat droppings out of my tonsure.

'That was different. He was a child. A-and he was dead.'

'That is the one fact of which I do not need reminding,' I said heaving myself out of the wooden tub and grabbing a towel to dry myself. I must say it felt good to have rid myself of the stench of that prison cage with its detritus of vermin excretions and lice. I could begin to see what it was about bathing that so charmed King John although I would not go so far as to indulge in the dozen or so immersions he is rumoured to enjoy in a year. The body, after all, has its own natural oils which should not be removed and Jocelin is at least partially right in thinking the body uncovered like that of the animals can lead to other unwholesome thoughts. I had only to think of the girl in John's bedchamber to remind me of that.

'It's all right,' I said slipping my habit back over my head. 'You can look now. I'm decent.'

Jocelin opened his eyes. I nodded to the servant who clapped his hands together upon which signal four more servants entered like genies, two to lift the bath and the others to take the towels and buckets away.

'Well,' I said when they were gone. 'We have our work cut out for us.' I had already given him an outline of my morning interview with Samson.

'I don't see why,' said Jocelin. 'As F-father Abbot says, we are in God's hands now.'

'So we give up? Nothing more to be done? Let God alone decide?'

'Is there a b-better judge?' he asked piously.

I almost replied, Yes there is: Judgement by a dozen of a man's peers using their wits to assess the evidence laid before them. But he would have assumed I meant God is fallible when what I really mean is that man's *interpretation* of God's intentions is fallible. God Himself, of course, is perfect.

I felt like being mischievous. 'Have you ever witnessed a trial by ordeal?' I casually asked him.

'No,' he replied suspiciously. 'Why?'

I sucked my teeth. 'Not a pleasant sight. I had to attend one once in a professional capacity in order to dress the hand. Ordeal by fire this one was.'

'And d-did you?' he asked hesitantly. 'D-dress the hand, I mean.'

I shook my head. 'There wasn't much of the hand left to dress.'

Jocelin cringed and I smiled slyly. I could tell from the look on his face that he wanted me to say more but was hesitant in case he didn't like what he heard. Like most people, his natural thrill at hearing the gruesome details vied with his fear of being revolted by what he heard. But having warmed the pot of his curiosity, so to speak, I continued to stir the contents:

'You see, what happens in the case of ordeal by fire is this: A piece of iron – say a horseshoe or something of similar size and weight - is heated in a furnace. I don't just mean warmed up, I mean really heated, hotter than that bath water you tried to scald me with just now. So hot it glows white and you really do have to shut your eyes or they will burn out of your head just to look at it. Imagine that,' I said holding out my hand to demonstrate. 'Holding a white hot poker in your bare, naked hand.'

Jocelin flinched pleasingly. I licked my lips and continued:

'But then you have to walk with it – not run, mind you, *walk* - five paces, and slowly. After the first step you can already see the smoke coming off the hand. At the second the flesh begins to sizzle and fall away. At the third the hand is barely recognisable as such anymore.' I nodded at the memory. 'It's actually quite a pleasant smell you know, burning human flesh. Rather like pork.' I chuckled. 'Now there's an amusing irony, fried Jewish flesh smelling of pork. That should cause a stir on Monday morning, don't you think, when Isaac's flesh starts to sizzle and fry and fall off? And then, of course, the bone beneath the skin starts to crack and splinter and -'

'Oh stop!' said Jocelin who was starting to turn green. 'You've m-made your point. There's no n-need to be quite s-s-so g-graphic.'

'Isn't there?' I frowned. 'Anyone who has seen a horse branded knows what hot metal does to flesh. Only this is not animal hide but human skin, and in Isaac's case the very softest white skin of a man accustomed to living not by his hands but by his wits, with few calluses to cushion the pain.'

'If he is innocent, God w-will provide,' insisted Jocelin wiping some beads of sweat from his forehead.

I nodded. 'Maybe so. And I will remind you of those words as Isaac takes hold of the poker's end – if, that is, you can still hear my voice above his screams.'

'What d-do you want of me, Master?' he asked sitting down heavily and putting his head in his hands.

'For us to do the job we were engaged to do.'

'I th-thought we had done. We examined the b-body. We know how the boy was k-killed and we have a credible suspect.'

'You forget, we concluded that it took two people to kill the boy - one to hold him while the other slit his throat. Even if Isaac was one, who was the other?'

'Perhaps he will tell us b-before the – the –'

'Disfigurement?' I supplied. 'And how reliable would that be? He could name anyone under that amount of duress, just for a moment's relief. We need to investigate in order to find out for certain.'

And in the process, I thought, we might just discover who the real murderers are.

'There's something else,' I said seriously. 'I don't believe the boy was as innocent as we have been led to believe.'

I could see my words did not find favour with Jocelin. 'N-now you go t-too far, brother. Everyone attests to his saintliness. His m-mother, those Knieler women.'

'Ah yes,' I interjected. 'The Knieler women. I'm sorry to disillusion you but they are fakes. They're not religionists at all.'

He slumped deflated. 'H-how can you know that?'

I told him about my conversation with Mother Han, how the women were from Scotland, not Holland, hired by someone to whip up sentiment against the Moys. I also told him what Mother Han had said about Matthew's character.

He clearly didn't hold much store by Mother Han's word. 'It is easy to s-say such things now he is d-dead and cannot defend himself,' said Jocelin morosely. 'You complain we don't f-follow the evidence. Well in this case the evidence is clear. He took care of his mother and provided for his siblings. He was even about to t-take holy orders. What more evidence of saintliness could there be?'

'His murderer clearly didn't think so,' I said. 'He must have done something, or known something that was so dangerous that it was worth taking away his young life for.'

'But h-how much harm could a twelve-year-old boy do?' scoffed Jocelin incredulously.

That suddenly reminded me. 'Speaking of which,' I said as casually as I could. 'I never had time to finish your fascinating study of the life of Saint Robert of Bury.' It was a tenuous connection but I could think of no other way to raise the subject.

If Jocelin noticed the incongruity he gave no sign. He attempted a smile. 'Hang on to it for a while l-longer, of you like. Give it back to me when you've f-finished it.'

'Yes,' I nodded. 'I'll do that.'

Well, that settled one question at least. Jocelin didn't retrieve his treatise from my cell, *ergo* he didn't have Isaac's testament either. Nor from our earlier conversation did Samson. I realised despondently that there was only one person left who could possibly have it: De Saye. My chances therefore of getting it back were probably nil.

'So w-what next?' Jocelin asked.

'Hm?' I said coming out of my reverie. 'We continue to dig of course. We have very little time so I suggest we split up. You go and talk to Ranulf, the boy's tutor. I think he will speak more openly to you than to me. See if he can shed some light on Matthew's private life. He must have spent many hours getting to know the boy. Find out anything you can about him that might be of use.'

'What will you be doing?'

'I'll tackle Isaac again. It may be my last opportunity to do so before the trial.'

As I'd suspected, Isaac had already been arrested and was being held in my erstwhile abode, the gatehouse gaol. In a way I was relieved. At least up there he was out of harm's way. My friend the dumb gaoler would be equal to anyone trying to harm him, even more so than the captain who, unlike the gaoler, would have to leave his post at some time. Yes, probably the tower was the safest place for him.

I was in such a hurry to get up there when I left Jocelin that I nearly collided with someone coming out of the abbey church. I recognised him as Sir Richard de Tayfen, a wealthy local cloth merchant whose daughter I had been treating recently for the cholera. Sir Richard was a widower whose wife had died in childbirth some years before. A local man of humble birth, he had done well in the new prosperity that came with peace after the Anarchy. When it came to his family's health I am happy to say he did not stint on the most up-to-date and expensive remedies. Although I was reluctant to delay my interview with Isaac, Sir Richard was not the sort of man I would wish, or could afford, to brush aside lightly.

'Master Walter,' he said with some surprise stepping back and bowing.

I bobbed too. 'Sir Richard. My apologies. I was preoccupied and didn't see you.'

'You were just in my thoughts,' he said pointing to the church door. 'I had been doing as you suggested, giving thanks for my daughter's recovery. I had been meaning to come before and to thank you personally but I have just been too busy.'

'Never too busy for God, I trust,' I beamed at him. 'How fares my young patient? Well, I take it, since you are offering thanks.'

'Every day she grows a little stronger, brother – all thanks to you.'

'I am delighted to hear it. Now, if you will excuse me.' I bowed and turned to leave.

'I had the well stopped up as you suggested,' he persisted stepping in front of me. 'And the cesspit moved according to your instructions, although I could not see how that would help. I also had a pipe laid to bring fresh water in from the little brook above the house. That has been a popular move. My other daughters find the cooling spring water refreshing in this heat.'

I nodded politely. 'Good, though I shouldn't let them drink too much of it. The female sex is particularly susceptible to too much water. Salad rather than raw water, perhaps. And now, Sir Richard, by your leave.' I tried to move off again, but he put a hand lightly on my arm.

'There is not much you could teach me about the needs of the female sex, brother. With five daughters mine is a household of females. Oh, I am not complaining for they are a delight to their father in his old age. But a business like mine really needs a son.' He leaned over and lowered his voice catching hold of my sleeve further preventing me from leaving. 'Confidentially, Master Walter, they are a worry to me. They will all need husbands in time and no would-be husband wants damaged goods - pardoning your cowl, brother.'

'Damaged goods?' I frowned at the hand gripping my robe. 'Oh yes, I see, damaged goods. Yes - quite.' I could see the entrance to the tower frustratingly just a few feet ahead of me though it might as well have been half a mile for all the chance I had of reaching it.

Sir Richard nodded knowingly as one man of the world to another. 'But what am I to do? I can't lock them up for twenty-four hours a day. Their mother is dead, God rest her sainted soul, and I have only my dwarf servant, Ruddlefairdam, to look to their honour and he cannot be everywhere at once.'

'I trust your daughters have not been compromised, Sir Richard,' I muttered absently while peering anxiously up at the tower.

He shook his head vigorously. 'No no no, as far as any man can be certain of anything I am certain of that. But it's not for the want of trying. A houseful of fillies always has some young colt sniffing around. That young vagabond who got himself killed for one.'

I stopped. 'Matthew? You mean Matthew the fuller's son? The murdered boy?'

'Aye, the same.'

'But surely you are mistaken,' I grinned nervously. 'The boy was barely twelve years of age. He could not – with young ladies - could he?'

He shook his head. 'There's no mistake. He used to come to the house to sell his earth – for the cloth, you understand. But he was a sly one. Far too familiar with my eldest. In the end I had to confine him to the yard outside. Twelve years old you say he was?' He shook his head sorrowfully. 'It's a sad sign of the times. Lads are starting earlier and earlier these days.'

'Erm, forgive me Sir Richard, but you are sure we are talking abut the same boy: Matthew the son of William the fuller, on the Haberdon. Not some other boy?'

He was starting to look irritated, unused, no doubt, to having his word questioned. 'I know the boy well enough, brother. As does that poor wretch up there,' he said nodding to the tower. 'He's up there, am I right? The Jew?'

'Yes yes,' I said, squinting up through the sunshine at the tower. 'He's there.'

'Then ask him. He knows the truth of it.'

I looked at him steadily. 'Let me understand you, Sir Richard. You're telling me that Isaac ben Moy knew the boy who was murdered?'

He looked at me as though I were a simpleton. 'Of course he knew him. It stands to reason, doesn't it? He killed him, so he must have known him.'

'But you know this for a fact. You don't just surmise? You are sure they knew each other before the murder?'

'Brother, I know what I saw. I've seen them together.'

'Yes, I'm sorry Sir Richard, I didn't mean to doubt your word. I just needed to be sure.' I smiled and bowed. 'And now please forgive me but I really must go.'

Bad form or not, I could delay no longer nor hold in my excitement at his words and tugged violently on my sleeve at last releasing his grip. He let out a startled noise of protest but I did not wait to see if I'd offended him, I just had to get away.

'I am pleased that your daughter is on the mend,' I called over my shoulder as an afterthought. 'Give her my blessing.'

But how unpredictable was the goddess Fortuna. If I had not bumped into Sir Richard by chance at the bottom of the tower I would have had little to say to the man at the top. This new piece of information changed everything. Before I was unsure what I was going to say to Isaac. Now I knew exactly what to say to him. With a lighter step than of late I bounded up the tower steps two at a time to the gaol room above.

Chapter 15
AN APOLOGY AND A REVELATION

I felt a slight shiver of apprehension as I rounded the stairwell and stepped out onto the gaol level. I hadn't expected to be back here quite so soon. Mother Han's "husband", the dumb gaoler, was sitting in his usual cubby-hole by the window. He looked a little confused at seeing me, not being quite sure if he was supposed to be locking me up again. But a silver penny unscrambled his mind enough to let me approach the cage while he went back to killing cockroaches with his thumbnail.

Isaac was kneeling in prayer in just about the same position that I had been doing a similar thing twelve hours earlier. Odd to think that we had both been addressing the same God. I coughed lightly and waited. He finished his prayer and came over to the side of the cage.

'Master Walter. It is good to see a friendly face.'

'Is that what I am? I thought I was gathering the means to hang you.'

He smiled. 'I know you will gather it with an even hand. That is a godly thing to do.'

'Hm. Well, let me take care of your earthly needs first. I expect you're hungry.' I held out the basket of bread and eggs I had purloined from the pittancer's range. Slightly more wholesome than

Mother Han's mutton and cabbage I might hope, and certainly easier on the gut, but evidently not wholesome enough for Isaac.

'Abbey food?' He smiled and shook his head. 'I cannot eat it.'

'I thought eggs and bread were permitted under your dietary laws?'

'It is not just the type of food but how it is prepared. It is complicated.'

'Even in your hour of extremis? Is your God so heartless?'

'It is at such times that we are tested most, brother.' He frowned. 'Forgive me, I do not mean to lecture.'

'Well,' I said holding out a flask of water. 'Adam's Ale is the same in any faith. Will you drink?'

'Thank you, yes,' he said taking the bottle. He took a long draught before offering the flask back. I told him to keep it. It seemed the gaoler was no more considerate of Isaac's physical comforts than he had been of mine.

'Now,' I said, 'there is little time and much to discuss.'

I laid out the case against him: The similarities between Matthew's death and those of Saints Robert of Bury and William of Norwich both of whom had been accepted as martyrs and both thought to have been murdered by Jews; the crucifixion-like wounds found on the body albeit that some of the wounds had been placed there *post mortem*; the universal presumption that no Christian could have made such wounds in mockery of Christ; the miracles performed by the boy and the mother's oath corroborating early holiness and thereby confirming God's special purpose for him; the chains discovered in Moy's cellar that could have been used to restrain and torture the boy; the Knieler women being drawn apparently through divine revelation to Isaac's house as the place of his martyrdom; and finally the fact that Matthew's mutilated body had been discovered in Isaac's garden.

When I'd finished I looked up. Isaac's face bore the expression of stoic resignation.

'I notice you do not challenge any of this,' I said.

He splayed his hands. 'To what purpose? The evidence is overwhelming. On the basis of your indictment I am already convicted.'

'God in Heaven, man,' I spurted angrily. 'Won't you even fight?'

'God in Heaven knows the truth of it,' he countered. 'If He wills it, I will be saved; if not, then who am I to disagree?'

'I see,' I nodded. 'You're going to play their game too, are you?'

'If this is how people are thinking, brother, how can I gainsay it? A mere Jew.'

'Do you deny the charges?'

His eyes filled with sudden anger and frustration. 'Certainly I deny them. There is not a scrap of evidence for any of it. The list is entirely circumstantial.'

'Of course there is no evidence,' I agreed. 'But as the Abbot says, your case will not turn on evidence.'

He gave a sick smile. 'Ah yes, trial by ordeal. Tell me, how do you rate my chances of surviving that?'

'None. You will be agonisingly mutilated and then hanged.'

'Oh please brother, don't spare me with soft words.' His body shook as though he had been suddenly thrust naked into a world of ice. 'You know,' he shuddered, 'I have never understood the Christian hatred for members of my faith. We honour the same God as you; we cause no wars; we keep the King's peace. We harm no-one. It baffles me what we are that makes you despise us so.'

'I do not see why it should baffle you,' I dismissed blandly. 'To me the answer is obvious. You are guilty of being different. You represent the unknown. Every man fears the unknown. It may herald good or it may herald evil, but why take the risk? Safer to strike it out before it has a chance to do damage. And most unforgivable of all, not only are you different but you choose to remain different. That is why you are despised.' I leaned forward close to the bars of the cage. 'And, Isaac ben Moy, you are also a *liar*.'

He looked at me in shocked disbelief. 'How so?'

'You told me you did not know the murdered boy,' I said quickly. 'I have a witness who says you did. That you knew him – *intimately*.'

'That is a lie!'

'My witness is unimpeachable. He has no reason to lie.'

'Neither do I.'

'Indeed you do. Any association between you and the boy implicates you in his murder. You knew that when I first interviewed you and you chose to hide it. You placed your hand on the Old

Testament, the Tanakh, and you deliberately dissembled.' I grabbed his hand through the bars. 'This same hand that will justly burn on Monday if you do not tell me the truth now.' The gaoler stirred behind me wondering whether to interfere.

'I did not lie,' Isaac insisted panicking to retrieve his hand, but I held on tight. 'I did not know him. Not in the way you mean.'

'What way do I mean? Isaac, tell me now while you can, what was this boy to you?'

He managed to free his hand from my grip and cradled it like an injured puppy, whimpering.

I slammed the bars of the cage. 'Tell me, God damn you!'

I heard the gaoler again shuffle behind me but he did not intervene. There was a long pause while Isaac rocked in despair. I thought for a moment he would tell me, but in the end he just lowered his eyes and shook his head.

'Then you are lost,' I said.

'You were pretty h-harsh with him,' said Jocelin later when I told him. We were sitting in the north range of the cloister enjoying the warmth of the midday sun. The sunshine was making me quite drowsy, my interview with Isaac having exhausted me more than I realised and the lack of sleep was beginning to catch up with me. Jocelin had his inevitable knapsack propped between his knees.

'Shock tactics,' I defended casually, watching the comings and goings of the other monks. 'I was hoping to frighten him into telling me the truth.'

'And what is the t-truth?'

'I don't know. Something is stopping him from telling me. I think he's already given up. He spoke like a man resigned to his fate. Before I left the gaol he made me promise again to give the casket to his wife when he's gone. But I don't know how I will be able to do that now. Samson has it in his study but he may not release it to me. He certainly won't if the King gets to hear what's in it.'

'And Lord de Saye, no doubt, will be h-happy to tell him,' nodded Jocelin.

'To be sure,' I agreed bitterly, 'if only to ingratiate himself further with King John. One thing I'm pretty certain of, though, is that he won't have told him about the testament.'

Jocelin raised his eyebrows. 'Testament?'

Oops. That was a mistake. I must be more tired than I thought. I still hadn't told Jocelin about the testament fearing he would reveal its existence to Samson. Even now, I realised, I was suspicious of Samson's motives in assigning Jocelin to be my assistant. If there was a question of divided loyalties I couldn't be certain which way he would lean. Too late now, the genie was out of the bottle. There was nothing for it but to come clean and tell Jocelin how Isaac had given me the testament the day we recovered Matthew's body and how it went missing at the same time as the casket - omitting the one small detail about my hiding it inside his treatise on Saint Robert of Bury thereby losing that too.

'What was in this t-testament?' he asked when I'd finished squirming my excuses.

'I don't know,' I said. 'It was sealed.'

'S-so it could be anything – a confession even. Have you m-mentioned it to Father Abbot yet?'

'No, not yet,' I grimaced. I was sure now Jocelin would want to tell him.

He thought for a moment. 'Then don't. Samson will be the officiating judge at the trial. If he, too, suspects it might be a confession it could colour his j-judgement. That would be unf-fortunate to say the least.'

'Oh quite – well yes. I couldn't agree more,' I said, relieved. I looked at him sheepishly. 'Look, I'm sorry I didn't tell you about the casket and the testament. The truth is, until today I really didn't know if they had any bearing on the murder. And you have to understand that Isaac took me into his confidence.'

'Oh, I understand p-perfectly,' said Jocelin.

'Good,' I smiled.

'I understand that you didn't t-trust me – that you still don't trust me – to be impartial in this investigation. You think I am spying for Father Abbot.'

'No, really I -'

'I b-believe he thinks that too as a m-matter of fact,' he continued as though delivering an academic treatise to a class of students. 'Although he has not asked me in s-so many words. As for this other matter - I don't b-blame you for having sympathy with Isaac ben Moy - we would not be human if we did not pity him. But it was extremely stupid of you to have allowed yourself to become his confidant, and even more stupid to have kept the fact to yourself. Had you told me about the testament I would almost certainly have advised you to read it. You had the authority to do so. Now that opportunity is lost. S-similarly, if you had told me about the casket you would almost certainly not have spent last night in the tower for I would have been able to vouch for you. That was a failure of duty on your part for it helped no-one having the chief investigator locked up, least of all Isaac ben Moy. You have squandered a whole day with your secretiveness and suspicions when we have precious little time left and we will now have to work twice as hard to make it up. But worst of all I thought that you might have r-realised by now that whatever my own personal beliefs about the boy Matthew I am as keen on finding the truth of what happened to him as you are. Oh, and while I am putting matters straight, it was not I who betrayed your comment to Father Abbot about the state of Saint Edmund's body the day of the King's banquet. I am saddened that you should have thought me capable of such a thing. B-but we did not know each other so well then. I had harboured the hope that our work together these past few days might have engendered a better understanding between us, and m-might even have extended as far as… friendship.'

I was speechless. He was right in what he said, every word of it – again delivered, I noticed, barely without a stutter. The catalogue of my transgressions and idiocies would have filled several pages of his tight script. I was guilty of arrogance, conceit, stupidity, suspicion, vanity, deception, contempt for others – most especially for Jocelin. My confessor, Brother Ronald, will be weary of my litany of self-complaint before I am finished. What could I say to this man who I had treated so abysmally? I vowed there and then that I would never again treat him so contemptuously.

For a few minutes all I could do was stare at the wall opposite the silence hanging heavily between us. Monks came and went along the cloister wall without my seeing them. Finally I was able to find my voice again:

'What, erm, did you manage to glean from Matthew's tutor?'

He shook his head. 'Ranulf would hear n-nothing against the boy. He claims he was a model pupil. In his eyes Matthew is already a saint. However,' he smiled, 'there is one interesting fact I m-managed to find out about him. It has to do with his age. He wasn't as young as we've been led to believe. I got the p-parish p-priest of Saint Botolph's Haberdon, Father Paul, to show me his baptismal records. I was puzzled at first because I could not f-find Matthew's name in the rolls for eleven-eighty-seven. So I looked at the rolls for the years either side. Matthew was named for his saint's day in the thirtieth of Henry. Now, King Henry,' he said rummaging in his knapsack, 'came to the throne on December the nineteenth *anno domini* eleven-fifty-four, s-so his thirtieth would have been - let me see -' He pulled out a scrap of paper. 'Eleven-eighty-five making Matthew fourteen when he died, not twelve as we p-previously thought.'

'That's very interesting,' I said and realised immediately it might explain another inconsistency. I told him what Sir Richard de Tayfen had said about Matthew's interest in his daughter. Difficult enough to believe in a child of fourteen, but not as difficult as in a child of twelve. It also rendered the boy less than the pure in heart we were led to think he was, and certainly no pre-pubescent child.

'Didn't you say part of the reason these boys are chosen by the Jews for sacrifice is for their innocence? If Matthew wasn't as young as we thought then that surely weakens the argument against Isaac.' I grinned rubbing my hands together. 'Things are looking up.'

Jocelin studied me for a moment. 'Forgive me for saying so, brother, but you're sounding more like Moy's defence c-council than the chief investigator.'

I shifted awkwardly. It was something Samson had also noticed. 'It's as you said before, I pity his plight,' I defended. 'A-and with so many eager to hang this crime on him I think it reasonable to have someone on his side. And as you so rightly pointed out just now, I betrayed his trust. Because of my incompetence he may well die and his wife and family end up penniless. I have ground to make up. A slight leaning in his direction I feel is not amiss - to redress the balance somewhat.' I grimaced, unconvinced myself of my own argument.

Jocelin thought for a moment. 'Have you considered that may be part of his strategy - to influence the c-course of the investigation? To win your sympathy?'

'I prefer to think that it is a sign of his desperation that he had to turn to me, a complete stranger, a Christian and possibly his chief persecutor, to help him.' I frowned at the sunlight. 'It seems to me that everywhere you look someone has something to gain from finding

Isaac guilty: The King covets the man's wealth; our brother monks wish for a new saint to venerate. No-one seems to be bothered about finding the truth.'

'The elusive truth again,' smiled Jocelin.

'Indeed,' I said resolutely. 'And I intend to get to it even if that means upsetting the Abbot, Geoffrey de Saye, or even the King himself. But mark me,' I put on what I hoped was my sternest face for Jocelin. 'If it turns out that Isaac ben Moy really is the murderer of this boy then I will be the first to put the rope around his neck, make no mistake.'

Jocelin smiled and nodded. 'S-speaking of mistakes, I noticed that Matthew's mother d-didn't try to correct the one about the boy's age when we spoke to her. '

'Yes, you're right. Perhaps we should tackle her about it. God, there is so much to do and so little time.'

Jocelin looked thoughtful. 'It seems to me we are dealing almost with two completely d-different people. There's Matthew the child saint eulogised by Egbert, Ranulf, Jeremiah *et al*. And then there's the urchin Matthew described by your Mother Han, who r-runs about the streets and lechers after girls. Which is the real Matthew, I wonder?'

'When we know that we'll know which one got himself murdered, the saint or the sinner. And then perhaps we will know the reason why.'

Two young monks I knew to be among those who had supported the canonization of Matthew at his requiem came out of the inner parlour. They were in animated conversation which stopped abruptly when they saw me. I was dreading they might come over and braced myself for another barrage of abuse. But they merely nodded politely, if coolly, and walked off the other way towards the church. I could sense Jocelin tense and then relax next to me again.

'What happened to the four Knieler women?' I asked him gazing up at the brilliant round globe of the sun. 'I haven't seen them beside the grave today.'

'Samson had them removed,' he said. 'He d-doesn't think they are genuine either. I think they may have resumed their vigil outside Isaac's house.'

Poor Rachel, I thought. That's all she needs.

'I think that's where I should go next, see how she's faring. God knows what the poor woman must be going through alone in that house with three young children. But she showed herself to be a woman of spirit when we were there. Maybe she can animate Isaac into fighting for what is undoubtedly going to be his life.'

'Do you want me to come too?' Jocelin asked.

'No. She thinks poorly enough of our Christian ways. One monk is intimidating. Two may clam her up completely.'

On my way to the Moy house I thought I'd make a quick detour to Joseph's shop again to see how things were there. I hadn't been for a few days and it was an insubstantial structure vulnerable if left unattended, and though it had appeared to be all right on my last visit I felt a duty to go up there again to keep an eye on it. It would be one less worry on my mind if I knew it was safe and one less distraction from my difficult task. As before, I went out of the town through Risbygate, turned right and walked the few dozen yards to the shop.

When I got there I was appalled at what I found. It had always been such a welcoming place, lively, busy and filled with the most wonderful artefacts, exotic plants and herbs, spices and potions in colourful bottles and glorious silks and fabrics from the East. All had gone, the shop entirely empty, shutters up and blinds down. My eyes filled with tears at the sight of such dereliction. I was almost too distraught to go inside but I forced myself to push at the door and step across the threshold.

The interior was dark and damp where just a fortnight earlier it had been light and airy, and where there had been the fragrance of incense now was the stench of dereliction and decay. I had no doubt animals and probably vagrants had been in. I knew Joseph had intended going but I had thought he meant to leave the place ready for his return as soon as the King and his entourage had left the town. But this was total abandonment. Coming on top of my concerns over the murder I suddenly felt very weary and realised the events of the past two weeks and lack of sleep had taken a greater toll on me than I had thought. The emotion must have got to me then because I let out a sob of such despair I surprised myself. The sound must have disturbed someone in the inner sitting room because I heard a noise.

'Who's there?' I called angrily and readied myself to fight whoever it was. But the screen parted and a tall lithesome figure appeared in the doorway. The possessor was in shadow at first and I could not see who it was, but then I recognised the young man who had served the tray of spiced must and sweetmeats the last time I was here. I hadn't liked the look of him then and finding him alone now when Joseph was away annoyed me all the more.

'You,' I said. 'I thought it was a vagrant.'

'There was someone until two days ago, but I threw him out. I am alone here now.'

I didn't believe that. By the look of him he couldn't have thrown a cat out never mind a vagrant. He was clearly up to no good.

'You know who I am?' I demanded.

He nodded. 'Joseph's brother.'

I bridled at his impertinence. 'You call your master by name? I wonder if he knows. Where is your master?'

'Gone.'

'I can see he's gone,' I said sharply. 'I'm asking you where?'

'I do not know.'

'You do, you just won't tell me. And by the way, what is your name? I don't think I heard it. Do you not know to show courtesy when you address a brother of the abbey?'

He did not flinch but spoke steadily. 'My name is Chrétien.'

I snorted. 'That's a name for a French ponce. What's your real name?'

'It is the name Joseph chooses to call me.'

'Oh, does he?' I wagged an admonishing finger at him. 'I'll tell him all this when next I see him, don't think I won't.'

I'd had enough of his insolence and was about to order him out of the place when I noticed something he was holding behind his back.

'What have you got there?'

He produced the object, a money purse which I snatched from his grasp. 'I'll take that, thank you.'

I opened the purse and saw that it was indeed filled with dozens of silver pennies - doubtless takings from Joseph's business. This was probably the real reason the boy was here today. I'd clearly caught him in the act of stealing it and was in two minds whether to call the Beadle. But I reluctantly concluded that anyone on the premises, even this ne'er-do-well, was better than no-one.

'I'll keep this,' I sniffed turning to leave. 'And tidy the place up a bit. Living here as though you owned the place. I shall be back to make sure you do, probably when you least expect me. So beware.' And giving him one last sneer of disapproval I marched smartly out of the building.

Outside I felt oddly elated by the encounter and relieved at least to have heard news of Joseph. I set off back towards the town feeling unexpectedly refreshed and ready to tackle the harridan who was Isaac ben Moy's wife.

Chapter 16
THE STREET URCHINS

The week of hot dry weather continued but I was beginning to sense a subtle change in the wind. As I looked back from the top of the town over the abbey below me white fluffy clouds scuttled maniacally, so it seemed to me, across the otherwise clear blue sky. As they did so the west end of the abbey church, now completely encased in scaffolding for Samson's towers, cast intermittent shadows over Palace Yard, the space through which Isaac ben Moy would be brought for trial in three days time. Just three days to save a man of whose innocence I was more and more convinced.

The scene outside Isaac's house as I arrived was more or less the same as it had been the previous week. The sturdy little captain of horse was still there but had been joined by two more soldiers who were guarding the doorway to Isaac's house. I noted with dismay that several pieces of vegetation had been flung at the door and were lying rotting on the doorstep but otherwise it had remained unmolested. The 'whining wenches' as I had privately come to think of the Knieler women were back and still on their knees outside the house babbling in what I now knew to be Gaelic and not heavenly 'tongues'. Their presence was drawing unwelcome attention to the house inciting curiosity and ill-will in equal measure against the family – which no doubt was their purpose. It was just a pity I did not know another Scot who might be able to challenge them in their own language and put an end to their ridiculous blathering once and for all. Someone had put them up to this and I was sorely tempted to tackle them on the spot to find out who. But confrontation would simply cast them in the role of victim while doing nothing to help the Moy family. All I could do was bide my time and pray for some miracle to remove them.

In contrast to this and adding a welcome note of levity to an otherwise dismal scene was a gaggle of half a dozen street urchins who were clowning about, having fun mimicking the women's attitude of devotion and inventing a very plausible gobbledegook of their own. It crossed my mind these might be some of the waifs Mother Han had referred to in the gaol. The captain certainly was enjoying their antics and the ones who particularly took his fancy were rewarded with the occasional quarter-penny which he flicked high into the air for them to catch. It must have been very irritating for the Knieler women to have these human hornets buzzing around their heads and being unable to swat them but to do so would have meant they'd have to reveal themselves for the charlatans they were. Still, I had to admire their forbearance in the face of such provocation. Some passers-by slowed their pace to watch the fun but most seemed content merely to hurry by leaving the captain and his men with little else to amuse them on this sultry afternoon.

'These young tykes, brother,' chuckled the bearded captain as I approached. 'They put on a good act. That one with the mizzened hand is a born showman. I'd wager he'll be in one of the Easter plays before he's much older. His face is as pretty as a girl's, make a bonnie wife for one of Noah's sons. Ha ha, look at him! Here, a whole penny this time.' He pinged the sliver of silver high in the air whereupon all six scamps dived for it. But it was the boy with the mizzened hand who managed to catch it despite his handicap.

'See?' grinned the delighted captain. 'He may have half the limbs of the others but he has twice their wits. He gets the coin every time.'

I laughed too, but I was more interested in one of the Knieler women who was evidently in not quite so blindly euphoric a state as the others for although she didn't stop her gabbling I noticed her eyes followed the line of the captain's little shiny charm as it arched its way through the light-filled air. This gave me an idea.

'Why captain,' I said, beaming at him. 'A penny's a paltry reward for such excellent sport. Let's raise the wager a little.' I reached inside the purse that I had taken from Chrétien and withdrew a handful of coins. 'Here boys,' I yelled holding out the pile temptingly. 'Something this time for everyone.'

Upon saying, I scattered the coins high in the air so that they rained down like a sparkling shower of Italian comfits landing all about with a very pleasing tinkling sound on the ground. This time it wasn't just the urchins who scrabbled in the dust for the money but one or two of the watching adults also. But still the Knieler women held their ground and stoically carried on their charade of pretend-gibberish. So I tried another handful of Joseph's bounty and then a third just for luck. I would have thrown a fourth but I didn't need to. First one, then a second, and finally all four Knieler women, their nerve finally gone, were screeching and scratching and shoving each other and the urchins out the way to get at the money. Wimples askew, hair flying, they fought like dockyard drunkards to scrape up the money accompanied by much shrieking and spitting in both Gaelic and English.

The captain's eyebrows shot to the top of his head. 'Well, I'll be damned! You know, I thought there was something fishy about those women.'

Fishy being the operative word for these herring-gutters, I thought to myself. We watched the women for a few moments more all pretence now abandoned as petticoats flew and fingers scrabbled for the remaining few half-pennies, much to the amusement of the men watching, some of whom threw up their own few coins just to keep the entertainment going.

I turned away with a mixture of disgust and satisfaction. 'Captain, I've come to see the Moy family again. I'm the chief investigator in the murder case. You remember I was here a few days ago.'

'Aye,' nodded the captain. 'I remember you, and the fuss you caused last time.' He nodded toward the fracas on the road. 'Seems havoc has a habit of following you.' He signalled to the soldier by the door to let me through the gate.

'I'll try to be less bothersome this time,' I said kicking aside a rotting cabbage that was lying by the door. 'And thank you.'

The gruff-looking, late-middle-aged woman dressed entirely in black who I had seen on my last visit let me in.

'You are Matilde? The Moys' servant?' I said as she shut and bolted the door behind me.

'*Oui, mon frère,*' she bobbed politely.

Her reply in French took me momentarily by surprise until I remembered what Isaac had told me that three generations of her family had served the Moy household. In all probability they had hardly been out of the house in all that time and had no lives of their own, passing on their skills and ancient version of the language from one generation to the next. I had heard of such servants before but usually they were of Arab or African descent, never French.

'I have come to see your mistress on a matter of some urgency,' I articulated as clearly as I could. 'I do not have time for the usual courtesies so I would be grateful if you could just tell her I am here. I am sure she will see me.'

She seemed to understand well enough my purpose and led the way to one of the side rooms on the ground floor.

I couldn't help noticing as I walked through the dark and empty hall that the house was still as shuttered and cold as it had been the last time I came, giving the house a depressing but serene atmosphere as though it were waiting for something to happen. The side room turned out to be a sort of scullery not a living room at all. There was no window and the only light was from a single candle that sat on a table in the middle of the room. Next to it, huddled together on a wooden settle, sat Rachel Moy who was cradling the two little girls, one in each arm, while the boy stood close by. It was a moment or two before my eyes adjusted sufficiently to see them all properly.

'Mistress Moy,' I said, slightly shocked by her appearance. 'Are you all right?'

At first she seemed not to hear me, her eyes glazed and unseeing. But then she curled her lip to reply. 'They throw missiles at the house,' she said in a voice empty of emotion. 'Shout at night. Sometimes they try to get in. We are safer in here.' She leaned over and kissed the heads of the two little girls.

My heart filled with desolation and compassion at her words. She sounded so hopeless. 'Rachel, is there nowhere you can go? Surely now to your husband's family in Norwich? For pity's sake – for the *children's* sake?'

She snorted. 'Who would carry us there? You?'

I looked at Rachel Moy's face. It was the face of a rabbit caught in the jaws of a stoat, hypnotised and resigned to a fate that was beyond her understanding or control. I didn't know what to say to her.

'If it is any comfort, those women outside are gone now. I don't think they will be back.'

She merely snorted. 'They have done their work. Everyone knows we are here now.'

There was a sound behind her and I stiffened as I realised that there was a fifth person in the room standing so far back in the shadows that it was almost impossible to see him. He must have seen me start for he came forward and I could see from his attire that he was a rabbi. I wondered how he had got in to the house for I doubted if the captain would have allowed him to pass. But then I guessed he must have come in through the secret shaft at the side of the house leading to the cellar and in so thinking it occurred to me that that was probably the reason they had kept the shaft and the cellar clear. The Abbot's ordinances against Jews living in the town extended to visiting rabbis. This way he could come and go discreetly. The man now stepped between me and Rachel holding out his hands protectively.

'We are all praying that Isaac will soon be back and this nightmare will be at an end.' He gestured towards the door for me to leave. But I had no intention of being so summarily dismissed.

'Rabbi, I have to ask her some questions,' I insisted.

'To what purpose?'

I bristled. 'In order to fight, of course. You can't just do *nothing*.'

'I told you, we are doing something. We are praying.'

'I too am praying,' I said. 'And I think God has partly answered my prayer. He sent me a messenger with some unexpected information that I believe may be critical. I asked Isaac about it but he was reluctant to discuss it. I want to see if Rachel can throw any further light.'

'Forgive me, brother, but that is your desire. It is not Rachel's. And from what you say it is not Isaac's either. So please, leave now. You cannot help.' He stepped forward with his hands held out to usher me away.

This was maddening. What was wrong with these people? Why were they being so defeatist? It was almost as though they welcomed their own martyrdom.

'I just want to ask,' I insisted, 'did the murdered boy Matthew come here to the house? I mean, I know he did but I need to know why.'

'You already have the answer to that. He came to be crucified by the Christ-killers.'

The phrase infuriated me. It could have been uttered by Egbert. 'I don't believe that,' I frowned. 'And I don't think Rachel does either. There has to be another reason.'

'Then you are the only one to think it.'

From behind the rabbi Rachel spoke at last, though not to me but quietly as though reminiscing to herself. 'At first he came to sell us earth – the clay of Adam's body. It was a kindness. Useful.'

She was referring to the fuller's earth used for cleaning clothes. I understood that. 'Yes?' I said encouragingly. 'That's right. The earth. But something else. Some other reason for his visit. What was it?'

'They became – friends.' She curled her lip and spat the word again. 'Friends!'

'Matthew and Isaac. Yes, yes. Go on. What passed between them?'

Her mouth smiled but her eyes showed her mind was elsewhere. 'The Devil passed. He comes in many guises, old Ned. Sometimes with the sweet face of innocence.'

The rabbi swung round. 'Say no more, Rachel. Your duty is not to this man but to your husband.'

'Please,' I was almost begging. 'Don't stop now.' But it was no good. Rachel's face crumpled as Jacob put his arms around his mother and she broke down in silent sobs clutching her children to her. I knew I would get no more from her. With all the stress of the past days her wits had finally left her.

The rabbi looked almost as distraught as she. 'You must go now. Can you not see you only distress her more with your questions? Her mind is in turmoil. Leave her to grieve in peace.' We had reached the door which Matilde stood ready to open. As she did so the rabbi stepped back into shadow so as not to be seen from outside.

'Grieve?' I snorted angrily as I paused on the threshold. 'You speak as though Isaac were already dead.'

I could not see the rabbi's face, only hear his words: 'Isn't he?'

Outside the air seemed clean and the day bright. I felt angry, frustrated, useless. I'd been so close to knowing the truth and in the end I was thwarted. What had passed between Matthew and Isaac? What was their secret? My temper wasn't improved by once again having the feeling that I was being watched. Frustration finally got the better of me.

'Come on!' I yelled spinning round. 'Show yourself!' I ran to a corner but there was no-one there. I ran back again. I squinted hard into the bright sunshine and shook my fist impotently in the air. 'Coward!'

'Feeling better now?' said the captain once I was a little calmer. He must have thought I'd lost my senses. 'I think I preferred it better with those wailer women. Here.' He held out his hand in which there were half a dozen of the silver pennies. 'I found these among the weeds. These little rascals will have the eyes from your head if you let them.' He nodded to the street urchins who were still hanging about waiting for the next opportunity to present itself.

'Keep them,' I said dismissively. I could hardly care less for the money.

The captain shook his head. 'No, it's more than my job's worth.'

'Why should it matter?'

He shrugged. 'Who knows? I've been a soldier for a long time, fought in the King's wars in Palestine – King Richard I mean, not this new one,' he added, lowering his voice. 'I've learnt the safest road is the straightest one. Do your duty, don't ask questions and act dumb, that's my rule. It's thinking that does for people.'

'What a sad comment on the state of humanity,' I said with sincerity.

'Aye, mebbe. But I'm forty-seven now. In three years time, God willing, I shall retire with enough money to marry my sweetheart, buy her father's assart from his lord in Lincolnshire and build a little cottage to see out our days.'

I managed a smile at that. 'Good for you, my friend,' I said sincerely. 'It is cheering to hear a glad tale in these sorry times. I wish you well indeed.' I laughed and took the proffered money returning it to the purse and intending to put it in the poor box and say a prayer for the captain and his family. 'Will you be here tomorrow?'

'I will. Tomorrow, Monday and for three days after the trial.'

'Ah yes,' I nodded. 'For the judgement. Well, I must be getting back to the abbey, there is so much to do. I'll bid you good day.'

'Good day to you too,' he sniffed looking up at the sky. 'Doubtless we'll be seeing each other again.'

He was right, we would indeed be seeing each other again, but in circumstances I would have given the bag of coin and half my own wealth not to be.

I was beginning to build up a picture of the boy Matthew whose character was slowly coming into focus. The image of the child saint who could do no wrong was gone, replaced by something far more complex, far more *human*. Something had passed between Isaac and Matthew, but exactly what my imagination could not fathom. Rachel said they had become friends, but what sort of friendship could it have been between a fourteen-year-old boy and a man old enough to be his father – indeed, who was a father of a boy of the same age? Matthew had begun visiting the Moy house, Rachel had said, to bring them fuller's earth. This in itself would have been theft since the mill and all its produce belonged to the abbey. It seems Matthew was making a little extra income illicitly. But that, surely, would not be sufficient motive for murder.

Matthew had gained entrance to the Moy house – that much had been endorsed by Sir Richard de Tayfen and by Rachel's somewhat more ambiguous replies. Having thus won their confidence he continued to visit them. Why? And what happened next? Did they have a falling out? Was that what led to Matthew's death? Over what? And by whose hand? And what had Isaac's testament to do with all this? The more I pondered the conundrum so the mist seemed to return to obscure the scene. I needed time for the picture to clear further but time was rapidly running out.

As I walked down the hill towards the abbey I became aware that I was being followed this time not by my phantom shadow but by the same street urchins who had been tormenting the Knieler women outside the Moy house. They had been watching, I noticed, when I came out of the house and must have seen the captain give me back my money. Perhaps they were hoping I'd give them some more. Now like jackals on the scent of a kill they were keeping pace with me but just a few feet behind. I stopped and turned. They stopped too but maintained their strict distance of two or three feet just out of arm's-reach. If I took a step or two towards them they melted back again. I shrugged and continued nonchalantly on my way but after a few more steps I turned suddenly and roared towards them like a lion so that they squealed in fright and scampered away in all directions. I stood in the street with my arms akimbo laughing as one by one half a dozen faces reappeared from behind walls and bushes. They were like a troupe of monkeys and a variety of ages and heights they were too. No doubt this was how they survived by being ready to take any opportunity as it presented itself. I noticed the boy with the mizzened hand was still among them.

Doubtless his deformity made his life even more of a struggle than the others. But he was still alive and thriving, *Deo favente*.

'Who deserves a penny?' I grinned round at them. That drew them a little out into the open though they still kept their distance.

'All right,' I said fishing out the coins that the captain had returned to me and holding them out in my tightly-clenched fist. This tempted the bravest of them closer until one, the bravest, finally came right up to me and tried to prise open my fist with his grubby little fingers. I was astonished at just how determined and persistent he was. It was a struggle but I managed to keep my fist closed. Frustrated by their friend's failure, the others now tried too biting, scratching, pinching – anything they could think of to wrench my fingers apart. But though pained and scratched I just proved the stronger and managed to keep hold of the money. Eventually they pulled and twisted my hand so hard that I went down, laughing and panting, onto my knees where, being now at their eye-level, I decided to remain.

'All right, all right, I tell you what, you can have one each,' I yelled above their squabbling, 'in return for –'

'What?'

'Information.'

'In-form-?'

'-mation,' I repeated. 'Information. Do you know what that is? It means telling me something I don't already know.'

'Like what?'

'Like the name of the boy who got murdered?'

'That's easy!' said one.

'You already know,' said another.

'We all do!' came a third.

'Matthew!' one of the littlest ones said and grinned his gappy-tooth grin.

'That's right,' I said, smiling and nodding. 'Matthew. He was a friend of yours, yes?'

They all nodded confirming something Mother Han had told me about Matthew "running with the strays". So far so good.

'Now, what else can you tell me about him?' I sensed there was some kind of code of silence going on, so I upped the bribe. 'Two pennies for anyone who can tell me what sort of boy he was.'

This drew some more nervous giggling and two of the youngest did some odd sort of wriggling dance that was comical and strange at the same time. I frowned at them and they pulled faces back mimicking me the way they had the Knieler women.

'So?' I said.

'He was bad,' said one of them at last but he was immediately pounced upon by one of the older boys. 'He was a saint,' he insisted. 'Haven't you heard? The God says so.'

'You mean *God*,' I said gently, frowning. 'There is no "the". Just "God". And He hasn't said so, not yet.'

They all looked vacantly back at me so I tried again:

'All right, then. In what way was Matthew bad?'

'He…' began one of the smaller boys but he was smacked hard by the other one who had spoken. It must have hurt but the little trooper stoically refused to cry, God bless him.

Their obstinacy was beginning to annoy me. 'You wouldn't lie to me, would you?' I said. 'You see this robe I'm wearing? That means I'm a monk from the abbey. You know it's a sin to lie to a monk.'

At this they just laughed. I looked round at their faces, childishly innocent and worldly-wise beyond their years at one and the same time. I sighed, exasperated. I could see that I was going to get no further with them, so I turned my, by now, scratched and bruised hand over and opened it. They grabbed hungrily at the coins like so many starlings pecking at an ear of corn, and in a moment every penny had gone. As they ran off with their prizes I made a grab at the boy with the mizzened hand and caught him by the actual hand itself. He struggled in panic for a moment making a pathetic mewing sound in his throat like a trapped animal. I realised in addition to being deformed he was also mute and my heart went out to him. I smiled and nodded trying to reassure him that I meant him no harm and gently drew him closer. I wanted to look at the hand - I was, after all, a physician. I could see it was deformed but from birth not from any accident, and not from leprosy either. The thumb was fully formed but the fingers were little more than pea-sized stumps. I had never seen a hand quite like it before and wondered what sin he had committed to deserve such a terrible burden to have to carry through life. There was clearly nothing I could do for him, so I stroked the hand even making myself kiss it in order to prove to him that I wasn't repelled by it.

'You know,' I said gently, 'you could try praying to Saint Giles of Nîmes, the patron saint of cripples. Miracles do happen.'

The boy looked at me blankly. Then a thought struck me:

'You have heard of saints, have you?' I ventured, but he simply continued to stare at me with his huge innocent eyes as though I were speaking Persian.

And then he did something truly horrible: He coughed up the biggest gob of phlegm I have ever seen and spat on the ground in front of me. I was so shocked that this time when he tugged at his hand I let it go and watched him run off after his friends.

I was shaken by what he'd done. As I was already on my knees anyway I thought I'd say a prayer for the boy. Clasping my hands together tightly and shutting my eyes there in the street, I bowed my head, 'Oh Lord, Jesus Christ, if it be your will, restore this child to wholeness I earnestly beseech you, and protect and comfort all these the least and most vulnerable of your children. And also bring comfort and justice to Isaac ben Moy and his family, for your name's sake, Amen.'

When I opened my eyes again the bright light dazzled for a moment, but then I glimpsed a flash of colour disappearing around a corner. Was this my elusive shadow again? Quick as lightning, I was on my feet and ran into the alley after it, but whoever it was had eluded me once again.

Chapter 17
TRIAL BY ORDEAL

For the rest of that Friday and all through Saturday and Sunday Jocelin and I did our best to get the trial annulled or at least delayed in order to give us more time for our inquiries - all to no avail. Looking back now I can see we were foolish to even try. Powerful interests were set upon a trial and nothing that Jocelin or I could have done would have dissuaded them. I tried to petition Samson one last time but he refused to see me, claiming pressure of getting the court proceedings in order before Monday morning. So I left Jocelin camped outside his office and told him not to move, even to relieve himself, until Samson came out and then he was to use all his guile to persuade his old mentor to grant us a hearing. But if Samson was in there he must have superhuman bladder control for he never appeared out of his office once in ten hours.

Every attempt to petition the King also came up against similar intransigence. I doubt if my increasingly desperate notes made it further than the King's lowliest clerk. By compline on Sunday night it was clear that we had lost. The notices went up on the abbey notice boards and in the refectory: All those with interest before the King's justices in the case of Saint Edmund versus Isaac ben Moy were to present themselves to the court summoner by terce the next morning. I had now only the maxim of the Law to fall back on: *Dura lex, sed lex*. The law is indeed harsh, but it was all we had.

It was clear from the beginning that this was not to be a trial in the normal sense of determining guilt and administering punishment. Rather, it was to be a formal hearing to decide whether or not to proceed to trial by ordeal. Elsewhere in England pleas of the crown like murder are reserved for judgement by the royal justices but in Bury the Abbot had this right granted since the time of King Cnut and it was a privilege jealously guarded by Abbot Samson. Normally hearings like this are held in the Abbot's Hall but such was the public interest in this case that it was realised a bigger venue would be needed to hold all who wanted to witness the proceedings. The case was therefore to be heard in the larger Hall of Pleas which stands next to the cellarer's gate and faces onto Palace Yard.

Abbot Samson sat in the middle of the semi-circular bench at the far end of the hall adorned in his formal robe as Baron of the Liberty of Saint Edmund while ranked either side of him were the chief obedientiaries of the abbey, each in his own robe of office. Before them sat the clerks busily scribbling and ready to record every jot and tittle of the proceedings. There was some curiosity over a single vacant chair which had been placed just below and to the left of the bench but which so far remained empty.

Facing this formidable array of worthies in the middle of the hall were two tables, one on the left, the other on the right. At the left-hand table sat the prosecution team among whom I had to sit uncomfortably prominent as the chief investigative officer in the case. My function was not to prosecute but to give support to the abbey's prosecutor-general, Sir Fulk de Warenne, beside whom I sat. I'd only just met Sir Fulk that morning and fully expected - indeed *wanted* - to loathe the man, but in all fairness I could not. He was a career lawyer, one of those infuriating men who knew his business to the finest measure but managed to maintain a professional detachment. He exuded charm as he explained my function which was to provide the evidence when called upon to do so. He understood completely that I did this reluctantly and that every investigative officer he had ever dealt with had gone through the same agonies of conscience which in the case of a monk must be all the more intense. But, he reminded me gently, it was my duty to do all this clearly, thoroughly, to the best of my ability and without fear or favour to any man. By the time he had finished prepping me I was completely in his hands - damn the man's eyes. He sat nonchalantly cross-legged in his lawyer's gown radiating quiet confidence, his black beard which was flecked with grey twitching like a mouse's whiskers and his sharp little rodent eyes under his lawyer's cap missed nothing.

On the other side of the gangway was an identical table to ours at which sat the defence team which totalled six in all, three lawyers in their black gowns and caps plus their secretaries. I was secretly pleased to see that the Moy family seemed to be sparing no expense in providing

Isaac with the best defence they could buy. In the middle of this gaggle sat Isaac, soberly dressed in the garb of a prominent local Jew, stoically dignified and rigidly erect. You'd have been forgiven for thinking he was the person least connected with the drama which was about to unfold instead of being its central player.

Behind all were the common throng of the people standing in serried ranks below the bar of the court and spilling out into Palace Yard, a goodly cross-section of the populous of Bury from rich merchants to lowly serfs, each craning his neck to see over the man in front of him and each hoping to catch a glimpse of the defendant. With so many human animals in such a confined space the doors of the court were left open to catch any cooling breeze on this hot June morning while at the same time letting out the stench of so many unwashed bodies.

All the major players were now on stage in their places and waiting for the drama to begin, but the appointed time for the commencement of proceedings came and went and nothing seemed to be happening. Even with the doors open it was stiflingly hot in the hall making short tempers shorter, especially when no-one seemed to know what was going on. After several minutes of confused inactivity the usher of the court, dressed in his long black robe and carrying his rod of office, made his way quickly over to the Abbot and whispered something in his ear. Whatever it was he said to him Abbot Samson frowned and shook his head whereupon the usher shrugged and went away again. It was all very intriguing.

At this point Jocelin came bustling into the hall pushing his way through the crush and beaming all over his face as he hurried over to the prosecution table. 'It's all right', he whispered excitedly to me as he sat down. 'It's n-not to be ordeal by fire but ordeal by w-water. G-good news, eh?' I was not so sure. Then someone broke wind behind in a very loud and irreverent way which met with a roar of approval. The trial was in danger of descending into farce.

Then just as it seemed the day was lost and the usher might have to clear the court, horses were heard outside the hall and heads turned to see the King appear at the bar of the court accompanied by a dozen of his courtiers. The party were all dressed in their hunting array of browns and greens, long leather riding boots and even some of their greyhounds panting and yelping on leashes - quite inappropriate for such an august setting. All heads craned to see them – all, that is, except for Isaac who alone continued to stare stonily ahead. The King looked dusty and hot after his ride, his retinue full of loud and boisterous chatter in Norman French – discussing, as far as I could follow it, the doe that had eluded their arrows and the King's excellent shot at downing an antlered buck. You'd have been forgiven for thinking they were in a private hunting lodge somewhere in the forest rather than a court of law where a man was about to go on trial for his life. Many among the throng pressing around him frowned in disapproval and could be seen muttering among themselves – though none loud enough to be heard. To give him his due, the King did seem to realise their behaviour was out

239

of place and with a gesture silenced his noble companions. Even so, he was not to be hurried. In the silence that followed and with exaggerated care he peeled off his long gloves and handed them to a page. He then looked about him with a bemused expression as if seeing the court for the first time and then, noticing the Abbot, addressed him in a loud and confident voice:

'My Lord Abbot,' he bowed. 'May I be permitted to observe the proceedings of this illustrious assembly?'

Ponderously, deliberately and with exaggerated gravitas, Abbot Samson rose to his feet, and with him the entire court also stood. The Abbot then bowed formally to the King. 'My Liege, you do our humble gathering great honour with your presence.' And with that he gestured imperiously to the vacant chair below him.

So that's what it was for. I should have guessed. No casual happenchance this but a carefully stage-managed little scene. The King then bowed theatrically to the Abbot in return and strode purposefully down the gangway towards the bench. As he passed me I could smell the scent of the kill still upon him and winced, realising that Isaac must have smelt it too. When he got to the vacant chair he turned and sat down with a flourish and took up the pose of a curious but neutral observer, whereupon Samson also sat, and we all resumed our places once more.

With everyone at last in position the business of the court could get under way. At a signal from Samson the chief usher wrapped three times on the floor with his rod to bring everyone to order and called for the accused man to stand up. Slowly, Isaac rose to his feet.

'Isaac ben Moy ben Moses ben Sechok, you stand accused of the wilful torture and murder of Matthew, son of William the Fuller, on the ninth of June last against the peace of our Lord the King and the dignity of Saint Edmund. How do you plea?'

There was total silence as Isaac's clear voice uttered the two words, 'Not Guilty,' at which the court erupted into noisy babble. The usher banged three more times with his staff and called above the din for the tithing-man of the district in which the murder had taken place to present the case. Everyone looked round straining to see who this was. After a pause a frightened little man, unshaven, dishevelled, cloth cap held in both hands against his chest and clearly overwhelmed by the whole proceedings, blinked and rose hesitantly from the body of the court. Giggles and guffaws ran around the court as they saw the identity of the tithing-man. I heard the name 'Cuthbert' whispered several times followed by hoots of laughter and incredulity. The usher, seeing who it was, shook his head in dismay.

To explain: You have first to remember that this was forty years ago and we do things slightly differently now, but in those days everyday policing in Edmundstown was organised by dividing the town into units of ten households known as 'tithes'. Every male over the age of twelve had to join his local tithe whose leader, known as the 'tithing-man', was elected by the other members. It was the tithing-man's responsibility to make sure anyone accused of a crime was arrested and brought before the justices. This was a lonely, difficult and often dangerous job and therefore unpopular. Usually the least appropriate person was designated to do it whether he liked - or even knew - that he had been chosen. This was evidently the case here for the funny little man who was clearly perplexed and, stumbling over his words, had to be led through the presentation by the court usher, to much jeering and whistling from his neighbours. By the end of his performance, though, he had begun to enjoy the unusual attention he was being given and it was the usher who finished it for him, frowning and still shaking his head. It did, however, provide a brief interlude of levity in an otherwise sombre occasion.

That marked the end of the preliminaries. Now the meat of the case could begin and people settled down to enjoy hearing the juicy details of Isaac's purported crimes. But in this they were to be disappointed. What followed was an hour of heated legal argument between Sir Fulk on one side and the Moy team on the other, each bobbing up in turn with legal technicalities incomprehensible to everyone but themselves and the court recorders. The crux of the dispute, as far as I could follow it, was over the legitimacy of the court to even hear the case with Isaac's lawyers vehemently protesting that as a Jew Isaac was the legal property of the King and therefore not subject to the common law. This problem was eventually resolved rather neatly: Since the King himself was present, Sir Fulk suggested, surely he could be appealed to directly. The King duly rose and graciously dispensed with his royal prerogative then sat down again. It was presented as a spontaneous decision by the King but anyone could see it was just another piece of theatre pre-arranged between the King and the Abbot in order to speed matters along. The strategy of the defence team had evidently been to lock the court in lengthy legal wrangling in the hope that the case would simply collapse for lack of time, but they were being thwarted by the wily Samson. It made me glad I was not a lawyer but a mere physician. The human body with all its baffling cogs and whirls was a child's toy compared to the complexities of the *body juris*.

Having had their first fox shot Isaac's lawyers immediately moved their second objection: Under one of King Henry's laws, they affirmed, Isaac had to be tried by a jury of his peers consisting of six Jews and six Christians of good character. This started a flurry of activity among the court's clerks to try to find the citation, much to the amusement of Sir Fulk who clearly had anticipated the tactic beforehand. It was another legal ruse by Isaac's team because, as everybody knew, since the 1190 expulsion there were no longer six Jews to be found anywhere within the Liberty. As a result, they urged, the case could not legally be heard. Sir Fulk simply argued that since this was a crime against the person of Christ Himself judgment could safely rest with God alone and so there was no need of a jury.

Next came the testimony of the murdered boy's mother. The usher banged his rod thrice on the floor and called her by name:

'Call Margaret, widow of William of the Haberdon, miller.'

All eyes turned to the back of the court and the crowd hushed as she appeared alone at the door, pausing before slowly making her way down the centre aisle to the front. She was soberly-dressed and clutching a shawl about her as though the freezing wind of desolation blew about her. Even I shivered as she passed in spite of the stifling temperature. She was indeed a formidable woman.

Her function was simple and obvious: To win the sympathy of the court. It was a role for which she had been well primed by Sir Fulk. In a quiet, trembling voice she eulogized her exemplary son's heroic support of his brothers and sisters since her husband's tragic death. She told of how little Matthew had been training at the abbey to take the cloth and recalled the last time he had walked out of the house on that fateful evening never to return. In all this there was much weeping but I have to say I saw little sign of actual tears. I did see real tears, but only in the eyes of those listening. We were left with the impression of a saint in the making. I was much impressed. It was a consummate performance.

One aspect of her demeanour in particular interested me: On her way to give evidence at the front of the court she had to pass quite close to Isaac's table. I would have thought given the ferocity of her attack on him in his garden that she might at least have glanced at her son's murderer. In fact she did not; her deportment registered his existence not at all. It was as Jocelin had said after our interview with her when he noticed then the change in her attitude towards Isaac. "Resigned" was the term he used. "Indifferent" was mine. Seeing her today I think mine was the truer description. The tingling in my spine returned as I realised just how cold and calculating this woman truly was.

We now came to the part of the proceedings I had been dreading and from the murmuring and excitement clearly the part most people wanted to hear: The detailed description of Matthew's injuries. I went through my evidence as meticulously and dispassionately as I could trying to leach all emotion from my words. At first I was listened to in respectful silence, but as I progressed listing all the injuries the level of disquiet gradually increased.

I began by citing the marks on the boy's forehead and wrists and gave my opinion that they had occurred as a result of the boy being restrained. Sir Fulk swooped on this like a falcon to its prey. While the marks were not a precise imitation of Christ's wounds on the Cross, he suggested, were they not close enough for their purpose to be clear? I didn't comment but then I didn't have to, the point was made. In the mind of the common people the image of marks on the child's head was damaging enough: They were a mockery of Christ's wounds. I then went on to describe all the other marks on the body in response to Sir Fulk's detailed questioning. He had clearly done his homework and knew as much, if not more, about Matthew's injuries as I did.

I wondered as he quizzed me who he could have got the information from. At first I thought of Jocelin, but then I realised it must have been Egbert or one of his cohort who had dug the body up from its first grave. Judging by the gasps coming from behind me people were more interested in the injuries caused by vermin than in anything that suggested ritual sacrifice - doubtless Sir Fulk had anticipated this too. He wanted to paint as graphic a picture of the horrific condition of Matthew's body as he could and for this to remain in the minds of the listener. The process brought home to me once again the truth of Jocelin's comment about the mother's oath: That the details mattered less than the impression it created. Sir Fulk also wanted a detailed account of the autopsy which although - or possibly *because* - I gave it in cold, clinical terms it horrified people all the more. They considered it sacrilege to carve up a human body in this way, especially a saint's body. All this further added to the impression of ritual desecration. The chains in Isaac's basement were mentioned (though never linked to the wounds) as was the fact that the body was found in Isaac's garden. Both facts were circumstantial but that didn't seem to matter. By the time I got to the actual cause of death, the slashing of the boy's throat, it seemed a relatively minor injury compared with the rest. Most people by then had made up their minds and although I repeated at the end my conviction that many of the injuries had occurred after the boy had died this simple fact was lost in the hubbub that followed.

Together, my testimony and that of Matthew's mother, did the job intended. I could not help a wry smirk to think that she and I had been put in this tandem together in order to convict poor Isaac who clearly stood no chance from the beginning. Revulsion was written on most faces around me and one man even went so far as to spit on Isaac's back. But it was all innuendo and suggestion, nothing substantial. Analysed coldly the evidence would evaporate like the morning mist. But as Samson had said, evidence was not going to be the deciding factor. Finally, and disgracefully, Sir Fulk asked me directly in my role as the chief investigative officer, did I believe Isaac was innocent of the crime of which he was accused, namely murder of the boy Matthew. The question should never have been allowed and although I looked to Samson to overrule it he did not. For the first time since I stood up I also realised that Isaac was looking at me with intense eyes, but like the coward I am I could not bring myself to return his gaze as I gave the only honest answer I could: I did not know if he was guilty or not.

When I sat down Sir Fulk patted me on the arm as though I had provided the *coup de grace* of the prosecution case. He then rose once again and quoted a different law of King Henry which directed that anyone accused of the crime of murder had to suffer 'ordeal of water'. No flurry of clerical activity this time, I noted, the clerks having been well-primed by the court in advance. Up till now the case had been a matter of procedure but now it was coming to practicalities. I had almost hoped against hope that judgement by ordeal could be avoided even though I knew it was the course Samson and the King had determined upon.

As a matter of record, since King Henry's time there had been a gradual shrinking away from the notion of trial by ordeal in favour of trial by jury - indeed that had been a central tenet of the old king's reforms. Trial by ordeal depended on church support since it required priestly cooperation to carry it out. Unfortunately for Isaac, so far the new Pope, Innocent, had been reluctant to give up this vestige of papal control. The conceit was that man was not competent to judge, only God could do that. And how was God's judgement to be interpreted? By how He treated the injury received during the ordeal. Trial by fire was plainly horrific, but trial by hot water was no less so. This was why Jocelin's optimism had been so misplaced. The accused was required to put his hand into a kettle of boiling water and retrieve a stone.

Now, anyone who has accidentally scalded himself with boiling water knows how painfully the hand blisters and the skin peels leaving a scar. Imagine the damage a prolonged immersion of an entire limb would cause. The skin swells and cracks, the live flesh actually starts to cook, the blood congeals in the veins and the fat melts away. A wound thus inflicted would be bound and if by some miracle after three days it started to heal then God was presumed to have judged the accused innocent. If, however, the injured site showed no sign of regeneration the accused was adjudged guilty.

It hardly needs saying that Isaac's lawyers wished to avoid such a process at almost any cost and in so doing they made their fatal error. After more lengthy, and this time quite acrimonious, consultation between themselves and their client the lawyers proposed to the court that Isaac change his plea from Not Guilty to Guilty with the corollary that Isaac should pay a sum of money to the murdered boy's mother by way of compensation. There was plenty of precedent for this course of action in Saxon law which was the ancient law in England. But Saxon law had long since given way to Norman - and besides, the mood of the court would not tolerate it. The very suggestion that a Jew could commute Divine Judgement in the case of a murdered Christian child to a few pence or even a considerable sum was greeted with outrage. It would be Judas and his thirty pieces of silver all over again. The lawyers' mistake sealed Isaac's fate. There was only one course of action the people were willing to accept and that is what they now proceeded to exact.

But before anything else could happen the Abbot had to give his decision which was merely to confirm what everybody already knew: The verdict of the Court was that Isaac should be handed over to the Sheriff and to suffer Ordeal by Hot Water. Amid cheers of approval the court rose and the King, the Abbot and all the chief officials of the court filed out, with rather unseemly haste it seemed to me, while two armed guards led Isaac away through another door. It appeared neither the Church nor the Crown wished to be seen to witness the unpleasant business of carrying out their commands; that pleasure was to be reserved for others.

Poor Isaac. I could hardly bring myself to look at him. He was utterly destroyed, his head for the first time hanging in despair. Amid some turmoil the court was adjourned by the usher, only to be immediately reassembled outside in the Palace Yard where a kettle of boiling water had already been merrily bubbling away for a quarter of an hour or more. The atmosphere out here was quite different from what it had been in the courtroom, more like that of a carnival or a bear-bait, except that the bear is not usually hated the way Isaac clearly was. It was not something I would normally wish to see but despite my revulsion I felt it was my duty to remain and witness that which my pitiable efforts had failed to prevent. I thought at one point Isaac even searched among the faces of the hostile crowd for my face. I hoped so and that he saw me for he had few enough friends in that terrible place that day. I had further hoped that someone might have taken pity and kept the temperature of the water below boiling point, but I could see from the bubbles that it was as hot as it was possible to get. To my further horror they had chosen the deepest bucket they could find so that Isaac's hand would be covered all the way to the elbow.

The crowd, which by now had become an ugly mob, fell over each other in their rush to find the choicest positions to see. Isaac was at least allowed the courtesy of having a rabbi administer to him - the same rabbi, I saw, who I had met at the Moy house the day before. But Isaac was a lonely figure that day standing in the circle of rabid hyenas eager not to miss a single scream of agony or glance of terror. Trembling uncontrollably he began rolling up his left sleeve, but the crowd were having none of that. They set up a chant of "Dex! Dex! Dex!" which echoed round the enclosed courtyard like a battle cry and sent a shiver down my spine - "dex" being a corruption of "dexter", the Latin word for "right". What they were calling for was Isaac's right hand – his writing hand - to be the one sacrificed to the cauldron.

Three times his hand came near the bubbling liquid but each time he lacked the final courage to plunge the limb in. In the end it was the rabbi who took hold of the hand and staring hard into Isaac's eyes pushed it under the bubbles accompanied by screams from Isaac and whoops of delight from the crowd several of whom had the decency to faint. Isaac quickly found the stone and tossed it away, but from where I stood I could see the skin was already a crimson red and blistering where it had touched the scalding water. Quick as lightning the limb was bound in clean linen and Isaac was half-carried, half dragged away faint with pain and followed by hissing from the crowd. The entertainment now at an end, there was a sense of anti-climax as the crowd slowly dispersed back to their homes equipped with a satisfying tale of just deserts to while away the long sultry summer evenings.

Chapter 18
FIRE!

'S-sometimes the old ways are the best,' said Jocelin when we returned to his office. 'I'm sure G-god will not allow an innocent m-m-man to s-suffer un-n-necessarily.'

'You don't think what we just witnessed can be called "suffering"?' I said bitterly.

'I d-don't know,' said Jocelin shaking his head disdainfully, 'I don't know.'

I could tell he was in some distress over what had happened if only by his almost uncontrolled stuttering fit. I felt more anger than distress and I wanted to vent it on someone but realised it wouldn't be fair to do so on him so I said no more. I sat down on one of his chairs surrounded by the piles of documents we had hurriedly assembled for the trial.

'What will happen to him now?' he asked when he had calmed after a minute.

I let out a long sigh. 'He'll remain in custody for three days, at the end of which his bandages will be removed. If the wound has healed, or shows signs of healing, God will be assumed to have judged him innocent and he will be released.'

'And if not?'

I shrugged. 'He'll hang.'

Jocelin shuddered and, typical of the man I was coming to esteem more and more, he had the generosity to say a small prayer. 'Well, at least your p-part in it is over,' he said kindly. 'You look exhausted. You should rest now, certain that you have done all in your power, and leave matters to others.'

I snorted. 'To God, you mean.'

'Yes,' he nodded firmly. 'To God.' He looked at me with deep concern. 'Brother, I hope your experience through these troubles has not destroyed your f-faith. It is at such times that we need to hold on to our certainties with g-greatest tenacity. If we lose them, w-what else is there?'

He was in such earnest that I couldn't help but smile. His features were screwed into what looked like such pain he appeared even more shrew-like than ever.

'Do not fear, my good friend,' I said to him. 'I am not losing my faith. It is simply that God's voice sometimes gets so drowned out by the clamour of man's petty squabbling that we have to listen all the harder to hear Him.'

At this his face relaxed. He beamed and nodded, evidently delighted at my reaffirmation. But I went in to vespers that day with a heavy heart, my thoughts entirely on the man with the bandaged hand who at this moment must be suffering unspeakable torments both physical and mental in the tower gaol. He now had but three days before he learned his fate, three tortuous days of uncertainty and unimaginable pain. Not that any of this was anything more than of academic interest. In all my time as a physician I had never seen anyone recover from an injury like the one he sustained today. A mere spillage of boiling water leaves a horrible scar once healed, if it heals at all. More often the injury turns septic, then gangrenous, a tertiary fever affects the heart and brain and the patient dies, usually in agony and fever. In Isaac's case it was unlikely to get that far. He will hang well before infection kills him. What was most difficult for me as a physician was the frustration of not being able to dress his wound which would at least make it more comfortable for him. But of course I wasn't permitted to do so. The whole point of the exercise was that natural processes – and God's intentions judged therein – had to be allowed to work without interference.

As we filed into choir I deliberately kept my eyes lowered for fear of catching sight of Egbert or one of his colleagues. I could not have borne the look of triumph on their smug faces or the answering scowl on my own. Even so, I could sense their disapproval. As far as they were concerned I was taking the side of a Christ-killing Jew against that of an innocent Christian boy-saint and they were not going to forgive me easily. Jeremiah was the only one to have the decency to come up to me after the service. He laid his own arthritic hand on my arm gently. 'We will pray for him brother,' he said. In spite of myself I smiled and nodded, grateful for this small sign of humanity.

Later at supper in the refectory Jocelin sat with me again – it was becoming something of a ritual.

'It s-seems there is to be a candle-lit vigil tonight for the soul of the murdered boy,' he whispered as he sat down.

I was appalled. 'That's tantamount to confirming Matthew is already a saint,' I said. 'And by implication that Isaac is guilty. Surely Samson hasn't agreed to it?'

He squirmed. 'He will not raise objections provided it is solely within one of the s-side chapels and not open to the general populous.'

I shook my head angrily and started to rise from my bench. 'No, this cannot be allowed to happen. I must try to prevent it. At the very least it's prejudicial to Isaac's case.'

Jocelin put out a restraining hand on my arm. 'Samson is trying to tread the m-middle path, Walter. He does not want to deny the devout their r-right to honour a martyr. If he did they would make even more of a fuss. B-better to have this private devotion than a public p-protest.'

He was right of course. A service at night in a side chapel with only the choir monks present would keep the publicity to a minimum. I would be doing Isaac no favours by turning it into a noisy battle of wills. 'So long as they don't expect me to come,' I said sitting down again heavily.

Jocelin smiled wryly. 'I don't think our presence will be missed.'

I looked up and smiled. 'Thank you for that "our" at least.'

A brother I did not know well but whose name, I think, was Valentin had been eating next to us and apparently listening to our conversation. He now slammed his spoon down and glared at me with what looked like pure hatred. 'Have you no conscience at all?' he demanded of me before pushing his plate away heavily and getting up.

'Now, which camp is he in, I wonder?' I asked Jocelin watching the man storm out of the room. '*Pro* or *anti*? I must say I'm getting confused. Depending on your point of view, I either saved Isaac in court today or put the final nail in his coffin. It seems I can do no right for doing wrong.'

'He probably just didn't like having his s-supper interrupted by idle chit-chat,' said Jocelin watching the monk leave.

I poured us some thin beer. 'Well, we can do little to obviate Isaac's suffering but we have three days before judgement. Let us hope nothing else happens in that time to make matters worse.'

Jocelin looked at me sheepishly. 'Th-there have b-been more m-miracles.'

I groaned. 'Tell me.'

He glanced at the reader at his lectern: Brother Nicholas today, a quiet, self-effacing monk too immersed in the text he was reading to notice anything else.

'It seems that during the trial a woman was cured of a lump in her b-breast. Unbeknown to her, she was leaning against Matthew's grave in order to remove a stone from her shoe as the judgement was read. The stone miraculously swelled and jumped out of her shoe leaving her free of both pain and lump. It is being seen as a sign of God's favour for Matthew.'

'Leaning against what?' I snorted. 'There's nothing to lean against. The grave is but a flattened pile of earth. Another fabrication.' I closed my eyes and shook my head. 'What else?'

'A carp hauled this morning from the river near the fuller's mill. The fisherman opened up the b-belly and found a silver penny with the cross of Saint Matthew the Apostle.'

I was bewildered by man's seemingly unquenchable thirst for self-delusion. 'It is only a matter of time before one of the chapels gets re-dedicated to this new saint.'

'Oh, I doubt that,' said Jocelin. 'You know, one of the reasons I wr-rote my *Life of Saint Robert* was because he was being neglected. I had hoped the work might reignite some interest. Alas, to no avail. You still have it, by the way? My treatise?'

'Hm? Oh yes,' I smiled reassuringly. 'Safe and sound.' I didn't have the heart to tell him I'd lost it.

Jocelin nodded and drank some beer. If only I'd examined Isaac's testament when I had the chance – as Jocelin counselled I should have done - his treatise might not have been stolen and an awful lot of what happened since might have been avoided. I was sure it was somehow critical to the whole case. The one person who knew what was in it, of course, was Isaac and he was saying nothing. I wanted to visit him again in the abbey gaol to try one last time to persuade him to tell me. I also wanted to see Sir Richard de Tayfen again. He was another who knew more than he was saying. As I toyed with my pot I reflected again that with just three days before Isaac's final judgment there was still much to do.

Sir Richard's house was a grand two-storey affair fronting directly onto a narrow avenue in the centre of the town in that area known to Mother Han as "pennypinch hill". Built of flint stone with a wattle-and-daub frontage, it stood out from its neighbours in its lush livery of a lime-wash mixed with ox-blood to make that deep, rich reddish-pink pigment so typical these days of town houses in Suffolk. The house was no less than six mullioned-windows in length with a vast gateway at ground level to allow the easy passage of carts into the yard at the back, one of which was just driving in as I arrived nearly knocking me down in its haste. The top floor was one large hall running the full length of the house where Sir Richard conducted his business of buying, treating, sorting and selling cloths of all descriptions.

Sir Richard's dwarf, Ruddlefairdam, answered the door when I called the next morning. I'd seen him before on my several visits when I was treating his master's eldest daughter.

'Ah, good day to you my man,' I smiled my most professional smile. 'Remember me?'

He nodded mechanically.

'Good. I, er, was wondering about the health of your master's daughter, erm - Marian.'

'Miriam.'

'That's the one. I was wondering how she was, erm, faring.'

'Well, thank you.'

I nodded. 'Good, that's good to hear. I, er…that is to say she, erm… Look, is your master available?'

'Do you have an appointment?'

'Do I need one?'

'He's a very busy man.'

'I know, but I happened to be passing and…'

Just at that moment, *Deo gratias*, Sir Richard entered the hallway behind Ruddlefairdam who was fortunately small enough that I could see and be seen over his head.

'Oh, Sir Richard!' I called waving furiously. 'What a lucky coincidence that we should meet thus!'

Sir Richard, who had been engrossed with an employee discussing what appeared to be fabric samples, stopped and squinted.

'It is I,' I said smiling broadly and stepping back for the sun to illuminate my face. 'Master Walter. From the abbey?'

'Master Walter,' he nodded courteously but briefly. 'Did you wish to see my daughter?'

'Yes, yes indeed I do - erm – well actually, no. Might we have a word?'

I was fearful that he might still be harbouring resentment over my discourteous behaviour at our last meeting outside the abbey church when I brusquely dismissed him. But he seemed in genuine preoccupation with his work.

'I am extremely busy, brother. Can it not wait until the end of the week?'

Four days away? Isaac would be dead by then.

'Sir Richard, truly, it cannot.'

He spoke confidentially to his employee and handed the pile of fabric samples to him before turning back to me. 'Very well.'

We were sitting in a plush parlour that I imagined was normally reserved for entertaining important clients. I was not surprised to find myself there. Sir Richard had never struck me as a man especially swayed by the trappings of rank or formality, except where it was necessary in the furtherance of his business interests. Ruddlefairdam had just put down a silver salver on which were a flagon of wine and two silver goblets, and then he left closing the door quietly behind him.

'This is not about my daughter, is it?' said Sir Richard when we were alone. 'It's about that Jew.'

I smiled non-committally. 'Sir Richard, when we met outside the abbey church the other day you told me some things that may be of extreme significance in this case. I was taken rather by surprise at the time and was not quick-witted enough to grasp what you were saying.'

'Yes, you did seem somewhat preoccupied.'

I inclined my head apologetically. 'I was on my way to see Isaac ben Moy and in some trepidation as to what I was going to say to him. Please accept my apologies, I did not mean to be rude. The thing is, I have now had time to digest your observations and would like to follow up one or two of them.'

From his manner I got the impression he had been thinking about our previous conversation too and was not entirely surprised to see me. He poured wine into the two goblets and handed me one. After swallowing a mouthful he studied the bottom of his goblet.

'You know, I was there yesterday. At the trial.'

'Yes, I saw you,' I lied. 'Were you impressed?'

'To be truthful, I was bored out of my wits. Lawyers!' he snorted. 'They could skin a fart with their nitpicking. And it was hellish hot in that place. I didn't stay till the end. Better things to do back here.'

'So, you missed the, erm…business…in the yard afterwards.'

He drew himself up. 'I wouldn't have stayed for that in any case. I'm no ghoul. But I know what happened. There's been talk of little else among my people today. And that's another thing that infuriates me, people taking leave to gawp when they should be working. It's worse than cock-fighting.'

I could feel my pulse quicken a little. I had been right about the man. Beneath that gruff manner beat a humane heart. I could only hope he would do as his conscience bade him and tell me what he knew. But he would not be hurried despite my urgent need that he should.

He poured himself some more wine and studied me carefully before looking away again. 'I'll be open with you Master Walter, I don't like Jews. They're parasites. They pay no taxes, they charge exorbitant rates on their money-lending, and they make – nothing.' He took a mouthful of his wine. 'My father was a journeyman tailor. He worked hard all his life and paid his taxes. No-one ever gave him anything. When he died he left me the little he could and with it I built this business and was honest in the doing of it – not many can say that with a clear conscience. So when the Abbot threw the Jews out back in '90 I was pleased. Good, I thought, that's what they deserve. They plead for special protection, let the King protect them now.' He took another large gulp of his wine, wiped his mouth with the back of his hand and glanced sheepishly at me. 'That was barbaric what they did to that man yesterday.'

'Sir Richard,' I said quietly. 'As you know, I have been given the duty of investigating the death of the murdered boy, Matthew the fuller's son. Anything connecting him and the accused man may be of significance even though it may not appear so at first sight. You intimated the other day that you saw Matthew entering and leaving Isaac ben Moy's house. May I ask how you saw it?'

'I wasn't spying. My work-room is on the upper floor above most rooftops. I can easily see into surrounding gardens, the Moys' included.'

'You've seen the boy entering the Moy house?'

'He's been there several times.'

'Are you sure it was the same boy.'

He nodded. 'I told you the other day that I know him. He supplied me with scouring earth from time to time. We don't use a lot of it - we don't really deal in that sort of cloth. I didn't like the lad but the clay he supplied was good quality and in business you have to deal with all sorts. But I never trusted him and I made sure he was never left alone in the house especially after he – showed interest in my daughter.' He took another mouthful of wine. 'I believe he also supplied the Moys.'

'Illegally if he was,' I commented without thinking.

Sir Richard scowled defensively. 'I assure you my business with him was entirely above board. I have all the receipts.' He made to rise.

'Sir Richard,' I said quickly. 'Please do not stir yourself. My concern is with the murder of a child, not with the sale of a few illicit bags of clay.'

He grunted and sat down again.

'You say he'd been to the house on several occasions,' I continued gently. 'Why did you mention this particular occasion?'

'Because this time he didn't have his barrow with him. That seemed odd to me and as I say, I have never fully trusted that boy so I took note. Plus they left the house together.'

I leaned forward. 'By "they" I take it you mean the murdered boy and Isaac?'

'No, I mean the son, Jacob. That too struck me as odd. Jews generally don't like their children to mix with ours. Besides, I've known Jacob Moy all his life. He is a quiet sort of lad, quite different from the fuller boy who as I say was canny beyond his young years.'

More years than he thought. I felt a pang of excitement over the news.

'What day was it you saw them together, Sir Richard? Can you remember?'

He considered for a moment tapping his jaw with a finger. 'It was a week or two ago. It would have been the day after the King arrived. Yes,' he nodded. 'We'd just had a delivery of Genoese velvet. Excellent quality.' He went to his desk and opened a drawer. 'Yes, here we are. It should have arrived the day before but the town gates had been locked for the King's pageant. I was concerned it might not arrive at all. Would have cost me a lot of money if I'd lost it.'

'So no fuller's mud that day,' I mused aloud.

He looked at me with pity. 'Not for velvet, brother.'

'Nor for the Moys, either,' I suggested.

'As I said.'

I nodded thoughtfully. 'Well, thank you Sir Richard,' I said putting down my goblet and rising. 'That was extremely helpful.'

He shrugged. 'I don't see how. Two lads out for a bit sport. Lassie-baiting, I shouldn't doubt. That's all right, so long as it's not my lassies they're baiting.' He smiled evidently relieved his own ordeal was over and I wanted to ask no more. I had the impression he could have chatted on but I was in a hurry to leave. He saw me personally to the door where Ruddlefairdam was waiting.

As the dwarf opened it to let me out Sir Richard said, somewhat apologetically, 'I did not speak of this before when you asked, Master Walter, because in my view it's no-one's business what a man does in the privacy of his own home. Even a Jew is entitled to that.'

My mind was in a whirl. The implication of what Sir Richard had told me was devastating but unavoidable: That it was *Jacob* Moy and not *Isaac* who was Matthew's killer. It certainly would explain Isaac's refusal to defend himself for a father's natural instinct would surely be to protect his child even at the cost of his own life. But was it possible? Could Jacob truly have been Matthew's killer? I'd seen Jacob Moy in the flesh and had examined Matthew's body. There was no doubt which was the bigger and stronger. And by Sir Richard's judgement Jacob was by far the less worldly of the two – a conclusion I would be inclined to as well. Would Jacob have been able to overpower Matthew? It didn't seem likely.

But I was forgetting, there were two murderers. So could Isaac have been the other?

Try as I might I couldn't imagine a circumstance where Isaac and his fourteen-year old son Jacob would want to kill Matthew – unless it really was a ritual killing after all. But I refused to believe the suggestion for all the reasons of timing and character that had made me dismiss it before. Nor was I ready to act as though I did. I couldn't in all conscience put another member of the Moy family through what Isaac had been through on a mere suspicion. I needed more concrete answers first and if Isaac was unwilling to provide them then there was only one other person who could - Jacob. I presumed he was still with his mother at the Moy house so that was where I headed after I left the house of Sir Richard de Tayfen.

As I turned up Churchgate Street again I became aware of things floating in the still warm air - tiny pieces of soot-blackened straw. Fires are all too common in a town of open hearths and reed roofs and with the unseasonably dry weather of late the only surprise was that there hadn't been more of them. The abbey has had its fair share of fires, the one that destroyed the martyr's tomb almost exactly a year ago being just the latest. Somewhere in the distance a cow-horn was being blown which is the usual means of alert, its doleful bleat hallooing above the rooftops. I presumed the fire must be over that way. As I climbed further the smoke was increasing in thickness smarting my eyes and making me cough. I was about to try another route to avoid the smoke when I saw hurrying down the hill towards me a crouched, round figure I thought I recognised.

'Matilde? Is that you?'

It took her a moment to focus, but then recognising me she gave me a curt nod before continuing on her way.

'Is everything all right?' I said catching her up. 'You seem upset.' She was struggling with a huge and ancient valise that looked as though it held her entire worldly possessions.

'*Non,*' she insisted stoically. 'All is well.'

I could see from her expression that all was far from being well. Matilde was no longer a young woman and this vast portmanteau was far too heavy for her. It occurred to me that she might have been dismissed from her position or left of her own accord. Either way it would be another sad consequence coming on top of the other troubles afflicting the Moys.

I took hold of the handle of the valise. 'Please let me help you with that.' After a moment's hesitation she reluctantly relinquished it. 'Where are going with it?'

Before she could answer a gang of men rushed between us carrying pitchforks and other implements nearly knocking us down in their haste. I drew Matilde to one side.

'It must be quite a conflagration,' I muttered to myself, and closer than I thought as I watched the men disappear up the hill. 'I wonder where it is.'

'I have to go now,' said Matilde trying to retrieve her valise from my hand. She seemed unconcerned by the fire. Unnaturally so.

I looked into her face. 'Something's happened. Matilde?'

She scowled and tried to wrestle the bag from my grip again, but I held it tight. 'Why are you in such a hurry? What's happened? *Qu'est-ce que ce pas?* Tell me, Matilde. *Dites-moi. Dites!*'

But now she pulled ever more frantically at my fingers accompanied by a string of incomprehensible Norman French. I would not relinquish my hold. Then in sheer frustration she said something I did understand. '*C'est le Monsieur*,' she blurted angrily. 'He is *re-tour-né.*'

I was stunned. 'Isaac's back? You mean he's *escaped*?'

'*Oui!*' she snarled into my face. 'Es-caped,' and with a final tremendous tug she managed to wrench the bag from my grasp and with it scurried as fast as she could down the hill as another gang of men ran up past her.

I let her go and turned looking towards the direction she had come from. Had I a moment I might have wondered why, if Isaac had returned to the house, she was hurrying as fast as she could away from it. But I didn't have time to think about that, for despite the hue and cry it was clear now that the pall of smoke was rising from the place where I estimated Isaac's house to be, and it was then that I started to run.

When I got to the Moy house the roof was already well alight and smoke was pouring out through the shutters. A little group of onlookers were standing a few feet away idly watching the flames roar upwards towards heaven but no-one was attempting to put out the fire or to try to get in - indeed, some were actively discouraging anyone who tried. I realised then that the men I had seen running with pitchforks had not been coming to put out the flames at all but were part of a posse hunting Isaac. No-one was concerned for the house or its occupants. On the opposite side of the street stood the captain who had moved away from the burning building and together with half a dozen of his subalterns were keeping others well back from the flames. But they, too, were doing nothing to get into the burning building. It seemed to me insanity for apart from anything else adjacent houses were in danger of catching alight. From inside came the sound of crashing glass and splintering wood. If there was anyone in there still alive they surely would not be for much longer.

'Who's in there?' I demanded of the captain who nonchalantly shrugged his shoulders.

'No-one. The fire started and they all came out.'

'All?' I said. 'Who exactly?'

'The wife, the maid and the three children.'

'No-one else? What about the man?'

He looked at me as though I were a simpleton. 'You should know – he's in the abbey lock-up.'

'You're sure?' I asked. 'He hasn't been seen?'

'Not by me.' The captain looked at his men who all shook their heads and for a moment I was relieved. Maybe they had all got out. But Matilde had been alone when I saw her. She surely would not have left the children. And why would she say Isaac had come back if he hadn't? Something was very wrong. I studied the house carefully. Smoke billowed from the upstairs windows now and the roof was sagging.

'I think there are people in there,' I said. 'Maybe they got back in.'

But the captain replied impatiently, 'I'm telling you they came out and no-one went back inside.

Neither the front nor the back.'

'But what about the side entrance?'

'There is no side entrance.'

'But there is, into the cellar.'

He frowned and shook his head. I leapt back to avoid a rush of flames and sparks that shot from the house as a wall collapsed inside. And then I suddenly had a vision of those people in York who had chosen death on their own terms rather than wait to be murdered. Somehow I knew Isaac planned something similar for himself.

'How did the fire start?' I asked the captain quickly.

'How does any fire start? An accident. It'll burn itself out soon enough.'

'No,' I said. 'This isn't right. I think they went back inside. I think Isaac ben Moy has escaped and has returned.'

The captain looked at me sceptically. 'You want me to send a man to the abbey to check?'

I shook my head. 'There's no time. Please, captain. I'm certain I'm right. You must help. I beg you.'

But he was still reluctant to move apparently transfixed by the flames that were by now engulfing the entire roof and the upper floor. 'I can't risk my men over a hunch.'

Frustrated, I went over to the house and tried the door. The handle was red hot and I seared my hand.

'It's locked,' I said. 'Who waits to lock a burning house?' I crouched and peered at the lock. 'The key is inside. I tell you they're in there,' I barked trying the red hot handle again. Frantically, I turned to the watching crowd. 'Will no-one do their Christian duty and help these people?' I yelled at them, but although some shuffled awkwardly looking at their feet, no-one stepped forward. I implored the captain again. Tears of frustration welled up in my eyes not helped by the fire and smoke that grew more intense with every second and I had to step back further from the heat my burnt hand smarting badly. In desperation I turned to the captain one last time: 'For the love of God!'

Something must at last have stirred in him and he set his jaw. 'You!' he barked at one of his men. 'Find some buckets. And you help him!' he said to another. 'Get water from the horse troughs. Find rakes and a ladder. Don't just stand there, *move!* And you two – over here. Get your lances in here under the lock. Move out of the way, brother, or the blast may consume you when the door falls out. Right, ready?' he said to his men. 'Heave!'

I stood back, coughing, to watch. In a moment they had the door open while other soldiers were pulling the burning thatch from the roof. It seemed an age but in fact it was barely a few minutes before they had the fire under control enough for the captain and me to get inside. My eyes and lungs stung from the smoke and heat and I had to hold my robe over my nose in order to breathe. Surely no-one could have survived in there. It was unrecognisable as the house I had last visited barely a week before. Everything was blackened, charred beyond recognition, choking fumes everywhere. At first I was relieved for there seemed no sign of anyone being in the mess, indeed, it would have been impossible for anyone to have survived in that heat and smoke.

And then I saw a sight that made my heart stop. There were people in there. Two blackened shapes in grotesque poses twisted further by the heat. I had no doubt they were Isaac and Rachel. They were lying together in the middle of what was the hall in a final embrace of death. But it wasn't the fire that had killed them. As I bent to turn the bodies over I could make out enough of the remains to realise that Isaac and Rachel had both been stabbed through the heart, the knife that killed them still embedded in Isaac's chest and the hand that wielded the knife, the unbandaged left one, still gripping the knife-handle. Clean deaths both of them.

I knelt in the middle of this carnage to weep and to pray. From behind me at the doorway I heard voices whispering in awe: 'See, we were right. They have committed self-murder. Heathen bastards. Murdered the children as well, I shouldn't wonder. Animals, they are.'

The words made me catch my breath. The children. Where were the children? I looked but could not see them. And a quick search of the rest of the house revealed nothing more. Jacob, Jessica and Josette were missing.

Chapter 19
THE HUNT FOR JACOB

Isaac and Rachel's funerals were carried out the next day. This may seem like undue haste but under Jewish burial lore the body is a gift from God and must be returned to Him as soon as possible after death wrapped only in its *tallit*, or prayer shawl, so that the body is in direct contact with the earth. I was not able to be present at the funeral which in any case had to take place outside the walls of the town, but I sent one of the abbey servants along to keep a discreet eye out for the Moy children. He reported back that he saw no children even though he hung about the graveyard until late into the evening in case they came to pay their last respects.

The apparent rush also appealed to Samson who was keen to get the whole business wrapped up as quickly as possible.

'Well, I suppose that more or less concludes the case,' he said when I relayed the details of the funeral in his study.

'Far from it,' I countered. 'Isaac's death poses more questions than it answers.' I was still very angry over what had happened and the pain from my burned hand wasn't improving my mood.

Samson sighed heavily. 'The man killed himself. I'd say that was pretty conclusive.'

'Yes, I was meaning to ask about that,' I said licking my lips. 'How exactly did he manage to break out of gaol, given that we'd crippled him? I wasn't able to do it and I had four fully functioning limbs - at least, I did when I was put in there.' I lifted my bandaged hand in the makeshift sling that Gilbert had tied for me.

'Bribery,' said Samson. 'He paid the gaoler.'

'Nonsense!' I snorted. I couldn't say so because I had no proof but I strongly suspected someone had deliberately let him out knowing what he was likely to do.

Samson was beginning to lose patience with me. 'Walter, you cannot carry on defending a dead man. It's irrational. I know we cannot say for certain that he was little Matthew's killer but we do know he murdered his wife and that he committed self-murder. In most people's eyes that is tantamount to a confession.'

My jaw dropped open in incredulity. 'How on earth do you make that equation?'

He held out an entreating hand. 'Because if he'd been innocent he would have waited for the bandages to be removed at which point he would have been exonerated – by the divine judgement of Almighty God. The fact that he chose not to wait can only be because he knew the verdict would be guilty.' Samson smacked his outstretched hand down resolutely on the desktop signalling an end to the discussion. He sighed sadly. 'This has all been a trying experience for everyone involved. Naturally we will pray for the souls of the dead – *all* of them – but then we must move on.'

Oh yes, I could quite see how eager Samson would be to draw a line under the affair. With Isaac dead the town will settle down again, the abbey will get its new saint to further swell the pilgrim purse and - most importantly from Samson's point of view - King John will have no reason to remain here consuming the abbey's resources.

'And the Jews will get the blame yet again,' I muttered finishing my mental list of consequences. 'A result that I'm sure will not displease your grace.'

He shot me look of impatience. 'Brother Walter, I have been willing to overlook your impertinence because you are plainly upset. But I would remind you who I am, and that is not one of your medical students. Do not test my patience too far. You have a laudably compassionate nature that has led you to sympathize with the plight of this man and his family. That is perfectly understandable especially given your own family circumstances. But you mustn't allow your private prejudices to cloud your professional judgement.'

By my "family circumstances" I took him to mean my relationship to Joseph but that had nothing to do with my belief that what we had witnessed was a gross miscarriage of justice.

'*My* prejudices!' I sneered contemptuously.

'Face facts man!' he barked back angrily. 'We are in a life and death struggle here against the forces of Satan. Christ's enemies are many and everywhere - damn it, what do you think this place exists for?' He held out his arms to encompass the entire Benedictine Foundation of Saint Edmund, King and Martyr. 'The blessed

Edmund himself died fighting the heathen and we continue that fight in his name, here as much as in the Holy Land. That is my priority and as an ordained member of Christ's holy army it should be your priority too, not the fate of one unbelieving Jew.'

He glared up at me from his seat behind the desk and I have to admit I was momentarily humbled by his words, enough at least to lower my eyes and bow my head dutifully. He was reminding me that I had solemnly given up everything - kith, kin, home and hearth, even my own will and desires - when I took the cowl and devoted my life to the service of Christ. I must never forget that simple fact.

'You are right father, of course. I spoke out of turn. Please forgive me.'

'Hm,' he nodded rubbing his chin with his beefy hand. He scowled painfully. 'Walter, I have no wish to chastise you. You have done a splendid job, arrived at a solution – the *right* solution. But you are tired and you are injured.' He nodded at my bandaged hand then looked at my feet. 'And I see you've also ripped your boot.' He tutted. 'How on earth did you manage to do that?'

I looked down and smiled. 'Running to the fire, I expect.' I hadn't noticed it before.

He shook his pink and white tonsured head kindly. 'It seems that every time you appear before me you've had some new mishap. You need to rest. That is why I want you to go to Thetford for a while. The Sisters of Saint George will minister to you. I've had a word with the

Prioress who is a good friend. She is in full agreement.'

'Oh, but father -'

He held up his hand. 'No more arguments. I have told you the matter is closed. And this is not a request, it is a command. As your spiritual father I have to do what I think is best for you. You will go to Thetford. The weekly dispatch of supplies will leave for the nunnery in a day or two, you can travel with it.' He started to rise.

'What about the money in the casket?' I said quickly.

He sighed. 'What about it?'

'Isaac entrusted it to me to pass on to his survivors should anything happen to him. His three children did not die with their parents in the house. They are still alive somewhere and should have it. They will be destitute without it.'

Samson shook his head. 'Out of the question.'

'But your grace -'

'You said it yourself Walter, there were two involved in this murder. If the father was one then the son must be the other. Until Jacob Moy is found and is either convicted or cleared of the crime he remains a fugitive – and that means he cannot inherit from his father. The casket remains here in the abbey treasury.'

It was an obscene conclusion to draw. 'Jacob an outlaw?' I scoffed, suddenly angry again. 'The boy is barely fourteen.'

'Old enough,' sniffed Samson. He looked at me. 'I'm sorry Walter, that is the law. Jacob Moy is the only remaining suspect in a capital crime. He stands accused and must answer the charge.'

'The law, oh yes, the law,' I said bitterly. 'But what about justice? We hounded his parents to their death and we are still hounding their son.'

'He can have justice,' said Samson. 'Here, in my court. But first he must give himself up. The matter is out of my hands.' He gave me a look that told me it was futile to persist.

I pursed my lips. 'Let me at least hold the casket for him. I can do it as well as the treasury.'

'Like you did last time.'

'It was his father's last wish. I swear I will not give it to him until he is proved innocent and will do all I can to encourage his surrender to your grace's mercy. But I beg you, allow me to do this one last thing for him.'

Samson hesitated. 'Strictly speaking all Isaac Moy's assets now belong to the King.' He stroked his beard thoughtfully. 'But I doubt anyone has told him about the casket. Oh, I daresay we can make an exception in this case - as a gesture of Christian charity. All right, you hang on to the casket for the present. But mark me Walter, you are forbidden to give it to the boy or to aid him in any way while he remains a fugitive. If you do you will be committing *couthutlaugh* and that means you may legally be banished yourself. If you see him you are to arrest him, understood? I have your solemn oath on that?'

Reluctantly, I agreed.

At that his manner softened as he led me to the door. 'If it's any comfort, I doubt the boy will ever be found. And I daresay the King will be wanting to leave now that the matter is resolved, *Deo gratias*. By the time you get back from Thetford he and his entourage should be long gone, all this unpleasant business will be forgotten and we can start getting back to normality, for which blessing I for one will offer thanks to God Almighty.'

Since the King's departing entourage would include the appalling Geoffrey de Saye, I said a heart-felt *Amen* to that myself.

'He gave you the c-casket, then,' said Jocelin who had been waiting for me outside Samson's office. 'I m-must say I'm surprised.'

'Yes,' I nodded cradling the damaged box under my good left arm. 'He gave in a little too easily I think. I imagine Samson will be putting a watch on my cell to see if Jacob tries to retrieve it.'

Jocelin's eyes lit up. 'You could k-keep it in my office. Samson won't think to set his spies there. A-and it would be safer than your cell – b-bearing in mind it was already lost from there, I mean.' He looked away shyly. 'Th-that's if you w-want to.'

I hesitated but realised there could hardly be a more secure place in the abbey to keep it with all those locks and bolts. It was just a pity I hadn't put it there when I first got it.

'Are you sure you want the responsibility? Samson would be furious if he knew. I wouldn't want you to get into trouble.'

'That's all right,' he grinned. 'I enjoy frustrating Father Abbot occasionally. It is a game we have played b-before.'

I looked askance at him. There really was more depth to his character than I had given him credit for.

'B-but the casket is only half of it,' he continued. 'The testament is still m-missing.'

'I know.' I looked at him hard. 'You haven't mentioned it to Samson, have you?'

He shook his head. 'I said I wouldn't and I haven't.'

'Thank you. You and I are the only ones who know about it.'

'And the thief,' reminded Jocelin.

'Oh yes, of course the thief. Mustn't forget him.'

'You think it's your f-friend, Geoffrey de Saye?'

'He's no friend of mine.'

'What exactly is it he has against you?' Jocelin asked as we walked to his office.

'I don't know and I don't suppose I shall ever find out now. Samson wants me to go to Thetford. I think he'd like me to stay there until de Saye has left Bury with the King.'

'S-so he considers the m-murder solved?'

'He certainly wishes it so. With Isaac dead and Jacob missing it does look as though everybody's suspicions have been confirmed. But I'm not so sure. If Samson really believed Jacob was the accomplice he would be raising a hue and cry for him right now. As it is, he's only had Jacob declared an outlaw.'

'That was to be expected.' Jocelin unlocked his office door and pushed it open for me to enter ahead of him. 'I d-don't think he had any choice. A-and the evidence does seem compelling. Matthew was a frequent visitor to the Moy house, there's n-no disputing that. And you have a witness confirming that M-matthew and Jacob were together on the night of his murder. We agreed that it needed two people and now Jacob has gone m-missing. Add to that the fact that Isaac made arrangements in anticipation that he would not be around for very long, wh-which could be interpreted as another indication of guilt. It all makes a forceful case for Isaac and Jacob committing the murder together, f-father and son.'

'Yes yes, everything you say is true. But still it doesn't add up. You said yourself what a strong young man Matthew must have been. He wasn't a pre-pubescent child like the other boy martyrs. You've seen Jacob, too. Picture them side by side. Matthew towers above Jacob. Can you really see Jacob holding Matthew's arms down and Isaac slicing through his neck? Or perhaps Isaac doing the holding down and Jacob wielding the knife?' I shook my head. 'No, I think the real killers are still out there, and from Samson's reaction I think he does, too.'

It was a mess and I was largely responsible for it. If I hadn't lost that blessed casket in the first place I might have been able to give it to Jacob and he could be far away, with his father's family in Norwich if he had any sense. That, at least, would be some justice. But where was he? And where were his sisters? Were they even together? They surely couldn't be living wild in the forest, the usual refuge of outcasts. I decided I had to tackle Matilde again. If anyone knew where the children were she would. With the Moy house burnt down she'd had nowhere to go. I'd found her in the infirmary garden sitting forlornly on her giant valise. Out of compassion I'd sent her to Thibaut, the sub-almoner, who was technically my assistant since in addition to all my other duties I was also the almoner, although in practise Thibaut did most of the work of ministering to the poor. He was the obvious person to look after her now until she could find somewhere else. Although born here in England both Thibaut's parents were from Angoulême in the middle of France so he spoke both *oc* and *oïl* forms of French. The almoner's office was behind the abbey church near the infirmary so that was where I headed.

I found both my targets in the almoner's lodge. Thibaut was on his knees on the floor clearing up a mess of cooked rice while Matilde sat rocking on the only chair weeping profusely into her smock as no doubt she had been doing ever since she arrived, her enormous valise propped up in a corner.

On seeing me Thibaut pulled a face conveying what I had suspected, that he was just about at the end of his tether with the wailing Matilde. I tried to smile reassuringly at her.

'She refuses to eat,' he said sadly. 'I keep giving her food but she just leaves it to one side and I come back later to find half of it on the floor.' He shook his head looking at the upturned bowl.

'Has she said anything?' I asked him.

'Oh, loads, but nothing that's made much sense. She's completely batty.'

I gestured to him to temper his comments in front of Matilde. He made a mooing sound. 'I shouldn't worry; I don't think she understands much English. In fact the French she speaks is very strange too, rather like I imagine was spoken a hundred years ago.' He smiled condescendingly at the grizzling Matilde who eyed him mournfully.

'I think that's because she learnt it from her mother who learnt it from *her* mother,' I said rolling a figure eight in the air to indicate infinity.

'Ah, that would explain it,' nodded Thibaut. 'It's really most peculiar. Do you know what word she uses for "dinner"? It's -'

'Yes, that's all very interesting,' I interrupted him. 'But have you heard her mention the name "Jacob" at all?'

He frowned and shook his head. 'No, I don't think so. Mind you, she could have done for all I know. I was asking her about -'

'Yes, I'm sorry to keep interrupting, brother, but I really have very little time. Do you think your French is up to asking her a few questions if I put them to you in English first?'

His eyes lit up enthusiastically. 'We could certainly give it a try.'

So we began. I gave Thibaut the questions I wanted answered in English, he translated them into Northern French. Matilde gave her answers in her own idiosyncratic version of French and then Thibaut translated the answers back into English for me. It was a tortuously slow process made all the more difficult because Matilde was weeping so much and tended to blub her answers. Plus the fact that she liked to embellish her responses with copious meditative ramblings that had nothing whatever to do with the questions and in which Thibaut got hopelessly lost. I gathered, however, that she did not know where the children were and could not offer a suggestion where they might have gone. Trying to get from her any further insight into Matthew's visits, in particular the last visit on the day before he died, was even more fruitless although she did confirm that it was Jacob he had come to see, not Isaac which corroborated what Sir Richard had told me. I got the distinct impression that she was on her guard with her answers. But the one thing she did let slip was that Jacob had gone out with Matthew *only reluctantly* that evening.

'Well,' said Thibaut scratching his youthful and stubbly pate, 'I hope you got more out of that than I did.'

'Yes, quite possibly,' I said vaguely. 'Er, thank you brother. And thank you,' I said at Matilde.

'Pah!' she snorted. 'There is no need to yell I am not deaf.' And then in a very thick accent: 'And I speak better English than he speaks French,' she said jabbing an index finger at Thibaut.

'Well I'm blessed!' said Thibaut grinning all over his face. 'She understood after all, the crafty old French maid.'

'What will you do with her?' I asked when we were out of earshot. 'She's nowhere to go.'

'I know,' sighed Thibaut. 'We don't really have the facilities to deal with a woman. I've put her in the infirmary for now. I've screened off a corner next to old Osbert. He's blind and a bit gaga so he probably won't notice. Hugh is being terribly sweet about it but he won't like his infirmary disturbed for too long. I fear we will need to make alternative arrangements soon – before the next bleeding when we will need all the beds.'

'Thank you, brother,' I said. 'I will speak to the Abbot when I can and see what can be done with her. But if you would indulge her a while longer I would be grateful.'

As I was leaving, Matilde muttered one more thing in French that made Thibaut spin round.

'What did she say?' I asked.

He looked a little reluctant to tell me but in the end he did: 'She said it was your fault they died. The Moys, she means.' He gave an embarrassed grin. 'Sorry.'

I couldn't face going back to my cell knowing Samson's spies would be watching. Instead, I walked down to the river between the fish ponds on one bank and the vineyard on the other. It was a relatively peaceful part of the abbey grounds where I often went to think and pray. Given space and time the mind often comes up with answers which in any other circumstance would seem insoluble. As I gazed across the river at the serried ranks of the vines I once again had the feeling that I was being watched but this time by someone clumsier than on previous occasions. One of Samson's spies, perhaps? A pretty inept one if it was. I could distinctly hear rustling in the bushes above my head which stopped when I stopped and started again when I moved. I paused by a small outcrop of woodbine, probably some that had escaped from the Abbot's garden, and pretended to enjoy its fragrance. Without turning my head, I said, 'It's a pity I cannot reach you from here or I would have to detain you. I am sworn to do so.'

There was a pause. I had never heard Jacob's voice before but as soon as he spoke I knew it was him. 'I didn't do it, brother. I didn't kill Matthew. Nor did my father.'

'But you know who did,' I suggested squinting across the river.

Another pause. 'No-one will believe me.'

'If you are telling the truth they will. Come with me to the Abbot. You are in mortal danger while you remain abroad. You have been declared an outlaw. Do you know what that means? It means I cannot give you aid and anyone can take your life at any time without penalty. If you are truly innocent then let the law deal with it. I promise you will come to no harm. You have my word.'

I could hear him breathing and, I thought, crying. I was forgetting in all this his vulnerable age. It reinforced my view that he was not the murderer. He was barely two feet behind me, now. I could easily have made a grab for him. I had given Samson my oath to do so if I saw him, but so long as I stared at the vines on the opposite bank of the river and did not turn round I could not see him.

'Father said it will be my word against his,' he said when he'd recovered sufficiently. 'And if he escapes justice a second time then my life will be in danger, and those of my sisters. We will be hunted. He will never rest. So you see, brother, it makes no difference that I am declared outlaw. I am already dead.'

'*Who* will never rest?' I blurted in my frustration, but he remained silent. 'All right, if you won't tell me who then at least tell me why. What hold did Matthew have over you?'

'I cannot tell you that either.'

I nearly turned around but stopped myself in time. 'In the name of God why not? If you were being coerced then it will be evidence in your favour. We can protect you. *I* will protect you.'

He hesitated but finally he said, 'Father said you are an honourable man. But he also said you must find the evidence yourself. Only then will you be believed.' There was a rustle of leaves.

'No wait,' I said. 'I have your father's money for you. Jacob!' I darted into the bushes after him, but he had already gone.

He said I needed to seek out the evidence for myself. That was what he had risked capture to come and tell me, not to give up. If I'd been waiting for inspiration out there among the fishes and the vines then that was it. I knew now what I had to do the next day and who I had to see.

Chapter 20
THE MIST BEGINS TO CLEAR

Saturday 19th June dawned bright and early. It was one of the longest days of the year, practically the longest. I have no idea why days grow longer then shorter and then longer again with unerring regularity although I fancy it can only be God's gentle ordering of the universe like the rhythmic breathing in and out of the body reminding us that all Creation is connected by but a single thought. I'm sure Joseph has other explanations gleaned, no doubt, from the ancient wise men of Greece and the East which he studies assiduously and is always quoting. I often wonder if Joseph's wise men were from the same tribe as the three who had followed the star to Bethlehem. It would seem likely to me for surely the Magi would not have been the only ones, though unquestionably the wisest. I wonder where that tribe is now or whether the wars in the Holy Land have destroyed them. We could use their council now for so much of the world is in turmoil that I fear the Day of Judgement itself will be upon us before God finally reveals His true purpose for mankind. That day, surely, cannot now be long in coming for all the signs favour it. In the meantime all we can do is live each day as it comes and try to solve our own puny man-made problems as best we can.

With this purpose in mind I set off shortly after lauds when the sun was already well above the horizon. It didn't take me long to reach my destination. I lifted the latch of the garden gate and walked up the path. Matthew's mother was just coming out of the house carrying a basket of washing. She stopped when she saw me approaching and put the basket down on the ground.

'I was wondering when I'd see you again,' she said straightening her skirts. 'You'd better come in.'

I followed her into the house where she stood with her back to the far wall and waited. With the daylight flooding through the open door I saw again what I'd seen at the trial: From the set of her mouth, the coldness of her eye, I could see that she was a hard woman - or perhaps *hardened* would be a more generous description, a woman accustomed to making difficult choices. But then, who could blame her? In this forlorn, isolated place what prospects had she, a woman of perhaps forty summers, widowed with five young children to support? Fulling is heavy work, as Jocelin so graphically pointed out, man's work. With her husband and eldest son both dead and five hungry mouths to feed she would have little prospect of finding another husband. I had had a charmed and trouble-free life so who was I to judge? What would I know of the struggles a woman in her position was likely to have to bear and the daily decisions she would have to make just to survive?

The five little ones were grouped now on the one big bed that filled half the room, as they had been last time, wide-eyed and silent - oddly silent it occurred to me now - and I wondered why they were not out in the yard playing in the morning sunshine. I went over to them, smiling, but they did not smile back but stared at me with doleful eyes.

'When I was last here,' I said to their mother, 'you told me these little mites wouldn't starve. Why were you so sure?'

She linked her hands in front of her and lifted her shoulders. 'God will provide.'

The slick answer made me smile. 'Indeed,' I nodded, 'but in addition you are being maintained, are you not? Someone is giving you money. Who, I wonder? Not the monks who were here last time. They paid you a fee to sign that absurd oath, but that won't last long. So where is the rest coming from?' I waited but she did not reply. 'Your silence does you no credit, mother.'

'People are generous,' she sniffed. 'They know my situation.'

'If you are in need of alms I can help,' I offered. 'I am the abbey's almoner as well as its physician. But funds are scarce and the poor are many. I have to be sure of deserving cases. Of course, if you have another source of income…'

She looked away. 'I have no need of your charity.'

That confirmed that I was right and there was indeed someone else paying her. But who? And why? What had she to sell that others might give good coin to secure? She plainly wasn't going to volunteer the information.

'If you won't answer me that then let me try a different question. You told my brother monks that Matthew was twelve when you knew full well he was fourteen. Why did you do that?'

She shrugged. 'They said he was twelve, not I. He might have been.' She nodded toward the other children. 'With so many it's easy to forget.'

I snorted with contempt. 'No mother forgets the ages of her children. You let them think Matthew was two years younger than he really was because it fitted better the story they wanted to believe, that an innocent babe was crucified by Jews. But Matthew wasn't a babe. In law he was a man, old enough to swear an oath, old enough to die for his King. Nor was he as innocent as others would have me believe. You let that charade continue even though you knew it to be untrue.'

The smirk on her face forced me to suppress a moment of anger. My investigation, the trial and the suicides of Isaac and Rachel Moy could all have been prevented with a single word from her. Yet she chose not to speak it. She permitted a family to be hounded to death simply by her silence. The sin of omission. I shivered at the cold callousness of it.

'Something else you told me. About the day Matthew's body was found. You said you knew how to get into the Moy garden because some man – some *gentleman* you said – told you. There was no gentleman, was there? You knew how to get there because you'd been there yourself with Matthew. You encouraged him to go there. Why?'

'We had something to sell that they wanted to buy.' She smiled. 'Fuller's earth.'

'It was not yours to sell,' I countered sharply. 'It belonged to the abbey. There are severe penalties for theft. Flogging – even hanging.'

If I was hoping to frighten her into revealing more by threats of that nature I was underestimating her. She merely smiled her lop-sided smile again. 'I have already confessed it to the Abbot and he has forgiven me. I have learned my lesson and am contrite. There will be no more thievery.'

I was appalled to hear that Samson had spoken to the woman without telling me. Once again he was cutting my legs from beneath me. No wonder she was looking so self-assured. She had it all worked out.

'Matthew wasn't selling fuller's earth to the Moys on the night he died,' I said. 'I have witnesses who saw him. He didn't have his barrow with him. And he came alone. What was he really doing there that night?'

'Ask your witness.'

I was flailing in the dark hoping to stumble on some truth. She knew I had nothing and the more I staggered the more confident she was becoming.

'You know, don't you? You know it all yet you won't tell. I wonder why.'

She simply lowered her eyes, then raised them again defiantly. No, she was not going to tell me.

'He was also seen leaving the Moy house with Jacob Moy,' I blustered on. At the mention of Jacob's name her self-assurance did seem to falter momentarily. Was I on to something at last? I pressed the point home: 'I know that Jacob was reluctant to go with Matthew that night. Whatever they were doing together it was Matthew who instigated it. Why don't you tell me what it was? If it was innocent it will do no harm.'

'Ask him yourself,' she said recovering her poise once again.

'Oh I will, do not fear.'

I was getting nowhere. It's a good physician who knows when the symptoms defeat him and it's time to stop the treatment. To continue might even kill the patient. I took a step as if to leave but couldn't resist one last stab.

'Do you know what I think? I think you not only know what Matthew was up to that night, you instigated it. I think you know who killed your son and why. Rest assured I will soon know, too. It may take me longer without your help but I will get there. Inch by inch I will get there. And when I do I will know the true depths of your crimes and then all your conniving with the Abbot will avail you nothing. For your silence I will demand the harshest punishment I can.'

A mistake. I sounded pompous even to my own ears; to her I must have seemed ridiculous. And worse, my rash threat will probably put the already vulnerable Jacob in even greater danger. I cursed my own impetuosity. She smiled arrogantly, confident that I had no more bolts in my quiver. The wall of silence that encompassed Jacob, Matilde and this woman was proving impenetrable. Why won't any of them speak? The silence hung heavily between us, only broken by one of the little girls on the bed who started to hum a song. It was the same little girl whose hair I had stroked the last time I was here. I went over to her as I had before and sat on the bed next to her. She smiled sweetly as I stroked her blonde hair again while she continued to sing.

'That's a pretty tune,' I said. 'What is it?'

'A ditty,' replied the mother casually. 'Something her brother sang to lull the babes to sleep.'

I continued to stroke the little girl's hair while she sang. It was clearly irritating the mother. 'Be quiet, Esme!' she barked and the little girl instantly stopped with a jolt.

My God, I thought, the woman has these children on a tight rein. I wondered if that was how it had been with Matthew, how she had persuaded him to do whatever it was he had been doing. I could sense her anxiety growing behind me. She wanted me to leave, which out of devilment made me linger longer. But there was clearly no point in remaining. I was about to rise when something caught my eye.

'Where did Matthew sleep?' I asked over my shoulder.

The mother snorted contemptuously. 'How many beds do you see?'

I gently lifted the little girl out of the way and felt among the bedclothes which were damp and grimy from so many grubby bodies, not somewhere that got turned out too often. Perhaps the mother had intended doing so today with the rest of her laundry. I was glad she had not.

'What are you doing?' she asked trying to see, but my body screened her view. I picked the object and concealed it in the palm of my hand. I knew, of course, what it was and where it had come from, there could be no mistake. And in that moment like a house of cards toppling on a conjuror's bench a whole cascade of apparently random events seemed to tumble through my head each knocking the next over. I gasped at the simplicity of it. How could I have been so stupid as not to have seen it before? Hiding my trophy from the mother's eyes, I stroked the little girl's head once more and rose to leave feeling my hand tremble as I did so.

'Is that it?' said the mother suspiciously. 'No more questions?'

'No, no more.' I forced myself to smile. 'Thank you.'

As I left, the mother went over to the bed and started to feel frantically beneath the folds herself, but I had left nothing behind. I walked up the path towards the abbey. Behind me Matthew's mother came to the door to watch me go and for the first time I thought I detected fear in her eyes.

Chapter 21
UNMASKING A MURDERER

I now knew the identity of Matthew's killer although I still did not know the reason. That I hoped to learn once I'd confronted his murderer which was where I was headed now. Whatever the reason turned out to be I was certain it had nothing whatever to do with boy-martyrs or Jews wanting to return to their homeland. Had I been a little smarter - or at least quicker – I might have been able to prevent the deaths of Isaac ben Moy and his wife Rachel and avoid the tragedy of the past few days. All this was going through my mind as I turned in at the tower gate and crossed the expanse of the Court of Hospice, passing the spot where Isaac had been so cruelly tortured, and out through the cellarer's gate. My heart began to thump with anticipation for as I drew closer I could hear him singing the same tune that little Esme had been humming just as I remembered he had on each occasion I'd visited him. His sleeves were rolled up this time and I could see now they had concealed a pair of powerful forearms, certainly powerful enough to restrain the limbs of a fourteen-year-old boy.

At first he did not see me but when he did he stopped singing and his face broke into its usual jolly smile.

'Well, good day to you Master Walter. Have you come to tend my injuries again? There is no need. As you can see, I am fully recovered now.' To prove it he slapped and pummelled the dough on the bench before him shaping it and reshaping it with his big strong fists. I did not reply but instead placed the little almond macaroon I had retrieved from Matthew's bed in the middle of the table. It was broken and shrivelled but still recognisable for what it was.

Alric glanced at it briefly and raised his eyebrows. 'That looks a bit stale. Would you like another? I've plenty made.' He nodded to a plate of freshly-baked Venus Nipples which were identical to the one I'd brought, his signature confection, his own speciality that only he baked. That was how I knew, of course. It could be no-one else.

He carried on working but gradually his kneading slowed and the smile on his face faltered. He glanced again quickly at the macaroon and then at me before looking away again. 'I don't recall giving that to you, brother. May I ask where you got it?'

'It was concealed amongst the soiled linen of a child's bed.'

For a moment he did not respond, then he said quietly, 'Ah. That was careless. Boys of that age can be clumsy, can't they brother?'

Though neither of us had mentioned Matthew's name it was clear we both knew who he was talking about. Alric finished kneading his dough and placed it into a mould, sprinkled flour over the top and covered it with a linen cloth to rise. Then he wiped his hands on his apron and turned to face me. What was he going to do? Attack me? I braced myself for the blow but all he did was to sit on a little three-legged stool in the corner where he remained silently in the shadow for a long minute, his big hammy hands resting immobile on his knees.

'You know,' he said quietly, 'I have in me such love, brother, such…longing.' He frowned. 'I think maybe his father dying like that when he was so young had a lot to do with it. Fathers are so important to a boy, don't you think? It's a terrible thing to be forced at such a tender age to provide for all those little brothers and sisters. I didn't blame him for making the most of any opportunity to make life easier. He saw my weakness and exploited it.'

My jaw dropped in amazement. 'You are saying it was his fault?'

'No,' he frowned, 'of course not. But Matthew was special. He had wisdom beyond his years. The others merely teased and ran away, but Matthew – he had the measure of me from the start.'

'Others?' I frowned. 'How many others?'

'Over the years?' He shrugged. 'Dozens.'

I shut my eyes. 'Dear God.' Images came into my mind of the urchin boys I had met on the street outside Isaac's house – Mother Han's "waifs and strays". How many of those, I wondered, had he abused? They knew all about Matthew – that was obvious from their curious behaviour now when I thought back. It was what their funny little dance had been about and their reluctance to speak to me. And how could I blame them? Even if they knew who or how to tell, who would have believed them? Who could they have trusted? Certainly not me, a stranger in a monk's habit, the same habit that Alric wore. I was a fool to think that they would.

Then a horrific thought occurred to me. 'These boys. Did one of them have a deformed hand? Like a fist that has not opened?'

He smiled. 'You mean Onethumb – that's what the others call him. A strange, quiet boy. But – how shall I say? - *accommodating*.'

Christ in Heaven, what must he have thought of me when I kissed his hand that day on the street? No wonder he spat at me. I had been simply trying to show compassion but he probably thought I meant something else. How dreadful to think that he must see all who wear the cowl in the same light as Alric. My monk's habit, my belt, my tonsure – all supposed to be a symbol of humility and service. But to these boys it must have been a badge of menace. Anger welled inside me and I dare not speak for a moment for fear of what I might say to the man.

He, by contrast, seemed to want to speak: To confess, maybe, or at least to share the secret he had kept hidden to himself for so long relieved at last to unburden himself.

'You don't remember me do you, Master?'

'Remember you? No, I don't remember you.'

'It must have been a year ago. I wasn't a baker then. I was the assistant novice master.'

Of course! Yes indeed, I did remember him now. It had been nagging at me and now I knew. My mind suddenly hurtled back to an incident that occurred last summer, something of nothing really - or so it seemed at the time. The details were coming back to me. It was one Sunday morning. I had been tending a sick patient in the town and was late back for the beginning of mass. Rather than interrupt the service I decided not to take my place in the choir but stood at the back of the nave with the general throng. Near me was a group of postulant boys. They were a little bit rowdy - boys of that age can be a challenge to discipline. One tries to make allowances for youthful high spirits, but even so postulants are supposed to be in training for holy orders and their behaviour was attracting some disapproving glances. I looked around for their novice master but seeing none I thought I had better admonish them myself which I did with a stern stare. But soon their sniggering returned until it was becoming quite a nuisance, so at a suitable moment in the mass I went over to have a word. It was then that I realised the cause of their bad behaviour: They were drunk! I could smell the alcohol on their breath.

Shocked, I quickly herded them out of the side door into the yard. I warned them I would report them to the Prior to be punished for their behaviour and demanded to know where their novice master was. Just at that moment one of the brothers had come running towards us from across the cloister garth. I realised now that brother was Alric. Breathless from his exertion, he was full of apologies claiming he'd been answering a call of nature. He assured me he'd been gone just a few minutes. I can't remember now what I said in reply - some trite little speech about duty and respect, no doubt. The alcohol problem did give the incident a more serious slant than mere misdemeanour and one that should have ended these boys' careers in the convent and possibly Alric's too. But out of charity – or more likely laziness - I went back into the church and promptly forgot the whole affair. Now another terrible thought struck me: What if I had reported the incident as was my clear duty at the time? Would Alric have been disciplined, perhaps lost his position? And if so, would Matthew still be alive now?

I do not pretend to understand what passions drive men like Alric. The simple answer is that it is the Devil's work - but that is too easy. There has to be a deeper reason. I wanted to understand.

'I know what you're thinking, Master,' he said watching me. 'But there was no real harm done. It was just a game to them. To most of them at least.'

'But not to Matthew?'

'No,' he smiled. 'Not to Matthew. As I say, he was different. With him I was the prey and he played me as the angler plays his catch. Once he'd hooked me there was no escape.'

'Or what?' I asked, incredulous. 'What did – what *could* he threaten you with?'

Alric shrugged. 'What else? Exposure.'

I nodded. 'If you didn't give him what he wanted?'

'Yes.'

'And what was that?'

Alric sighed deeply. 'Not very much at first. Bread for his family. He has a large family, so many small children. I gave it willingly. I knew his father was dead and there was no income. Pity and compassion were my motives then.' He looked down at his hands and smiled again. 'I don't expect you to believe that but it's true. That was how clever he was, you see? I did not know then that I was dealing with a devil.'

'He was a child!' I protested angrily.

'Oh yes. And all children are innocents, aren't they?'

'Yes,' I nodded fiercely. 'They are.'

He smiled wryly at that but didn't reply.

'When did it start?'

'With Matthew? Oh…All Hallows Eve was probably the first time. I'd noticed him already, of course, as one of the new postulants. Such a beautiful boy. I could not take my eyes from him – and he knew it. He came with some other boys wanting wine to spice their pleasure - they like to dress as creatures of the night to terrorize the townsfolk. They knew I would not refuse them.'

'In return for…favours,' I suggested.

He glanced away, embarrassed by the word. 'When the others left for the town Matthew remained. We talked. I genuinely liked him as a person. He seemed brighter than the others, more thoughtful, sensitive. I didn't know then it was all an act. Oh he was clever, my bright little angel.'

First a devil now an angel. The double personality of the boy again.

'But things soon changed?' I suggested.

'Oh yes.' Alric took a deep breath and shuddered. 'At first he was very sweet, and willing. But when he didn't get what he wanted he changed, became spiteful, vicious. And always he was asking – *demanding* - more. He wanted beer from the cellars. Then wine - not like the others, to get drunk. In fact, I can't remember seeing him actually drink himself.'

'To sell, then?' I suggested.

'I suppose so. But that was just the beginning. Soon he was wanting other things, things I could not conceal. Plate from the vestry, coin from the Pilgrim Box. Quite a lot from the stores. The losses were being noticed. Brother Jocellus started complaining of items going missing from his cellars. It could not go on. I told Matthew to leave, to never return. I told him I would confess all to Abbot Samson.'

'And that was when his mother paid you a visit,' I guessed.

'Yes, that's right,' he smiled at my insight. 'I admit I was shocked. You wouldn't have thought it would you? I mean, his own mother.' He shook his head incredulously. 'She threatened me. Said I wasn't the one to tell Samson, she would do that and Matthew would be seen as the victim and I would be hanged.' He curled his lip. 'And she was almost right wasn't she?'

So I was right about the mother. She must be a hardened woman to have used her own son in that way. I shuddered at the unfairness of life's gamble.

I hesitated before I asked my next question, the one burning in my mind. 'Now tell me about Jacob Moy.'

Alric's eyes widened in surprise. 'The Jew boy?' He shrugged. 'Not much to tell. Matthew brought him like all the others, but as soon as I saw him I knew he was the wrong type. He was too shy, not at all like the others. I was surprised they even knew each other. He was very nervous at being here and just wanted to leave.'

I clenched my fist tight as I asked my next question, dreading the answer: 'Did you…violate him? The truth, Alric, upon your oath.'

He shot me a haughty look. '*Violate*? Is that what you think I did? No, brother, I did not *violate* him. I told you, he didn't want to be here. Matthew made him come.'

His words filled me with inexpressible relief. I realised I had been holding my breath waiting for his reply. So in that case why? What purpose did Matthew have in bringing him? Jacob was no street urchin. He must have realised he was as Alric said, "the wrong type". Why did Matthew bring him? There had to be another reason.

'When was this? When did Matthew bring Jacob to you? Can you remember?'

'Clearly. It was the day after the King's banquet.'

'You are certain of that?'

'Do you think I could forget the most humiliating day of my life? That brute of a guard dragging me from my ovens, accusing me of poisoning the King's food.' He snorted his contempt. 'It was later that evening they came - Matthew and Jacob. Shortly after you'd left from tending my wounds, in fact. I was still angry from how I had been treated and in pain. Matthew was showing off in front of the Jew boy.' He shook his head. 'I didn't want them here. I'd had enough of insults for one day. I told them both to leave. Jacob didn't need telling twice, he ran off immediately. That made Matthew furious. He wanted him to stay and blamed me for not stopping him. But the bell for compline began ringing. All I wanted to do was go to hear the office and to lose myself in prayer and meditation, not listen to more abuse. We argued. I lost my temper.'

'And that's when you killed him.'

He laughed. 'Oh no, brother. I didn't kill him.'

'Don't lie to me now, brother,' I said angrily frustrated. 'You've told me practically all, now go the final step and confess to the murder.'

But he just looked at me bemused. 'I didn't kill him, I swear.'

'Then who -?'

'Geoffrey de Saye, of course.'

'*De Saye?*' I was staggered at the sudden mention of that name.

'Yes,' he smiled. 'I thought you knew. Everyone's heard how he harasses you. I just assumed it was because you knew he was the killer.'

My mind was spinning unable to follow this latest twist. 'Tell me what happened – precisely.'

He shrugged. 'It was all very simple really. As soon as the Jew boy left de Saye arrived. It was as if he'd been waiting outside. I was surprised to see him, but then de Saye was always turning up unexpectedly, him or one of his thugs. They thought it fine sport to torment me knowing I could say nothing. I thought for a moment he had come to beat me again, but it was Matthew he was angry with this time, not me. Lord de Saye is easily angered.'

I could hardly believe what I was hearing. 'They *knew* each other?' I said incredulously. 'Matthew and Geoffrey de Saye?'

Seeing my face Alric realised what I was thinking and laughed. 'Oh, not like that, brother. Lord de Saye has other appetites. Nothing so prosaic as mine.'

'Go on,' I said.

'He started shouting at Matthew. Matthew shouted back. I must say I was shocked. Boys of Matthew's rank do not normally dare even look such men in the eye but to his credit Matthew stood his ground. I was proud of him then. But that merely served to enrage de Saye all the more.'

'So he killed him. Simply because he refused to give in?'

Alric curled his lip. 'The man is a bully like all his type. I tried to get between them, but...' He shrugged helplessly.

One to hold the boy the other to wield the knife, I thought to myself. 'You held the boy's wrists,' I said.

'Only to protect him. He looked as though to strike de Saye and I feared what de Saye might do to him if he did. But then he did it anyway. He drew his dagger from his belt and sliced through poor Matthew's throat as if through butter. It was all over in an instant.' Alric's eyes had filled with tears. 'He died right there in my arms.'

'And you did nothing? You raised no alarm? You knew all this and all that happened in the days that followed and still you did and said nothing? What kind of man are you?'

'A frightened one, brother. I freely admit it, I am a coward. You saw what de Saye did to me in the King's chamber. What would he have done this time?' He quietly sobbed.

'So what happened next? Who dumped the body in the Moy garden?'

He took a moment to recover. 'Me. It had to be me,' he said wiping his eyes. 'De Saye would have been too conspicuous. But no-one took any notice of a monk with a bread barrow. There was a lot of commotion in the town that night.'

I nodded. 'The night of the football match. But why the Moy garden?'

'That was de Saye's idea, but I could see the sense of it.'

'To save your own miserable necks,' I snorted.

He turned on me his mouth twisted into an ugly grimace. 'Oh no, brother. I did it for Matthew.'

Stunned by the abomination of his words all I could do was stare in disbelief. But Alric was in earnest and I could see again the light of wonder I had seen in the eyes of Jeremiah and Egbert, even Jocelin.

'Don't you see? The Jews would get the blame and Matthew would become a martyr like little Robert. He would become one of God's chosen, his past sins washed clean. The Jew had to die to save Matthew from everlasting torment.'

I was feeling giddy. I stood with difficulty finding that my legs were shaking. 'Of all your crimes, Alric, that is the most monstrous.'

'Is it? *Is it?*' he shouted after me. 'The Jews are condemned anyway. They deny Christ. It was the Jews who murdered Christ, brother! They deserve to pay.'

'Possibly. But not these Jews,' I said backing away from him as he groped towards me. I stumbled for the door and the light anxious now to get away. 'The Abbot must be told. It will go better for you if you own this deed yourself. But if you will not tell him then I must. And may God in His mercy forgive you.'

'God may well forgive me,' said Alric quietly behind me. 'But I won't.'

Chapter 22
REVENGE IN THE FOREST

I didn't know what to think. De Saye the murderer? Much as I disliked the man the suggestion seemed preposterous. What possible reason would he have? Why would he even have dealings with a miller's boy, someone who to a man of de Saye's standing barely ranked above the rats that infest his privy? On the other hand, why would Alric make up such a dangerous lie? He had already felt the sting of de Saye's wrath once before and even Samson would not be able to save him this time. And if it was me who voiced the accusation then my future, too, could be counted in hours. Yet conscience would not allow me to simply ignore what Alric so passionately affirmed was the truth and permit Jacob to remain a hunted outlaw. If only I had some proof to take to the Abbot, but I had none, not even that damned macaroon anymore since in my haste to get away from the place I'd left it at the bakery. And in any case, would Samson believe it? Given our last conversation he would more likely dismiss the suggestion as a desperate attempt by me to clear Isaac and Jacob's names, which to some extent it would be. And all this was assuming de Saye really was the murderer and Alric wasn't just lying to save his own neck.

I needed time to think. Maybe a few days with the Sisters of Thetford was a good idea after all to help me get things into perspective. If nothing else I could blame Samson for my procrastination - or was I just looking for an excuse to do nothing? No, my duty was clear and I made up my mind: If nothing had happened by the time I got back from Thetford I would take what I knew to Samson whatever the cost to me, that much I owed to Jacob and to his father's memory. Perhaps by the time I returned Alric would have done the right thing and gone to Samson of his own accord and saved me having to do so. I could only pray that it would be thus.

Saint George's Priory on the outskirts of Thetford town is but a dozen miles from Edmundsbury's north gate. It was said to have been founded by the canons of Saint George in memory of those who fell in a great battle nearby between King Edmund and the Danish hordes. Later, the canons were replaced by Benedictine nuns as a daughter cell of our abbey and the two houses have retained close ties ever since. One such tie is for the abbey to supply the nuns with bread, cooked meat and some of our brewed ale for which the Prioress, Mother Cecilia, is said to have a particular fondness. Needless to say, this weekly transport is bedevilled with robberies and assaults on the wagons and servants of the convent and so they were quite pleased, this fine midsummer morning, to find in me an extra pair of hands to ward off any such attack – or rather, *one* extra hand since the other was still heavily bandaged inside its sling and healing only slowly.

Loading up in the Great Court, we found we were not alone in making ready to depart for it seemed Samson had been right and the King was at last preparing to leave. With the dismantling of dozens of tents, the loading of scores of wagons, the hitching of an army of mules and the kicking out of a hundred fires, there was a general air of excitement to be moving on in advance of the King's own departure. The effect of all this was that they were creating even more chaos than when they arrived two weeks earlier. It would take weeks, if not years, to clear up the mess. But at least they were going and Abbot Samson, who I could see watching from his study window, would be viewing the scene with satisfaction.

I must say I was finding the prospect of my own journey rather thrilling. It had been a long time since I'd been as far as twelve miles from the abbey. With all the other activity there was something of a holiday atmosphere about the place. I was looking forward to putting my recent preoccupations if not behind me at least to the back of my mind for a while.

'Good gracious me,' I said, watching Jocellus the Cellarer supervise the loading up of our own poor wagon. 'How much do the good sisters of Thetford consume in a week?'

'Ninety-six gallons of beer, thirty-five loaves of bread, fourteen hides of mutton, ten of beef,' he said, ticking them off his list. 'Plus an assortment of pies, cakes, fowl, poultry - and this week, fifty pounds of trout.'

'Will there be room left for one small physician?' I grinned.

He assessed me with a professional eye. 'Ten stones? I should think so.'

'I've been meaning to ask,' I said before he marched off. 'Your problem with stock disappearing - has it been resolved at all?'

'There has been less of it in recent days, I will admit.' He eyed me suspiciously. 'Why do you ask?'

I shook my head and smiled. 'Oh, no reason.'

'Then have a good journey, brother. And pray God that you, and my dispatch, arrive in one piece.'

'Amen to that,' I said doubtfully.

He helped me up onto the over loaded wagon with its two oxen at the front and I sat between a grinning, gangly youth who was pulling nits from his greasy hair and the ugliest snaggle-toothed midget I had ever seen. The midget was the driver.

'Good God, what an awful stench!' I said to him as I clambered aboard. 'Are you sure those trout are fresh?'

'Oh, that'd be me, brother,' said the midget. 'Sorry 'bout that. Tch tch Lightning, get along now Fury,' he encouraged the two lumbering beasts who slowly, painfully, eased the wagon between the thronging hordes and out through the Great Gate of the abbey. As we turned northward along the dry and dusty road to Thetford I looked up at the sky and saw with dismay that thunder clouds were gathering. If we made it to the convent before the rains started it would be a miracle.

There was to be no miracle. Sure enough, we had been travelling barely half an hour with the sky darkening all the time when the wind suddenly rose, the temperature plummeted and soon we were engulfed in a torrential downpour of hail and rain – the first real rain we'd had in nearly a month. My cowl which I pulled up over my head was soon dripping wet and useless. My two companions looked a no less sorry pair with just an oil skin each to ward off the worst of the deluge - though the rain, according to them, made the threat of attack less likely, highwaymen being disinclined to get their felonious feet wet. There was not much we could do for cover short of climbing between the wheels of the cart and sitting out the worst of it. On a vote we decided to press on since we could hardly get any wetter, the gangly youth whose name was also Walter being out-voted by me and the midget who turned out to be yet another Walter. With so many Walters and so much rain there was a joke to be made there somewhere, but it did not seem a propitious moment to make it. Besides, I was too miserably sodden to make jokes. I pitied poor Noah having to endure forty days and nights of this - and worse if the whole world was to be engulfed in so short a time span. Our own little ark was sodden and dripping fish oil all over the road while the road itself had all but disappeared beneath a river of mud.

Once in the forest the rain eased a little and we all stopped to relieve ourselves each choosing a separate tree. I knew the area well, my family home being but half a dozen miles to our right. There was a break in the cloud before the next shower so it seemed a good moment to dismount, stretch my aching limbs and worry about the state of my battered kidneys. I squelched across the muddy road to my chosen tree while my companions went to theirs and I stood with the rain dripping from the canopy above, adding my own small contribution to the swell of puddles.

I was so concentrating on the awkward task of holding up my robe with my injured hand while relieving myself with the other that I barely registered the crack of a twig behind me. A hand was already over my mouth before I could take breath and my cowl was pulled hard down over my eyes. I was so taken by surprise that at first I was not sure what was happening – maybe one of my companions playing games. But it quickly became clear the assault was in earnest and I was locked in a deadly struggle. I wrestled with my assailant blind and mute while all the time hearing the chatter of my two companions just a little way off and oblivious to the peril I was in. I was sure a single cry from me would have brought them instantly to my aid but the hand that was tightly gripping my throat stifled any hope of that. Out of sheer desperation I did manage to get a purchase on my assailant's arm and took breath but a punch to the ribs winded me and sent me sprawling onto my hands and knees. Then an arm came up under my windpipe yanking my head up to expose my neck and I suddenly knew that my last moments on this earth had arrived.

But then just as suddenly I felt another arm come between my neck and the first and a terrific contest of limbs ensued that seemed to last for minutes but could only have been for seconds.

Then a thump, a cry of pain and the weight of a body came crushing down on top of me pinning me to the ground. I blindly struggled with it for a few seconds before I realised it was limp and lifeless. Eventually catching my breath, I managed to wriggle myself out from under it and at last, pulling the cowl out of my eyes, I looked up to see, staring down at me from atop his magnificent gelding with its harness of blue and gold silk, the splendid figure of Earl Geoffrey Fitz Peter, Chief Justiciar of England. With him were ten or so mounted guards one of whom had dismounted and was standing between me and the Earl who was looking down at me with a mixture of curiosity and disdain. Another guard appeared from the bushes dragging my two protesting companions, a Walter in each hand, and threw them to their knees before the Earl where they remained squealing for mercy. 'Shut up!' the guard barked at them and they instantly obeyed.

'Is this all?' the Earl asked of him.

'Aye my lord, and a cartload of victuals standing on the road. These two were running away no doubt part of the murderous gang of robbers. Should I dispatch them now?' He took out his sword ready to decapitate the pair at a nod from the Earl.

'No wait!' I protested stepping forward and slipping in the mud as I did so. 'They are my companions.'

Earl Geoffrey nodded for the guard to sheath his sword then he scrutinized me more closely. 'You're the bone-breaker from the abbey, aren't you?'

'Indeed so, my lord,' I replied struggling to bow and remain upright at the same time. The bandage on my injured hand had become unravelled and was trailing in the mud, the sling having disappeared completely in the scuffle. As I rewound my filthy bandage I looked down at the body of the man who had attacked me, his face turned towards the ground. 'This – er – gentleman is the robber. I would introduce him to your worship but I'm afraid I do not know his name.'

'He's my uncle,' replied the Earl curtly.

I looked down again at the man and to my astonishment saw that it was indeed Geoffrey de Saye. He was alone. I glanced quickly about but saw no sign of the third man in the struggle who had saved my life. It couldn't have been one of the Earl's guards for they were all wearing mail hauberks to their wrists while my rescuer's arm I'm certain had been bare. Besides, the guard who had dismounted was looking at me with barely concealed astonishment that such a weakling monk could have fought off the much bigger de Saye.

Whoever my saviour was he can't have done more than lightly knock de Saye out for he was already coming round holding his head and moaning. The guard helped him to his feet and I could see his face at last. Earl Geoffrey was regarding him with a mixture of disgust and contempt though whether because of his criminal attack on me or his inability to overpower a weakling monk I could not tell. He looked up at the sky that was beginning to threaten rain again, and sniffed. Then, turning his horse's magnificent head toward Bury, he barked his order at the dismounted guard.

'Bring him.' Then with a curl of his lip: 'Bring them both.'

Chapter 23
EXPLANATIONS AT LAST

Geoffrey de Saye sat glowering at me across the antechamber outside Abbot Samson's study while we listened to the voices raging inside, and a sorrier pair of half-drowned rats there never was on God's good earth. We looked as though we'd both been in a mud fight – which was exactly what we had been, of course. His nephew, Earl Geoffrey, had marched straight in to Samson's study without so much as a by-your-leave still in his riding boots and leaving a trail of muddy footprints on the scrubbed floor of the antechamber. I could not but admire the length of his stride as evidenced by those footprints and saw clearly why he was the chief minister of the land while I was a mere lowly cloister monk.

De Saye was still looking a bit groggy from having been knocked out but managed to retain that air of superiority that is natural to his rank confident, no doubt, that his version of events would be accepted before mine. If I had any doubts before that he was capable of murdering little Matthew I had them no longer: He'd nearly done the same to me. I was trying to work out, as I studied him now across the ten feet that separated us, why he had attacked me in the forest. It can't have been a comfortable ride in all that rain so he must have been pretty desperate to persist. The only explanation I could come up with was that everything Alric had told me must be true, that de Saye was indeed the murderer and learning that I knew the truth of it he had followed me out of the town in order to silence me before I had a chance to tell anyone else. It wouldn't have taken much to persuade him to kill me since, judging by the expression on his face, his hatred for me remained as keen as ever. Indeed, I was sure he would be upon me in a moment if it wasn't for that giant of a guard who had been in the forest with Earl Geoffrey and who was now posted in the anteroom to keep us apart.

'You're for it this time, bone-breaker,' he smirked confidently and cracked his knuckles like a schoolboy bully. 'You can count your days in digits.'

'As God is my witness, my lord,' I replied, 'I truly do not know what injury you think I have done you. But be assured, I will not flinch from my duty. Whatever you may do to me I will tell all I know before I expire.'

It was a bold threat and I meant every word of it though I had no idea if I would ever be able to carry it out. The only effect it seemed to have on de Saye was to increase his smirk further.

Not much could be gleaned through the thick oak door of Samson's study but the rising and falling of voices made it plain that the two men inside were having what I believe in diplomatic circles is known as a lively exchange of views. Ten minutes later the door burst open and Earl Geoffrey stormed out, his face livid with anger, and with a flick of his glove he signalled to the guard to follow him and to bring de Saye. His stride, I noticed with awe, had if anything increased in length. He didn't acknowledge me as he stormed past, for which oversight I was deeply grateful.

In a moment the whirlwind had disappeared down the stairs and I was left alone in the calm after the storm with the inevitable gaggle of bewildered petitioners peeping out from the shadows like rabbits after a squall. Through the open door of his study I could glimpse Samson still seated behind his desk, his face, too, as black as thunder. When he saw me his eyes narrowed and he beckoned me in with one fat forefinger

'I cannot trust you out of my sight for five minutes, can I Walter?' he growled when I had closed the door.

'I'm sorry to have displeased you yet again, Father Abbot.'

I glanced at Jocelin who was in his usual position just behind Samson's shoulder. He looked traumatized, poor old thing, his face as white as a sheet. He must already have been with Samson when Earl Geoffrey burst in and started ranting.

'You were supposed to spend a few quiet days in Thetford for prayer and contemplation, not brawl on the forest floor with a member of one of our leading noble families. It was with the greatest difficulty I managed to persuade Earl Geoffrey not to have you publicly horse-whipped for your insolence.'

My mouth dropped open in astonishment. 'It was de Saye who attacked me, father, not I him.'

Samson waved aside my protest. 'When will you learn the realities of life, Walter? The likes of Geoffrey de Saye are never in the wrong. It was only the fact that you are in holy orders that I was able to persuade his nephew the Justiciar to leave the matter with me, for which you can give your thanks and prayers to Saint Thomas of Canterbury.'

He was referring, as I knew, to Becket's battles with King Henry over the rights of the clergy to sit in judgement of their own and for which dispute he had been martyred – not the happiest of comparisons in the circumstances. Jocelin looked as though he might launch into a detailed explanation of the reference but Samson waved him silent. 'Just sit down the pair of you. You're giving me a crick in my neck.'

We each pulled up a chair while Samson went over to a side table and poured three goblets of wine. I took mine gratefully not having eaten or drunk anything since early morning. Samson sat down again and with a flourish produced a parchment from beneath a pile on his desk.

'This is what it's all been about.'

It took me a moment to recognise the document, but when I did my jaw dropped again. Despite his anger Samson chuckled. 'Never play dice with a con-man, Walter. He will read you like a book. You know, of course, what it is? Yes, I can see from your expression that you do.'

'Isaac's testament,' I said pointing stupidly at it. Jocelin and I were the only ones who were supposed to know about it. I shot him an accusing look but he just shrugged and shook his head evidently as dumbfounded as I was. 'Where did you get it?'

'Not from you, obviously,' retorted Samson sharply. 'Even though you had it in your possession when I asked you for it on several occasions, and then denied the fact. Before, that is, you managed to lose it.'

'I didn't lose it,' I protested feebly. 'It was stolen from me. And I never actually *denied* having it specifically. I just never admitted it, that's all.'

Samson shook his head disdainfully. 'Well, it was fortunate that others were ahead of you and managed to spirit it away before it fell into de Saye's hands. For believe me, if he had been the one who'd taken it, it would not be sitting here on my desk now. He'd have destroyed it.'

'Because it's a loan bond issued to him by Isaac ben Moy.' I was guessing, but I was sure now that was what it must be. But who had taken it? Presumably the same person who had saved me in the forest today as well as being my elusive shadow, my guardian angel, over the past few days. That could only be one person, surely?

Jocelin had already picked up the document and was scrutinizing it closely. 'It is a bond,' he confirmed, and then he whistled through his teeth. 'F-for an extremely l-large sum of m-money.'

Samson nodded. 'Which de Saye never had any intention of repaying and which was why Moy gave it to you for safe keeping – a grosser case of misplaced trust there can hardly ever have been.'

Samson's slight went unheeded for into my mind once again had reared the story Isaac had told me about the Jews in York. They too, I remembered, had granted loans to noble families and the documents relating to them had been burnt on the floor of York Minster so that there was no record that they ever existed. It was all making sense now, even down to his suicide pact with his wife. He reckoned to be in the same hopeless position as those wretched people in York castle and saw for himself and his family the same terrible solution.

'Hold one moment, though,' I said frowning and trying to remember something. 'I thought it no longer mattered about these documents. Jocelin, you told me in the light of the York massacre that King Richard had passed some law requiring loans to be officially recorded.'

Jocelin nodded. '*The Ordinance of the Jewry*, it was called. B-but that law wasn't passed until eleven-ninety-four.' He tapped Isaac's document. 'This is dated eleven-ninety-two.'

'So this is the only existing record of the loan,' I nodded. 'And that is why de Saye would want it destroyed.' Then another thought struck me. 'That must be why de Saye is here in Bury.' I said it to myself but loud enough for the others to hear. 'He came in order to get Isaac to hand it over.' My mind was racing now. 'And that was the reason he killed Matthew.' I slapped my forehead. 'Of course!'

Jocelin looked at me in horror nearly dropping his goblet. 'D-de Saye killed M-m-m-matthew?' he stammered.

I'd done it again, not given Jocelin a vital piece of information. 'I'm sorry brother. Until this minute I couldn't be sure.' I turned to Samson. 'But I can see from Father Abbot's face that he already knew that Isaac had no involvement in the murder. In fact he knew all along, before the trial, before the ordeal by hot water. Was that why you didn't wish to witness it? Because you couldn't bear to see the consequences of your duplicity?'

Jocelin was clearly disturbed by this sudden rush of revelations. He looked beseechingly at Samson who at least had the good grace to lower his eyes. 'Not duplicity, Walter. That implies disloyalty. And the one thing I have been throughout all this is loyal.'

I shook my head incredulously. 'You allowed an innocent man to be tortured, reviled and persecuted to the point where he preferred to take his own life and that of his wife rather than have it stolen from him by the hangman, and you call that being loyal?'

Samson shifted awkwardly on his chair and this time his discomfort had nothing to do with his haemorrhoids. 'He wouldn't have hanged,' he muttered shifting papers about nervously on his desk. 'I'd have commuted his sentence.'

'Well, he cheated you out of that satisfaction, at least.'

'I had no choice,' grumbled Samson. 'There were other matters to consider. Important matters you know nothing about.'

I snorted contemptuously. 'Like what? What could possibly be more important than harrying an innocent family to death?'

He grimaced again, his bushy white eyebrows almost knitting together in what was a clear agony of conscience. 'Matters of state. State *security.*'

'Indeed? Then tell us, good father,' I goaded.

'Let us all into the secret. What are these "great matters" that are so important you could connive at persecution, torture and murder?'

My words must have hit their mark. He hesitated for a minute glaring at me as though wishing to throttle me, then he set his jaw.

'Brother Jocelin,' he said quietly. 'Would you mind leaving us? I'm sorry – please obey me in this and ask no questions. I will explain later.'

Jocelin's face was drained of colour, sadder and more confused than I had ever seen it before. But ever the good and faithful servant he did as his mentor asked. He got up without another word and left the room closing the heavy oak door after him.

When he had gone Samson turned his pained face towards me. 'I took no pleasure in doing that but you left me no alternative. Oh, I know what the other monks say about Jocelin, that he is a fussy old maid and a sycophant. But he has been a loyal servant and friend to me over many years. I feel I have betrayed him.'

'I am sorry indeed for that, father,' I said sincerely. 'Personally, I would have been happy for Jocelin to stay. If only to corroborate my version of events.'

Samson slammed his hand down on the desk, his expression angry. 'You think this is about you? Such arrogance! If I am prepared to imperil my immortal soul by covering up the murder of an innocent child and colluding in the suicide of two others, do you think I would blink before throwing you to the lions too?'

The ferocity of his outburst took me aback. But

it confirmed what I had already suspected, that he was indeed deeply troubled over the actions he had taken in recent days. That did not excuse what he had done but it did go some way to mollifying my fears for the safety of his soul. For that at least I was glad.

After a moment he'd calmed down sufficiently to regain command of himself. 'You want to know what matters are so important that I am prepared to sacrifice innocent lives. Very well, I'll tell you. But knowledge is a dangerous thing, Walter. Are you prepared to have it? Are you prepared to keep it and not to let it travel beyond these four walls? Because on peril of your life you had better be.'

He got up and refilled our two goblets with wine before sitting down again with a weary sigh.

'The last time we spoke on the subject I told you that King John's hold on the throne is tenuous. I'm afraid it's worse than that. Quite simply the Angevin Empire is finished.' Samson ran his hand wearily over his pink pate. 'Much as we all admired King Richard as a warrior, his foreign adventures drained the country over the ten years of his reign and left nothing for his brother with which to start his. Now Richard is dead, England is a wounded lion and the wolves are circling. Next year or the year after John will lose his territories in France, and when he does those English barons with estates on the other side of the Channel will join their French colleagues in rebellion. The loyalty of those remaining on this side cannot be guaranteed either. The Earl Marshal and Archbishop Hubert both agree with me that we cannot afford another distraction at such a time. Peace hangs upon a thread. If de Saye's…indiscretions…were to become public knowledge our enemies abroad would use them to attack his nephew the Justiciar and weaken the government further. Rebellion will turn to civil war and we will have the Anarchy back again. That cannot be allowed to happen. England needs firm government now as it never needed it before.' He looked at me with piercing eyes. 'Now perhaps you will appreciate how difficult my position has been. I spoke of loyalty. If it's a choice between one dead Jew and the security of the realm I know where my duty lies.'

I thought for a moment. 'Father, I do not pretend to understand the complexities of government. I am a simple country doctor, I can only deal with the symptoms that present before me. You say you didn't want de Saye's part in this murder to become public knowledge, but if that's the case why did you have it investigated? Surely it would have been better to have no investigation and allow matters to take their course. You had your motive for the murder – a boy martyr. A Heaven-sent motive, you might say. That being the case, de Saye's name need never have been mentioned.'

'I had to give the appearance of doing all we could to solve the murder,' he explained. 'Too many people were watching us – you've no idea.' He looked at the window as though expecting to see one of King Philip's spies crouched on the ledge. 'If it had looked like a cover-up the consequences might have been even worse. I needed someone to investigate the case convincingly – at least to *appear* to be doing so.'

He looked at me sheepishly. 'If you want the truth, I never thought you'd be successful.'

I felt my face colour at his words. 'I see. So when you said you chose me because of my investigative skills the opposite was actually the truth. You were expecting me to fail.'

This brought a wry smile to his face. 'But you didn't fail, did you? You managed to work it all out.' He studied me thoughtfully. 'You have worked it out haven't you, Walter?'

I frowned, shaking my head slowly from side to side. 'No. Not all of it. There's something more, something you're still not telling me. Anyone else – Jocelin, say - could have done what I did and probably finished this case much more quickly and neatly. There's another reason you wanted me, something to do with de Saye's hatred of me.' I drew myself up. 'You know the reason for that too, don't you? Isn't it time you told me?'

Samson sat thoughtfully for a long minute. I could see the turmoil going on behind his eyes. I waited. Finally he said quietly, 'Does the name Mandeville mean anything to you?'

Of course it did. Who in the east of England had not heard of Geoffrey de Mandeville, the so-called *Scourge of the Fens*? My father told me about him when I was a little boy. Geoffrey de Mandeville had been a nobleman at the time of the Anarchy and had fought at different times for both Matilda and Stephen, switching sides according to whichever he thought would profit him the most at any one time. Eventually he committed one treason too many and was arrested. As punishment he was given the choice of execution or of giving up all his possessions.

He chose life and fled to the marshy swamps of Cambridgeshire from where he and his private army of mercenaries plundered, tortured and murdered anyone unfortunate to fall into their hands and lived by extorting ransoms from their families. No-one, regardless of age, sex or rank was safe. King Stephen was unable to get an army through the impenetrable Fens to rid the people of this menace leaving de Mandeville to carry on terrorizing the east of England for more than a year.

'Eventually he was killed,' concluded Samson. 'Rather as King Richard had been, struck down by a sniper's arrow while he was besieging a castle. This time not a French castle but an English one not far from here. Burwell Castle, near Cambridge.'

'Yes, I know,' I said shortly. 'My father was one of the defenders.'

Samson nodded. 'Did you then also know that it was your father, William de Ixworth, who fired the fatal shot that killed Mandeville?'

I was stunned. I knew my father had seen action during the civil wars but I never knew before that he'd killed anyone. He had certainly never mentioned it to me. Maybe that was what had turned him against war when he was sent to the Holy Land and why he devoted the rest of his life to saving others instead. I sincerely hoped so.

'So are you now going to tell me that Geoffrey de Saye is somehow related to Geoffrey de Mandeville?' I guessed, almost chortling nervously at the absurdity of the suggestion. 'It would certainly explain where he got his character from if he were.'

Samson continued to study me stoically. 'Geoffrey de Mandeville's sister, Beatrice, married a man called de Saye. Geoffrey de Saye is her grandson.'

Now I was angry. Not that de Saye hated me because my father killed his uncle but because Samson knew all this, must have known it even before de Saye arrived in Bury. My life had been in danger from the moment he set foot within the town walls and yet Samson had never warned me, never even mentioned it. At the banquet, in the King's bedroom and any time thereafter de Saye might have murdered me and I would have been completely unprepared. It was what Joseph had come to warn me about the night of the football match, the night Matthew was killed.

'So I was to be the bait. That's the real reason you chose me to investigate the murder, to provoke de Saye into doing something foolish. If he'd managed to kill me it could have been explained away as the actions of a man obsessed with revenge and de Saye could then have been quietly disposed of. No messy business involving fraud and blackmail, just the simple case of settling old scores.'

'*Attempted* to kill you, Walter. There was never any possibility of him succeeding.'

'He very nearly did this morning.'

'But, God be praised, he didn't and you are still here to tell the tale. And de Saye has compromised himself just as we hoped. Believe me, you were never in any real danger. I took care of that.'

'Are you telling me it was one of your spies who saved me in the forest this morning?'

'Naturally,' Samson nodded modestly. 'How could you think otherwise?'

'So it was your man all along. The same man who's been following me around the town for the past two weeks?'

He looked puzzled. 'Following you round the town? No no, I meant the wagon driver and his sidesman.'

Yet again my mouth dropped open. 'You mean that smelly snaggle-toothed midget and his lice-ridden pal?' I guffawed. 'They ran away at the first sign of trouble.'

Samson flapped his hand in the air. 'That's neither here nor there. The point is de Saye was unsuccessful and now he will pay the price.'

'Oh?' I fumed. 'And what price is that?'

Samson grinned broadly and raised a fat finger in the air. 'Until now Earl Geoffrey would never hear anything against his uncle – you know what these old families are like, they stick together like dog-shit sticks to fur. And by the way, you've nothing to fear from the Earl over this business with your father. He's not like his uncle where blood feuds are concerned – different generation, d'you see?'

'I'm relieved to hear it.'

Samson nodded. 'But now the King is involved. He knows about de Saye's attempt to defraud him of his rightful inheritance and he is displeased. Mightily displeased.' He rubbed his hands together gleefully. 'Oh-ho yes, he's tripped up there and no mistake. De Saye has queered his pitch with the King. So that means he's finished. No amount of toadying will get him out of this one. Naturally he won't have a trial for all the reasons we've discussed. But there is a vacant manor in the gift of the Earl which would more than liquidate de Saye's debts – provided he remains on it.'

'I see. Exile. To where?'

'Shropshire.'

I snorted. 'So, in the end de Saye escapes justice. Like all of his rank.'

Samson mooed coquettishly. 'I wouldn't exactly say that. Have you been to Shropshire?' He smiled, rising from his seat. 'I think you'll find things will quieten down now.'

'What if I don't want them to quieten down?' I said remaining seated. 'Suppose I decide to expose the whole shoddy business.'

Samson stared at me. 'Did you not hear what I was saying? This is all to be kept strictly between us. Babble any of it about and it could be construed as treason.'

'Not if it was the King I babbled it to.'

Samson eyed me suspiciously. Slowly he sat down again. 'I've told you, the King already knows. And besides, he won't see you again.'

'He might,' I said. 'If he thought there was the possibility of a year or two's income - from a vacant abbacy.'

I paused to let the implications of my words sink in. As Jocelin had mentioned much earlier, Saint Edmund's was one of the richest abbeys in Europe. In law the income from any abbacy that fell vacant defers to the crown until a new abbot is appointed – a very tempting source of money to a cash-strapped monarch, and John was greedy enough to encourage it. And what will happen to my lord abbot in that case? Exile back to

Norfolk? Or worse.

'Treason, Walter,' warned Samson quietly. 'The penalties are not pleasant.'

'Then I suppose it comes down to which of us has most to lose. As I said, I am but a humble physician. My concerns are with justice not with the whining of some faceless nobles in France. However,' I continued quickly before Samson could respond. 'If Isaac Moy is shown not to be involved in the murder, and there was a public exoneration of all the Jews of Bury naming Isaac and Jacob Moy specifically, then I might feel I have no need to go to the King.'

Samson sat thinking for a long minute. Finally he smiled. 'Well, we don't want another Palm Sunday massacre, do we?' He started to rise again.

Inwardly I sighed with relief. I didn't know whether I would have had the courage to carry out my threat but was just thankful that I wouldn't have to find out.

'It may already be too late,' I said. 'The common folk have taken Matthew to their hearts. Jocelin may even write another history, God help us.'

Samson seemed unconcerned. 'Memories are short,' he said coming round to my side of the desk. 'These things come and go with fashion. I have told Egbert and Jeremiah that they will not have my support if they appeal to the Pope and the Holy Father has enough problems of his own at the moment without our parochial squabbles. It will all blow over, you'll see. And now that Brother Alric is dead...'

'What?' I interjected. 'Alric *dead*?'

'Yes,' said Samson. 'Haven't you heard? His body was fished out of the Lark this morning. A tragic accident.' He frowned shaking his head.

'Oh no,' I said, sincerely shocked by the news, and lowered my head in a moment of silent prayer.

Samson drew himself up haughtily. 'By all means pray if you think it will help him where he's going.'

'Alric was a victim too,' I said.

'I doubt if Matthew's mother would agree with you. I have made provision for that woman, incidentally, even though it pained my hand to authorize it. She will be allowed to keep the fuller's cottage together with a pension - on condition that she does not visit her son's grave in the abbey grounds. No doubt in the fullness of time his body can be moved to a churchyard closer to her home – once things have quietened down. Don't take it so personally, Walter,' he said placing an arm round my shoulders. 'You have your reputation restored and you can carry on doing what you do best - healing the sick and comforting the poor.'

He gently coaxed me towards the door.

'By the way,' he said in a confidential tone. 'Speaking of healing the sick, I've been meaning to ask your advice on another, *personal* matter. This whole unfortunate business has been playing havoc with my digestive system – something not dissimilar to the King's as a matter of fact,' he laughed nervously and lowered his voice. 'It's a little embarrassing.'

'You are constipated, father?'

He grimaced. 'It's a little more advanced than

that,' he said rubbing the back of his thigh. 'Some, erm, *protuberances*. I was hoping you could suggest an infusion I could take? Something perhaps a little less drastic in its effect than the opiate you gave the King.'

I thought for a moment and then nodded. 'Rhubarb, liquorice and goose fat, father.'

'Really? How interesting. I'll try it.'

He frowned thoughtfully as I opened the door and stepped out into the now crowded antechamber. 'Erm - just one thing. The rhubarb and the liquorice I understand. But the goose fat - how should one take it?'

I mumbled my answer as I threaded my way through the petitioners.

'Hmm?' said Samson cupping his ear. 'What's that? Put it where did you say?'

I turned and replied in a clear voice for all to hear: 'Up your arsehole, my lord abbot. Put it up your arse-hole.'

Chapter 24
SANCTUARY

By the time I left Samson's office it was coming up to noon and the cloud that had been hanging over us all day, both literal and metaphorical, seemed to have lifted and a sort of calm had descended on our little town of Edmundsbury. At this distance of forty years it is difficult to remember exactly what my mood was then but I sense I had come to something of a hiatus. I didn't know that there was a turn or two more to come before the top had finally spun out of this tale.

I was still feeling grubby from my encounter with the dread de Saye in Thetford Forest so I went into the abbey church early before sext stopping at the cloister lavatorium on my way to sluice myself down. I suppose I could have bathed but two baths in the space of a single week seemed to me excessive.

There were even more people in the church than usual, no doubt anxious to get out of the rain as much as for spiritual renewal, but the monks' choir is the one area of the church that is always closed to the public offering an island of peace as the river of pilgrims flows around it to and from the shrine. My intention was to do as our Lord taught us and to pray for my enemies as well as my friends: For Matthew, for his mother, for

Alric and even - God help me - for Geoffrey de Saye. But mostly I wanted to pray for the souls of Isaac Moy and his wife Rachel in the hope that when they come face to face with the Lord Jesus Christ, as surely we all must in the end, He will forgive them their error and not cast them aside with all the other unbelievers. As for their three children, Jessica, Josette and Jacob, I saved a special prayer for them fervently hoping that they were alive and safe - and a very long way from here. However, I wasn't to get very far in any of this as I saw that Jocelin was already sitting in the choir stalls ahead of me. He saw me first and nodded as I entered through the screen. There was no help for it but to join him.

Poor Jocelin. Samson really did treat him like one of his docile mules at times although in part he brought it on himself so willing was he to do Samson's every bidding and be grateful for the least sign of affection. After the briefest of prayers I lifted myself up onto the seat feeling I had to be the first to speak.

'Brother, I'd like to apologise for what happened back there. I did not know Samson was going to do that. I should have insisted that you should stay – after all, you did as much as I to uncover the truth about Matthew's murder.'

But Jocelin wasn't in the least offended. 'Oh no, brother. If F-father Abbot thinks there is s-something I should not hear then I must respect his d-decision. He is G-god's appointed after all, a v-very great and wise m-man.' Then he chuckled. 'You should have seen the way he stood up to Earl Geoffrey. He was m-m-m-magnificent.'

I sighed. I should have guessed that would be

Jocelin's reaction. To him Samson could do no wrong. It was hero-worship bordering on love - it *was* love. Even so, I thought he deserved some kind of explanation even if I could not disclose the important 'matters of state' that Samson had warned me to keep under my cowl. I kept my voice low so as not to be overheard as I rehearsed the litany of Alric's and de Saye's crimes. When I came to describe Alric's peccadilloes, however, I did not feel the abbey church was quite the place to be too explicit so I couched my explanation in inference and metaphor. Jocelin listened to it all in stoical silence though I'm not sure how much he understood. When I'd finished he still seemed puzzled. Clearly some more elucidation was required.

'Go back to the day of the King's illness,' I whispered. 'Remember I told you the guard who was sent to find the King's so-called 'poisoner' returned with Alric who he referred to as a 'pervert'. It struck me at the time as an odd thing to call a poisoner but I just assumed that all he meant was that any attempt on the King's life was to be regarded as a 'perversion'. It was only later that I realised he meant something rather more specific. There never was a poisoner, but the guard was obliged to provide one and he chose Alric probably on the principle of his being hung as much for a sheep as for a lamb.'

'Sheep as a lamb?' said Jocelin, frowning.

I pursed my lips. 'The guard already knew, you see? About Alric and his…weakness. It was common knowledge among the lower orders, apparently. He evidently thought Alric deserved a thrashing and didn't much mind what it was for.'

Jocelin was shaking his head disapprovingly. 'How long was it going on for – Alric's *weakness*? Do you think Matthew's poor mother was aware of it?'

'*Aware* of it?' I snorted contemptuously. 'She *instigated* it. All that nonsense about Matthew being a postulant. She was never going to allow her breadwinner son to become an impoverished priest in some far-off parish. No no. It was a ruse so that Matthew could have easy access to the abbey without attracting comment. And she made sure Alric paid for the privilege.' I looked at him. 'You do know what I'm talking about don't you, brother?'

Jocelin nodded slowly. 'I think so. B-but I still f-find it hard to believe a mother would prostitute her own s-son in that unnatural way.'

I shrugged my shoulders non-committally. 'I don't think the actual sin amounted to very much. Those street boys seemed to treat it all as a bit of joke. And I suppose it's debatable whose sin was the greater - the mother's for putting temptation in his way, or Alric's for succumbing to it.' I leaned my elbows on the bench in front of me. 'Anyway, the crucial point is that somehow Geoffrey de Saye got to learn about it – probably from that guard - and that's when it became serious because he saw a way to twist it to his own purpose.'

'W-which was what – precisely?'

'To unburden himself of Isaac's debt, of course.'

Jocelin nodded. Then he frowned. Then he shook his head. 'I-I'm still not clear how the two f-facts are linked: De Saye's debt to Isaac and Alric's sin?'

I could see this was going to be more difficult than I thought. I marshalled my thoughts again and took another deep breath.

'Look at the personalities involved. My lord de Saye, I think we would agree, is a man for whom the normal mores count for little – yes?'

'Indeed,' nodded Jocelin vehemently.

'Well, such a man would hardly concern himself with the morals of a mere monk, much less those of his catamite. He didn't care what they got up to. His only interest in Matthew and Alric's relationship was the opportunity it offered to put pressure on Isaac.'

'But how exactly?'

I opened my palm to explain. 'Matthew already knew Jacob through his dealings with the Moy household. De Saye simply got Matthew to introduce Jacob to Alric...'

'...e-expecting Alric to take his usual interest in the boy...' nodded Jocelin,

'...de Saye would then threaten to expose the relationship...' I continued,

'...unless Isaac agreed to release him from the debt,' completed Jocelin nodding furiously. 'Yes, of course. I see n-now.'

I nodded my agreement. 'At the very least the scandal would have brought shame to the Moy family - and probably been harmful to Isaac's business affairs, too. Except it didn't work out like that. Alric wasn't interested in Jacob – apparently he wasn't "the right type".' I nodded with satisfaction. 'Jacob wasn't like any of Alric's usual boys. I doubt he even knew what he was getting into.'

'I see,' said Jocelin. 'B-but that being the case,

and de Saye's plan having failed, why did it not end there? Why did not Isaac s-simply call de Saye's bluff? After all, Jacob had done nothing wrong - *ergo*, there was no scandal to expose.'

'Because by then it was already too late. Matthew was dead and the body lay in Isaac's garden. I think Isaac realised then that de Saye would stop at nothing, even murder, to get his way. That, I think, is what prompted him to trust me, a complete stranger, with his 'testament' which was the only proof of de Saye's debt. The desperate act of a desperate man.'

'Looking at the personalities involved,' smiled Jocelin kindly, 'I think Isaac recognised the kind of m-man you are and trusted you. That's w-why he gave the testament and the casket to you for safe-keeping knowing you would do the r-right thing in the event of his d-death.'

I shook my head. 'No, he didn't. Not really. And that is my burden I have to carry. Isaac had been gambling that I would open the document and once I knew its contents would take them to the Abbot who alone had the authority to bring de Saye to book. I think that's what he was hoping right up to the moment his hand was plunged into the boiling cauldron and why he refused to say anything, that I might be able to save him. And maybe I could have done except like the fool I am I didn't read it. And then to pile folly upon folly I lost it.'

'You j-judge yourself too harshly, my friend,' said Jocelin. 'No-one tried harder than you to clear Isaac's name.' He thought for a long minute. 'Forgive me, but still none of this explains why Matthew was m-murdered.'

'Hm? Oh that was a mistake.'

Jocelin looked horrified. 'A *what*?'

I glanced about me as curious eyes looked over. 'The sin of anger, brother,' I said lowering my voice. 'Matthew failed to give de Saye what he wanted. De Saye lost his temper and lashed out at the boy accidentally killing him. It was entirely unintentional.'

'And that's *it*?' said Jocelin, appalled. 'The only reason p-poor Matthew had to die was because he was *in the way*?'

I shrugged. 'The death of a miller's boy would have meant no more to de Saye than crushing a beetle beneath his boot. But from that single act everything else followed: The body being dumped in Isaac's garden; the Knieler women with their flimflammery nonsense – paid for by de Saye, of course; the martyrdom myth; Isaac's trial and his eventual suicide. It all played to ready prejudices.' Some of which, I might have added, Jocelin himself harboured. But there was no purpose in rubbing salt into what was clearly a painful wound. There were tears in his eyes when he spoke again:

'Then why did Matthew's mother not speak when she had the chance?' he objected fiercely. 'I saw her when the body was discovered in Isaac's garden. She was in g-genuine distress.'

'I'm sure she was – then. Remember, at that stage she still thought it was Isaac who had killed her son.'

'But when she found out the truth of it she could have s saved Isaac,' said Jocelin bitterly. 'Instead she allowed an innocent man to suffer and die.' His eyes filled with tears again. 'Oh, is there no-one in this whole sordid affair possessed of a Christian c-conscience?'

Heads again turned from among the passing pilgrims to look at us and I lowered my voice further.

'Would it have put de Saye on trial if she had? It hasn't now. And she is not entirely innocent in this business. She could have ended up in the dock alongside de Saye. Whatever else that woman may be she's no fool. And she still has her other five children to think about. Putting de Saye on trial would not fill their bellies. She made a cold hard calculation. She wanted de Saye to pay all right but in a currency less tenuous than justice – hard coin.'

I could hear the bell announcing sext and the choir was beginning to fill up with our fellow monks getting ready to sing the office.

'O-one thing still puzzles me,' said Jocelin hurriedly. 'Why did de Saye come after you in the f-forest? He must have thought he was in the clear. Isaac's suicide was tantamount to a confession to the murder and the bond of debt he owed Isaac was lost in the flames – or s-so he believed. Why risk all by attacking you?'

'Because it was me Alric confessed to, that's why. When de Saye learned that he must have thought the vengeance of God was upon him. After all, not only was his secret no longer a secret but the author of his impending nemesis was the one person he hated most in all the world - me. And with all that had passed between us he knew I would not remain silent. So when he saw me trundling out of town on an open wagon with only a couple of yokels as companions he couldn't resist the temptation to follow and do what he had been itching to do since he first saw me in the King's banquet.' I ran my finger graphically across my own throat.

'Th-then it was lucky you had your guardian angel to protect you,' Jocelin said under his breath. 'P-presumably the same mysterious presence you kept seeing around the town. Who was that, I wonder?'

On that subject, too, I had an idea and might have told him except at that moment we were interrupted by a commotion near the choir altar. All the while Jocelin and I had been talking one of the sub-sacristans had been laying out the altar cloth ready for the high mass following sext. I'd been vaguely aware of him genuflecting and fussing about with candles and tapers, but had been concentrating too hard on explaining matters to Jocelin to pay him much attention. Now he abruptly disappeared behind the altar ducking down behind it only to bob up again a moment later looking very angry and holding between his finger and thumb the ear of a small boy. Fortunately the ear was still attached to the boy who was dirty and dishevelled as were two little girls who also suddenly popped up beside him and were complaining very noisily. It took me but a moment to recognise who they were under their grubby faces and as soon as I did I was on my feet and rushing towards them. From the state of them Jacob, Josette and Jessica looked as though they had been hiding there for a week, which indeed they probably had. But mere commotion was about to degenerate into out and out pandemonium:

'Sanctuary! Sanctuary!'

We all looked round in astonishment to see the squat but sturdy figure of Matilde barrelling down the central aisle of the nave towards us with a face of thunder, scattering pilgrims like alehouse pins in her wake and waving her fists wildly in the air.

'Sanctuary!' she yelled again, her voice echoing like a banshee's in the cavernous church. 'I claim sanctuary *en nom de Jésus-Christ!*' her bulbous frame wobbling perilously as she careered down the aisle towards sub-sacristan Gerard and the children.

Startled as he was, Gerard was not about to relinquish his prize so easily, not at any rate until Matilde had arrived and landed him such a hefty wallop that it sent him flying backwards against the chancel screen with a teeth-splintering crunch. She then cradled the three children's heads in her arms and backed against the screen glaring fiercely about her and making an odd growling noise in her throat like a cornered animal.

'Quickly,' I whispered to Jocelin. 'The casket.'

'W-What?' he stammered.

'The casket,' I repeated. 'From your office. Fetch it now. *Run!*'

Turning, he picked up his robe and rushed down the aisle towards the west door of the church nearly knocking over a family of pilgrims who had just come in.

Matilde was still looking like a mother lioness protecting her cubs and whining maniacally as I gingerly approached hands held out to show I meant no harm.

'It's all right, Matilde. It's me, Brother Walter. I'm not going to touch them, I promise. You have been hiding them, yes? Here behind the alter - erm, *vous avez été les cacher ici?'* I spluttered. *'Derrière l'autel, oui?'*

'Oui,' she whimpered defensively and bared her teeth at me.

As I later discovered, she had indeed been hiding the children and feeding them from Thibaut's bounty ever since the day of their father's suicide. That was where she had been going the day I met her on the street, not to the church to pray as I had thought but to meet the children and to hide them. But they had been discovered too soon. Samson had not yet had time to rescind Jacob's outlaw status. There was still a hue and cry for him and he could be killed at any moment with impunity.

People were rushing about now and several monks were approaching from both sides trying to pincer the cornered Matilde and her brood. Others hearing the commotion had appeared at the west end of the church blocking any escape that way. There was no point arguing with them. Action was what was called for. I thought quickly. I would use the confusion to get them all safe. Jocelin arrived back with the casket and I pushed it into Jacob's hands.

'Take this,' I said to the boy. 'Don't argue, just take it. It's yours anyway. Take your sisters and Matilde and get to Norwich. Find your relatives – they are there. You know them.' I looked back. Guards had appeared at the west door now – I could just make out the tops of their pikes as they started towards us. But the door at the far end of the south transept was still clear. I pointed towards it. 'Go now. Go. *Go!'*

A moment more of hesitation and then they turned and the last I saw of the four of them was as they pushed their way into the throng of milling pilgrims and disappeared from view. One of the monks had tried at the last moment to grab them as they passed, but Jocelin had tackled him successfully to the ground, God bless his bony white knees.

Chapter 25
A DEPARTURE AND A RETURN

At last the day came for the King to be on his way. It was a relief to see him go on many levels but for me personally it would mean that Joseph might be able to return to his shop. I hadn't seen him since the evening of the football match two weeks earlier when he came to warn me about Geoffrey de Saye. So much had happened since that night. I was looking forward to telling him all the news and hearing his comments which I was sure would be succinct and perceptive.

For the past week the King's agents had been picking over Isaac's property removing anything of any value that could be salvaged and sold. Most of the furniture had been destroyed in the fire but some that had survived had been offered for sale to Abbot Samson who had graciously declined. However, I believe Prior Robert bought one or two fine pieces to grace his fine house overlooking the banks of the River Lark. Indeed, so eager had the King been to liquidate his newly-acquired assets I was surprised he didn't simply hold an ad hoc auction on the road outside the burnt-out shell of Isaac's house and have done with it. All this stocktaking of Isaac's wares was, I gather, the reason Earl Geoffrey Fitz Peter had been on the Thetford road the day I was attacked by his uncle having been summoned by the King to make an inventory. Evidently de Saye had not informed his nephew about the existence of the casket of treasure any more than he had the King and for much the same reasons I expect. The loss of any treasure would, I am sure, be a devastating blow to King John.

As the hour approached for the King's departure the sense of anticipation was palpable. The entire abbey, obedientiaries, choir monks and servants all, turned out to wish the King a fond, speedy and hopefully final farewell. The three weeks of his stay had all but bankrupted the Abbot who now in exquisite irony would have to borrow the funds to finance it from Jews in neighbouring towns since, by his own ordinances, Bury no longer had any Jews of its own to scrounge from. Jocelin told me that as a token of his gratitude for our hospitality King John was to give back to the abbey the very silk cloth that his servants had borrowed from our sacristy when he first arrived and which normally adorns the High Altar of the abbey church. Since John hadn't even paid for the cloth most of the monks were outraged by this display of shabbiness – though not, of course, out loud. They would have been even more outraged had they seen the cloth in question, as I had, draped around the naked body of John's fourteen-year-old concubine. But I couldn't help laughing at the joke. I also noticed, incidentally, that the monk who received the cloth from the King was the same sub-sacristan, Gerard, who'd had the tug-of-war over Jacob's ear a few days earlier and who evidently was still nursing bruises from the encounter. I do hope he remembers to wash it before it gets used again.

As a final act of blasphemy the King went to mass the morning of his departure, the first since his arrival three weeks earlier, and made great play of his donation to the poor of Bury. Considering how much he must have made out of the estate of Isaac ben Moy I thought he could have been a little more generous than the paltry twelve shillings he ostentatiously dropped onto the collection plate. But just as the plate was about to pass from the royal hand the King seemed to have second thoughts and called for its return.

What was this? Had the King been toying with us after all? Was he now to make the generous departing gift so earnestly desired and expected of a visiting monarch just as his brother and father had done at the end of their royal visits?

We craned our necks to see what bounty the King might be bestowing upon the abbey, but all he did was to borrow another shilling from one of his courtiers and tossed it nonchalantly onto the plate thus bringing the sum total of his gift to thirteen: 'One for the baker,' he announced in a loud voice, 'to make a round dozen,' and then proceeded to snigger at his joke throughout the remainder of the mass.

With that the King took his leave and disappeared out of the East Gate of the town with the remnants of his army, his courtiers and his baggage train bringing up the rear all heading towards lucky Ipswich as the next stop on his journey back to London. *Sic transit gloria mundi.*

I would add one post-script about the King's constitution – his *corporal* constitution that is, not his political one. Abbot Samson had been right when he said that King John would have no wish to see me again, but he did send round a messenger to ask my professional opinion – unremunerated, naturally - concerning the bowel problem that had been the original cause of his extended stay at the abbey. He wanted to know what I would recommend so as not have to suffer a recurrence of the problem. I suggested a supplement to his diet of soft fruit in order to keep his bowels open: Plums, cherries - or perhaps, since he had an apparent fondness for them, peaches. But not too many, I cautioned, or he may have the opposite problem from the one that laid him low for so long. I have no idea if he ever took my advice.

Even as the gates were closing on the last of the King's wagons I rushed in the opposite direction up to the top of the town and through the Risby Gate to Joseph's shop my heart pounding with anticipation at what I might find there. When I arrived I could hardly believe my eyes. All was magically back to where it had been the day before the King's arrival, even down to Joseph's staff which was in its usual position lying across the entranceway.

'It won't be for long,' he said after I had embraced him and slumped exhilarated on his ubiquitous and infuriating cushions. 'The Abbot has relented on his expulsion of the Jews and is to allow some back into the town – those who can contribute to his taxes.'

'Into your old shop near the market?' I said with a twinkle in my eye.

'Possibly.' He eyed me suspiciously. 'I don't suppose you have any idea what might have changed his mind?'

'None whatsoever,' I grinned.

So, I thought, Samson had kept his word to me about relaxing his policy towards the Bury Jews – and maybe a touch of conscience might have sweetened his decision, although it was more likely pressure from the Jews of Thetford and Cambridge whose loans he was even now negotiating. I was glad for I did not wish to harbour bad opinions of Samson who I knew at bottom to be an honourable as well as deeply religious man. But like all men he was prone to the climate of other men's thoughts and the exigencies of the times.

'Dear God, it's good to see you again,' I said to Joseph. 'You have no idea how much I've missed you. Yet, you know, even in my darkest hour I had the oddest feeling that you were never far away.'

'Really? I can't think why.' He lightly clapped his hands together.

'Mind you,' I went on, 'I had no need of anybody's help, if truth were known. When de Saye attacked me in the forest, I was equal to him. It was lucky, really, that Earl Geoffrey arrived when he did or I don't know what I might have done to the poor wretch even with one of my hands injured.'

'Indeed?'

'Oh yes. A flick of the wrist, a duck and a dive and I had him on his back laid out cold like a stunned rabbit.'

'A stunned rabbit, eh?' He clapped his hands again.

I burst out laughing and threw one of his cushions at his head. 'You old goat! I knew it was you all along watching over me, disappearing round corners, thwarting de Saye's attempt to cut my throat in the forest. And I also know that it was you who stole Isaac's testament from my cell. So, come on now, admit it.'

His smile faltered slightly as he shook his head. 'Not me, my brother. Quite impossible.' He raised his leg and I could see that he had his foot heavily bandaged. 'I badly twisted my ankle escaping from the abbey the night of the football match. I have been unable to do more than hobble about ever since which was why I went to stay with friends in the country. I haven't been near the town since. It is nearly mended but I will be incapacitated for some days yet.'

My mouth dropped open. 'But I saw you. It must have been you.'

I was baffled. I had been sure it was Joseph who had done all those things. But as I examined his foot I could see the bone was badly bruised and quite impossible to put any weight on it. I shook my head in bewilderment. 'If not you, then who?'

At that moment the screen parted and the boy Chrétien entered bearing a tray of refreshments. He set the tray down on the floor and proceeded to pour us a cup each of the steaming herbal tea. As he handed me mine I noticed one of his arms was scratched as though he'd been in some kind of violent tussle.

No, I thought, that was a foolish notion and instantly dismissed it from my mind. Impossible. He was too light, too *effeminate*.

Seeing him, though, reminded me of something else I needed to settle. 'By the way,' I said turning again to Joseph. 'I believe I owe you some money.'

He gazed vaguely into space stroking his brown beard. 'No, I don't think so. The abbey accounts are fully up to date. You paid me for that last purchase you made – have you forgotten?'

I was growing frustrated. 'I don't mean my purchase account. I mean the bag of coin your boy here gave me,' I said indicating Chrétien.

But Joseph was shaking his head sadly. 'My dear brother, I think in your tussle with Lord de Saye you must have hit your head harder than you thought. I have no idea what you're talking about. And since you mention him, Chrétien is not my servant. He's from your mother's household.'

My jaw inevitably dropped. 'My *mother*?'

'Yes. Did I not say? The Lady Isabel came to see me the day before the King's arrival and brought him with her. She was quite insistent I should take him. Among his many attributes he is apparently a champion wrestler – are you not, Chrétien? I daresay she knew Geoffrey de Saye was to be among the King's entourage and thought Chrétien might be useful to you. I hope he was.'

You see now why I regretted not mentioning him the first time I saw him all those weeks ago, for had I done so I would have learnt all this sooner and might not have attacked him when I found him alone in the shop; might not have wasted my energies chasing shadows around the town; and might have joined forces with him to defeat the dread de Saye sooner. Mortified by my stupidity, I glanced again at Chrétien but he replied to none of this and was already disappearing behind the shutters and silently closing them after him.

So there you have it, the chapter missing from Jocelin's *Chronicle* that should have been written but never was – until now. It has taken me forty years to summon the courage to do so and though I say so myself I think I have made a fair fist of it, although perhaps not as fair as Jocelin would have done. I would, however, add one final footnote to the tale: Despite his best efforts, many of Samson's fears about the break-up of John's empire did indeed come to pass - although Samson mercifully never lived to see its final demise. But his machinations had been for nothing for matters followed their own path which meant the whole tragic business concerning the fuller's son need never have happened. In light of this it is ironic that the events leading to King John's ultimate defeat were in part precipitated by a scandal involving the death of another child not much older than Matthew: Prince Arthur, the boy Samson was so scornful of occupying the throne and John's greatest rival, was dispatched in the spring of 1203 aged just sixteen, many say by John's own hand. That in turn led indirectly to the signing of his Great Charter which many Englishmen regard as marking the beginning of their freedom – an event, incidentally, also fermented within the walls of our abbey of Saint Edmund. But that is a tale for another time.

A few months after the King's departure I received a parcel from an unknown origin in Norwich. It contained no note or indication as to who sent it just a portion of a beautifully-carved piece of rosewood of the type that often adorns the sides of wooden caskets made in the East. It was from Jacob of course letting me know that he had arrived safely in Norwich. I have kept the carving ever since as a memento and can see it propped on a shelf above my study desk even as I write. Its exotic carvings and subtle colouring look slightly out of place against the unadorned dark oak of my lectern.

Later still I heard that Samson had been as good as his word and given Matthew's mother a pension out of his own purse, which was more than she deserved. I could be cynical and say this was to buy her silence but I know Samson's character well enough to know it was probably done out of charity.

The verdict of the King's coroner, by the way, was that Matthew had been murdered by person or persons unknown. But the Jews were exonerated from all blame, I'm pleased to say, and specifically Isaac and Jacob ben Moy, Isaac receiving a posthumous pardon. This again I think was Samson's doing for shortly after that some of the restrictions on the movement of Jews within the town were eased as Joseph had predicted and while suspicion did not entirely disappear, no more violence was perpetrated upon that unhappy race. Once again I will resist the temptation to cynicism and instead make recourse to the wisdom of Scripture: "And behold, there was in the carcass of the lion a swarm of bees and honey" – in other words, out of depths of evil comes sweetness.

Dear God, I'm even starting to sound like Jocelin.

HISTORICAL NOTE

The basis for the story is the spate of child murders that took place in 12th Century England. All these murders were blamed on Jews thus turning the victims into martyrs (the first victim, twelve-year-old Saint William of Norwich, is still venerated in a chapel in Norwich Cathedral today). The murder of another twelve-year-old boy called Robert occurred in Bury St Edmunds in 1181. Partly in response to this fifty-seven Jews were massacred in the town on Palm Sunday 1190.

Jews in twelfth-century England were a useful source of finance before the invention of banks and at a time when the usury laws prevented Christians from lending money at interest. It was not unusual to try to get out of repaying these loans by destroying the records - or better still, by murdering the lenders as well.

Many of the characters in the story existed in real life. Abbot Samson and Jocelin of Brakelond are well-known figures and were written about by Jocelin himself in his *Chronicle of the Abbey of Bury St Edmunds*. Walter the Physician also existed as did Geoffrey de Saye who was the real-life uncle of the Chief Justiciar of England, Geoffrey Fitz Peter, and great-nephew of yet another Geoffrey - the infamous Geoffrey de Mandeville, *Scourge of the Fens*.

Jocelin records that King John did indeed visit Bury St Edmunds shortly after his coronation in May 1199 although he does not say how long he stayed. He did give the abbey its own silk cloth as his parting gift along with thirteen shillings. He may or may not have suffered from constipation during his visit, but he did die seventeen years later probably from eating too many peaches.

SWW August 2011

ABBOT'S PASSION

Easter 1201. Following a treaty between King John and King Philip of France, England is at last at peace. Alas the same cannot be said for Saint Edmund's Abbey. The pope's new legate has arrived determined to stir up controversy. For Abbot Samson this brings the possibility of a new ally against an old enemy. But his intrigues lead to disaster with Brother Walter being placed in mortal danger and a full-scale battle in the nearby village of Lakenheath.

In the middle of all this the legate's clerk is murdered and a London merchant is wrongly accused. In desperation the man is granted sanctuary at the abbey's shrine, but it is only a brief respite. The whole weight of the judiciary and the church are against him.

Amid rape, religious bigotry and trial by combat Walter has to find the real murderer before a terrible injustice is done and the wrong man is hanged.

WALTER'S GHOST

Summer 1206. Before it was renamed, Bury St Edmunds was known as Bedricksworth after the ancient family who lived there. Now the last surviving member of the Bedrick clan, Arnulf Bedrick, wants an heir to carry on the family name. Marrying for a fifth time, this is his last chance to achieve it. But Arnulf has a secret.

Now jump forward seven hundred years to New Year's Day 1903. The antiquarian and celebrated writer of ghost stories, M. R. James, is excavating the graves of five medieval abbots of Bury. But in one of the graves he discovers something that shouldn't be there.

How are the two events connected? What is the secret found buried in the abbot's grave? Over it all hovers the ghost of Brother Walter who drives the investigation on to solve not only a seven hundred year old murder mystery but also another in the twentieth century in the way only Walter can.

MONK'S CURSE

December 1211. After thirty years as abbot of Saint Edmund's, Samson is dying. Before he takes his last breath, however, he calls Brother Walter to his bedside in order to recite the tale of the Green Children of Woolpit. This is a well-known local legend about two children who were found wandering in a Suffolk field half a century earlier.

Samson also reveals he has recently been visited by a mysterious woman who claims a murder is about to take place. But Walter cannot find out who the woman is or anyone else who has seen her. Did she really exist or was she, like the green children, just another product of a dying man's imagination?

Walter is reluctant to get involved but as he starts to investigate he realises there is more to both tales than first appears and eventually unmasks a tale of abuse and corruption going to the very heart of government.

Can Walter finally solve the mystery of the Green Children of Woolpit and prevent a murder being committed, or is he already too late?

BLOOD MOON

November 1214. King John has returned to England having lost his empire to King Philip of France. Humiliated and desperate for support, he again travels to Bury St Edmunds where Abbot Samson has died and a battle is raging among the monks over who will be his successor.

In the midst of this there arrives in the town a seemingly inconsequential young couple and their maid. The wife is heavily pregnant and gives birth in the night to a baby daughter.

But then the maid is mysteriously murdered and it is soon apparent that the family is not all that it appears. With rebellion looming, abbey physician Walter of Ixworth is drawn once again into investigating a murder and a conspiracy that threatens to engulf the country in civil war and ultimately leads to the final nemesis that is Runnymede and Magna Carta.

DEVIL'S ACRE

January 1242. Brother Walter is dying. He is an old man but the prospect of death does not disturb him - indeed, he welcomes it to meet with old friends and see God in the face. But before he finally joins the heavenly host he is determined to solve one last mystery that has been plaguing him for decades.

But there are dark forces afoot that want to frustrate his efforts and are prepared to go to any lengths to keep secret events that even now could disturb the government of England - even murder.

In his mind Walter returns to those far off times when Abbot Samson took him on a bizarre journey away from the comforting familiarity of Bury Abbey and into the wilds of barbaric Norfolk where the abbot's power is limited and be met by a far greater one in the guise of the Warenne family of Castle Acre - or as some still choose to call it, the *Devil's Acre*.

THE SILENT AND THE DEAD

Winifred Jonah seemed like an ordinary Norfolk housewife, jolly, plump and harmless. Yet her bland exterior concealed a sinister secret. At fourteen she had already murdered her aunt and uncle and forty years later it was her husband's turn to die. Even so she might have made it to her own grave without further incident if she hadn't met Colin Brearney. He thought she was going to be a pushover, but he had no idea who he was taking on. The day Colin knocked at her door was the beginning of a nightmare that could only end in blood, silence and death…